The ultimat___

By Pe___

THE ULTIMATE INSTRUMENT OF JUSTICE

© Copyright P. J. Ljung 2015 - 2019
All rights reserved. No part of this publication may be reproduced, distributed, or transmitted in any form or by any means, including photocopying, recording, or other electronic or mechanical methods, without the prior written permission of the publisher, except in the case of brief quotations embodied in critical reviews and certain other noncommercial uses permitted by copyright law. For permission requests, write to the publisher

THROUGHOUT THE BOOK
THERE IS A MIXTURE OF ENGLISH AND SWEDISH STYLES

This is a work of fiction. Names, characters, businesses, places, events, and incidents are either the products of the author's imagination or used in a fictitious manner. Any resemblance to actual persons, living or dead, or actual events is purely coincidental.

THE ULTIMATE INSTRUMENT
OF JUSTICE
This book contains explicit sexual content,
some swearing,
& graphic descriptions of murders
If you are easily offended.
#Please do not read this book#

Chapter   1
Justin Webber

Göteborg present day.

One of the best eating places in Göteborg was the choice of Justin Webber. An American
 national, now living in one of the busiest cities in Sweden.

" Tin Tins, " a modern cozy place, with some of the best-filled sandwiches ever. Justin's favorite
was chicken, with a sauce filling to die for. " To die for, " an unusual few words, but, words that

 are just about to change his life forever.

Placing the delicious sandwich in front of him, the waitress smiled at Justin and turned to head
 back behind the counter. Justin smiled to himself, as he looked up and down the perfect legs

walking away. He liked the good things in life, like most people, and her legs looked as good as the chicken to eat.

Justin moved over to Sweden in the mid-1990´s, after his mother and father were murdered in their own home. A friend of the family invited him over to Göteborg to recover from the traumatic experience. He was 15 years old at that time. To lose one parent was devastating, but two, at the same time, was catastrophic. The scars ran deep for all these years, and the killer, or killers were never found. Every time he heard of a murder anywhere, he felt sick in his stomach and knew he was powerless over these cowardly bastard´s.

Justin´s job was of all things, a gravedigger, in one of the biggest cemeteries in East Göteborg. On occasion´s, there would be funerals of murdered victims, buried, and in time, forgotten. Where was their justice? Justin so wished he could do something to bring justice to these criminals. An old saying arises. " Be careful what you wish for, you just might get it! "

Finishing his Café Latté, he took his dishes over to the counter and complimented the mid-30s looking girl for the delicious sandwich and service. He placed a 100kr note on the counter and told her to buy a drink for herself some time. She smiled so kindly to Justin, and said " Thank you, sir! " Touching his hand on the counter at the same time, she drew her fingers over his and winked at him flirting. "I will definitely be back again," He said smiling at her.

This weeks' vacation was nearly at an end, and he
was going to spend the rest of the day looking
 for new work clothes, and Göteborg was fantastic for
these types of product.

Looking in the changing room mirror, he was pleased
with the fit body he now had. He had
 worked hard on his " six-pack, " and his long-shaped
legs were the correct proportion in size,
 almost athletic looking. His blond ponytail hanging
neatly at the back of his head towards his
 shoulder´s. The checkered wool shirt was ideal for
the up and coming cold weather, and would
 keep the icy winds from his skin. Spending over
3000 Kronor on work clothes was worth every
cent, as the winters in Sweden can go to -35 in a
very short time. People still died, no matter
 what the weather was, so, digging a two-meter
grave had to be done, even if the ground was
 pack ice.

It was changed day´s from " The States, " where "
Miami " was beautiful sunshine nearly all year
 round. Justin spent most of his days in the summer
vacations at Miami beach, hanging out with
 his school buddies. He remembers well the day a
police officer came along the beach with a
 megaphone. " Justin Webber? We are looking for
Justin Webber," came the echo from the
 portable " Personal Address System. " Waving to
the officer, he announced he was Justin.

From the serious look coming from the officers face,
Justin knew there was something wrong,
but what was wrong? The officer leads Justin to the
edge of the water, looked at Justin with a

sadness in his eyes. " I have some bad news for you young man, and I need you to be strong." A
coldness came over him, he had this terrible feeling it was to do with his Mom or Father. The
next words from the officer confirmed his worst nightmare. " A neighbor had reported a
shooting at your house when officers arrived, they found your parents had been shot many
times, and when the paramedics arrived, they declared them both deceased at the crime scene."
The officer continued with the terrible news and put his hand upon Justin's shoulder. " We have
been in touch with your uncle Zac in the next state, and he is driving to us now as we speak."
Justin fell to his knees, and held his face in his hands, hiding the tears now rolling down his
cheeks. " Ok! We are going to drive to the police department, Address: 400 NW 2nd Avenue.
 You can call any of your friends or family to give you support."

Justin was numb, from the brain down, and did not notice anything as they drove the short
 distance to the police precinct.

In the precinct, there were several arrested people sitting with an officer. Hookers, thieves,
drunken bums, all protesting their innocents, and most of the individual officers smiling and
saying. " Yeah yeah! - We heard it all before bud. "
The door at the end of an office opened, and coming towards Justin, was a man dressed in civilian
clothes, with an id tag clipped to his suit jacket. " Hey! You must be Justin right?" Justin
nodded to the man. " I am Captain Alejandro Santino, I am investigating homicide officer in your

parent's case, and I need to ask you a few
 questions that might help us catch the perpetrators
of this terrible crime." The officer continued.

 " You want a soda?" Justin nodded as he looked at
the captain with still numbness written all
over his face. " This can´t be happening, he thought
to himself. " It was almost like living in a
 nightmare movie when sleeping, and he was going
to wake up very soon.

Justin approached his apartment in Göteborg with
several bags of new clothes and noticed a
 familiar face from earlier. The legs were the first
things he noticed, and as he raised his eyes
higher, he could see the smiling face, it was of the
waitress from " Tintin,s. " " You either have
 just moved into one of the apartments, or you are
stalking me!" Justin laughed as he looked
 straight into her bright sparkling blue eyes.
Returning the smile, and moving slowly towards
 him, she put her hands on his shoulders and pulled
him closer, and with that second, she placed
 her lips on his, and passionately put her tongue in
his mouth, and licked his tongue and lips firmly.
 Dropping the clothes bags to the ground, he held
her waist tightly and moved his left hand to
the back of her head, then pulled gently, so to get
her lips and face closer.

" I am Bernadette!" she said staring into Justin's
eyes. " Hi! sweet Bernadette, I am Justin.
"Are we going to stand out here all day? or are you
going to invite me in for a coffee?" Justin
 jerked his head to signify going into the apartment,
with his right arm around her, and all the
 bags in the other, they proceeded to the elevator.

Opening his apartment door, he placed the bags in the hallway and leads Bernadette to the living area. She is amazed at his decor, as young guys usually have a cluster of mess everywhere, in this case, he was tidy, clean, and really good taste in furniture and wall fixings, that just oozes class. The centerpiece had to be the three-meter square aquarium expanding the length of the left wall. " Oh, how beautiful, what a fantastic amount of fish you have," she said smiling as she walked closer to get a better look. - So many different shapes and sizes, she continued. The tank had a coral centerpiece in the middle of the tank, with every color available. Although Sea Anemones look like flowers, they are predatory animals, and Justin had five species of them attached to the living coral. Bernadette was drawn to the seven seahorses of different sizes, and a yellow one, in particular, she loved at first sight as yellow was her favorite color. " I love your apartment, Justin," she said walking back over to him. " I do not have visitors very often Bernadette, and this is my peace and serenity bolt hole, and sometimes I can gaze at the tank for a long time, up to 4 hours at a time on occasion´s, and I feel a peace within me so deep, it calms my soul to the very center."

" Do I dare ask how you got my address?" He smiled at her waiting for an answer. Slipping her coat off over her slender arms, she draped it over the coat rack and moved over to Justin to sit next to him. " I saw you once many months ago, I was walking by these apartments looking to maybe lease one, but, there was none available at the time." "They are hard to get," Justin

7

replied
Now holding her hand gently, as they sat back on
the deeply padded couch. " When I saw you in
 Tintin's, I knew it was you, and my heart skipped a
few beats, I think because you are so
handsome, and I would be so lucky to have a
soulmate I feel you might be!" Justin started to
 blush a little, and smiled, and then told her. " I
watched you earlier, and I could not keep my
 eyes off you, and as you walked back behind the
counter, I was looking at the beautifully shaped
 legs you have, and if I was judging them, it would
be 10 out of 10." She smiled more, as she
 placed her hand on her left leg, and slowly raised
her short dress, just enough that he could see
 the outline of her pink underwear. - I have one more
like this, she laughed, as she placed her
 dress down neatly. - Time for coffee, Justin laughed,
and strolled into the kitchen to place the
kettle in its cradle.
"Thank you for trusting me Bernadette, it has been a
long time since I had a relationship, and I
just might be a little shy!" She had that beautiful
smile on her face again. Replying. " I have a
 sixth sense when picking boyfriends, and I go with
my gut feelings, and I got really strong
 knotted feelings with you. I feel as if I have known
you before in a previous life, and now I
have met you, I don't want this feeling to leave me."
Placing her coffee on the glass and chrome
 table, she moved closer to him, and pulled his head
to hers, and started to kiss him all over
 again. Justin started to have tingling feelings all over
his body, from his toes to his head, and all
 places in between. He was starting to get aroused,
as she put her hand inside his shirt, rubbing his

8

slightly hairy chest. She got her forefinger, then her thumb, gently holding his nipple, then gently twisting it so it became hard and pointed. " What a beautiful day this was turning out to be, " he thought, as he started to unbutton her lacy blouse.

Bernadette stood in the bathroom doorway; she was wearing Justin's bathrobe. This robe in brilliant white was knee length and made of thick fluffy strands of cloth. Her hair was shoulder length now, she had let it down when showering, and the blond strands of her hair dripped water on the robe, as she smiled at Justin. He gazed at her so intently, as he lay on the queen size bed. He was naked except for his underwear, and the skin-tight cloth showed his aroused manhood to the point of Bernadette sighing, as she looked on his beautiful body. " I want you so much Justin," she said with a velvet sounding voice. She loosened the robe cord, then let it open, unwrapping her self like a present at Christmas time, showing her gorgeous legs and her tight waist, that followed by her very curved breasts. Her silky pink skin was goosebumps all over, and her hard nipples pointing towards Justin. She was certainly all woman, and Justin felt so pleased she had found out where he lived. Slowly walking on to the bed, she knelt down with her legs astride him, then took both hands and gently lowered his underwear, until they slid off his legs. Justin could see that she was so excited, she was trembling a little, as she placed his manhood inside her aching flesh.

He held her tightly from behind, spooning her sexy butt in his lap. She was making purring type noises, as she half slept. Justin felt so happy, contented, and a new sense of good things to come with her being around. " Wake up you beautiful lady," he said, as he placed a chrome tray with coffee, milk, and sugar, with two china mugs side by side on the fleece blanket. She looked and smiled at him, sitting up with her silky butt indenting on the mattress. Justin reached to the bedside table, and took a red rose, and handed it to her. " I hope this is the first time of many that I can make love to you again and again? " Justin said." If you give me a red rose every time you make love to me, you will have to take out shares in a flower boutique!" She replied and laughed as she took the rose and placed it to her cute little nose. He leaned forward, took her delicate chin between his thumb and finger ran his nail along her lip, then kissed her like no one had done before. They both knew from that first kiss; they had fallen for each other. No bells, or fireworks, but plenty of chill factor vibrations, and a feeling they both were meant to be close to each other. " Tell me about you, Justin," she said, as she held on to his hand and looking up and down his glistening blond haired body.

Captain Santino placed the can of soda on the desk that they were now sitting at. Opening a folder in front of him, he started to ask Justin some questions, that just might help catch these murdering thugs. - Firstly, I am so sorry for your loss Justin, and we are going to do everything we can to catch and bring them to justice. Justin had an odd tear run down his face, as he listened to the Homicide Captain. Sometimes he heard the

questions, and other times, the Captain asked him
again, if he could shed any light on this horrific crime.
When he left his mom and dad earlier that
 day, there was nothing out of the ordinary, not even
a phone call, or knock on the door, no one
 had visited. Justin felt helpless as he nodded, shook
his head, and said " No, " to many questions,
 15 was a young age to be told that someone had
taken his parents away from him, and they were
 never coming back.........

Chapter 2

Two Meters Deep

Bernadette had been with Justin over the last few days, and in just a short time, they were getting very fond of each other. Making the most of each other's company, they were like flies to fly paper stuck fast. Bernadette had placed a vase on her side of the bed, and in it, was eleven roses, it was so nice to see them in full bloom, and she realized that they had made love exactly the same amount of times like he said he would, he kept his word. She knew he was a good person, she knew now of the trauma he had to bear when he was a teenager, and she knew he may be the person she could be with for eternity.

Monday morning time and Justin kissed her as she lay sleeping. She looked so warm and inviting, but he knew he needed to move his ass to work.
Starting his " SUV, " He placed the stick into the drive position and headed along the road for the
The 15-minute ride to the Graveyard.

" Good morning you Yankee blond bastard!" The voice laughed, as Justin shook his working buddies hand. Lars was one of those cheeky sarcastic types and had worked with Justin on the graves for a few years. " So how was your last weeks' vacation then?" he asked as he poured some black coffee into some tin mugs. Justin knew as soon as he told him about Bernadette, he would come up with some jokes, and usually sexually orientated questions. "You actually look like your glowing, and that usually means you scored over the weekend," he laughed as Justin held his hand over his eyes and laughed. " I think this one is for keeps," he said with a smile.

Most of the morning was taken up with Lars asking question after question about Bernadette and making fun of Justin's sexual aerobics. Like most times, Lars changed subjects like the weather changes and then proceeded to tell Justin about his weekend.

After digging 3 graves ready for that afternoon, Justin looked at the schedule for the rest of the day, saw Lars was to dig four at the East side of the cemetery, and he was to dig three in the Southside. Justin climbed into the mini digger, and fired up the engine, it purred into action and puffed out some black smoke clearing the tubes. Driving just a few miles per hour, he was looking at the graves as he drove to the next plots. One grave that always made him laugh, was the engraving on the tombstone. It read. " I told you I was unwell! " with a smiley picture in yellow beside it. As he slowly guided the digger to the first grave plot, he smiled to himself as he remembered one funeral, where the deceased man had such a sense of humor, his last request was for one of his friends to dress up as the " Grim Reaper, " and just stand there, and that nearly started a riot with some of the mourners. Pulling up just short of the plot, he positioned the extending arm shovel just above the turf and got out to mark the ground he had to dig up.

Listening to his headphones, and his favorite music, he started to remove the earth from the area marked for the grave. The ground was quite soft, and there had not been any rain for a few days, so the earth was easy to dig. Reaching the two-meter depth, he scraped the ground in the grave at the bottom to flatten the base.

Part of his job was to inspect the grave, making sure that there were no un-even areas, and making sure there were no holes in the ground outside of it, so there was no chance of mourners twisting their ankles or breaking a leg. He unrolled some artificial grass, and placed it around the top of the grave, then jumped into the hole he had dug to test it. Taking his measuring tape out of his pocket, he measured the depth of the hole and saw it was exactly as it should be. All the years he had been doing this now, was paying off, and it was not often he had got the depth wrong.

Justin stood at his mother and fathers graveside and stared into the hole that had been dug earlier that day. There must have been eighty people there to pay their respects to his parents, and standing beside him was his uncle Zac, who had picked him up from the police precinct a few days earlier. Justin was still in his numb state of shock, and still thinking that he was going to wake up soon. But, here he was, in real life, burying his dear parents, who were taken away from everyone, by a person, or persons unknown. At the far end of the mourners, stood Captain Santino, he was dressed in a dark black suit and was

surveying all the people there. As both
coffins were lowered into the ground one at a time,
and side by side, there were sobbing sounds
 coming from the small crowd, mainly from the
women, and an odd cry coming from two of the
 male mourners. Justin hardly knew most of them,
but he knew in families that some members
 just showed up at funerals.
" We lower these children of God into the earth, and
ask him to take their souls into his
kingdom, and wipe their tears and pain away." The
priest said his Catholic ritual, then. " **In
nomine Patris et Filii et Spiritus Sancti. "** Some
mourners replied with " Amen! "

Walking away from the graveside, Justin looked back
towards the last resting place of his dear
 mother and father, and under his breath, he said
these words. " Mom, Dad. No matter how long
 it takes, I will make sure the people who did this to
you, will pay. " At that point, he realized the
last man standing there was Captain Santino, he
waved to the officer, then turned to get into the
 funeral car.

Justin pulled out a tree root that was sticking out of
the side wall of the grave, and when he
 looked back at the small hole, he noticed something.
" What the..?" As he looked closer, he was
unsure at first what it was, then as he reached into
the hole, he saw it was some kind of jeweled
wood. He forced his fingers from both hands to pries
the wood out, then as he tugged a little

harder, the wood slid into the bottom of the grave. Justin stood there, he was shocked, as below him, was a miniature treasure chest type thing. It was about eight inches square and had four diamonds on each side where the two handles were attached, they were rusty, but he knew this must be an old treasure of some kind. At the front of the chest, there was a hinged bracket, and a shiny square patch, where you might expect to see some engraving. This Patch, looked like it was brand new and looked out of place on the box.

He peaked out of the grave, and made sure no one was around, or looking, and placed the wooden chest at the edge of the grave. Scrambling out, he picked it up and then went to the tool box at the back of the digger to get an old towel that he used for wiping oil or dirt away.

He kept looking nervously to see if anyone was around, but the graveyard was empty of any living life. Wrapping the box up carefully, he placed it in the towel, then slid the contents into the toolbox, making sure he locked it first, as Lars had a habit of taking Justin's tools. He was being so cautious because in Sweden if you find anything valuable, you need to give it to The government and this just might contain a fantastic treasure, and he had no intention of giving it to anyone.

He was getting quite excited as he wondered what could possibly be inside. The exciting feeling was with him most of the day, and all the graves were dug, and he started to head back to the compound where the diggers were stored. " Have

you had sex in the graveyard today?" Lars
laughed as he continued. "You got that look on your
face that says you did." Lars laughed as
Justin shook his head with a smirk. A few moments
later, Lars had as usual changed the
conversation to suit him, and even though Justin
looked like he was listening, his thoughts were
of when he could rescue the box from the digger and
place it in his SUV!

Finishing off all their last-minute chores, Lars and
Justin washed their hands and faces and
changed into some more casual clothes. " I´m
walking over to Paddington´s bar Justin, are you
coming for a couple beers?" " Not to-night Lars!"
Justin replied, " I have some stuff to sort out."
Justin knew he looked guilty, but Lars was too busy
walking out the door to notice. "No
problemo!" Lars said and continued. " See you in the
morning, we have about nine graves to do
tomorrow, so early to bed after my beers. Night
Justin." Justin continued to pretend he was still
washing and sneaked a peek through the door of the
working cabin, he saw him get into his car,
and then drive out the graveyard.

" Good! " Thought Justin to himself, as he shut the
cabin door, looked all around him again, just
to check no one was watching and walked over to the
digger toolbox. Pulling the wrapped item
out, he again looked, with that still nervous look, and
placed the item in his trunk. No one was
there, no one was watching him, he knew he had to
get it home and discover what was in the
box.

Turning the key in his apartment door, he gently
pushed the door open, then holding the box in
the towel, he pushed the door shut with his back.
Tonight, was Bernadette's all-night shift at
Tintin's, " so he had the place to himself. Whatever
was going to be found in the next ten
minutes was so exciting to Justin, and he was
counting the dollar´s in his head, as this could be a
small fortune. The four diamonds on each side, if
they were diamonds, were probably seven
karats in total size, so the eight of them would
certainly be worth a few thousand bucks he
thought.

He was so nervous and decided not to cook anything,
he was hungry, but this was too important
stopping to eat. He unwrapped the towel, then
placed the box on the glass table. He was
trembling as he gazed at this magnificent item.
Studying the box closely, he was trying to
determine how to open it, he went to the kitchen to
get a sharp knife, and a wet rag to also wipe
the dirt off and sat down in front of it.

Cleaning all the stubborn dirt off, he wiped it clean,
and the difference was amazing, it looked
brand new to a point. The handles were still rusty
looking, but a little cleaner, as he looked at it
in anticipation, he thought he could hear a faint
humming coming from inside, but instantly
dismissed that, and thought his ears were just
playing tricks on him. The square chrome looking
patch was gleaming under the living room light, and
again Justin had no clue as to what it was.
Twenty minutes passed, as he tried every way to
open the box. He tried to force it open with the

knife, and attempted to force the hinges off, but no! Nothing he tried would help it to open. He
kept getting drawn to the shiny patch, it was almost like it was calling to him, " but that´s not
possible, " he thought.

As if from nowhere, a thought came to him. " Place your right thumb on the square plate. "
Doing what he thought was a crazy thing to do, he reached forward and placed his thumb on
a patch of shiny metal.

The next sound was spooky, as the sound of humming he thought he heard earlier was back, and
this time, he knew it was real, he heard it getting louder, then a little louder, almost like turning
on an amplifier and hearing the hum from the speakers. Without warning, Justin jumped up
from the seat, as a pain came from his thumb, as a piercing piece of metal stabbed his skin, and
holding his thumb dripping with blood, ran to the bathroom to get a band-aid. looking in the
mirror, he had no idea why this just happened but thought it might be some kind of booby trap
when trying to open it.

" BLOOD ANALIZED, " BLOOD TYPE, A POSITIVE. YOU ARE JUSTIN WEBBER! "

Now Justin really did think he was going crazy as he ran to the box, and stared deep into it, with
the now opened lid......

Chapter 3
Instrument Of Justice

As he gained his rational thinking, Justin knew he
was sane, he knew what he heard, it was just
so strange to have some machine that knew who he
was.

" Awaiting voice recognition. " Justin´s eyes widened
in surprise, as the voice from the inside of the
 box spoke again. "What the hell is this thing?" He
said aloud enquiring. " Voice confirmed. " I am
 Justice instrument 2077! State your request! Justin
reached into the chest, and lifted very slowly and
 gently, an object that could only be described as a
mixture between an " Xbox controller, a
 miniature tv screen, and a small computer surf plate.
" Justin looked at the metallic chrome
 looking object, he was thinking this was something
out of a science fiction movie, and again
 questioned his sanity.

The light reflecting from the object was bright and
hurting his eyes, so moved it slightly to the
 left to avoid the ceiling lighting. He could now see
the object more clearly, as he gazed his eyes
 all around the weird gadget. At the base of this
futuristic looking thing was a symbol. It was
 about five inches in a complete circle, with what
looked like rolling waves on the inside, and
 encompassed the 360-degree circle. Underneath, the
etchings looked like pyramids, and finally
under that, was what looked like four swords crossing
each other, and there was no beginning to
 it and no end. As Justin stared at the etched picture,

he felt like he was one with the object, he
felt a calmness in his mind, he knew this thing meant
him no harm, and somehow, this was
going to change his life forever.

He thought back to a few minutes earlier, he
remembered the voice asking him to " state his
request. " Feeling a bit stupid, he started to ask the
thing some questions.

What are you? " I am justice instrument 2077, I am
here to serve you, and bring justice to major crimes."
Justin´s face went from surprised, to confused, and
decided to get the machine to clarify itself.

" When you say major crimes, what do you mean?"
He asked. The voice came back with. " I
detect fugitives from justice, Murderers, Rapists, and
administer punishment for their crimes. My system is
100%
accurate, and I do not make mistakes, as my
program is infallible. The human race needs help with
crimes, and I am
programmed to do that task, where humans can miss
clues, I can detect them. Justice instrument 2077
standing by!-
----"

" Wow! " Justin could not believe all this, it was like
all his Christmas gifts had come early, and
" Oh my God! " If this thing can do what it says, then
he was going to have a hell of a time with
it. He walked into the kitchen with the machine still

in his hand, and saw that some chrome
looking bars had started to extend from the body of
it, they were slightly curved, and he just
knew that this had to wrap around his upper arm.
He placed the machine under his shirt sleeve,
and as he did, the curved bars joined together, if like
magic, and no join could be seen. At the
same time, it changed shape slightly and looked just
like an exercise monitoring gadget. Justin
was like a young boy, he felt like he was invincible,
and if this machine can do what it says it
can, then he knew soon, that he was going to head
for the States, and find his parents killer or
killers.

Justin thought deeply for several seconds, he was
going through so many different things in his
mind. Bringing himself back to " Is this reality? " "
Have I finally fell off the edge of my sanity?
He knew deep down, this was really happening, it
was as real as the clouds in the sky. Justin
Was also an avid science fiction fan, but this! This
was science fact, and staring at him was this
gadget, that says it can detect clues to criminal
cases, and solve them. " My God! What a
discovery. Speaking aloud again, he said. - I wonder
if this device is " Alien? " Straight away,
the machine answered his question. " I have been
on this planet since the year 1352 AD, I have had
many
controllers like you! My designers are from an
alternate dimension, their quadrant of existence is "
Nebular 03990.
I have been created to be the Ultimate Instrument Of

Justice. "

The machine's voice was calm, it was soft-spoken, it pulsated a tone that could be described as soothing to the brain, almost like subliminal. Justin had this feeling that it knew everything he was thinking, his every deep secret, probing his every memory cell.

Glancing at the clock by the aquarium, he noticed that it was now the middle of the night, he was overdue his bed, but he was too excited to sleep. As the excitement grew within him, he just knew he had to try this machine out, " and the sooner the better he thought. " He decided he would try it out after work the next day, but in the mean time, where was he going to hide it? Bernadette was going to return early in the morning, so it had to be hidden. Slowing his mind slightly, he looked around his apartment and was drawn to the Aquarium. If he lifted the top panel from the tank, he could slide the chest with the machine inside the center hollow part of the coral. Closing the lid, he looked at the fish and seahorses, they almost looked sedated as a gentle hum came from the center of the tank. Smiling to himself, still with all the excitement, he thought deeply of how the next day was going to play out.

" Hello, beautiful man!" came from Bernadette, as she kissed him on the forehead. "And why are you sleeping on the couch?" she smiled as she walked towards the kitchen. She glanced at the fish tank and said. " Good morning beautiful creatures, and how are we today?" she asked as she passed into the kitchen. A panic came over Justin as he had this fear that the machine was going to answer her! Jumping to his feet, he stood in silence, listening hard for any reply, but, then remembered that the machine was programmed for his voice, and his only. Wiping the sudden perspiration from his brow, he relaxed slightly, as the sudden fear he had, vanished as quickly as it had arrived.

If there was ever a day that went slower than time itself, then this was the day. Work was not enjoyable this day, as all he could think about was later when he had the chance to test out the " the instrument of justice. " Was this real? or was this some kind of giant hoax? He thought deeply as the minutes passed but seemed like hours.....

Chapter 4

Ultimate Test

Night time had now come to Göteborg! The hustle of people walking around the city was like
 electricity, sparks of life flowing through the streets of this magnificent Swedish location. Neon
lights lit up the tall shopping areas, and clubs with people eagerly waiting to have their drinking
 and dance time. Walking slowly along the sidewalks, Justin stared at men and women going
about their exciting night-life. Street entertainers playing many different musical instruments,
 each carrying their own sound, penetrating the ears, then flowing to the brain for stimulation.
As he walked, he slowly lifted his sleeve up, to reveal a little of the machine now attached to his
arm. There was a pulsating running green light, like " LED " dots running back and forward
over the small screen. Justin knew that it was doing something, but what? Again, Justin felt like
 he was attached to it mentally, connected to the heart of the justice machine. His only goal now
was to test and see the results.

Anticipating Justin's thoughts, the machine started to send messages to him, not by sound, but by
a form of telepathy. " Searching for fugitives! " Justin heard so clearly the words being projected to
his brain, and looked at the screen to see a newly appeared diagram in thin lines, and resembled a
 sonar screen, just like they have in submarines.

Justin walked into a red-light district of the city, where hookers were there in doorways, and bars, and were plying their trade to fill their purses
with money from the perves and crazies of the city. Someone once said. " Sex sells! " They
were right! This was still one of the oldest professions in the world, and even with the fear of all the sexual diseases around, people still plied their trade for money, regardless of the
consequences.
Blocking his way, he saw a woman who resembled an all-in wrestler, with muscles on her
muscles, and a pair of breasts that would knock you out if she turned quickly. " Want to have fun
with these? " she asked smiling and looked at the large breasts in front of her. Justin smiled back
at her. " Not tonight thank you," he replied, as he sidestepped her and passed her now growling
face. " Your loss! " she replied as she turned her back on Justin, and walked back to the doorway
from where she had come from. Only a few minutes had passed, then without warning, the
machine spoke to Justin again. **" Crime scene detected, analyzing data! "** Justin stopped in his tracks,
as he waited for the machine to give him more information.

" Continue 150 meters, go down side ally. " He started to walk forward with a little more speed, he was
perspiring a little, still excitement in his mind, as he turned the corner into the back alley. On the
screen of the justice machine, an image of the ally appeared, it was identical to the exact place

he was now standing. Suddenly, an amber light
started to flash Intermittently, then followed by
 a projected light coming from the front base of the
machine. A holographic display started to
 project itself on to the alley wall. Justin thought this
part could have come straight out of " Star
 Wars " movie, and pictured " Princess Leia " putting
a message into " R2D2´s " memory slot.
 Smiling to himself, which was then wiped off his
face, as a man and woman came into the ally.
 The projected images were that of a hooker and a
client who were obviously looking for a place
 to have sex.
The man had a half-burned cigarette in his left hand,
and the other he held the woman close to
 his side. The machines sound came to Justin's ears,
as the man's voice asked her how much she
 was going to charge him? " 500Kr for full sex! 350
for me just to masturbate you," she replied
smiling at the man.

" What if I tell you I will screw you for nothing, then
cut you up into pieces?" Justin was glued
 to the spot he stood in, he shivered to himself as he
saw the man grab her with both hands
tightly, and threw her to the ground like a rag doll.
As she hit the ground with a hard thud! she
fell into unconsciousness. Underneath the back of her
head, blood was running along the grooves
 between the cobbled stones. The man took a knife
from his jacket pocket, looked straight at the
 razor sharp blade, it was reflecting light from the ally
lamp above him. The man smiled to
 himself in such a way, that it looked like he was a
sadist, he gave an evil type laugh as he started
 to kneel down over the hookers body. Taking the

knife closer to her clothes, he lifted her white
blouse as far as he could, then cut the flowery bra
from the straps. He tore at the blouse, he was
like a rabid dog, even to the point he was drooling
white saliva from his mouth.

He gazed at her breasts, pink and silky, his eyes
slightly bulging with excitement. He tightly
held her left breast in his hand, and with the other,
he placed the blade of the knife on the top of
her shining pink flesh. She never flinched an eyelid,
as he moved the blade along her breast,
the trail of blood running down her side and joining
the blood trail from the wound in her head.

Justin at this point felt sad, as he saw the life
draining out of the young woman's body. She was
turning pale white as more and more blood seeped
from her wounds. Blood was starting to soak
into the man's clothes, his jeans were like they had
been dragged through a slaughterhouse, as he
still smiled. Raising her dress, he took hold of her
underwear, then cut them away revealing her
private soft flesh. More blood was gathering at her
navel, then trickling down and running
between her legs. Justin didn't want to watch
anymore, but, the machine had not finished
displaying the crime yet. Just before Justin threw up,
he saw the man force himself on the
woman, she was lifeless, he screamed with a chilling
tone in his voice, as he ejaculated inside
her. Struggling to breathe, Justin was choking on his
vomit, as he could not believe what he just
saw. Silence fell around him as his ears struggled to
hear anything, not even a car on the main
road at the end of the ally did he hear. He was pale
white, just like the poor woman he had just
seen. A horrible numbness returned to him, just like

when he had been told about his parents all
them years ago. As he tried to compose himself, he
slowly walked out of the alley towards the
main road. As he surveyed the whole street, he
looked at people going about their business and
thought how unreal, but real this was. This was
happening, and it had happened, as he saw a
police help poster pasted to the wall at the
beginning of the ally. He missed this as he walked
into the ally, but he sure didn't miss it on the way
out.

**" MURDER HERE AUGUST 17TH. DID YOU SEE
ANYTHING?
ANY INFORMATION TELEPHONE
POLISINSPEKTÖR MAXIMUS LINDSTRÖM
KRIMINALINSPEKTÖR : : : GÖTEBORG ! "**

Looking at the poster, Justin thought carefully about
sharing the information with the polis, but
then decided that they would lock him up, as a prime
suspect for the accurate information, and
only the forensics and the killer would know the true
nature of her death. " Not a good idea! "
He thought.
Justin lit a cigarette, and inhaled the aromatic smoke,
breathing deeply, and thinking about what
he had just seen. This poor girl deserves for her
killer to be brought to justice, but how was he
going to achieve this without incriminating himself?

**" I am programmed to help you in any way, and I
can make files available, and clues to crimes can
be sent via
computer without incriminating you! Do you**

wish to find the fugitive of this crime?" Seeing what he had

seen, of course, Justin wanted the guilty man to be caught, so with those thoughts, the justice instrument spoke to him again. **" Searching!!------Fugitive located, setting directional route--------Continue**

walking forward towards road bridge. "

Justin was now thinking what would he do. What would he say? If anything! Coming face to face with a killer was not the one thing he wanted to do this day, but, knew if he was going to be the girls champion, he had to face this fear and help her in any way he could. Walking towards the bridge, he took another cigarette from the pack, placed it in his mouth with his hand shaking a little then struck the lighter flint with the button and inhaled deeply again. Thinking all the time, and trying to figure out what he could do when and if he came face to face with pure evil itself. **" When that moment arrives, I will activate my justice systems, and the procedure will take place to dispense the correct form of punishment. "**

Everything was happening so quickly, Justin thought, and how was the night going to end?

" Justice will be served. " The machine answered his thoughts yet again.

Reaching the bridge, the dial on the screen went into radar mode! One of the flashing running lights went from side to side; it was green in color. The light suddenly changed to orange and flashing a little faster than the green had done. A

few hundred meters later, the road slightly
deviated to the right, and as Justin came around the
corner, he saw a bar café with all its bright
 lights blazing along the road. Like a very fast heart
rate, the blinking light went extremely fast,
 and turned to red in color. Justin knew he had to go
into the busy looking pub! " This was it! He
 thought, as he approached the door entrance, took a
deep breath in, and opened the bar door...

Justin could hear the thumping of his heart through
his chest, it sounded like a deep jungle drum,
 it pounded on his chest, and the speed increased,
making him a bit breathless. Approaching the
 bar slowly, he asked the barman to get him a large
beer, and a whiskey chaser. "You sound a
 little out of breath sir!" the barmen said, then
pointed to the machine on Justin's arm which was
 showing slightly. " Do these monitors bring you back
to life if your heart stops?" laughed the
 barman. Justin smiled through his nervousness, then
picked up the beer, and took a big swallow,
 it cooled his throat and ran into his stomach, which
was now feeling like it had knots inside it.
 The cold beer hit the spot, and wiping the foam
away from his mouth, he glanced around the
 packed bar.
A bar stool became available as a man got up and
left, Justin sat quickly before anyone else
could take it. Nursing his beer with both hands, he
surveyed the people in the bar area looking
 just over the rim of the glass. The foamy beer was
leaving a scum mark on the glass, as the
 beer was getting less and less as Justin drank and
looked slowly all around him.
The voices of all the customers were deafening, as

each tried to talk louder so they could be
heard. At the far end of the bar from Justin, he could
see a man sitting with his glass of whiskey,
this man was unshaven, long shoulder length hair
which did not look like it had been washed in
months. As Justin looked more closely at him, the
machine spoke to him in thoughts. **" Fugitive
identified..... Do you wish to administer
punishment now? "** Not knowing what the hell this
machine was
going to do, Justin panicked at the thought of this
thing using some kind of ray gun on the man.
**" Ray guns are for movies! I am the Ultimate
dispenser of justice, and I will serve your
command. When you are
ready, just say Activate Justice punishment 2078!**
Justin's eyes bulged in his head as he heard those
words, he was going to have to tell the machine
himself to do whatever it was going to do.
Maybe it would subdue the fugitive with a tranquilizer
or sedative, maybe a stunn of some kind,
whatever it was, Justin was nervous about the whole
situation. Bringing himself back to his
reality, Justin looked as the man got up from his bar
stool, then turned to head for the toilets
behind him. This was the time! It was now! Justin
thought as he also raised his body and headed
for the toilets behind the man.
As Justin opened the toilet door, he gazed inside as
he moved towards one of the stainless steel
urinals. With the mirror in front of him on the wall,
he used it to survey the washroom.
Standing at the far end, the man he was following,
stood, relieving himself of his alcohol. The

man looked over at Justin and quickly looked away again. Zipping up his trousers, the man started to head back towards the exit. He side glanced Justin as he walked passed him.

Justin's heart was racing fast as he knew he needed to act now, or it was going to be too late. " Activate justice punishment 2078! " Came the words from Justin's mouth. The man stopped, turned towards Justin. "What the fuck did you just say?" the man said angrily with his face glaring at Justin with a twisted look. In a split second, a powder blue light pulsated in a fan shape over the man. Struggling to move, he looked like he was paralyzed, he was fixed to the spot he stood in. A fear came over the man's face as he attempted to break free from whatever crazy thing had him. Moving his mouth was the only thing he could do, but when he spoke, his words were coming out quiet as if he had a silencer on his vocal chords. Justin was shaking with not knowing what was to happen, and how this was going to play out. " What do you want? what´s happening to me?" The man's voice shook with fear as the two men looked directly into each other's eyes. Justin spoke directly to the man and asked the question. " Have you murdered any women lately?" Looking back at Justin, the man's eyes opened wider, at that point he knew exactly what Justin meant. You could see the puzzled look on the man's face as he tried to figure out how Justin knew. The light was still pulsating, it kept him in his space, and as Justin thought back to what he had seen earlier, he got angry. "You rape a woman, you then mutilate her body with a smile on your face and watch her die as her blood drained from her body. You sick bastard! You had no right to take that young woman's life." The man still staring at Justin's eyes looked more afraid now and muttered a few more words. " So, arrest me, and they will say I am insane! I will get 5 to 10 years, then let me out for good behavior." The man's face looked twisted with his fear. At these words, Justin was enraged! He had got the confession from the man, openly admitting his guilt. **" Ready to administer justice! Do you wish to proceed? "** Justin flinched as the machine asked the question. What was going to happen? How was the justice machine going to deal with this? With those thoughts, the machine answered again. **" Request to demonstrate! I will reveal the answer! "** Justin got a little spooked as again the machine knew what his thoughts were. " What the fuck is that thing on your arm? Who are you?" Asked the man, who now looked like he was going to burst into tears with fear. " I am here to help people like the one you murdered and this machine will help with that." Puzzled, the man smirked a little, then asked. " What's it going to do? Disintegrate me?" **"Alan Iseburg, you are a rapist and a murderer. You will pay the price for the crime. Teresa Ljung will be avenged! "** In the next split second, a red flickering beam of light landed on the man's trousers, right where his private parts were, followed by a faint buzzing sound, and then followed by a scream that would have woken the dead!

"AHHHHhhhhhh!" Justin looked on in disbelief as the

man's groin area started to bleed profusely!
Almost like someone had thrown a bucket of blood
over his lower part of his body. The man was
in agony, he was shedding tears as he tried to break
free his restraint. With a few seconds
passing, Justin looked at the floor where a pool of
blood was gathering in front of him. Justin
once again wanted to throw up as he saw in the
middle of the blood pool the man's testicles and
penis! **" Final stage! Alan Iseburg. Justice
administered! "** For a split second, Justin panicked
as he
thought someone could walk into the toilet area at
any time. Before he finished that thought, the
red pulsing light moved to the man's forehead, blood
filled the man's white bulging eyes, it filled
every area of his eye sockets, as the man became
lifeless, but still standing up straight in the
restraining beam. **" Justice instrument 2078,
punishment complete! "** Backing slowly away from
the
extending blood pool, Justin had to move quickly out
of the toilet area. " What if he was caught
here right now? " He thought quickly for an escape
route. One thing he didn't notice when
entering the restroom area, was at the far end of the
urinals, was an emergency exit, and without
thinking, he ran to the door forcing the emergency
bar on it down and forward. Finding himself
in another back alley, he ran quickly to the light at
the end, stumbling a little with the speed, he
composed himself as much as he could, as he
entered the main road along from the bridge. At a
further distance from the bar, he stood at a parked
dump truck and shaking, he lit another

cigarette, drawing hard on the smoke he was inhaling. He crouched down towards the ground like a tight ball and could not believe that he was partly responsible for the man's death.

He asked himself," 2078? That means that it was counting up every time it dispensed justice! " White and shaking with fear, Justin moved quietly out of the area before all hell was going to break loose!....

Chapter 5

Polis Inspektör Lindström

Justin looked at himself in the mirror of his bathroom as he waited for the shower to heat up. He looked pale as he checked to see if there was any blood on his clothes. Not a single spot could he see, not even on his black shoes. Still shaking, he slowly removed his clothing, then walking into the shower naked, he stood there trying to warm himself up. As he trembled, the drops of water vibrated on his arms, he looked down where the justice instrument had been attached, no marks, no sign anything had been there, but Justin knew what had taken place. His thoughts went back to him entering the apartment and going straight to the fish tank corral to hide the machine again. The warm water was having a slight effect on his cold shivering body, as he stood there motionless wondering what was going to happen next.

Sliding the shower door open slowly, Bernadette stepped into the shower behind him, it took a couple of seconds before he realized she was there. Placing her arms around his waist, she picked up the block of soap and started to wash and lather him slowly. She put her hand on the soap around his butt, then moved her hand so she was slightly touching his manhood. Her finger nail ran gently over his raising flesh, it pullsed in front of them, as she held tightly and squeezing it so it became harder." You seem a bit tense Justin!" She said, still holding him in

her hand. " Oh, just been a strange day," he replied
squeezing her hand around his penis so the
blood flowed more. His thoughts ran through his
mind, as he could still see the man's penis and
testicles lying in the pool of blood. " I feel so low at
the moment, he held her close as the soapy
bubbles slid their bodies together with her private
flesh rubbing along his throbbing penis. Still
thinking, he felt so damn guilty, as if he had
murdered this man, but trying to shake that thought
off, he knew he was only dealing justice with this
machine. How could he justify this action? He
kept beating himself up with every negative thought.
" Maybe you are sickening for something!"
She said caressing the wet body. She kissed him on
the chest, with water flowing over her head
and face, then knelt down so she could kiss the lower
regions.
Running the thick pile towel over his body, she moved
her hands slowly as to make him feel
good, and pressed gently on his groin, as she dried
his pink flesh. " I might just take a couple
extra days from work and go visit my friend in Borås."
"Ya! do that, a change is good as a rest!"
She said smiling and kissing him on his lips.
Continuing, " But you need to make love to me
before you go anywhere," she smiled again with her
eyes sparkling with the thought of feeling
him inside her again.

Inspektör Maximus Lindström stood one meter away
from the corpse in the men's room of the
pub. He looked puzzled as he gazed at the dead man
in the blood. There in front of him lay the
penis and testicles soaked in his own blood; the

blood was looking thicker now as it dried in the
 air of the washroom. A policeman stood next to him
looking as puzzled as the Inspektör,
wondering how the hell he could have his parts cut
away from his body, and yet, the jeans he
 wore had still been on and zipped up. There were no
tares in the fabric and no sign of a struggle.
The biggest puzzle of them all was how the hell did
this man meet his death with his body still
 standing up? The Inspektör looked closely at the
blood-filled eyes, with some blood that had
 dripped like tears over the man's unshaven chin.
Blood droplets were thick and still now, as he
 looked up and down the man's lifeless corpse. A
Polis photographer flashed all around the crime
 scene making sure he had every angle of, and
around the body. The barman in the main bar was
 drinking a large whiskey as the Inspektör walked
towards him preparing to ask the important
 questions.
The Inspektör stared the barman straight in the face,
as he asked the man his first question. " You
 told my officer that no one heard any screams or
shouts, so how the hell did a man get his balls
 and dick cut off without anyone hearing a thing?
Take your time, as I have all the time in the
 world, and you better tell me everything that
happened up to fifteen minutes before the body
 was found!" The barman started to say how the bar
was quite busy, and that he only noticed the
 murdered man getting up to go to the toilets. He
was busy serving drinks and had his back to the
 bar area as he did so. " Do you have close circuit
cameras in the bar?" The Inspektör asked
 looking up at the ceiling and around the bar walls."
Just the one up in the downlighter over the

drink display, and only to cover anyone near the cash register, in case of theft." The inspector looked up at the direction of the camera, then as his detective mind looked, he saw the mirrors above the till and wondered if the camera had caught anything from the reflection. " I need to see the nights footage of the till. Is it DVD? Or memory card?" He asked looking back at the barman. " It´s memory card," replied the barman. As the barman went to the office to get the memory card, the Inspektör was trying all the bar stools to see the different angles the camera might have picked up on. Placing the card on the counter in front of the Inspektör, he asked if there was anything else for now? Answering him, Inspektör Lindström told him to be near in case of any more questions.

Pushing the memory card into his laptop, he waited for the program to load, which only took a few seconds. He scrolled back until he saw the murder victim sit down on the stool at the far end of the bar. Judging the guy, he thought to himself if this guy wasn't a criminal, he would jump off the dock at the ferry terminal. His sharpness for detail was second to none, he was quick thinking, smart, and had a nose for inner instinct! Interrupting the Inspektör, a police officer brought a plastic evidence bag and placed it in front of the laptop. " We found this knife in the back pocket of the victim's jeans, and it is not the murder weapon, it doesn't have any blood on it, sir! " Looking right back at the officer, he sneered at the officer. " Are you a forensic expert?" "No sir," came the reply. "Then get that bag to forensics to get tested, and do not assume anything you flat foot cop. " Sometimes,

the Inspektör had some choice words for
officers who assumed, as he told himself many times,
" Assuming is a fucked-up word that
should never be used, especially in murder
investigations."

Walking back into the toilet area, the forensic doctor
was pulling the man's jeans down to
examine the wounds on the body. " Any idea
doctor?" The Inspektör asked. Looking over the
rim of his glasses, the doctor looked closely at the
groin area, where the penis and testicles were
severed from the body. " I have never seen anything
like this before in my life, the cut is more
like a laser cut and has burnt skin fused together
over the whole area." Continuing. "From first
impressions, the first few seconds would have
caused half his blood to be pumped out, then the
extreme heat has sealed it shut, in English terms,
this is called cauterized, so there was just
enough blood to keep him alive for a few moments.
His eyes are filled with blood, so to me, the
brain has just exploded inside the skull; I won't be
able to tell fully until I have done the post
mortem."
Two forensic officers were placing the corpse on the
stretcher, as Inspektör Lindström watched
them take the body outside to the waiting black
morgue van. There was flashing of camera
guns, as reporters were surrounding the cordoned
off polis crime scene tape. One reporter
ducked under the tape to get a closer picture of the
corpse and was quickly manhandled back
and put behind the polis line.
Sitting back down at a bar table, the Inspektör
opened his laptop again, pressed the play button,

then watched as the seconds counted upwards on the screen. As the murder victim walked to the toilet door, 27 seconds passed, when the camera had caught a blond ponytailed man walking towards the same door, hesitated for a couple of seconds, then went through the toilet door. He could only see the back-left side of the suspect, but his gut feeling told him, this was the man he was going to pursue.

Running the recording forward, he saw after 10 minutes, another man going to the restroom, and then run back out to raise the alarm. The Inspektör knew the blond suspect was the killer, as he did not come back out the same door.

Calling to the barman in the staff room, the Inspektör indicated for the man to come sit down at the table then turned the laptop towards him, then pointed to the blond guy walking into the toilet. " Do you remember him?" The barman looked closely at the screen, then said. " Yeah! I remember him, he was sat down the opposite end to the murdered guy, but I didn't see him get up and come to think of it, I didn't see him leave the bar either. " " Ok! If I need you to identify this guy, do you think you could pick him out of a lineup?" "No problem!" The man smiled as he thought he had said something right for the Inspektör. " One last thing before you go. Did anyone sit down on that bar stool when you saw that it was empty?" Answering the detective again, the barman looked deep in thought as he said. " No! I remember now seeing the guy´s beer glass, it still had some in it, so I did not lift the glass until after the customer found the body." " And you probably washed all the glasses waiting for the polis to arrive, right? " The man nodded with a guilty expression. " Fine! You can go for now," and the barman stood and started to walk towards the back exit through the staff room. At the door, the barman turned, then stated. " Oh! There is one more thing, the guy with the ponytail spoke with an American accent!" The inspectors eyes widened as he heard these words, then raised his eyebrow to signal his brain thoughts. " No wonder he is just a barman, he thought, there is more brains in my little finger than his head. Ge'ez! "

Standing at the place where the suspect had sat, Maximus crouched down to bring his head level with the underneath of the bar counter, he saw fingerprints all over the area where the stool had been, then hoped that the forensic guys could get good prints from that area. " Dust for prints here, and let me know in the morning if any good ones come up," he said talking to one of the forensic staff.

Raising his voice slightly to one of his officers, he told him he was heading home, and to bed, he needed to rest his brain to enable his expertise to be fresh for the next day.

Seven am sharp, and Inspektör Lindström pushed open the corridor doors and entered the office areas. " Good morning sir!" Greeted him as he walked through to his own office. The polis woman smiled at him as he placed the laptop, and his briefcase on his desk then headed to the coffee machine. Pouring the black gold into his cup, he raised it to his nose to get the aromatic smell, that usually works wonders for him, and today was no different. " Forensics have left a report on that knife that was found in the bar last night, and I think you should read it straight away sir!" She smiled as she closed the office door behind her. Opening the file, he saw two pages of writing in the report and started to read.

" The report on the knife found on the male murdered in last night´s homicide is as follows. "
" Under ultraviolet light, the blade was examined closely, and blood particles were discovered. After analyzing the samples, the results show that the blood is not of the victim, however, after running the samples through the database, the blood test came up with a match for murdered victim Teresa Ljung, who was murdered on 17th August this year! "

" Oh my God!! " gasped the Inspektör, as he spluttered out some coffee from his mouth.

" I have got a fucking Vigilante on my hands!! ".........

Chapter 6

Death comes at a price!

Justin sat on the edge of the bed, again he saw his reflection in the mirror, and still looking pale
 with the horrible guilt feeling. He was starting to feel he had unleashed a monster, then thought
 back a short time, to the time he wanted justice for murderers. " I have become Judge, Jury, and
 executioner, " he thought as he raised his body to go to the bathroom.
Holding his cell phone to his ear, he stood silently as the ringing tone echoed in his eardrum.

" Good morning! Thank you for calling Mumster´s, Rickard speaking!" " Hi Rickard, it´s Justin,
 How´s it going?"
Justin and Rickard had become good friends for a few years when they had met in Stockholm at
 a concert with 3 rock groups performing. They were always glad to catch up when they talked,
 and Rickard started to tell him how he had just started a new concept.
" It´s really good to catch up with you Justin," Rickard said, as he told him of the new baguette
 butik in Borås, which was only about 45 minutes from Göteborg. " My brother Roger and I
 started up in June this year, and the business is going great!" " Good for you my friend. I was
 wondering if I came down to chat, and maybe stay for a couple days, that you might put me up
 if you have space?" "No problem Justin, you can come down as long as you need buddy!"
" Fantastic!" Justin replied. " I will be down in the

morning tomorrow, so will see you about 11
am."
Justin knew he had to get away for some kind of rest
if it was going to be a rest. The events over
last few days have played heavy on his mind, and his
sanity. He knew he was sane now, and
this thing was in his life, so he needed to decide if he
was still going to use the justice machine.
Packing his backpack, he looked over at the fish tank,
then decided to leave the machine in it´s
hiding place. The elevator door opened, and as he
went to walk in, he stopped, then turned and
headed for his apartment again. He was starting to
get a little obsessed with this machine, then
thought how if he could solve other crimes that the
polis could not, then it justified the action he
was taking. " I need to help these victims, " he
thought, placing it in the pack.
Heading along the motorway, he was thinking about
what the machine did to the murderer, and
how was this possible? How could it dispense all this
powerful energy? Not knowing the
answer, but, Justin started to feel he was some kind
of avenging angel and was standing up for
the murdered souls. The justice machine did not
speak, it did not send a thought to Justin's brain,
and that brought a calming effect to him, and right
now, he needed that.
Hugging each other, Justin was so pleased to see
Rickard and walking into the new butik,
Rickard couldn't wait to show him around. "Wow!"
Justin said with wide eyes, this was a very
smart and double floored butik. " The feedback
comments have been awesome Justin, and we
have trebled our takings in just a few months, and I
will show you some of our filled baguette´s

which have given us the best part of our profits." Justin certainly liked filled sandwiches, but, it would be hard for them to beat " Tin Tins " back in Göteborg. He smiled to himself as he was lead to the kitchen. " Hello Justin," came the voice by the cooker, it was Violette, Rickard, and Rogers " Moster "(Aunty) who was apparently there a lot to help the boy´s out in busy times.

Cutting small portions of the baguette, Rickard placed some of the delicious looking fillings on each individual piece, then asked Justin to try them all, and placed a glass of water beside the plate so he could rinse his mouth after each one. When he got to the last one, it was a Räkröra topped with extra Räkor, and, oh my God! This was like tasting heaven, it melted in Justin's mouth, and the flavors coming through in the taste buds was exciting, to say the least. " This one is fantastic Rickard!" He said with a huge smile on his face. All in, every filling was top of the range in quality and when he saw one of the biggest baguette´s going out to the butik, he could not believe his eyes at the size of it. " People have commented as far as Stockholm, and we have done hardly any advertising, so word of mouth goes a long way when food is this good." Rickard and Roger were very proud of their concept and were even more excited at the prospects of expanding, sooner rather than later.

As Justin moved the last part of the delicious baguette towards his mouth, the Räkor, and Räkröra slid down his throat like fingers being placed in a silk glove, smooth and full of tasty heaven.

Feeling very good for the boy´s, Justin was told that they hoped to have many " Mumster
Butik´s " up and running in the next two years, and even being as big as " Burger King, " " Mc
Donald's, " and " Kentucky Fried Chicken. " " If I know you and Rickard, you will do it," Justin
said smiling.
Rickard handed Justin a set of keys and showed him on a map where his new house was. " The
new basement apartment has been finished, so you can stay in there, and I put some food in the
refrigerator for you, so you don't go hungry." Rickard laughed as he knew Justin certainly liked
to eat well. Hugging Rickard and thanking him, he walked through the magnificent butik,
passed through the chiming door chime, and left in his " SUV: "
Unpacking his few clothing items, he placed them in the walk-in closet. For a moment, he had
forgotten the machine, he lifted it out from the bag and placed it on the single bed. Justin stared
at the shiny metal in front of him, he was wondering what crime he might discover in Borås!
Leaving his SUV at Rickards house, he ordered a taxi to go to town, and then would see what the
night would reveal. He glanced down at the justice machine around his arm again, it was pulsing
the chasing green light, side to side it went, as it did previously. " Searching for crime scenes. " Came
the voice from the now activated justice machine. Knowing what Justin was thinking, this clever
piece of metal guided him to exactly where he needed to be.
Justin leaned over a railing by the river in town. As he looked behind him, he heard many

voices coming from the bus stands depot. Several
busses passed to and from the terminals,
quickly picking their passengers up, then moving on.
" Crime scene detected. " Justin looked at his
arm, the machine was pulsing steady, the light just
blinking at the spot he was standing. Staring
at the river before him, he gazed into the dark water
slowly moving. The leaves in the water
floating on the surface, gently rotating and being
blown by the slight wind running the length of
the river. Ripples could be seen, as at times the wind
blew stronger for a few seconds, then died
down to a gentle breeze. As Justin stared at the
water, three small ducks paddled in front of
him, looking up as they swam by, probably looking
for bread that some people would throw to
feed them. Suddenly! His mind became a movie
screen, as the machine was now projecting
images of the spot he was standing. This time it was
different, there were no holograms in front
of him on any walls, but was being passed to his
inner mind, but with crystal clarity. Justin's eyes
were like they were looking backward, and inwards
as the new crime was starting to play just
like a " TV Crime show, " but this show was for real,
and deadly.
The first image to go to Justin's mind was of two
men, both in their early 30s, they were holding
a large black cloth bag, it was about two meters in
height. They were in a deserted factory
building and started to walk towards a girl, probably
about 18, she was sitting with her hands
tied behind her back. Her once very pretty face was
covered in small cuts and slight blood trails
running from them. Her eye makeup was running

from the tears she was shedding and streaked
along her cheeks as the mascara mixed with the
blood spots. Once again, an evil looking smile
came from one of the two men. He was probably the
eldest of the two and took control of the
second man. " You can go first Steven, and I will
finish her off!" The voice sent more chills
through Justin's body, was this the way most killers
were? Were they this perverted and evil as
they carried out these horrific crimes. Justin felt sad
again for the girl he was watching. The first
man pushed her body to the ground and started to
rip her jeans and underwear from her body.
She screamed loudly as the man forced her legs
apart, then started to rape her for several
minutes. She sobbed and looked so frightened as the
second man undid his zipper, then lay on
top her, making her cry even more, then with
desperation, she managed to land a foot in his
groin, she connected her pointed shoe with his
testicles, he let out a cry of pain, and at the same
time, he forced himself inside her again, this time
with angry eyes, and an extra strength of his
body pushed her closer to the cold concrete floor. As
she lay there, cold, petrified, and unsure
what they were going to do next, she managed to
scramble to her feet, her shaking legs trying to
build up the speed in them to carry her to the double
factory doors a few meters away. Her
attempt was in vain, as the older man jumped on her,
and the force pushed her on to the ground
again. "Where do you think you are going? Bitch!"
He shouted as she sunk her teeth into his
arm. With that second, the second man swung a
metal bar as he stood over her head, then,
brought the bar crashing down on her skull with

bones cracking under her hair, she gazed lifeless
 at the ceiling in the roof. The older man put his
hands tightly around her throat, then squeezed
hard, he had to make sure she was not going to walk
away from this. He stared at her body, they
both knew she was dead, and now with that
realization, they had to get rid of the body.
Looking all around them, they stood at the river
railing, they had brought along two big suit
 cases and the large black cloth bag, so if anyone
was watching, or passing by, they would just
 think they were waiting for a bus or taxi. Twenty
minutes previously, they had placed her body
 in the bag, and added four concrete blocks, as their
next task was to throw the bag into the river.
 This would certainly weight the bag down, and
maybe no one would discover the body ever, or
 not for a long time, and then destroying any " DNA "
evidence. The rail at the river was high
 enough at the bottom, so they put their feet firmly
on the bag, then forced the bag under it, and
 watched as the bag splashed in the water, then sank
quickly. With just some little air bubbles
 breaking the surface, they knew that it was time to
leave, slowly picking up a suitcase each, and
 walked out of the bus area.
Justin felt cold, he felt shocked and sad as once
again he had witnessed murderous hands at
 work. " This world is so full of evil. " He looked at
the water again, then knowing exactly where
 the bag was, he spoke gently to the submerged
corpse in the bag. " I am going to get those scum
who did this to you, and then I wish for you to rest in
silent peace!"

" Do you wish to find the fugitives? " Justin had no
hesitation before saying quickly! " Find these
murdering pieces of shit now!"
A sense of responsibility came over Justin, he for
once in his life was doing something worthy
for murder victims, and this machine was now a focal
point, it was an instrument for putting
things right, where the law had failed. " Hello, my
handsome guy! I was just wondering how
you were in good old Borås?" Came the voice from
Bernadette through his cell phone. " Hi!" he
replied trying to put a happier tone to his voice so she
would not detect any problems, and
especially not knowing what he was doing. " I am
just in town looking for a nice woman to go
home with!" She laughed as she knew he was
kidding her. "Things are good, and I met Rickard
earlier, he and Roger are doing great, and their butik
is fantastic, I am sure they are going to do
well. I miss you already!" she said with a sad tone in
her voice. " Only a few days, then you can
have me all to yourself," He replied. With a reply from
her that would have made a monk blush,
he laughed, then told her to " be good."
Bringing him back to the present time, the machine
sent him messages again, this time with
directions to find the fugitives. **" Continue 8.5 km
South until you come to Rydboholm. "** Knowing he
had to get a taxi there, he walked the short distance
to the main taxi rank, then sat in the back
seat of the first taxi and asked the driver to take him
to that area. The driver did not take long to
go the short journey, and asked " where to let Justin
off? " Hearing what the driver had asked, the
machine sent thoughts again and told him to **" stop**

at the first railway crossing. "

Paying the driver, Justin watched as the car did a U-turn, then faded into the night along the dark road surrounded only by tall trees and some rabbits searching for food.

The night was very quiet, and Justin started to adjust his eyes to the blackness around him. There was the odd animal sound rustling in the forest, but if you had dropped a small pin, you would have heard it for miles. Looking over the railway crossing, he could just make out some house lights on a steep hill ascending up some granite rocks. Slowly walking up the hill, he was careful not to trip over any wood or stones. With eyes now watching the machine on his arm, he saw the blinking of the light, it was now pointing straight ahead, Justin knew he was close to the fugitives home. In the still of the night, he could hear his breathing, it sounded like thunder in the distance and trying to control every breath and doing it as quietly as possible.

Justin stood just a few meters away from the front door, his heart started to pound faster as he tried to gather his thoughts.

A cold chilling feeling pressed on the back of his neck, followed by a voice he recognized. "You better be lost, or a polisman!" The voice echoed around the front yard of the house, then he slowly turned around to see one of the fugitives staring directly into his eyes. Once again, he saw evil facing him, only this time, the man was holding a sawn-off shotgun. " What the fuck are you doing here?" The man demanding an answer. **" Do you wish to activate? "** The thought wave came straight into Justin's mind, and without thinking replied. " Activate. " A beam of light came from the justice machine, it surrounded the man just like it had done on the last murderer. The man was frozen to the spot, he struggled to move, but only his mouth and eyes were not restricted. Justin turned his body to the left as a man's voice came from the doorway, he was heading straight for Justin, then reached down to his waist fumbling for a pistol wedged tight into his jeans. Very quickly, he raised the pistol to Justin's head, then shouting, Justin commanded the machine to "Activate " again. A second restraining beam shot from the machine, once again the second man could not move, and was glued to the spot he stood in. Justin stepped back a few paces, then surveyed the scene. "What the fuck is going on?" The first man demanded to know, then a second later, a hologram projection shon between the two men. The men watched with horror as their rape and murder were played out right in front of them. They watched and said nothing as the machine captured every detail, then showed the men their crime. Still confused, the men looked at each other, then Justin. " Does that answer your question?" Justin asked with a stern voice. They still never said anything, they looked so guilty, but then they had been caught. The first man then spoke quietly to Justin. - We want a lawyer, he demanded. With a return look, Justin gazed straight into the man's eyes. " What´s going to happen next is not going to need a lawyer, so if you believe in a God, you better have answers to why you raped and murdered this young girl." Justin's anger started to rise again, then looked at the machine on his arm and stated without blinking. " Activate

Punishment. " Two red beams of light shot from the machine, one to each of the men. The beams caused blood-curdling screams in both men as blood soaked the men's trousers. A small thud could be heard as both the testicles and penises fell to the ground at the same time. Seeing two evil grown men cry was not a pretty sight, but this is what they got for taking that innocent girls life. The blood pools were trying to run along the path, but only a few centimeters, then it soaked into the ground like a large sponge. The red beam stopped, then reactivated on the heads of the murderers. With a snapping sound, both the men's heads exploded with skull bones sticking through their hair. It was almost like a small hand grenade had exploded within them. They became quiet, their eyes filled with blood and started to run from the sockets. Justin stood and watched; he now had no remorse for what he was seeing and doing. The beam from their heads stopped again, then finally, the beam shon around the men's throats, their throats were being squeezed by a hidden force, and when the light had finished its work; all you could see was a skeleton bone with the tightly stretched skin around it. " **Justice punishment 2079 & 2080 completed. "**

Staring at the open door, he was curious as to how the two men lived, what was their habits? The fear had left him now, he was satisfied, satisfied to the point he was starting to feel good that punishment had come to scum like these men. Walking through the door, he looked around the large living room, then his eyes opened wider as he saw two girls about the same age tied to a

chair each. Both girls in their early 20s, both had
been crying, they had a cloth gag in their
mouths, their eyes were sad and frightened, they
stared at Justin as he looked on in disbelief.
Untying the two girls hands, then giving them some
water, they were so grateful to Justin. He sat
on a third chair thinking as to what was going to
happen next.
"What has happened to the men?" asked one of the
girls. " When you leave the house, try not to
look at them, they are standing outside, but they
can't hurt you anymore." Justin continued. " I
want you to call the polis 10 minutes after I leave,
and tell them the truth, and I am writing down
details of a murder they committed in Borås, the
location of the woman's body in the river by
the bus depot! These men just paid the full price for
their crimes, and you girls were certainly
going to be next!" The girls looked horrified when he
said that but knew Justin had saved their
lives. With a shaking hand, one girl reached to
Justin, stroked his face, and thanked him again.
Smiling back at the girls, he walked through the door
and past the two men, they were lifeless,
slight blood still oozing from their wounds and
standing stiff upright. Walking slowly to the
train crossing, Justin knew that within the next few
minutes the whole surrounding area was
going to be covered with polis cars and ambulances.
Sitting on the rail track, he sat and knew his life was
just about to get messy. Headlights came
towards him, this was it, he was done for. Flashes in
his head told him he was just about to go to
prison for the rest of his life, with shame brought to
any family members still alive.
The car pulled up alongside Justin, he heard the

sound of the window winding down, the
window stopped halfway, then he heard a voice he
could not believe. " Going my way?" Justin
looked up and saw staring at him, the last person he
thought he would ever see. " Bernadette!!?? " ....

Chapter 7

Two for the price of one

Justin sat opposite Bernadette, they looked with smiles at each other. Stretching towards Justin, she held his hand tightly, her eyes shining bright with the apartment's lights.

His mind drifted back to the railway track, and Bernadette saying " hello! Going my way?"

"Bernadette!!??" Justin jumped quickly into the car, this was the first he knew she had a car, and what the hell was she doing on this dark road where he had just acted on two murderers?

She drove at a good pace and did not speed as they went through the forest filled area. Suddenly, they saw several police cars heading towards them, their blue lights blazing in the night air.

Sirens howling as they got closer, then passed them. Justin looked at them as they still drove in the other direction. Soon the blue lights went from their view, then darkness behind them again.

Bernadette very quickly leaned over to Justin, then kissed his cheek. Staring at her, he was waiting for an explanation! She looked down at her right arm, and when Justin followed her eyes, he saw halfway up, the identical metal shape that he was wearing! " I have known since the first day you met me at " Tintins. " My machine told me that a second device was going to be found very soon, and the new wearer was going to be you. So, I had to make sure you were going to be ok with it and safeguard you from any possibility of danger. My justice machine also has a link to your´s and alerts me to where you are. On the night you went into the ally, then found the murderer in Göteborg, I was watching as you went into the bar. The machine carried on to tell me you would be coming out the back ally of the pub, so I knew I had to make sure, you were safe then!"

"How long have you had your machine?" Bernadette smiled again. " Just over 13 months and I have been to 11 crimes, and each time the justice machine dealt with the criminals who had raped or murdered. - Many times, I felt lonely and afraid, I was unsure if to carry on after the first time, but, I knew like you, that if bringing the criminals to justice was the right thing to do, I had to carry on. I judged myself many times, but my gut feeling was to help the victims, as our own justice system had broken down. Many murderers are sometimes caught, but then they may only get 12 years in prison, and some let out after 5 or 6 years, which is no comfort for the victim or the family left behind." Justin knew what she was saying, he knew the feelings attached to all this, and now knew he was no longer alone.

" I fell for you when we met, and knew you were a person I could trust, I just needed to wait for the right moment to tell you, so Justin Webber, you and I are deep in the shit together." Looking at each other, they moved closer then passionately kissed and held on tightly. During the ride back to Rickards apartment, Justin called him to say Bernadette had arrived unexpectedly, and if it was ok for her to stay? " Of course, she can! " Rickard had answered.

At the apartment, they spoke of their encounters with

criminals and how they felt on each
occasion, going over in detail how horrified they
were, and then getting that deep guilt feeling of
remorse.
Hugging each other close, they fell into a calm sleep
and enjoyed a peaceful night.
On awakening to the sound of the TV, Justin forced
his eyes open to hear a special Polis report
from Borås! Bernadette was holding a cup of coffee
and looked at Justin as she said. " You
made the news last night honey! "

" **From Borås, we can now hear from Inspektör**
Patrick Jönsson in charge of the case! "
" **I have to report the two murders of two**
middle-aged men from Rydboholm, who were
found deceased at their home last night. On
arriving at the murder scene, we found two
young women who had alerted us to the crime
and appears that they had been held
against their will at the location. An
unidentified man in his mid-thirties rescued
the girls,
and told them to call the Polis. The man left
the area quickly, and the first reports we have
are that we have discovered and recovered a
woman's body from the river in town at the
bus depot. The man involved told the girls that
the two murdered victims had carried out
the crime, and where the body could be found.
This information has turned out to be
correct, and we urge this person to come
forward to assist us in our investigation! The
man
is said to have a deep Irish accent, long dark
shoulder length hair, and has a scar on his

right cheek about 5 centimeters. "
The TV screen then went to cameras overlooking the
river in Borås, and crime scene tents
erected around the area.
Bernadette turned to Justin again. " The girls are
protecting you, Justin!" she said with a smile.
"They were certainly grateful for you rescuing them,
and giving false clues about your accent
and scar, which you don't have." " If you had not
come along last night, I would be awaiting jail
now, so that is one good thing about this all, other
people are glad these two guys are dead.
When I think about how this machine is swift and
quick with the justice, I hardly have time to
think about it all, until I relax, then the adrenalin
seems to kick in even more, like a panic attack
making me shake like a washing machine."
Bernadette looked at him with those all-knowing
eyes again then hugged him to help him feel safer.

Inspektör Jönsson stood by his desk holding the
telephone receiver, his ears waiting to hear an
answer to the call. " Polis Inspektör Lindström
speaking, who´s this? " Maximus!? Patrick
Jönsson in Borås headquarters here." " Hey! Patrick,
good to hear from you, how are you these
days?" " Up to my ass in crimes like you!" " I am
calling because I read a report the other day
through channels about a crime you had in that
Göteborg bar, and I think we might have a link
down here with maybe the same death wounds. " I
´m listening, Patrick! Give me the details."
After 25 minutes, they both agreed they had identical
murders, but with some slight differences
in the wounds. The biggest link´s being that both

cases, the victims had their testicles and
 penises cut off, and they all were standing up dead
like rigamortis had set in. All three of the
 bodies had their clothes intact, and every detail
concerning the unscorched clothes could link
 them to the same person. Inspektör Lindström told
him about how the man he was looking for
 had an American accent and a blond ponytail! A
slight pause came over the phone, then Patrick
 answered. "The two eyewitnesses say he was Irish
with a scar on his cheek, but I got the
 impression they were covering for him." " Sounds
like it!" He said with a slight laugh. " I know
 mine is a " vigilante, " but I just don´t understand
how he managed to carry out this kind of
precision surgery in just a few minutes, and with
what equipment? This is a real puzzler!" He
said, sounding confused as hell. " The next question
for me is if this guy has nothing to do with
the victim's crimes, how does he know they are the
guilty ones? " Is he psychic?" Inspektör
 Jönsson thought for a moment. " If he is, he is one
of the best in the world, but, he is now guilty
 of murder himself." He continued. "My two victims
have crimes under their belt ranging from
 theft, to assault with deadly weapons, and the world
probably is better off without them, but,
 once I have the DNA report from the murdered
woman in the river, I will probably be looking at
 the same situation of a vigilante. Look! Keep me
informed, and I will get back to you as soon as
I know Max! Bye for now!... Click, the receiver went
down with Inspektör Jönsson looking
 more confused, but also concerned if the vigilante
was going to strike again?
Bernadette was really surprised as Justin introduced

her to Rickards and Roberts Business.
"Hello Bernadette, nice to meet you, Justin kept you quiet," laughing out loud. Bernadette
smiled as she replied. "Oh! he is quite good at keeping secrets!" She laughed back with
Rickard. " So, let me try one of your delicious "Räkor and Räkröra, (Prawns & Prawn Filling)
as he says they are the best in Sweden," she smiled again as Rickard walked through the staff
entrance into the kitchen. Rickard shouted through to the butik " Two for the price of one coming up!".....

Chapter 8

Miami Revisited

The whole town in Borås was buzzing with the three murders on most people's lips. News
bulletins were being shown on TV every day, also radio coverage on " Rix FM! " The latest
 news was a release by Inspektör Patrick Jönsson of Borås Polis.
" After examining the woman's body, we carried out post-mortem examinations, this revealed to
us that the two men who were discovered murdered, were involved in her death. There was
enough DNA found on her body to connect the two of them to her murder. The strange
circumstances of the two men's death´s, is still an ongoing investigation, so if anyone has any
information, please get in touch with me, or one of my officers." The TV broadcaster then
announced that they had spoken to the girl's parents, and the report then followed.
The Father and Mother stood motionless, they held each other bravely as the news reporter asked
 the questions. " The death of a young person is tragic, but to have their life taken away in this
 manner must be heartbreaking for you? " The Mother with so much sadness in her eyes lifted
 her head, she paused for a couple of seconds, then spoke, quietly, but firmly, you could hear the
trembling in her voice. " Her father and I have had some wonderful times and memories with our
daughter, and for this to happen even before she could marry or have children is devastating. I

am glad that the two men responsible are dead! I am glad whoever killed them did what he did. I
 want to thank him for doing justice for our daughter, and I pray he sleeps well knowing for us,
 he did the right thing. God may one day forgive me for my thoughts and bitterness, but today, I
 am glad they are gone from this world. "
Justin and Bernadette looked at each other, they both had tears running down their cheeks.
Hugging each other, they knew that they had brought some comfort to those grieving parents,
and, the Instrument of justice had done its job yet again, swiftly, and quickly.
Inspektör Jönsson leaned over the two men's dead corpses, the metal slabs where they lay were
ice cold, it was a cold and quiet place in this room. The only sound on and off was of the bone
 saw the pathologist was using to cut into the skeletons. Holding half of the top of one of the
men's skulls, he looked closely at the fragments of bone pointing outwards, the conclusion he
had was not making sense, but however it happened, it was staring him in the face. " Inspektör
Jönsson! You might like to take a look at this!" Gazing into the exposed brain, he saw that burn
and scorch marks centered on the area from where the bone forced its way upwards, and
outwards. " I have never in my 40 years as a doctor seen anything like this! I have seen some
 crazy wounds on dead bodies before, but this is the weirdest of them all! What I see is there in
front of me, but, my logic says it is not possible for these wounds to exist!" He continued. " If
 you now take a look at the lower groin area you can see the same burn and scorch marks! I have
looked into the files of the male victim in Göteborg,

each wound around the penis and
testicles area are cauterized with tremendous heat,
similar to a laser! but this is not a laser. As I
said, this is weird at its weirdest!" The Inspektör
looked at the doctor with confused eyes, he
looked again at both corpses wondering just what
could have caused these wounds. " If I was to
guess at what caused the injuries to their bodies, I
would lay my career on the line, by saying.
You are looking for an instrument from a science
fiction movie!! " Answering the doctor, the
Inspektör stared at him with contempt, " If I put that
in my report, I will be kicked off the polis,
and then waiting for me outside the polis
headquarters will be a crazy wagon to take me away!
Straight jacket free of charge!!" The doctor raised his
eyebrows, forced a smile and at the
same time shrugged his shoulders to state " I Know!
"
Reaching into his jacket pocket, the Inspektör pulled
out his ringing cell phone, looking at the
caller ID, he saw it was the polis desk at
headquarters. " Jönsson here! " " Hello sir! I have a
taxi
driver here who says " he has information that might
help you with the two murders in
Rydboholm!" " Great! Keep him there, do not let him
leave!"
Pushing the entry button on the polis office entrance,
the Inspektör calmly walked up to the
chairs in the waiting area and saw just the one
person sitting there. He knew this was his guy, as
the man was wearing a taxi badge ID pinned to his
jacket. " Hey! I´m Inspektör Jönsson, you
have some information about the Rydboholm
murders?" The taxi driver stood up and leaned

forward to shake the inspectors hand. " I think I do!"
The driver told him how he had picked this
guy up from the main taxi rank and had taken him to
Rydboholm, dropping him off at the
railway crossing. "So, he was mid-thirties, dark hair
with a scar on his cheek? Spoke with an
Irish accent?" "No! No! sir!" The taxi driver looked
confused as to the Inspektör saying that.
"Then what did he look like?" "He was mid-thirties,
however, he had long blond shoulder length
hair with a ponytail and he spoke with an American
accent!"
" Leave your taxi badge details with the desk officer,
and I will be in touch with you maybe in
the future." The Inspektör shook the man's hand
again and smiled at him saying. " You just
might have helped to identify the murderer, thank
you!
" Two sugars and milk please Linda! " Answering the
question from Polis Inspektör Lindström´s
assistant officer. Sitting down behind his desk, he
reached for the ringing telephone. Holding his
cup of coffee in one hand, and placing the receiver
between his chin and his shoulder, he listened
intently as Patrick told him of the breaking news with
the taxi driver coming forward. " Fuck!!
I knew it! " he shouted, as he once again sprayed his
coffee over his desk. " Ok! now we can
home in on this son of a bitch, and we will have
him." Both inspectors congratulated each other
on their teamwork and started to discuss their next
move to catch the guy concerned.

Rickard stood in the doorway of the apartment he let
Justin and Bernadette use, they both looked
at his face. It was not smiling, and he looked

concerned, as he said to them. " I think you had better turn on the TV set!" Justin said nothing as he walked the short distance to the remote control, turning the power button on.

In front of them was a TV news bulletin, and standing in the center of the screen was the Borås Inspektör.

" This is a further update to the two men murdered in Rydboholm! New evidence has come to our attention, and we can now give out a description of the suspect we wish to interview. After speaking with a witness, we can tell you that........"

Justin and Bernadette turned to look at each other, and then Rickard, as the Inspektör described the suspect.

" The male suspect is about mid-thirties, blond ponytailed hair, shoulder length, and speaks with an American accent. " Rickard stood there with a sad face, he knew this had to be Justin, there was no doubt in his mind.

" How open-minded are you Rickard? Could you possibly believe me if I told you the 100% truth? Rickard looked at the both of them and told Justin to " Try me! "

For almost an hour, Rickard sat there next to them, he listened with the confused and skeptical mind. Justin then took the justice machine from his arm and sat it on the coffee table. Rickard gazed intently at this strange object. " Justice machine, please playback first murder and justice administered in Göteborg. " Rickard moved further back in his seat as the machine played back the hologram right in front of him, it also showed the punishment it had given to the man. **" Do you wish for me to show the Borås murder and**

murderers punishment? " " Yes! " Replied
Justin. Rickard and Bernadette watched every
second of the gruesome events, as this was the
first time Bernadette also had seen the full events
unfolding.
Rickard turned to Justin, then told him. " I was going
to telephone the polis first, but, then
thought I wanted to see your face first and see if you
could talk your way out of this! As
incredible as this seems, I believe you, I believe what
I see on the table, and, what this thing!
says and records. Bernadette turned to her arm and
pointed to her justice machine. " I have one
too!" She said. " Mine for some reason can
administer a completely different punishment. She
continued. " Activate the last playback from Malmö
murder. " Once again a justice machine shone
a hologram in front of Justin and Rickard. Stood in
an apartment, was the mid-twenties looking
man, he was kneeling over an old woman, she was
about 65, he reached into her purse, then
took out a load of cash, then placed it in his pocket.
He then picked up a brass table lampstand,
and hit her hard on her skull, with blood splattering in
all directions, he smiled as he looked at
her eyes go dark and then still. Her lifeless corpse
laying there, with the blood running down her
head and face. Her justice machine then played the
recording of the punishment. Held tight in the
machines pulsing beam, Bernadette told the machine
to " activate punishment! " Both Justin and
Rickard watched as the machine sent another beam
to the man's mouth, then all you could see
was his mouth, head and throat turning hot red,
there was smoke starting to emanate from his

body as it started to rise in temperature. His body was starting to reach the temperature of a small star! Before all three of them, the man's body melted like plastic from a shop display model. In the final few seconds, all you could see was a blackened fine powder, the entire body, including bones was completely dust!

With his mind diverted from his intentions when he came to see Justin, Rickard had a slight smile, then said. " If you are going to be some kind of avenging angels, you need to lay low for a while, and Justin! Color your hair brown for now!" All three smiled at each other now, as a calm came over them, they all hugged, and Rickard said. "Your secrets are safe with me! "

In front of him on the highway, he could see Bernadette in her car, he was close enough to see her waving to him every few minutes, he had a smile on his face when he thought how much had happened in a short period of time, with catching the fugitives, and the punishments given out by the justice machines. Justin was so pleased he didn't have to justify himself to her, and she understood fully the situations, and she did not think he was mad or a bad person. Their conversation before they left Rickards was to get back to Göteborg, then phone into their works departments to say they were sick! Then after, they would go to the travel agents to book a trip to Miami and the states. Justin so much wanted to take and test this machine out and hoping he could catch his parents killer or killers.

5 minutes before they arrived back at the apartment, the clouds opened up to reveal the first

winter snow falling over the windshields. " Getting away to the sunshine was now the exact right time, " Justin thought.

Justin woke to the voice of the air stewardess! " Would you like a refreshment Sir, Madam?" The bright white teeth shining through from her slightly opened mouth. Bernadette asked for a double Scotch! and Justin a black coffee.

She leaned over Justin's shoulder and started to place her head on it to try to relax a little more before they arrived in Miami.

Being on a plane for over 9 hours was an exhausting time, then when you have to reset your watches back 7 or 8 hours, you can understand why many people have " Jet Lag. "

Justin sat in the window seat, he was staring out into the darkness with a wide-eyed gaze, not really fixing on anything, just letting his mind go back in time to when he was 15.

Remembering getting into the funeral car, he sat with his uncle Zac! His uncle was not a great talker, but, he had this calm smile look every time you looked at him. Zac was a gentleman, he dressed smartly, always neat in his appearance, and never swore. Being an ex-Miami polis man, he always obeyed the law and would do you a good turn, if he couldn't, he would do you no harm. He was the old school sort, he would see you struggling with something, then would walk over to help. Justin remembers a time he stopped the car when he saw an old man who was homeless, he had broken shoes with holes and splits, he went to the nearest shoe store and returned with some adjustable slip-on shoes for him. When he gave them to the man, you would have thought he had given him the stars! Zac wasn't looking for the pat on the head, his ego wasn't that big, but to see the smile on the old man's face was priceless, that was the sort of man Zac was. Justin thought back to when he was about 6 years old, he saw his uncle Zac, his fathers brother coming to the home with boxes of Christmas gifts, he always brought some " Eggnog! " and some " Apricot Brandy. " When Justin's mom and dad weren't looking, Zac gave Justin a small thimble full to warm the " Cockles of his heart. " An old English expression. With a wide smile, he told him " not to tell his parents. " Of course, his mom and dad knew, but they didn't let on and smiled about it often over the years.

At the funeral of his parents, Justin thought back to them standing at the graveside, and one of the men crying was Zac. He had lost a great brother and sister in law who was dear and close to him. Each person grieves in their own way, and Zac was grieving hard that day. These people had never done any harm to anyone, they lived very happily over the years, and no one could understand how two such sweet people could have their lives taken from them in such a murderous way.

" Ladies and gentlemen, this is your captain speaking. We will be landing at Miami International Airport in twenty minutes, please fasten your seatbelts for landing, and make sure your tables are in the upright and closed position. On behalf of our airline, thank you for flying with us, and we hope you will join us again in the future. "

Bernadette kissed Justin on the cheek, then whispered in his ear. " I hope you are not too tired to make love to me in the hotel my gorgeous lover? "

She smiled and winked at him, and with a
comforting feeling, he smiled back at her.
" Remember Justin! I am with you 100%! Whatever
happens here in Miami, I will cover your
back. The Justice machines will watch over us, and I
believe you will get closure to this twenty
year old tragedy! Justin stood at the hotel window
staring out at the beautiful landscape before
him. He was naked and calm, as he thought back
twenty years, and the day he left the States to
go to Sweden. Twenty years was a long time with no
clues to his parent's murders. Bernadette
slowly came up to him from behind, she put her arms
around his warm body, binding her hands
tightly around his waist. With a gentle breath from
her mouth, she blew on to his neck, and at the
same time moving her hand over his butt. She ran
her finger up and down his silky dry skin,
between the butt cheeks, then up and down his
spine, slowly, oh so very slowly! She could see
the goosebumps rise on his skin, he shook a little as
he felt her beautiful body close to his. The
body hair from her groin rubbing gently around the
backside area, creating a tickling sensation.
He turned to see her eyes glistening, she was
radiating color from her neck, the orange and red
mixing like the paint on an artist pallet. She sighed as
he placed his hand with a gentle caress
between her smooth silky legs, she had become so
sexually excited, so warm, so completely
satisfied with what he was doing. She had never felt
deep feelings for someone like this before,
and right now, she was ready for him to take her, all
her feelings, and all her moist areas, she
wanted him inside her now! She started to wrap her
right leg around Justin, and with a hand, she

placed his throbbing nakedness inside, deep and warm with a tenderness some women have never experienced! She pointed her breasts towards his face, as he licked her nipple, and gently flicked it with his tongue. If heaven was just a feeling, then they were both in heaven, they were happy and joined together at that moment. As they both climaxed with heavy breathing, they looked at each other's eyes, all four of them were shining like stars in the night sky, and smiles as wide as rivers coming from their content faces. Gazing at him, she looked at him, then said. " Welcome home you sexy man! ".........

Chapter 9

Swift Justice
With No Mercy!

From the hotel, Justin and Bernadette took a short taxi journey to a car rental company, then after signing the papers, they both got in, and Justin adjusting his mirrors to drive the twenty minutes to the old house. What was going to meet them? Justin went quiet as he thought of some of the old memories of the past. He knew the house had never been sold, and as far as he knew, the " Real estate " company had taken it off the market over 17 years ago. Bernadette glanced down at both their justice machines on their arms. Both were showing green lights running from side to side. " Are you ready for this Justin?" she asked holding his arm slightly, then squeezed it to give him support and comfort. Answering her, he gave a sigh, then said. " Guess I am as ready as I can be! My heart is racing high, but, this needs to be done, and I have waited twenty years to discover the true crime, and now I have the means to detect what went on. I miss them bad Bernadette, I have a heart that misses beats when I think back to the day on the beach, the day I was told they were dead! We are two lucky people who have got something special, we have each other, and we have the justice machines giving a kind of hope, but a hope some people don't even know they have. We have to live through murders and rapes, we have to see the precise details of the crime to bring these scum to

light! The victims only have us, and I am
coming to terms with it all now. When I see in my
mind the women and girls that we have
 helped in some way, it brings a smile to my heart,
my soul, it lifts me up to heights of "
Spiritual awareness, " even the punishments dealt by
the machines. Only some weeks ago, I
 didn't know if I wanted to continue with this so-
called craziness! But, I have changed, we live in
 a world where fugitives literally get away with
murder, and if we can make a slight difference
for the positive good, then we have done something
right."
Bernadette started to tell Justin her first encounter
with the justice machine, and after finding the
first fugitive, and then seeing the punishment, she
felt a little more at ease for the woman who
was raped and murdered, and reminds her self of
that constantly!

"We will get through this together Justin!" As they
both looked out the car windshield, they
turned the last corner before Justin's old house. The
start of the long driveway still stood the
proud oak trees, they had definitely grown in the
twenty years since he had been there.
Driving the 100 meters to the house took only a few
seconds, then arriving at the front door, they
looked hard at the newly painted entrance, it was
spotless, and everything was in nearly the exact
place, as when he left to go to Sweden.
They both stood gazing at the white painted house,
someone had spent a lot of time replacing
old wood panels, new window glass had been
inserted. Scratching his head, he was confused, he
was expecting decaying wood, broken windows, and

slates fallen off the roof, which was now
showing a brand-new roof, shining and clean.
Someone had taken a lot of time and money to
repair the old house, and it reminded Justin how
good this old place was to be raised in it.
As they walked to the door, both of their justice
machines announced precisely the same time! "

 Crime scene detected! " Standing at the entrance for
only a few seconds, Justin was about to tell the
machine to play crime, but then stopped quickly as
the front door swung open to reveal someone
familiar!
Looking pale and frail, stood his uncle Zac! He looked
unlike the man Justin knew, he was
shaking slightly as he looked at the two strangers at
the house. " If you look closely at my waist,
I am holding a Magnum 44, Clint Eastward said once!
"Probably the most powerful handgun
ever made! " Both Justin and Bernadette's face went
chalk white! Then quickly Justin shouted at
his uncle! " Uncle Zac!! It´s me! Justin!!"
Zac looked Justin up and down, focusing his eyes
with a squint, he realized it was his nephew.

" Justin my dear boy, it´s so good to see you, why
didn't you let me know you were coming? "
Lowering the cannon in Zac's hand, he pointed it
down to the ground and smiled at Justin. " You
nearly had new ventilation holes in you! " Justin
smiled back, then threw his arms around Zac's
body to hug him. Turning to face the beautiful
looking woman beside Justin, he asked. " And
who is this charming young lady you have with you?
" " Well! She is special uncle Zac, it took
me a long time to find her, but, I think she found me!

" Justin laughed as he introduced them to
each other.
Walking into the hallway, Justin stopped, looked at all
the old surroundings, it felt strange being
back after all this time. The last time he was here,
was a few days after the funeral, and it still
held the scars of the crime. Now, the scars that were
left, were just the ones in Justin's head.
Every wall and piece of wood was painted to a high
standard, and varnish on the old furniture.
The floor shone with a glare from the sun entering
the doorway, and the large crystal chandelier
hanging in its pride and place, reflecting color sparks
all around the lower floor.
His uncle sat down in Justin's fathers armchair, it was
strange to see his uncle there, as his father
never let anyone place their ass anywhere near it.
His uncle picked up a glass of Scotch, it was golden
yellow as Zac took little sips of the
Scottish Highland malt!
" I have been coming here nearly every day since you
left Justin, I have sat here where you know
your father sat for many years. I have been thinking
if we missed anything in the initial stages of
the tragedy, and going over the police file, which I
was allowed to see after the case was filed
 closed! I miss my brother, and your Mom Justin, as I
guess you do too? Sometimes I sit and
stare into the whiskey, it seems to calm me for a
while, but, I know that´s not going to solve what
happened." Justin looked at Bernadette, then as if
they were psychic! Bernadette turned to Zac
and asked him. " How much of an open mind do you
have Zac?" She smiled slightly at him, then
waited for the response. " Open mind? Not sure what
you mean by that, but, if you mean would I

consider anything to solve the crime here? The answer is " Yes! I have gone through every report, but nothing, no one saw anything, no one noticed anything out of the ordinary.

Justin looked at his uncle, he saw like himself, the stress of the trauma, even after all these years. Being an ex-policeman stood Zac on firm ground, he had still got that spark to deal with fugitives, and if there was a way of solving this double murder, he would jump at the chance.

Justin and Bernadette looked each other in the eye again, Justin knew instinctively that he had to share the knowledge of the machines to his uncle. What was concerning Justin, was what would he say or do after he was shown the murders? and could his mind and spirit take it? There was only one way to find out!

Justin looked down at his arm that had the justice machine securely attached, it was flashing amber now, but not a sound came from the machine. " Uncle Zac! You are about to see something that your mind might not allow you to believe, but, this is as real as you and me! You are not going insane, and afterward, Bernadette and I will tell you more of this seemingly impossible science fiction type thing." Zac's eyes opened wider as he heard Justin say those words, but you could see on his face that he was trying to prepare for maybe something good being shown to him, even if it did sound crazy.

Justin placed the machine on the coffee table, then looked at Bernadette, then his uncle, then spoke allowed. " Instrument of justice, play crime scene! " A silent pause came over the house, then a voice came from the machine! **" Activating**

crime scene now! " Zac's eyes opened even wider, with a disbelief, he watched as a hologram projection shone from the machine. The light beam flickered as it centered the middle of the scene to exactly where they were sitting now. Suddenly! There she was, Justin's wonderful mother, then walking into the living room after her, his father! Laughter was coming from both of them, they were kidding each other on, and play fighting.

With so much laughter, they didn't hear the doorbell ringing, then they caught a glimpse of a shadow at the front door window glass. The glass was made out of bubbled French glass, so it was hard to make out who it was calling. Justin's father walked to the door, and as he opened it, he was pushed back in by a hand, the hand was covered by a glove, and fitted with a black skin-tight sweater. His mother screamed as she saw in the man's hand, a large caliber handgun.

Raising their eyes higher, they saw the man standing now in the doorway, he was also wearing a ski mask that had the eye holes cut from it. The man shut the door, then demanded cash and jewels, as he threw a black cloth bag on the floor next to them. At this point, Zac shouted at Justin. "Stop!! Stop now!!" Justin told the justice machine to pause the crime scene!

Zac's breathing was faster and harder, he looked confused and angry at what he was seeing.

" How is this possible Justin? Answer me!" Justin picked up a glass and poured some whiskey into it, then stretched over to Zac, then filled his glass with more." Take a good slug of that, and I will tell you the story.

Justin sat back in the chair, he tried to get

comfortable as he told Zac of the day he found the machine in the jeweled box, and what happened after that. He went on to tell him of his first murder suspect, and the first murder of the woman in Göteborg. He continued to talk to him of the machines justice punishment, and that its power was enormous! It was bigger than anything he had ever come across in his life! Zac swallowed most of the whiskey in one gulp, then poured himself more. " So, this thing! This gadget! can detect crime scenes, and administer justice?" Zac waited for Justin's answer, you could also see the strain on Zac's face, he was weighing all the things he had heard, and with seeing the hologram, he knew if he watched more, it was going to show his brother and sister in laws deaths!! " Uncle Zac! This is my chance to find out who my parents killer is, it might just help us both to finally find closure to this shit we have had un- answered for twenty years!" Zac went quiet for what seemed like hours but was only seconds in reality. " I have a pretty good level head Justin, and as crazy as this looks, I get the feeling of this is real, and right! " Justin raised that little smile again, as he looked at his uncle then told him. " The machine can link to you in some way uncle, and the feelings manifest within you, that is when you get that kind of psychic link with it!" Zac moved towards the justice machine, as he did, he felt a surge of energy pulsating from the machine, it buzzed louder as he got even closer. **" Permission is not granted for you to touch this justice instrument! If you come any closer, I will**

activate against you! " Zac stopped in his tracks as

he and Justin stared at each other. Now Justin
knew that is why the machine took a DNA sample of
his blood, it was like a security key, only
Justin could access. Taking another full measure of
whiskey, Zac sat back in the chair and
muttered! "Now I´m taking orders from a machine!
Ok, Justin! Let´s find out who this bastard
is!"

Bernadette excused herself to go to the bathroom,
and left the living room and smiled at Justin
as she left. Justin noticed on her face a kind of
knowing something, but never said what it was.
" Continue to play on the crime scene!" Justin
watched, as he and his uncle continued to see the
Crime unfold.

Justin's mother nervously picked up the bag, then
walked over to the Bureau where they kept
some of the jewelry. She fumbled through the
drawers then picked up a couple thousand dollars
cash from one of them, then placed it in the bag. The
masked man stood there, he was standing
straight, he had a steady hand with no visible signs of
nerves. She walked slowly towards the
man, handing him the contents, he looked inside,
then in a sudden burst of rage, he started to
shout in an evil type of way. " Is that all? You are
kidding me right!?" With a trembling sound
coming from her, she told him, " that's all they had! "
Now with a calmer voice, he said. " I don't
like liars." At the end of those words, he turned the
barrel of the gun towards Justin's father.
"Bang!!! " Followed by another 4 shots one after the
other. Justin's mother ran towards his father
picking him up with blood everywhere. She looked up
at the man, as now he was pointing the
gun at her. A heavy sobbing could be heard around

the house, as she held her dying husband.
"Why? Why this?" She knelt there lonely, frightened, and so much wanted to fight back, but she was powerless and helpless all at the same time. She could do nothing!
Zac and Justin looked at each other, their eyes were filled with water droplets, Justin tried to force back the tears as he wanted to focus on the crime, just in case he missed something. "You have what you came for, just go now and leave us alone!" She was getting hysterical now and holding her husband tighter and tighter, she so much wanted him to live. Justin's father started to cough and choke on the blood that was now pouring into his lungs and chest cavities, blood spurted from his mouth as he was gasping for air. " Go!! Just go!" she screamed as the gunman stood there aiming the sight right at her. She saw him raise his left hand towards his face mask, then placing some of his fingers below the material, he slowly started to lift the mask off. With more hysterical behavior she shouted at him. "No!! No! don´t do that!" The fear in her eyes worsened because, at that point, she knew if he took the mask off, she was dead!!

" Oh, I think you need to see who I am!" He smiled beneath the moving mask, then shook his hair as his face was exposed!! Holding her lifelong partner tight, her eyes looked petrified and confused, as she stared at the now naked face. Zac and Justin again looked on in disbelief, they were gazing into the eyes of the long-lost murderer!.....
Zac stood up quicker than an " Olympic athlete! " His mouth gaping open as if his jaw had

collapsed! There standing in the hologram, was the killer, it was one of Zac's old police buddies. Captain Alejandro Santino!! Both Justin and Zac now stood in the middle of the room, disbelief on both their faces. Seconds, and more seconds ticked by as time seemed to stand still. A void of unreal horror, as after 20 years, they could see the cold-blooded man before them, this so-called man, of law, this upstanding citizen, this murdering scum bastard!!

Justin's mother looked into his eyes, her mind was racing, now, it all made sense! Her memory activated from a few months previously. She spoke to the twisted cop! as she knew he was rejected by her 3 months before. " You have done all this because you made advances to me the night my husband and Zac went for some more beers, you tried to unbutton my dress and put your hand inside my underwear. Underneath that badge Alejandro! You are filth! You are the lowest form of scum on Gods earth! You did this because you were rejected?? Get the hell out of my house!! " The fear left her quickly, she still looked straight into his eyes, they had grown dark in color, like oil pools in the sunlight, empty, and pure evil!

Alejandro smiled back at her, he didn't care, you could see by the expression on his face, he was getting some kind of sadistic pleasure from it all. She spoke to him with a little more calmness with her next words, when she said. " I know I am dead, so pull the trigger now!!

" BANG!! " As he went to pull the trigger for the second time, the gun just clicked, he had used all the chambers bullets, at that point she lay there, bleeding heavily and fell back on the floor

hitting her head. " Nooo!! " Justin burst into tears
heavily sobbing as he witnessed yet again
another parent dying right in front of him. Seconds
passed, then! "Bang!! bang!" right into her
breasts and finally, he took aim at her head. " Bang!!
" In a few moments, he had reloaded the
revolver had clicked it shut, then re-aimed. "You
won't reject anyone else again bitch!!"
Zac and Justin were speechless as they saw the
woman's head explode with the force of the high
caliber gun. Bone protruded from the back of the
skull, with grey strands of brain splattered all
over the room and walls.
A twenty-year-old crime had just been solved, but,
the murderer, was probably the last person
anyone would have thought of.
Trying to compose themselves, Zac and Justin wiped
their teary eyes, Zac reached into his inside
jacket pocket for a handkerchief. Wiping his eyes and
nose, he had seen their murders but found
it so hard to believe who the killer was. Both of them
reached for the whiskey at the same time,
as if that was going to make everything better, if
anything, they both felt angry and slightly
intoxicated!
" How the hell are we going to prove all of this
Justin?" Looking empty, Zac turned to Justin for
the answer, and replied very quickly, Justin said. "
Uncle Zac! You are forgetting something, we
have the Justice machine! After 20 years, we still
don't have evidence that a jury would believe,
so, the punishment needs to be done by the only
thing that knows the truth!" Holding his head in
his hands after everything they had seen, Zac
pinched his eyes with his thumb and forefinger,
and at the same time wiping more moisture from

them. " I am going to kill that son of a bitch my
self! I don't need any machine to do that for me." "
Please listen, uncle Zac! Taking his life will
leave clues somewhere around, forensics would pick
up on it in minutes, so let the machine do
what it does, and they will not understand how it was
done, but it will be done."
Facing away from the front door, none of the two
men standing there noticed the front door had
been opened, and standing there, the murderer
himself!
"Well! Well! Well! the voice interrupted them as they
spun around quickly to face the murdering
cop. " So that´s how you discovered me huh? After
all these years I had the feeling that young
Mr. Webber would come looking for answers, but this
machine! This is something else!" The
cop stood there pointing a gun directly at the two of
them. " And in case you are wondering,
Yes! " this is the same weapon I used! Would you like
to know another crazy thing? It was the
same neighbor who tipped me off that some
strangers were at the old house, and sadly, the 89
year old won't reach 90, she has gone to meet her
maker, I guess the old nosey bitch won't be
reporting any more shit huh?" As Alejandro had been
talking, he didn't notice Zac reaching
slowly for his very big cannon revolver, at that
moment, Justin sent a thought out to the justice
machine. " Activate fugitive mode!! " Nothing! Again,
he thought the thought! " Justice machine,
Activate now!!" Still sliding his hand slowly towards
his gun, Zac stopped, as Alejandro caught
a glimpse of what he was trying to do. " If you want
to make the last move you ever have, try for
your gun for one more second!" Zac froze and

removed his hand away from the weapon.
"After all these years Santino! I just thought you
were a good cop! One of the good guys, and
yet, now your true colors have surfaced to make this
world even uglier!" With that response
from Zac, Alejandro gave one of those evil looks, just
like most of the killer's smiles that glued
to their faces, just before and after their vicious
crimes. Turning slightly towards Justin, he
remembered the day he was in his office,
interviewing Justin. " And you young Webber! I was
going to pin the murders on you! But! The time
frame was all wrong, you had too many alibi
witnesses. Over my career, I have enjoyed watching
people squirm like an insect when they see
me coming, they smell of shit and stench in their
cozy little hideaways. "Your mother was acting
like an angel, so " goody two shoes, " like " butter
wouldn't melt in her mouth. "Justin's face
went red, he hated what he was saying about his
mother, but trying to keep all his built-up anger
inside, that wasn't easy. " All women are nothing but
whores and shit under my shoes!" Courage
started to return to Justin, he began to rise from his
chair, slowly, but fast enough to make
Alejandro flinch and re-aim his gun at him. " OH! and
one more thing, I had an interesting
conversation with a polis Inspektör Lindström from
Göteborg! He is most anxious to talk to you
about some murders there and Borås! Tut tut! Have
you been a busy boy huh? So, what is going
to happen now. Any ideas Zac? Justin?" Silence fell
on the room again, all that you heard was
the ticking of the mantel clock against the wall.
Zac looked at Alejandro, then smiled in a knowing
way at him. " I have witnessed you murder

two innocent people, you say you killed the old lady next door, and I imagine you have more murder notches to your gun belt that we don't know about. Let me tell you how this is going to go, Alejandro!" The police detective stood more upright, he was really interested to hear Zac's comments on this situation. " I think that you underestimate this machine, Alejandro! You have no idea that in a moment, this device is going to capture your ass, then as we stand there watching you try to escape from it, we are going to watch as you get your deserved payback!" Silence again..... Then!... A thunderous laughter came from Santino's mouth, he laughed so hard, his side started to hurt, then as he laughed, he took aim at the machine, " Bang!! "A loud shot echoed around the room as instantaneously, the machine exploded into hundreds of smaller pieces with the force of the bullet striking it dead center! Tiny fragments of the justice machine spewed on to the floor, bouncing to every inch of the room. For such a small device, it was unbelievable the amount of splintered metal laying before them. " I´m sorry! What were you saying Zac, my old friend?" The silence that followed was deafening! " Tick Tock! Tick Tock!" Again, the sound of the clock boomed in their ears as the gun was trained on Justin and Zac. Smoke was curling its way out of the gun barrel after the shot, it floated higher towards the ceiling as Alejandro spoke yet again. " Well boys, I think it´s about time we wrapped this little party up huh? " Looking for their reaction to that comment, both of them smiled at Alejandro as Zac opened his mouth to speak. " As I said! In a moment, the machine is going to capture your ass, then as we stand there watching you try to escape from it, we are going to watch as you get your deserved payback!" " I think you boys have had too much of the Scotch whiskey! And I thought I was the crazy one here!" Laughing again he wiped the laughter tears from his eyes and then said. " Lights out time!! " He aimed the gun first at Justin, then.....

" Activate justice machine now!! " What a sound that was, as a humming sound came from the justice machine. Alejandro was paralyzed from the neck down, his eyes widened as the face expression showed his confusion. " Do you wish for me to activate my justice sequence? " The voice was soft and gentle, but so different to the voice of the last machine! Justin and Zac both at the same time sighed a sigh of relief, as they looked behind Santino, and smiled at the welcomed sight before them. " I thought you had fallen down the toilet Bernadette!" All three started to laugh as they started to calm down after all the trauma. Adrenalin pumped hard through their three bodies as the aftershock was taking hold. Zac turned to walk towards Bernadette, then approaching her, he grabbed her like an angry bear and squeezed her tight as tears dampened his cheekbones.

Thank you, young lady! He held her for a brief moment, as the voice from Santino shouted.

"You need to read me my rights! you need to take me in!" Demanded the now frightened looking detective. All three stood in front of him, staring wildly into his eyes. Zac looked to Justin, then nodded to him knowingly as to what to do next.

" Alejandro Santino! You are guilty of murder! To actually say for all these years that you were friends with me and Justin's parents is now an insult to their name. " Santino started to snivel and blubber like a little baby, he was whimpering like a frightened animal, but, animals deserved more respect than him. Justin leaned over to Bernadette's ear and whispered to her. Pleading for his life he screamed at the three possible executioners before him. " Mercy! Mercy!" he cried just as the words came out of Bernadette's mouth. "Activate instrument of justice punishment!! " Justin's last words before the machine activated were.." Mercy? You never showed Mom and Dad mercy!! Go to fucking hell Santino!! " A loud hum came from the machine as a red beam shot quickly from the metal object on Bernadette's arm. The next sound was of the beam pushing through Santino's stomach, the beam went clean through his body and fixed on the wall behind him, blood following the beam in the same direction, then stopped! As the three of them watched, they could see clean through to the back wall and then daylight through the hole that was now there. The blood stopped draining instantaneously as the heat from the beam cauterized the wound. Alejandro gasped for breath, but he was still alive, still breathing. A second beam, third, fourth, and fifth shot from the justice device Simultaneously! Each beam in the same pattern as Justin's parent's wounds, then, holes as the first wound appearing with daylight penetrating the freshly burned flesh. He started to smell like " burnt pig! " Zac thought, then said. " Rot in your own juices scumbag!! " The life you were watching, slowly draining from his carcass, as suddenly, the last beam shot through his cheek, then with a small explosion, his skull opened up on one side as the beam came to rest on the wall behind.!!

" Do you wish to use burn program? " Bernadette glanced at Justin, and as she did, he nodded to her to confirm the final action! Like standing next to a small sun was the feeling and heat for five seconds, as the complete dead body disintegrated into a small pile of dust particles!

" Justice instrument 4267 punishment complete!!

" Swift justice and no mercy was shown for Alejandro Santino. " Murderer! "......

Chapter 10

NEBULAR
03990!

A cloud of gas and dust in outer space. Visible in the night sky either as an indistinct bright
patch or as a dark silhouette against other luminous matter. Some people say that " Nebulas are
old stars that come to die! " Some say " This is a magical place that things from our wildest
dreams mature. Colors so bright, so radiant, shapes like horses heads, lions, and even unicorns,
 whatever your belief, " Space " is one of the unknowns, and man has only just begun to tap into
 this vast void! "
Justin lay with his head against the aircraft window, the night sky like a black canvas with bright
specs twinkling every few seconds. A new peace had fallen over him, with the pain of his
parent's death hundreds of kilometers behind him, he had serenity in his heart for the first time in
his life. He thought back to the last day in Miami and starting the journey back to Sweden, and
 the unknowing fate that waited for him...

"I guess you are going back then Justin?" His uncle Zac sad at the thought. " I need to! I can´t go
all the rest of my life looking over my shoulder uncle Zac! Maybe the one miracle I need will
happen to me, but I doubt it! I take the responsibility seriously for what has happened, but I don´t
regret anything now if my purpose was just to help a few good people, then I have achieved
that."
As Justin spoke, you could hear a sadness underlying

in his voice, it was quieter and soft, even
though he was 35, he had grown even more with all
the pain and emotions that had surfaced over
this short time. The justice machines had opened his
eyes to the reality of life, and how some
people abused and made others suffer. They made
sons and daughters parentless, and mothers
and fathers childless. This was a world that was
running out of control, and justice had to be
found another way.
" I see on the Miami news that they have put a
nationwide hunt out for Captain Alejandro
Santino!" "Yeah!" replied Justin with a little smile. "
News reports say that an email arrived at
police headquarters confessing to the murders of
twenty years ago of Mr. & Mrs. Webber! And
killing an 89-year-old lady in connection with it."
"Yup! Says also he could not live with the
guilt anymore, and the murder weapon turned up at
the precinct in a mailbox! with his prints all
over it. Makes you feel that he got his just deserts
huh?" Justin smiled again, then took his uncles
hands in his. Shaking them, he looked at his uncle's
eyes, there was a calmness about them now,
they had received the answers that had been evading
them for 20 years, and now they could let
the peace penetrate into his soul.
Justin looked at the garden just outside the house, a
single red and pink mixed colored rose stood
there, proud and upright, just swaying slightly in the
breeze. Justin knew within his heart that
this was his parents rose, the red for his father, and
pink for his mother and that they were
together somewhere in the vast universe, laughing,
kidding each other, and play fighting.
" Love is a wonderful thing Justin, your parents had it

until the day they died, and I believe they
still have it and enjoying a new peace of color and
light. If that is heaven, then that's just the
start of it.
Zac walked back into the house, pausing just for a
moment, then walked over to Justin's father's
chair poured out a large whiskey, then sat his aching
butt on the soft seat. Resting his arms on the
armrests, he lifted the glass with the golden nectar. "
Get your ass in here Justin! Pour yourself a
stiff one, then me and you are going to chat about
Bernadette and you getting married!"
Laughing again, they began to tell each other stories
of Mr. & Mrs. Webber, their crazy parties,
the strange things they did, and about their honesty
in their life that they gave to others, kindness
and hospitality to everyone. " Oh! And Justin, if you
find another of those justice gadgets, send
me one!" deep low laughter filled the house, the
house that held so much sadness for years, now
gone, just like the evil creature that caused it!
Bernadette came in and sat beside them. She could
see the relief on both their faces, but a slight
hint of worry on Justin's. " It´s easy to say " Don't
worry about returning to Sweden, But I have
a good feeling something good just might come out
of it all." Looking at her with that cute smile
of his, he nodded to her, then gently held her hand
and kissed it tenderly pulling it over his cheek
and chin.
Loading their luggage into the trunk, Justin pushed it
shut, at the same time, Bernadette was
hugging Zac, holding her as tight, the same way he
held her that day they dispensed the
punishment to Santino. He put his mouth to her ear.
" Look after him, honey! " He looked at her

out the corner of his eyes, then a slow wink followed
by a gentle kiss with her winking back to
reassure him...

Justin turned his head to see that the sweet lady
beside him was resting again on his shoulder,
now with a small pillow, the stewardess provided. Her
Justice machine was showing on her arm,
he looked at it with a smile, then, he saw scrolling
words running across the screen. Curiously,
he looked closer to see a message to him! **" In less
than two minutes, you will feel a small jolt of
electronic**

 **pulses do not be alarmed; someone wants to
meet you! "** Three worry lines appeared on his
forehead,
wondering what to expect next, he tried to calm
himself, thinking, " Just another weird thing
happening in his life again! " His next view was of him
standing in the isle of the plane, he saw
passengers reading, taking coffee, and a few were
using their laptop computers, some working
on reports, others playing cute games. He stared at
his seat. Seeing himself sitting there was
another crazy unexplained happening. Panic was
setting in. " Am I dead? " A clear thought came
to his mind. " No Justin, you are in an astral travel
state, I am here to guide you to a place of
serenity, a place where only a few humans have ever
been to." The voice was deep, soft, it was
like listening to a hypnotic voice, but you just knew it
was real. He wasn't dreaming, he felt that,
but his mind was trying to work out how this was
possible. " Walk to the middle right door,

Justin! Look beyond the metal and glass, you will
feel the energy of the atoms parting in front
of you, have no fear as you walk into the atoms. "
Glancing back to his seat, he saw how comfortable
Bernadette was, she had a sleepy smile as she
snuggled closer to Justin, he felt her closeness, but
at the same time, he felt he was being drawn
into this new unknown, an unknown so powerful it
excited him greatly! A famous quote came to
him as he walked into the metal and metallic light
that pulsated before his eyes! **"That's one
small step for man, one giant leap for
mankind."** Neil Armstrong July 20th, 1969!
He felt like a mist! being there and everywhere all at
the same time, even hearing soft musical
tones, deep bass, then high pings, almost like he was
inside an acoustic synthesizer. An
 unbelievable surge of energy rushed through his
very thought process, giving him thoughts of "
Everything and anything is possible, no boundaries,
no fears, no pain. " A Serenity,
peaceful, calming, and feelings of pure untainted
love. " Trying to describe the feelings, no one
would believe him, if God existed, he was 100% Love
and light! " Warm wisps of invisible
wind blew over his misty state as he floated more
along a path that he could not see.
How long had he been in this state? Was it hours?
Days? Time had stopped, only colors and
tones of fantastic vibrations rippled through him.
Each color that he passed through had a
different vibration, it made him think clearly, it made
him whole and part of the wide unknown
he was traveling in. If this was peace in his life, he
never wanted it to end.

Looking at a growing silver and red mist before him, it grew larger with every second, as he got closer he stared at the mist looking at its construction. Silver chrome and some alloy were swirling around like the gases around a planet. If you mixed metal and mercury together, that was the thing he saw before him. His eyes widened as he started to push through the atoms again, and then seeing a sight that could only be described as a Greek Amphitheatre! The semi-circle was vast in size, it stood there with pillars of marble looking stone, some white, some black.

Justin stood there, his eyes reached the space above him, gazing at the swirling colors of gasses, some even resembled the symbols of " Ying & Yang! " There black and white wispy circular movements, some spiraling one way, and others the opposite. Where or whenever he was, he was at peace, with life, with a positive energy, and a sense of belonging, he felt like he had always known this place, yet this was the first time! Or was it?

He found himself standing before a white marble altar, on it was a very familiar looking object. He knew he was smiling, but he didn't have a mirror to see, but he knew. It was a small jewel box identical to the one he found in the graveyard, with diamonds, but this time, it had gold inserts throughout the casket. It shone and pulsed as he stared at it. In his mind, he placed his thumb on the metallic square plate below the hinged catch. **" Master Instrument of justice 0001. You are Justin Webber!** " The voice echoed from inside the box, at that moment the catch opened by itself. There before Justin was a round object, it was

different to his first justice machine, but he
knew it had the same abilities as the other which had
served him well.
" You have proved yourself well Justin! " The voice
he heard on the plane was now around him,
but still no bodily form visible. As he stood there, he
felt a presence behind him, he slowly
turned. The body form in front of him was like a "
Native American, " his body was free of any
clothes, he stood there with his back to Justin. A
platted ponytail dark black in color hung down
past his shoulder blades. The body could have been a
contender for the best-kept torso
competition! This man had a physique to die for, any
man would have enjoyed this beautiful
body. Shinning bronze in color, he stood there,
saying nothing, Justin wondered why he had been
brought there, where ever " there " was. In slow
motion, the man turned to face Justin, staring at
each other, Justin felt an overwhelming burst of
energy bouncing from him, a warmth and
aura brighter than a street lamp. Coming from the
center of his forehead, Justin saw colored
particles of light heading straight for him, he wasn't
afraid, just curious, but knew any second
that he was going to get some answers. Penetrating
Justin's skull, he felt like he had been
 plugged into the national electricity grid. Energy
from every color swirled around in his mind
making him feel light and happy. The man had an
essence of tranquility about him, never
speaking, but his slight smile shone like perfection
itself.
Moments later, Justin heard it, he heard the thoughts
of the man before him.
" Welcome, Justin. I have a story to tell you. My

name is John, I am here in love and light. I am
light, I am here and everywhere. You are a part of
this great place we call " Nebular 03990! "
This dimension is home to many of our conscious
states, we are not physical in nature, but we do
take forms from planets in space! " Justin listened in
silence as he continued.
" In your realm of thinking, your timescale, this
dimension has been here since the dawn of
dinosaurs! This is just one of the thousands scattered
throughout time and space. Pure thought,
pure minds come here to look at the beauty that only
a few will get to see. " Justin with the new
glowing feelings inside his soul looked at John, he
had no movement from his mouth but heard
every word from Johns mind. There was something
so familiar about this man, but could not
pinpoint what it was. John continued. " Your earth is
decaying Justin, and within a few decades,
it will arrive close to its final destination! In ten of
your earth years, you will know that you have
never been alone, you will know that entities of love
have been watching over you all since your
dawn of time! Two thousand years ago, you had a
peaceful man walk upon your soil, he brought
a love to mankind that had never been seen before,
and he sacrificed his life so humans could
live. " Justin's eyes opened wider, seems to have
been doing that a lot lately. " Peace in your time
is possible Justin, and to feel as you do now, will be
spread to others, and the thoughts of love
will return 10 million-fold. A new beginning is coming,
and you will know the time, as they will
try to do to a man, the same things they did to the
Holy man! You are one of the chosen! The
new justice unit you have is the master version, and a

new responsibility will come with it. Your
new unit will also be able to predict crimes, it will
lead you to places before they happen, it will
be your choice what action to take. One day, you will
get the call to help a new peaceful man,
you will know him when you see him because your
heart will not lie to you. When you arrive
back in Sweden, you will be taken on a journey that
you might not want to travel, but this needs
to be done as you will alter the end result of your life
if you stray from that path." Justin's
emotions tried to rise to negativity but was
surpressed by the place he was standing in. " Do not
be afraid Justin, as your heart is good, and soon you
will see why you were chosen, and to be
chosen is a privilege. It is time for you to return now,
and my friend, until we meet again, Peace
be with you!"
" John! Please wait!" Justin looked on as John turned
and started to fade into a golden mist,
dancing like smoke as it vanished! Justin had so
many questions, so much he wanted to know,
but his thoughts moved around again telling him he
would know the answers soon!
Lighter and free was the next feelings as he was
being drawn back through the atoms, sparks of
charged particles burst in front of his face as he
floated in the nebula! " Justin! Justin! Wake up!
" With a fast jolt, he sat up straight in his seat as
Bernadette said. " Thank God for that! I thought
you had died on me. " Holding him tight, she flinched
backward as she rested her eyes on his
arm. " Oh, My God!! " Look at your arm!" Her eyes
bulged when she looked at the chrome and
golden sports monitor. His senses were returning to
him but felt light headed as he glanced down

at his left arm. A warm smile returned to his face as
he looked back at her with the knowledge
that he had just returned with. " Can you explain
this?" The facial expression was priceless, she
just couldn't work it out. " Well, I had better tell you I
think!" He smiled more as he told her the
story. " So, didn't you feel embarrassed standing in
front of a perfectly formed naked man? " A
small laugh rippled his throat muscles as he replied. "
The thoughts never crossed my mind. "
She smiled back at him saying. " If I had been in your
place, I would have asked to stay longer."
Both laughing now, they started to look more closely
at the new justice machine.

**" Master instrument of justice 0001! Standing by !
"......**

REVENGE
IS BITTERSWEET!
Chapter 11

Bernadette and Justin held each other's hand tight as
the plane touched down gently and safely
back on Swedish ground. Snow covered the airport
runways and entrances to the terminals, snow
ploughs scraping the white slush before them. Justin
was quite nervous now as he and Bernadette
entered into the arrival area. Looking at the desks,
his eyes looked for the polis, where were
they? They must have checked the flight passenger
lists returning from the States, but no! Not
even an airport polis man. Looking confused, Justin
was still on his guard, looking, watching for
them coming into the arrival lounge. Going through
the security gate and passport check, Justin,
held his breath as the officer scanned his passport. A
low sounding ping from the computer
terminal hit his ears like a church bell. " Welcome
home Mr. Webber " came the officer's
response. Bernadette gave the officer hers, then a
small ping! again " Welcome home Miss
Ljung!" They both picked up their hand luggage. The
carousel spun around the delivery room for
the main luggage, and only two minutes saw their
cases bouncing around on the rubber delivery
system. Making their way through to the terminal
main area, he took one last look, he saw no
one coming to arrest him. Inhaling on both their
cigarettes they were outside near the taxi
drivers and suddenly overheard two of them
discussing the horrific polis officers daughters
murder in Göteborg. One of the drivers pointed to the

daily Göteborg Times! " Poor bastard lost
his daughter to a small bike gang, I hope he´s as
good a detective as they say he is. Justin walked
over to the Nyheter stand and took out one of the
free papers. " Shit!" Justin said loudly and
walked faster back to Bernadette. " Look at this!" He
stood close to her as they both read the
chilling news.

GÖTEBORG TIMES
POLIS INSPEKTÖR DAUGHTER MURDERED IN SMALL BIKER GANG ATTACK!!!

**Kriminal Inspektör Maximus Lindström´s
daughter was found murdered in Göteborg
yesterday evening in an abandoned
warehouse. Two witnesses, a young couple
saw 5 bikers
hold down the girl, then ran away and called
the polis emergency number. The well known
Swedish detective was said to be devastated
when reporters tried to interview the
officer.........**
" I don´t know whether to be sad or glad! " " Justin
Webber! That poor girl!" " I know I know
Bernadette, just glad that he wasn't here to arrest
me!"

Returning to his apartment, they walked into the
elevator with their luggage, then saw the mail
box filled with unopened letters and sitting on top of
the box was a brown paper package. The
apartment was freezing after their time away, so
going to the electricity box he switched the
central heating on for the night.
With freshly brewed coffee they sat in their piece of
chill space. Justin went over to the aquarium

and checked on the fishes and seahorses, they were all fine as he had installed an automatic feeder for the time he was away. He stared at the yellow seahorse. and noticed it was swelling in the belly, it was expecting young ones. Out of everything that had happened, that was some good news.

Exhausted, Bernadette kissed him on his forehead. " Good night my handsome man! I am off to bed." " Night sweetheart!" Justin replied. She walked slowly to the bedroom and fell on the bed, sleep came quickly to her as she drifted peacefully away. Justin picked up the mail and started sifting through it. Putting them in order for bills and spam junk mail, he picked up the brown package. " I´m not expecting any packages! " he thought to himself. The wrapping paper came off quite easily, then, he opened the white box and took hold of a small business card.

" COMPLIMENTS FROM JOHN!! " The postcode was marked 03990! He smiled as he knew what was in the box. Holding the metal object in his hands, he noticed that it was definitely the old instrument of justice and attached to it was a small note. Justin! The unit failed in America because of an unexpected powerful solar flare, this has been rectified, and it will never happen again! " Bloody hope not!" He said. He smiled again and then thought how fortunate all of them were to be alive!

Lifting the fish tank lid, he reached in and placed the original machine into the box, then locked the old chest.

"Hello Lars, my old friend, how are you?" Justin had driven into work to check when it was ok to start back Grabbing Justin, he hugged him tight and

smiled as he missed him being away so
long. " Great buddy, I´m so glad to see you, hasn't
been the same since you have been gone.
The boss says you can start back on Monday, so extra
few days for you. Anything new
happening?" Lars asked him if he had heard about
the polis inspectors daughter? " Yeah, I saw
the paper yesterday," Lars explained that the girls
funeral was in two days, and they were
expecting at least 200 attending. " Ok pal, well I´m
heading home, and maybe get you up next
week, pre-Christmas drink before vacations." " You
are on permanent vacations at the moment,"
and then laughed his usual laugh.
No matter how much Justin tried to shrug off his
guilt, it surfaced time and time again. An after
thought crossed his mind, he knew the feelings he
had when his parents were murdered, and
Polisinspektör Lindström would be devastated and
torn-up inside. " The man was just trying to
do his job, and now something precious and good
was taken away from him. " Justin started to
think as to the situation of him being wanted for
questioning, how was this to be solved? At this
point, his SUV´s engine cut out completely and
steered the vehicle to the hard-packed snow
 along the edge of the highway, it stopped beside a
red and white snow pole marker. " Now
what!? " Justin shouted. Completely forgetting he had
the new justice machine on his arm, it was
beginning to hum loudly, then, a 3D hologram
appeared from the machine, it projected the small
image on to the flat surface of the car dashboard.
The Master instrument´s voice came from the
metal. **" Future crime scene detected! "** Justin

watched carefully as the machine not only projected the crime, but a time sequence scrolled under the hologram informing Justin that this was going to happen in 45 minutes time! He sat there thinking to himself for a few moments. **" Potential**

Rapist and murderer arriving in 42 minutes! " "

What to do? What to do?" He said out loud. He looked

out to the edge of the road, and a few meters back he saw a small forest road running back through the trees, and with the engine now starting by itself, placed the handle in to reverse!

Driving the few meters and hiding the car just out of view from the snow pole. Justin continued to watch the upcoming crime, he saw the man stop his car on the road at the exact spot Justin had been, then leaned over to the passenger seat and started to pull this 16-year-old girl towards him. The man was at least 40, and at that point, his intentions were not of that he showed when he picked her up hitchhiking in the snow. " What are you doing? No!! " She started to scream in a high pitch tone, then still struggling with the man, she bit his arm. He raised his hand and clenched his fist and forced the arm fast and vicious in its nature towards her head striking her between her cheek and eye. She was dazed and looking like she was going to pass out. He opened the car door then pulled her out his side dragging her limp body into the forest just off the road, then quickly snatching her jeans from her very cold body, ripping at her underwear.

Once again Justin looked on as the familiar evil smile came to the attacker's face! As she started to gain more consciousness, she looked around her,

she felt the ice-cold snow on her naked skin
as she felt his penis thrusting in and out of her tender
warm flesh. Numb with shock and cold,
she tried to lift her arms to fight him off, but her
strength was leaving her, her thoughts were of
the good life, that she knew was just about to be
taken from her. He pulled a knife from his
jacket and as quick as he did that, forced the knife
deep and quickly through her chest and
penetrating her heart. A very low sound of her last
breath being exhaled left her body with a little
misty steam coming from her mouth.
" 22 minutes to potential crime! " Justin now
realizing that this was different, this had not
happened
yet, it was now, he had to decide the best way to
prevent this happening, and being careful not to
get himself killed.
With a half-formed plan in his mind, he sat and
waited as time ticked by. **" Justin Webber! I can do**
many things to help, just think what you want help
with, then I will activate the best procedure for
this
situation!" That was comforting to hear from the
justice machine, and maybe this could turn out
well for everyone. The time on the counter on display
was showing 45 seconds left, whatever
had to be done, had to be done in the next few
seconds. **" Zero! Crime scene starting now!"**
Within a few seconds, the car he had seen in the
projection slowly pulled into the side and
Stopped in the same spot, the hologram said it
would. Running through the few meters of snow
which was hard, the snow was deeper at the forest

edge, he stood at the driver door, with
condensation all over the inside windows, he took his
forefinger knuckle and knocked on the
cold glass. A whirring sound of a small motor kicked
in as the window slowly lowered in front
of him. The man gazing at him with wide-open eyes
looked angry as Justin stood there. " Can I
help you, buddy? " The man's face was now full of
anger as Justin answered him back. He bent
down to window Hight, he could see the same girl he
had seen sitting there, she looked calm and
a slight smile on her face. " OH!! I think I can help
you more! Buddy!" Justin said it with a
sense of sarcasm, and then told the two of them to "
get out the vehicle. " `` Are you a cop?" The
man asked with a slight fear now appearing on his
face. Justin paused, then replied in a softer
voice. " Sort of! " Both the driver and then the girl
got out standing now in the snow. Flakes of
white fluffy powder fell between them as the man
waited for Justin to show him his polis badge!
" Activate restraining mode! " Within a split second
two glowing beams went in two directions
as the lights engulfed the driver and the young girl.
Their faces were confused as they tried to
break free from the beams. " What the fuck is
happening? Who are you? You frigging psycho!?"
The man demanded an explanation, he was just
about to get it.
In their encased light pulsating, they looked shocked
as Justin asked the justice machine to play
crime intentions! The young girls face looked
panicked as she saw what the man had planned for
her. " This is bullshit!! " Still the man shouting.
Turning her head to Justin, she asked " who was
he? " Continuing, " Is this true? " She waited on an

answer from Justin, and with a straight face,
he said. " " He was going to rape and kill you just like
in the hologram projection. In his pocket
is an 18cm hunting knife which has pearl and metallic
inlays with a stag with horns carved into
it!" Disbelief came from the man's face, then the girl
asked the man. " You were going to stab me
while you raped me!? You bastard!! " The hologram
played its last seconds of the yet to happen
crime and then silence. Looking at the confused and
frightened girl, Justin told her he was going
to release her, then let her sit in his car if she was ok
with that? Shaking with the freezing snow
falling, she agreed. Justin spoke to the machine
again. " Release girl! " Only a split second and
the beam to her stopped and she started to wobble
slightly, then getting her balance and ran to
Justin's car tracing his snow filled footprints.
" I haven't done anything cop! " The man sneered at
Justin as he spoke the words. Lighting a
cigarette Justin inhaled on the grey smoke coming
from the tip, the smoke was thick as the
temperature was so low, blowing through the
snowflakes Justin spoke again to the man. " If I let
you go, you will do to another girl what you intended
for her, so you and I know what was going
to happen, and I need to find out exactly what will
happen if you are released. " You could see
the thought process on the man's face, he was
weighing up the situation and trying to reach a
balance in his mind. But here was the problem, the
man's mind was unbalanced, he was a
future murderer and a walking time bomb waiting to
happen. Justin asked the Master justice
machine to tell the man with voice and thoughts at

the same time, of future events to unfold. **" Your thoughts**

are to break free and head to the nearest bar. From there you want to find another young girl to keep you warm

in a sexual way, you have been thinking for many days about committing these acts of violence, and your

fantasies have been increasing stronger as the days go on. Today was going to be your first attack, but you

would end up a serial killer, so justice needs to be implemented now! " " So, what to do with you is this! "

The man was desperately trying to get free, but it was impossible, he was stuck fast like glue.

Justin continued. " The intentions you had and have are dangerous to society, so there is only one course of action, your mind will be wiped clean, and you will live the rest of your time in some institution with doctors baffled as to your condition, but at least the women in towns and cities will be safe from you." If looks alone could kill, Justin would be laying on the ground now with snow floating over his body, but that wasn't going to happen. " You fucking crazy bastard fuck!! Let me fucking go!! " Justin flicked his cigarette butt towards the ground, looked the man straight in the eyes and spoke quietly to him. " No!!! Goodbye! Activate punishment!! " That now familiar hum from the machine kicked in as the new blue beam penetrated the man's skull, it did not smell this time as it entered his flesh then brain. The man's eyes swirled in his sockets as the beam got stronger until the machine reached its critical life-threatening stage. **" Master instrument of justice 0002 punishment complete, Releasing now! "** The man's legs gave way as he fell to his knees, his face blank and lifeless, but still breathing and alive. Walking through the thicker snow now, he headed towards his own car, and there standing, was the frightened girl with tears of relief but confused still. " Is he dead?" replying Justin said. "Nope, he´s alive, but in his skull, the lights still on, but no one is at home!" Again, she showed her curiosity. " What did that machine do to him?" " Just wiped his memory, but he won't even know what planet he´s on, and now it´s time to get you back to where you were heading, you are one lucky little lady."

Turning to Justin shaking, she forced a smile and said. " Thank you, sir!"

Turning the radio on after his morning coffee, he listened as a news report came over the speakers.

" A man was found kneeling in the snow along the main forest highway yesterday! An ambulance rushed him to the hospital where they gave him blankets and survival foil, then after examination, he was found to be mentally incompetent and taken to the city asylum. A doctor commented to this reporter saying. " The snow has bleached his brain, that is the only explanation! "

Justin choked a little as he heard that, then replied. " Stupid jerk!! But close! "

Justin stood by his grave digging machine, he had
dug another two graves for the day and was
about ready to pack in for the day. " I haven't
forgotten about you, Mr. Webber! " Came the
voice from behind him. Startled he spun around to
see Inspektör Lindström a few meters away.
Justin sat back on the machines foot plate wiping the
snow off that had fallen. " I was visiting my
daughters grave! Then what a surprise as I saw you
here working, so thought I would say Hello!"
Justin lowered his head a little, then sighed, and
looked the polis man straight in the eyeballs.
Holding his hands out clasped together, he said. " I
guess it had to happen Inspektör, so take me
in! " Maximus took out a pack of cigarettes, lit one,
and then held it out for Justin. If you had
blown on Justin at that point, you would have
knocked him over with surprise! Reaching out to
the lit cigarette he started to smoke, then Maximus
took another out and sat down next to Justin.
Staring at the polis man, he could see the sorrow in
the man's eyes and face, it was heartbreaking,
and Justin again remembered how that had felt.
" They still haven't got that Yank cop in Miami yet
huh? Strange how that turned around so
Quick. Do you agree on that Mr. Webber? So now I
know you are my avenging vigilante, and I
must admit I am surprised how so liked and loved
you are. To start with, I thought you were just
another piece of human garbage on a killing spree,
but lately, things, as you know, have turned
for me, so at the moment, you have got a break!"
Drawing on his cigarette the Inspektör looked
right at Justin. " What puzzles me is how the hell did
you do these scumbags? There is an
answer, but I don´t know if I am going to

understand it!" The polis officer was right, he did look puzzled, and all of this time thinking he was one of the best detectives in Sweden. Pushing his lips together closely, Justin thought carefully before giving the officer some facts.

" You are a good cop, sir! I know that and feel it; you are one of the few left in this world who would always do the right thing. You remind me of my uncle Zac Stateside, you would like him. Just like you, he did his job with great dedication, and in the end, it was his friend for many years that had killed my parents, so the crime was solved, and now justice has been done!" " We have courts and a system for all that Justin, and we break the law if we step over the line in any way. "Someone once said Inspektör. " The law is an ass!! I believe that because most of the law talk so much shit!!" Justin sat there in deep thought for a moment, then looked back at the officer.

"Would you like to know the truth about your deaths in Göteborg and Borås? Do you have the time to sit and keep an open mind?" Maximus lit another cigarette. " Try me!! " Justin took another few seconds, then. " Ok! Follow me to my apartment and I will tell you everything!" The Inspektör smiled enough to let Justin know he had agreed.

It was now getting darker as they drove out of the cemetery gates. There was no turning back for Justin now, and maybe he could rest peacefully later that night?

Opening the apartment door, they both walked in to see a bathrobe clinging to a newly showered Bernadette. " Oh, sorry honey! " Justin looked red in the face as he shut the door behind them.

" I´m early tonight Justin, I'll go get changed," she

hurried into the bedroom and shut the door.

The Inspektör surveyed the apartment, he really liked the setup, the fish aquarium was magnificent! " Wow! Your tank is fantastic Justin, and I love the seahorses." He looked deep into the tank as Justin poured out some Scotch whiskey for the two of them. " Scotch Inspektör?" Stretching his arm out to him. " Thanks " replied Maximus as he took the golden liquid from Justin.

For a few seconds, Maximus noticed the health checker machine on Justin's arm. " Are they any good?" He asked inquisitively. A pause again from Justin, then said. " More than you can imagine!" At this question, Justin removed the machine and asked the Inspektör to get comfortable. Placing it on the glass coffee table he sat down himself and waited for Bernadette to join them.

With a warm sweater and jeans, Bernadette strolled into the living room looking at the man now sat with Justin. " And who is this nice gentleman!? " Justin looked at her and then gave her the reply. " Let me introduce you to Polisinspektör Maximus Lindström! " Another case of picking someone's jaw up off the floor as she stood there opened mouthed. Justin sat her down and started to reveal the afternoon's events, then brought her up to date on what he was just about to show him. A worried look came over her, but straight away Justin tried to reassure her everything was ok! " If you are sure about that honey, then I am behind you!"

" Inspektör, what I am going to show you is going to be different to anything you have ever known, and as I said to someone once, do your best

to keep an open mind. What you see in front
of you is an object of great power, it is not a health
machine machine monitor! This in the wrong hands
could cause a shit load of trouble." Looking back at
Justin the Inspektör replied. " And your
hands are not the wrong hands?" There was a hint of
a smile as he waited for Justin's reply. " Sit
back and watch!!" Justin directed his voice at the
machine, then spoke the words. " Master
Instrument of Justice, play murders and punishments
for Göteborg and Borås with commentary,
also show the future punishment given to the man in
the snow on Forrest highway!" " That was
you too!!? Shit! "

**" Master instrument of justice 0002 replaying
crimes and punishment!! "**

Minute after minute the Inspektör watched the
hologram, as scene after scene played out in front
 of him, glancing at Justin and Bernadette who was,
in turn, watching his
expressions occasionally. At the last incident with the
man on the highway, the Inspektör was
angry at what could have been for the young girl,
then he looked sad as he thought of his
beautiful daughter who was taken from him only less
than a week ago! His eyes and nose started
to drip moisture from them as he picked some paper
tissues from a box Bernadette offered him.
Justin and Bernadette waited to see more responses
from him. How was he going to react now?
" I saw it, but I am having difficulty in believing it!"
He continued. " So, what you are telling me
 Is, you can get led to a crime scene, then it tracks
down the fugitive, then places a forcefield of
some kind that sticks him to the spot, and finally

gives them a punishment that fits most of their crimes to the way they murdered?" Justin thought carefully before answering, but he didn't have to as the Inspektör gave his response. " I believe that if every police force had one or two of these, we would start to wipe out every scumbag between here and Denmark! I was going to lock you up forever Justin Webber, but now I don´t know if I should do that or give you a medal!? "

" Your choice now Inspektör, " Justin replied. Bernadette was silent, just like she was most of the time, but today she was going to have her say. " Inspektör Lindström, would you like to catch these biker killers? " Silence again as seconds ticked by. " You know there can only be one answer to that question young lady. More than anything, but the law states that criminals deserve a fair trial!" Justin spoke again. " We can put an end to this with your daughters killer´s tonight because they could be ready to strike again! Whose daughter will it be next? A friend´s? A colleague? Maybe you do respect the law, but these assholes don´t!" Picking up his glass of whiskey he poured it into his mouth and let the warm glow hit his stomach! " Let´s go get those sons of bitches!! This is going to be Bitter Sweet Revenge!!! ".....

Chapter 12

BERNADETTE`S
DEATH!

Justin, Bernadette, and the Inspektör sat in the car in silence, as each one had their own individual thought´s. An anxious Inspektör sitting on the rear seats wondering what was going to happen next? Bernadette pleading with any God to help them in their next hours, and Justin, wishing that it was all over and catching the men responsible. Maximus pressed the button on his guns magazine clip checked that there was a full magazine, then placed the clip back in the gun. Pulling the top movable part back, he then let it slip forward by itself to push a bullet in the gun chamber, then put the red catch on to the safety position and put it back in his shoulder holster. Justin had been watching him closely as he had done that and felt it strange to have an active polis officer detective on their side. Bernadette checked her justice machine to make sure it was working good. An unusual event, but this was going to be one of the worst days in their lives for some people! The officer told Justin that " It was only five more minutes to the old warehouse, and drive slowly in case the bikers were back at the crime scene. " This wasn't likely but, caution was the evening's word as safety was paramount to survival.
The old track that led up to the warehouse was low in places, so slow, it had to be because of the deep holes all the way along it. With caution, the vehicle moved forward at about ten km´s an

hour. All of their hands reached for the car roof and side windows as their bodies were shook all around in the car. Driving a few seconds later, the SUV drove on to concrete, and there before them in the head lights was the old abandoned warehouse. Pitch black all around, it was silence as Justin stopped, then turned the engine off. No one to be seen, no life, just an old scary building and the blackness surrounding them. All three got out, then slowly with the Inspektör and Justin carrying flashlights, they moved towards the large open warehouse doors. Justin's justice machine came to life again. **" Crime scene detected! Do you wish to play crime? "** Sighing a little, Justin turned to the Inspektör, his face looked nervous as he had heard the machine too. " Go ahead, Mr. Webber! I am as ready as I will ever be!" Maximus and Bernadette waited as Justin told the machine to " Activate! "

Loud motorcycle engine noises could be heard as one after the other, five drove into the large empty warehouse. Behind one of the bikers sat a young girl. She was slumped forward and unconscious as they came to a halt. The motorcycles were placed in a circle with their head lights still switched on, and the girl's bike rider pushed her off the bike and watched as she hit the ground hard. The leader turned to the man. " How much chloroform did you use on her?" Replying, the man smiled and said. " Enough! " Being the gang leader, you could see the control he had over the other four men and demanded they wait until she was conscious before they had their fun! Beer, whiskey, cigarettes were taken from their jackets as they knew they would have several minutes to wait until she was fully awake. The young Rebecca Lindström started to open her eyes, still dazed from the drug she pushed herself up on to her feet, then tried to balance as she held her hands up to shield her eyes from the bikes head lights. " Welcome to our party! " The leader laughed at her, then he was joined by the other four who sneered and laughed with him. Trying to see an escape, she stood there, shaking and crying loudly, then pleaded with the men to let her go. Walking closer to her, the leader stopped only a few centimeters away, then raised his hand to her blouse. Suddenly, his other hand produced a large bladed knife. Slowly cutting the blouse from her body, it cut through the material like a hot knife through butter. She stood there still shaking and trying hard to cover her breasts with her arms. " Ok boys!! One Arm or leg each! " They all laughed again and cheered as they quickly went to her shivering body.

Each of the four gang members had taken hold of a leg or arm, then stretching her, the leader stood between her wide-open legs. Once again he took the knife and started cutting away at her underwear. The flowered panties fell in pieces as she screamed more and tried to struggle free.

That familiar evil laugh appeared again, this time on the leader's lips, as he demanded his gang lift her up to the Hight of his jean zipper. As quickly as she had started, she had stopped crying, she had gone into some kind of shock; she was motionless like a corpse but alive! Zipping his jeans up, the leader shouted at the girl. " Hey, you bitch!! Wake the fuck up! " He slapped her face hard as she still lay there suspended by being

held. No movement, just a large red mark
appearing on her face where he had hit her. Looking
beyond one of the gang, the gang leader saw
in the headlights of one of the bikes, a handle shaped
object. Walking over to it, he bent down
then picked it up. Looking it up and down he saw that
he had hold of an old wooden dusty tennis
racquet. A big smile came over his face as the evil
thoughts went through his mind. " Anyone
for tennis boys? " All five gave out a huge laugh,
echoing around the warehouse. He looked at it
with a knowing smile, stood back near her body, then
said in a put-on British accent! " My serve
I believe?"
Throwing a pretend tennis ball in the air, he lifted the
racquet in the air, then "Swish! " The
racquet made that noise as if cutting through the
night air quickly as it descended towards the
young girls face. It bounced quickly from her head as
it reached for the sky, then down fast again
as he repeated it time after time!. Her face looked
like it had been cut slightly in several small
squares as the blood started to leak from the little
square marks left by the weapon.
Suddenly! A car engine burst into life about a
hundred meters away, the men looked startled as
they tried to see who had driven away. They dropped
her like a rag doll as once again she fell to
the ground. " Go get that fucker!! " Shouting loud as
three of the men started their bikes and
went to look for the unknown unwanted guests.
The two men left, stood over her lifeless body, blood
slowly seeping through her wounds. Blood
spots had splattered over the warehouse dust as it
had fallen from her face. Only a couple of
minutes had passed, then with their blazing head

lights, the three returned shouting. " They got away whoever it was, we better get the fuck out of here now! " The leader and the last gang member jumped quickly on their bikes, kicking their engines into life, the leader signaled to the others with a circular motion above his head, his hand went through the air clockwise to let them know to get the heck out now! The leader looked to the side as he rode by the girl smiling that evil smile most murderers seemed to have!

The young Rebecca Lindström lay there, at that moment in time she was still breathing. Her eyes were open and staring at the roof of the building. Her chest naked to the air was moving a little, up, then slowly down, then nothing! Her life was gone!

A sudden burst of sound with someone throwing up could be heard, as the Inspektör puked hard wrenching his guts as liters of yellow crap projected to the floor. Then came the almighty cry of a tortured soul as he fell to the ground hitting the dust time and time again. Sobbing loudly and gasping for breath as he cried for the daughter he had buried a few days previously. His precious Rebecca was taken by men who could not be called animals, as that would be an insult to animals.

These men were monsters, and they needed to be exterminated like a rodent with a plague!

It must have been at least ten minutes before a silence fell in the warehouse. Taking two cigarettes out of a packet, Justin lit them both at the same time, then extended his arm to the Inspektör. Bernadette had placed her caring arms around the man, then reached to the cigarette placing it in Maximus's mouth. His lips bounced from each other as the smoke found its way to his lungs. Another silence came as all three were numb as to what just happened.

" Do you wish to find fugitives of this crime now? " The sound coming from the justice machine bounced around the echoing walls of the abandoned warehouse. With him stumbling as he rose, the Inspektör steadied himself, dusted his trousers and jacket with his hand, straightened the tie, and took a final draw from the cigarette. He raised his head so that his eyes were staring at Justin, looked at him with hatred filling them fully, there could be no more room left for the amount of hatred he had for these so-called human beings, and now was the time to spend the hate in return for whoever was responsible. Tonight! He was an unchained wolf! ready to tear fellow humans to pieces!

The atmosphere was tense as the three of them got back into the SUV. Tonight, saw a great detective change from a good level headed polis man to a hardened avenging father with a gun!

Tonight! nothing or no one was going to stand in the way of his vengeance.

The vehicle sped fast this time along the track, no one cared as the vehicle bounced like a football! throwing all three about inside. " Fugitives are 7.7kms away! Caution must be taken in the last 500 meters! Master instrument of justice! Standing by!!! "

The 7 km drive did not take long as Justin was speeding, he wanted to get these killers, all of them, he just hoped that all five were there! Once

again they had arrived at the location where
the bad guys were. This time, however, Justin turned
all lights out, and as they started to come to
the end of the farm road, they noticed a large stack
of straw next to a thrashing machine. Hitched
up to the towing eye, a large green tractor stood
motionless. Fifty meters ahead was a two-level
farmhouse, the lights were on lighting up the
foreground like a football field. At the bottom of
the three porch steps were four motorcycles. They
shone in the artificial light, the chrome and
 metal paint sparkling.
" Fugitives detected ahead!! " " This was it;
everything was just about to happen SHIT STYLE!! "
Whispering, Justin spoke to the Inspektör telling him
to lay as low as possible next to the front of
the tractor, and turned to Bernadette and told her to
stay with the wheel of the thrashing machine
and not move until Justin had them all in a locking
beam. Both nodded in agreement with him as
Justin got up, then started his cautious walk to the
farmhouse. The Inspektör held his gun sight
directed at the front porch, staring with eagle eyes at
every movement. Justin walked forward, he
turned slightly to look back at his accomplices. His
thinking process slowed down as when he
turned he saw a horror story unfolding behind him.
An ugly hairy all over biker was taking aim
at Bernadette and Maximus, shouting loud he
mouthed the warning, " BEHIND YOU!! "
Maximus laying on the ground rolled quickly and spun
and aimed at the man behind him.
BANG!! BANG!! Two simultaneous shots rang out in
the air as the bullets both found their
target. In a split second, Maximus fired four more

times as his rounds found the man's chest and one in his head. As the biker started to fall forwards, his trigger finger started to go into a spasm!
Hitting the ground, the semi-automatic weapon started firing by itself, bullets flying in the direction of all three of them. The inspectors gun was still aiming at the man on the ground.
Maximus started to gurgle from his stomach, he looked down and saw blood pouring out of three holes, he was losing a lot of blood, too fast for this to be recovery wounds. He propped his back against the tractor wheel, glad that he could ease the pain that was shooting through his body just like the bullets had done. Running from the farmhouse porch four bikers hurried into the open air carrying automatic weapons. It was like the American 4th of July as repeating bangs and flashes lit up the night sky. What seemed like an eternity, hundreds of bullets flew towards their direction, with every few seconds the men reloaded the guns.

" Activate the fucking restraining beams!!! " Justin shouted through the sound of the gunfire, and muzzle flashes nearly every second. With flashes of blue light, the beams caught their targets, one after the other capturing the four remaining murderers. They looked like they were frozen in time. Justin was heavy breathing, he turned to the Inspektör. " Oh no!! Maximus! "
Justin ran to the polis man, then put his hands firmly on Maximus's chest, trying to stop the bleeding. A faint sound came from the thrashing machine. " Justin Juustiinnn. " He could hardly hear it, but as he did, a horror came over his face again, and his heart started to miss beats as his eyes fixed on a blood-soaked Bernadette.

As Justin held her head next to his chest, she was struggling to breathe, every time she inhaled, blood pumped out of her left breast, he pulled her sweater up and forced a cloth handkerchief into the two bullet wounds. She managed to move her head slowly to look at the man she had started to love, his eyes dripping with tears like melting ice. It seemed like hours holding her as she gasped for every breath, trying to smile at him as he ran his fingers over her bloodstained cheek. He thought about calling an ambulance, but deep down he knew it was only a matter of seconds, and then the end would arrive snuffing her beautiful life from existence. He gently lifted her up more towards his lips, then kissed the bullet holes as she grabbed him tightly, then exhaled for the last time.

" Justin! " The voice repeated, " Justin! " Now a third time. " Justin fucking Webber!! "

Justin looked over to Maximus and saw he was still alive, barely, but still alive. " Before I leave this fucked up planet, go finish them sons of bitches off for me buddy! " Still having difficulty in breathing, he watched has now the hatred took over Justin's eyes that had turned black, for a moment evil touched his heart, and now it was time to become the devil himself!! He stood up, he looked at the four men before him, and walking closer to them all, he spoke. " I have only seven words to say to you guys." With pools of blackness all over his face, he stared at each one in turn. "You're fucked and you're dead!!!! ACTIVATE PUNISHMENT!!! ".......

Chapter 13

GOLDEN - CROWN!

" Jesus Christ!! " Justin Couldn't believe what he had just seen. The justice machine spoke
again!

" Possible future crime scene will present itself in 2 minutes 25 seconds! Evasive action needed! "

" We can´t let this happen! " Said the Inspektör, and Bernadette agreed. " That just frightened the
hell, out of me! " As she spoke, she smiled at Justin and uttered a few words to him. " You kissed
my bullet holes. From my angle watching, I thought you were being naughty! " None of this was
funny, but for a brief moment, it was! " This machine is fantastic Justin, to see into the future, it
could save so many lives! " Maximus said. They were all interupted as the machine came to life
again. **" Future crime scene in 1 minute! Take evasive action! "** Justin stopped the car at the same spot as
in the hologram projection, only this time, he was the only one in the car. **" Future crime scene active now! "** The justice machine then spoke to Justin.

"Bernadette's justice machine is now instantly connected to Master instrument, I await any commands for evasive action! " " Ok then! Let´s see how this
scene plays out!? " Justin started to walk towards the lit-up farmhouse, the bikes were exactly
where the hologram showed the four of them.

Looking behind him as he did in the hologram, he saw the first biker taking aim at Justin himself. At that moment He told the Master instrument to activate Bernadette's machine to restrain! Bernadette had been dropped off 20 meters before the area where the first biker was relieving himself in the long snowy grass, and slowly and quietly crept up behind him to within a safe distance. The biker didn't stand a chance of missing that beam, it fired out from her metal machine like a lightning bolt! Silver in color the beam held the guy and an invisible gag was placed around the man's mouth, now there was no chance of the man tipping his buddies off to warn them. Maximus slid around from the backyard, then moved slowly along the side of the house, keeping close to the wooden boards. He checked to make sure the area was clear, then as quick as he could sat on the first bike and kicked started the engine.

The 1200cc engine roared into action as Maximus ran back to the side of the house. He looked at Justin and put his thumb up to him for " Go for it! " Maybe 20 seconds past, then one after the other, all the bikers came out wondering why the bike motor was running. Inspektör Lindström spun around the corner house and shouted at the four bikers. " Halt!! Polis! " His gun was wavering between the four, and only two or three seconds, the biker nearest to the porch door started to lift his semi-automatic machine gun. With the now familiar shout, Justin raised his voice in an instant! " Activate restraining beam! "Four beams of silvery blue light fired out quickly from the master justice machine, each one freezing the bikers! Swear words of every description came from their mouths as all of them

tried to escape, but as usual, there was no
escape, and now it was close to their punishment,
but no one knew yet as to what that was going
 to be. What was known by Bernadette, Maximus and
Justin, was that they were just about to
 die!!
Justin walked up to the bike gang leader, stared into
his eyes, and looked hard to see if he had
any good in them. Black! Just completely dark black
with just a hint of white around the eye
pupils. " So, this is what evil looks like to-day huh!? "
With a twisted look, the gang leader
growled at Justin, then. " Fuck you asshole!!" then
spat into Justin's face! " Whatever the fuck
this thing is, release me and I'll show you evil!! You
fucking stupid cop!! " The anger on his face
was a pleasant sight as Justin replied. " OH! I´m not
a cop, but he is, " pointing to Maximus who
was now walking towards the captured four bikers.
Maximus stood there dead center in front of the four
of them. " Do you know who I am
scumbags!? " One of the gang shouted at him. " Who
gives a flying fuck man!!? " " " Rebecca
Lindström! Does the name jolt your memories? " One
after the other, each face looked shocked.
" I am not a cop tonight boys, I am just a grieving
father who just lost one of the most beautiful
things on this earth! You snuffed out a life that was
pure and clean, not that I can say the same
about you fucking shits!" Silence, they were lost for
words as Maximus glared into each face one
at a time.
" What about this scum here!? " Bernadette shouted
from the edge of the field. Justin spoke to
the master justice machine. " Can you bring the
fugitive in Bernadette´s beam closer to here

without releasing him!?" And with the next seconds, the machine answered him. **" No!! That is not**

possible Justin! " That wasn't the words Justin wanted to hear, but quickly thought about his next move.

With the gang leader and the three next to him, Justin knew he would need to get Maximus to go and help her, so gave the master justice an order to release the automatic weapon from the nearest biker. A scream penetrated the quiet surrounding the farmhouse, it was louder than the bikes engine which was still running. " Arrrggghhhh!!! " The bikers hand fell to the ground with the machine gun still grasped in it! Smoldering flesh could be smelt as it lay on the ground, with every second pushing sizzling flesh through the blades of grass. The man felt every nerve bursting into his brain, each nerve sending the signal of excruciating pain that brought a tough man, to tears like a small baby! The other bikers watched in horror as the man stood there bubbling like a coward. " Show you have a spine man!! You´re one of my gang, you sniveling turd! " The words from him didn't make a bit of difference, the other biker carried on with the pain he was now experiencing.

Maximus went over to the machine gun, and without flinching bent down to pick up the gun forcing the curled fingers from the handle. He thought for a moment, this hand was one of the hands that held his daughter so had no remorse for taking the gun from it. The hand once again hit the ground, this time it fell upon a light layer of fresh snow that had just fallen. Snowflakes 2 or 3 CMS wide came from the night sky as the

Inspektör walked briskly towards the biker and Bernadette. Bernadette was shivering as the new colder wind started to blow around her, making her shake a little, the snowflakes blew around in a small tornado shape circle, the wind unseen in the air. " What´s our next step!?" Asked Bernadette, with Maximus answering her quickly. " We need to release him and walk over to the others, Justin want´s them all together! So, you can tell your machine to release him in a moment, but not before I have a quick few words with him first!"

Inspektör Lindstrom turned to the biker, who now was petrified as to what was going to happen next? Maximus placed his pistol back in the holster, then held the machine gun tightly trained on the man before him. " Here´s what ´s going to happen in the next few minutes! Your puny little brain isn't going to understand about this piece of equipment that holds you, so don´t try. When the light releases you, all three of us are going to walk slowly over to the others, and if you deviate one centimeter, I'll blow you to hell right then, so your choice murdering scumbag! You will also slowly place your gun you are holding on the ground, then walk forward! If the barrel of your gun goes anywhere other than the direction of the ground, well!! Doesn't take a genius to know what´s going to happen to you! Ok, Bernadette! " Bernadette glanced down at the machine on her arm. " Release fugitive! " As quick as it had started, in a second it had stopped. Maximus had moved behind the man and was pointing the other gang members gun at the guys back. The familiar wobble came around the man as he got his balance on the fresh snow. You could see the relief on the guys face as he stood straight, then looked at the gun still in his hands. From the front view, the man's face started to smile as the thoughts went through his stupid head! " That was a mistake! " He thought! At that exact moment, the master instrument of justice alerted Justin to **"A potential future crime now!! "** Without hesitation, Justin replied in a stern loud voice. " Activate Bernadette´s justice machine and punish NOW!!! " All this happened so quickly, the biker only got three inches around in his swiveling body, but not enough to open fire on Maximus and Bernadette. Automatic gunfire again boomed in the night air with muzzle flashes igniting the air! "BANGbangbangbangbangbangbangbangg!!!!! with the echo of the last round bouncing over the field. Bullets had ripped through the man's body, they made gaping holes all around his back and stomach. In an instant, nearly every drop of blood in his body poured or splattered on the snow, the final bullet had struck the metal on the front of the tractor still standing there, it ricochet´s back and lands dead center on the man's forehead! He fell forward indenting his large built body in the white powder, was it over? The man lay there, no breath, no warm puffs of air coming from his lips, just a hint of gun smoke drifting over his dead body. This time the gunfire had happened, as before the hologram was just a possible future. Maximus in the heat of the moment was so hoping the biker would make a move for the worse, he wanted so much to take this scums life as he did his daughters. His wish had

been granted, and the justice machine had
been cheated of the death. It would have taken the
man's life, but maybe some justice had to be
taken by the father who´s sweet girl was no longer
walking on the earth. Showing nothing, he
turned to Bernadette who had thrown herself on the
ground and was brushing the snow from her
clothes and looking relieved. " You ok!? " He asked,
but he knew she was, as the man in front of
him stood no chance of living or harming Bernadette
with him there.

All three now standing together, they had slight
smiles of relief as to what just went down. " That
was too close for comfort, " then wiped some
perspiration droplets from his forehead. Justin
pulled his cloth handkerchief from his pocket and
started to wipe his brow, then looked at it, he
remembered the hologram, and of him pushing it into
Bernadette´s bullet holes.

" Are you taking us in!? Because all of this is bullshit!!
" Justin replied to the gang leader. " Was
it bullshits when all five of you held her and beat her
with the tennis racquet!? " " OH, fuck you
dick for brains! " It was difficult for Bernadette, the
Inspektör and Justin to see how this guy was
being such a jerk held by something they could not
possibly understand, and that only a few
minutes time, they were going to be no more. Justin
looked to Maximus; it was time for the
grieving father to take the action with the help of the
justice machine. He put the machine gun on
the snow-covered ground, then placed his hands in
his pockets to keep warm.

" I was going to say so much to you guys, with the
why´s! and what about´s! but you know
what? GO TO HELL!!! " He turned, looked at Justin,

and then came the words from Justin's lips!
" Activate punishment now!!"
A familiar noise entered the night air as the Master
instrument of justice started to do what it was
programmed for, to serve justice to fugitives that had
no remorse for their crimes. The three of
them waited for the usual humming sound to grow in
volume, then to see other beams of light
striking the bodies of the four men.
No!! This time there was no silver or blue beams, but
in its place was a golden glowing light that
projected a nearly perfect circle, nearly perfect was
the right word, as the golden circles hovered
over all four bikers heads to a distance of about 20
centimeters! Then the humming intensified
you could see a slight smoldering heat. The humming
got even louder, the golden strands of light
crossed each other between the circles. " Oh my
God!! " Bernadette said as the three of them
watched. As they looked at the circles, it had changed
slightly to resemble tennis racquets. The
golden light strands crossed each other as it took
shape. Another louder burst of humming could
be heard as the circling rings of intense heat and light
glowed like the midday sun! Then it
happened! Simultaneously, they all started to
descend towards the four bikers heads. A shock
and fear came over each of their faces. As Justin
Bernadette and Maximus looked on, they too
were a little anxious to find out what this thing was
going to do? This was the first time any of
the three of them saw anything like this, but, that
wasn't surprising as this machine realistically
shouldn't even exist! With a final burst of humming,
the Golden Crown looking objects
descended at a slow pace taking about five seconds

to reach the faces of the gang. If Bernadette Justin and Maximus could describe what happened next on paper, it would be something like this... " The Golden Crowns came into contact with all four faces, as the gang members were getting their justice. Their skin started to smoke and melt as the crossed lights entered deep into their skin. If you pictured a 5kilo block of square butter, then heated a metal wired tennis racquet up to temperatures that couldn't be measured, you would see how the wires melted through and came slowly out the other side, but afterward, it was like crushed ice being placed on the butter to cool it quickly so that the diced butter was in cubes but still standing firm in its place. Heated smoke came from all four of the men's faces, with hissing noises at the same time as the skin melted together. Basically, they ended their lives as objects that looked like they had been sliced and diced!! Cubes of slightly melted brains and skin fused together as the cold light had turned everything solid again! Two of the bikers had both of their eyes cut into cubes, and resembled something out of a horror movie! Not one drop of blood could be seen running from the men's heads as the three others watched with shocked faces.

Snowflakes still falling, the night was silenced now. Then it came like always! " Master instrument of justice 0006 punishment complete!!! " " Can I have a cigarette now, please!? " Came the voice of Bernadette. That to all of them seemed like a good idea as every one of them needed something to calm them as to what they witnessed! Justin asked Maximus " what he felt now!? " Drawing on the cigarette he looked

slightly more at peace with himself, but then
answered Justin. " Seeing them bastards fry was
good, I feel some relief, but that isn't going to bring
her back, is it!? " Shaking his head slowly
Justin took hold his hand and shook it hard and
firmly. " Thank you Inspektör for everything. I
guess if you had been another type of cop, all kinds
of different shit could have taken place, so
from my heart and Bernadette´s, Thank you! " The
Inspektör fumbled in his jacket pocket, then
sparkling in the night, he was dangling a pair of
handcuffs swaying left to right, then right to left!
Justin and Bernadette had shock written on their
faces as they gazed at the handcuffs!
A smile came over his face as he said. " Won´t be
needing these anymore then? " He watched
their faces as the breath and sigh of relief came over
them. Justin play punched the polis man,
then the three of them walked towards the SUV, then
drove from the crime scene!! ....

Chapter 14

(S-P-P)
SVERIGE PATRIOT PARTI!

3 years had passed since the Inspektör got his
revenge. Many things had happened in this time,
and the strange world they lived in, was still strange!
It seemed like the good guys were being pushed into
the minority, and vice versa. The bad guys
always in the media looked like they were edging
forward faster than the world had ever seen.
Murders, rapes, slave trade in humans, which we
thought went out with the 1800´s. And the
biggest happening of all. " Terrorism! " An evil thread
in the world that was spreading like
cancer.
After clearing through a mountain of paperwork three
years ago, the new Chief
Kriminal Inspektör Lindström was becoming an iconic
polis man as he was preventing crimes by
the dozens every month. His colleagues couldn't
believe the number of potential rapes and
murders he stopped. How the hell did he do it? We
have to go back to the day after the biker
gang was taken out when their bodies were
discovered.
The snow lay heavy on the ground in most of the
area of Göteborg. The call came in about mid-
day as the Inspektör was just about to go to lunch.
Acting surprised, he grabbed his winter coat
and headed out to the polis staff room. Pointing to
three of the polismen sitting at their lunch
table. " You! - You and you with me now! and bring
some lunch for me. " Trying to look like he

had no idea what he was going to find, he put on a
face of looking concerned as he told the three
men he was thinking this might be another vigilante
killing.
" Difficulty " was an understatement as the polis 4x4
drove along the snow-filled farm road and
managed to get to within about 50 meters from the
edge of the field. He knew what he was doing
when he told the officers to stand about 5 meters
away from him in a line when he was ready, he
would give the signal to move slowly forward.
Surveying the area with his eyes, he knew where
to look as his gaze headed to the spot he had opened
fire on the biker. Telling the officer on his
right to start walking slowly, he looked at the two on
his left, then asked them to move forward
too. The depth of the snow was about 1 meter, so
treading through it was hard going. As they
walked forward, he glanced over at the officer on the
right from the corner of his eye, as he knew
exactly the point where the first biker lay, he waited,
and waited, until. " Sir! Sir! I have found
something! " The officer slightly tripped then bent
down and started to brush the snow away
where he nearly fell, and within seconds he
uncovered the ass in jeans of the dead biker.
Inspektör Lindström ran as fast as he could over to
him and looked down. Kneeling with
the officer they both started digging through the cold
powdery snow and saw the white snow
wasn´t white anymore. The powder snow around the
immediate body area was crimson in
color. " Get some crime scene tape and cordon off
the body about 5 meters around him, then get
your ass back to me where ever we are! " The two
other officers and Maximus continued to walk

forward trudging through the deep snow.
As they approached the farmhouse, they walked
slower as the view they were looking at was
strange and creepy. " Hello, officers! " One of the
polis men drew his gun and pointed straight at
an old man. " Stay where you are and put your hands
up now!! " " Officer! Put your weapon
down, I believe this to be the neighbor who reported
the incident! " " Yes, sir! I´m Mr. Evertson,
I found them 10 minutes before I called you. I had to
go back to my farm to use the phone as
signals on the cell are difficult to get around here. I
was walking my dogs along the field when
as I looked over here, I noticed what I thought was
snow-men but, the dogs ran straight to them
and started barking. My dogs have never liked the
bikers who have lived here, and I try to stay
away from here best I can. When I tried to brush my
hand over the head of this guy, when the
snow came off, I saw this! " He was pointing to the
biker on the far right. Just a few feet away
was the other three, and the old farmer had not
touched anything else and called the polis! " His
face is strange and twisted, it scared the shit out of
me! " " Crime scene tape now boys, and make
it 10 meters around, I don´t want anyone in here
without my permission! "
The act he was putting on seemed so convincing, but
then it had to be to pull it off. Blue lights
flashing at the edge of the field, several more polis
vehicles surrounded the area and seconds
after, a forensic team walked to where the four were
standing. Three forensic officers started to
take pictures of the bikers, then got small brushes
and began dusting the snow from the heads
downwards. " What the fuck!!? " One forensic officer

shouted with shock as he was looking at
something so weird, he nearly shit his pants! It was
the bike gang leader, and staring back at him
was the face that looked like it had gone through an
industrial French fries machine, the kind that
has square holes. " If only they knew, " the Inspektör
thought.

" Keep me, informed men! I can be contacted on my
cell if anything else turns up, oh! and don´t
forget the fat ass one down there! As he went to
leave, the forensic doctor stopped him. " Sir! I
have no clue as to this, but maybe these are
connected to the so-called vigilante we were
investigating! The strange wounds are similar in
dimensional scorch marks, so whatever
happened here, could be connected to the same
weapon. " " Ok! Once everything is cleaned up
here, get them back for autopsies then let me know
what you find! " The doctor nodded and went
to walk away, then shook his head as he stared at the
gruesome heads before him.
Maximus headed for Göteborg center where Justin's
apartment was. Pressing the buzzer,
momentarily the door swung open. " Hey!! How are
you to-day Maximus? " Justin waved him
in, then started walking towards the kitchen. "
Coffee? " "Ya! Black and strong Justin, please. "
" Something happened? " " A farmer found the bodies
this morning with his dogs, and I think he
literally shit himself from what he saw. You could
smell his pants. When I saw the bodies
myself, they looked more of a horror story than last
night!" Maximus took the mug of coffee
from Justin, took some of the hot beverage then
placed it on the coffee table. " I have been

thinking! " said Justin as he walked over to the fish tank. He stepped up on to the small indoor step ladder and slid the tank lid over to reveal the top of the coral insert. Reaching into it, he grabbed hold of the chest and proceeded to fetch it to the table.

Before them was the original small chest. " I was asking the master instrument of justice questions last night, and I got some very interesting answers. " Justin leaned over to Maximus and took hold of his hand. " Trust me! " Justin said. Maximus looked puzzled as he allowed Justin to take his hand, then pushed his thumb outwards and slowly placed it on the shiny metal plate on the chest! Maximus was intrigued but skeptical as to why he was doing this, then he got his answer. As his thumb touched the plate, a small sting shot through Maximus's hand along his nerve endings. " You go up against machine guns and crazy bikers, and you are afraid of a little prick!? " Justin laughed with the Inspektör then said. " You leave my penis out of this!!" In light of all the sadness and pain, it was good to laugh, it mends so many scars, even if Maximus felt guilty for it only being a short time since everything had gone wrong for him and his daughter.

"So, remind me why we are doing this?" Justin smiled at him. " Wait a few seconds. " They did!

Then! " DNA analyzed!! You are Maximus Lindström! I am now Master Instrument of Justice Mark 2!!

Standing

 by!!!! "

" You are fucking kidding me on right!? " The Inspektör continued with his strange expression on his face, still puzzled! Justin started to tell him

about the conversation with his master justice instrument. " I discovered that we could upgrade all justice instrument´s, and Bernadette´s is also upgraded, I also thought you might like to have your very own! You deserve it Maximus, but this is your choice, however, this could help your career or ruin it and get you into a lot of trouble! "
" Trouble!? Trouble!? " he repeated. Laughing then, " I can't get into any more trouble than I am already in! Shit!!! They would lock me up and throw the key away if only they knew what went on with these things! And you!! You! Mr. Webber would be in the cell next to me, and Bernadette in a women's prison " Smiles came to them again as they continued their conversation and drank their coffee!

Maximus drove once again to Justin's apartment. Thinking to himself, and wondered if Justin would get on board with his latest criminal case? As the elevator ascended to justins floor, he stepped out and on to the corridor floor. The buzzer went into action as it made the inspector jump with a little fright!
The voice that greeted him was a joy to his ears as he heard. " Luncle Axmousee!! I hug preeeze! There holding on to his right knee and would not let go was Bernadette´s and Justin's 2 and a half-year-old son! "Frankie! " Said, Bernadette. " Let uncle Maximus come in first," then laughed loudly!
Frankie was a blond-haired blue-eyed boy that any parents would have been glad and proud to have. What was known is that Frankie had a powerful bond with Maximus, and Maximus vowed to watch over him until the end of time!

Bernadette took Frankie in her arms and gently carried him into his bedroom. " Say night night to uncle Maximus Frankie! " " Igt Igt Axmousee. " Frankie smiled and giggled as his Mom continued into the bedroom.

" So! What can I do for you Chief Inspektör? " Justin laughed as he asked, then looked at Maximus for the reply.

" Over the last couple of years Justin, we have come through some crazy shit! Preventing some murders, and finding and punishing others. Rapists behind bars with partial memory losses, and some with wiped brains in mental asylums! And some patches of long-gone dust that were murderers remains, but as we know, most of them were put on the missing person lists, and they will always be on it! I have been contacted by the Swedish Intelligence Agency! (S.I.A) They have a potential job that needs to be done, and the government wants me to gather a special team and help with national security! With my crime clean-up rate, they think I´m some kind of super cop!! " Both started to laugh again. Listening intently, Justin thought the time was right to pour some whiskey out. Passing a glass half full he sat again and gazed at Maximus to hear the rest of his talk." I can only tell you if you are in! But this is classified and top secret, and I have thought of a way to allow you to be involved. " Justin didn't hesitate as he said. "Count me in Maximus!"

" In front of you is a Swedish secret document, it´s basically the official secrets act that was passed through Swedish parliament, once you sign it, you will be subjected to the crime of treason if you break this contract, so don´t break it! " Smiles all round as Justin said. " Oh excuse me, sir! I am giving you all this information about a machine that turns peoples brains into chop suey and murderers into dust, I thought you should know that !!! Then I will end up in the same asylum as some we have put there!" Roars of laughter came from them as Bernadette pokes her head around the bedroom door. "AaHemm! Little quieter please, you drunks! " Silencers seemed like they were put on their laughs as they held their hands to each mouth.

Justin handed the pen back to Maximus after signing the document. " Ok! Now I can tell you about the assignment. " The chief continued. " In front of you is an envelope containing an official ID card authorized by the S.I.A! You are now a special intelligence agent, and you are on full salary as of now! The agency has already been in touch with your boss and given him a cover story, which is as follows. You have witnessed an event that more intelligence is needed, and therefore, you have been drafted to undercover work to help, which is true in a way, but it will stop him from mentioning anything about it, he also had to sign the secrets act!! " Justin looked at Maximus. " Don´t tell me he´s a secret agent too!? "Boys! Keep your laughing to a minimum, please!! " "Sorry honey!" And with that, Justin winked at her.

"Right! When we are anywhere in the polis station, you are working for me on special operations if anyone asks, and if they start to quiz you on anything, refer them to me!. " Justin nodded and put his thumb up to say " He understood. "
" Now to the heart of the matter. Have you heard of a Swedish man called Timmy Alekvist? "

Justin didn't have to think too long as his memory cells kicked in. " Isn't he the guy that runs that Political parti? SPP? Or SVP? " " You were right the first time Justin, Sverige Patriot Parti!"
The chief reached into the envelope and pulled out a photograph of the " SPP " leader. " He is
our mission! " Justin sat back in his chair as Maximus began to brief him on their task, and
intelligence reports they had received from operatives in Arpangistan. " We believe that in the
next three weeks, an attempt is going to be made on his life in Sweden, Göteborg to be precise.
The biggest plot to hit the world since 09/11. Here´s what we know! Twenty suicide terrorists
with 60 pounds of Semtex each will be gathered in Göteborg 8 days from now, 7 of them are
going to attack the main station in Stockholm and try to hit 4 trains and the terminal, this how
ever is just a bonus target for them, as the true motive is to take out Timmy Alekvist! "Justin's
eyes got wider as the information started to sink in. " Has he pissed them off for some reason!? "
Justin had not heard much about the guy but knew that a lot of people called him a racist!
Maximus continued and began again to answer Justin's question. " He is definitely not a racist,
and is probably one of the nicest men in politics! He even has close friends who are Arabs,
Africans, people with many different religions, he just wants what is good for Swedish people,
and to take the blindfolds off which many have been wearing for years. Some have opened their
minds more recently to the possibility of no true Swedish citizens in 30 years' time! Ridiculous!?
Many people don't think so. He is starting to win a lot of seats in parliament, and they are shit

scared of him. If they take him out, then the road is left open for terrorists from anywhere to come over the borders! Sweden needs to wake up because, like the great William Wallace of Scotland, he will get his ass blown off! So, to speak. " "Right!" Said Justin. " Starting tomorrow, you will be with me at a secret training site for special forces training, and I know we both have a justice machine, but you need to learn very quickly to shoot different guns. Rifle, small pistol, with a heavy hitting caliber machine gun. It´s always good to be able to shoot straight Justin! " "Too true Maximus! " Justin replied. " Ok then, I will meet you outside your apartment at 0700 hours, and I will bring some of your equipment you will be needing!"

" Be careful my darling and call or text when you can! " Bernadette held him and kissed a slightly nervous Justin as he turned to walk out the door. " Give Frankie a kiss and hug for me when he wakes up honey! " " Sure, I will!" She replied.
It was spot on 0700hours as Justin stood smoking a cigarette at the front of the apartment building. As he smoked, he glanced to his left, and coming towards him was Maximus along the sidewalk. " Did you forget to bring your vehicle with you getting out of bed too early!? "
Smiling, he kept looking at the chief Inspektör, but the smile left his face as he saw walking directly behind him, another man wearing a red bandana around his forehead, and what looked like to be an automatic rifle machine gun barrel pointing at the ground. The inspectors face

looked cold as he watched Justin in front of him as he got closer. Justin waited just that little longer until the men were close enough to act! Suddenly!! " Restrain man behind Maximus now!!! " Justin waited for the master instrument to take the action, but! Nothing!! Justin dived over Maximus's shoulder and struck the man with a heavy blow to his head, and while falling towards the ground holding on to the man to take him down!!

" Stop!! Stop Justin! " Just as Justin was bringing his fist down to the man's jaw! " He was your first test, Justin! He´s one of the good guys! We had to know what kind of response you have to these situations that might present itself! " " Fuck sake Maximus!!!! I nearly needed to go back and change my underwear! " Maximus smiled and then spoke to Justin again. " Why do you think the justice machine didn't work!? " Thinking for a moment, Justin answered. " Should we be talking about this in front of him? " " Show him, David! " Looking to the man beside him. David rolled his sleeve up slightly, then revealed another justice machine on his arm. " For shit's sake! Have they been giving these out at a supermarket chain store!?" David pushed his hand towards Justin, then spoke. " Nice to meet you, Justin, " Smiling back at him, Justin took hold of the man's hand and apologized for the takedown, and shaking his head, David replied. " No man!! You did excellently, and I´m glad to be able to work with you. "

At an unknown location, the three of them walked into a canteen where breakfast was being served, and picking up a plate each, helped

themselves to the hot steaming food before them. Wiping his mouth with the napkin, Justin turned to Maximus, then enquiring, started to ask him about the fourth justice machine. " When did you know about this one? " Finishing his mouth full of food, he placed the knife and fork back on the plate. " It was about 7 months ago when I came across a potential crime scene yet to happen, but the machine had projected another man hiding waiting to see what was going to take place, so to cut a long story short, we discovered we both had the same quest at the same time. " " Wow! " " Now you come to mention it, I have been picking up little blips of light on days when I go out past crime or potential crime scenes, so I guess it was you all along then David!? " " Yep! " David smiled as he replied. " I have watched the two of you on many occasions, so it was really good when Maximus and I started to see we had the same master justice machine´s, but we waited until just recently to tell you as I was already recruited for special opp´s! "
" Right boys! We are due on the firing range in 30 minutes, so best get moving! "

Standing behind tables on the gun range, before them was several weapons of all shapes and sizes. " The first gun I want you to use is one of the latest models out! The Glock 42S the .380 caliber update from the G19R This one has been reduced down in size but is very light and compact, and this weapon is our primary must carry, remember you only have to squeeze gently!"
Targets were placed at 50meters and one hundred meters and were now ready for them to train

on. " Each one of you has two magazines with 12 rounds in each, make them count lads, and take your time, one magazine for 50meters and one for one hundred! In your own steady time, Shoot!! "

" On many news reports over the years you have heard mention of the well known Kalashnikov AK (AK-47) 7.62mm caliber, this has been one of the terrorists favorite weapons, so again! Two magazines of 20 rounds in each, same as before, 50 meters and one hundred meters! "
Both Justin and David were pleased with their shooting skills, and David was just ahead on points for scoring perfect bullseye´s. 97% of all their rounds hit the targets, so Maximus was well impressed. The last to be tested was the .50 caliber, this weapon was a real body killer, it could cut a man in half with one bullet on impact with the body!
The smell of cordite hung around the firing range as other agents were trying their skills and expertise. "The last exercise for the day is grenade and claymore practice, " and this was going to be interesting.
After learning a crash course in explosives, they retired to the main building for dinner and showers, and then Maximus wanted to see them in one of the study rooms.
" For the first day, you have both exceeded my expectations, if we keep this up, you will both be reasonably ready in a few days, but remember the time is ticking down and we need to be ready as much as possible! "
Justin retired to his room and started to clean his

new weapon. I would rather have the
instrument of justice any day of the week, but I guess
I had better get a little more familiar with
this pistol! He thought.
As he cleaned and oiled the working parts of the
Glock, there was a light knock on the door.
" Justin my dear friend, I wanted to get you by
yourself for a moment to discuss a delicate
matter. " Continuing, Maximus sat on a chair against
the wall, then looked him straight in the
eyes! " I was putting questions to the justice machine
earlier, and basically the answers
concerned me a little! If we are in a situation where
we need the restraint beams, we can only get
a maximum of 4 from each machine, then it will use
too much energy in a short time period, so!
We need to be sharp-witted to use the potential
future unfolding crime scenes to best defend our
subject and ourselves! We could all go out with a big
bang in this one Justin, but, maybe with
some quick thinking, we can make it!! " Justin turned
to Maximus. " Each one of us my friend is
going to die one day when that´s going to be? I don
´t know! But with a lot of good planning
here, we can get to our next birthday and still have
saved the day! One last thing Justin. There is
a chance that there is a security leak within the
special forces section, so as an extra measure,
keep your justice machine on at all times, and unless
you have to use voice commands to it, use
your thought process to give it instructions, in some
way this might prevent big ears listening
in!"

A few days passed, then packing all their equipment,
they were going to head back to Göteborg

to meet their new assignment!

Arriving at the mansion where the conference was to be held, they were met by Timmy Alekvist himself! " Hello, gentlemen, and welcome! I am getting the paperwork ready for tomorrow, so go down to the end room on your left and help yourself to coffee! I also believe someone has set up a whiteboard in the room with the plan layout for this location! Forgive me for dashing away, but duty calls!! " As quick as he came in on the scene, he dashed away to take care of his business.

Straight away all three got down to studying the plan on the board, and making notes, they tried to come up with a working plan for the ministers meeting. After a few hours, Maximus opened up with a rough idea and opened the discussion up for changes if they needed.

" I think the West wall with the main building is most likely to be the weakest link, there is only one arched entrance to drive through at the north wall, so incased with a 15-meter brick wall, I don´t believe they will make a frontal attack! If I was them, I would breach the West wall first and then enter through the back of the conference room, that gives them an advantage instead of coming in the front door! Tomorrow morning, we will set up in three locations, so if it happens, we should be well covered! "

Maximus and Justin had come a long way since the discovery of the justice machines, and this type of operation was completely different from the rapes and murders they have been accustomed to! But! This was potentially planned murder, so the machines will do their job to help them. Maximus continued. " The meeting will go

ahead at 10 am, and they will take coffee
in the dining room next to the conference room, then
5 meters back into the meeting, then lunch
at midday precisely! We will scan the three areas we
are going to be positioned at, and each one
of the justice machines will warn of any future breach
in the defenses, but as we know, it can
only give us an hour heads up! I want you both to go
and get familiar with this building and the
inside and outside walls, check to see if anyone is
observing any of this mansion, remember to
send thoughts to the machines so we don´t draw
attention to them! "
Laying on his bed, Justin took his cell phone and
called his beautiful Bernadette. " Can´t tell you
much honey! But everything going well, this should
be over by tomorrow night, so fingers
crossed! " "Frankie keeps asking where you are in his
cute way, but you can see he looks for you
at the front door! " Hugs and kisses to him, and you
cute lady!! " " Take care, my handsome
man! Talk soon!"

" Potential future crime scene detected!! " On
Justin's dial on the justice machine was the possible
crime playing, no hologram, just projections on the
screen in front of him. Something was
wrong!! It was only 8 am and he had just walked
past the kitchen. Sure enough, as the screen
continued, a man dressed in a black suit and bow tie
came from the kitchen, he started to look
both ways, obviously checking to see no one was
around, then placed his cell phone to his ear. In
the next moment, Justin heard something in the one-

sided conversation he could hear! " Meeting
on for 10 am, coffee before at 09.30 in the dining
room! Then nothing! Justin casually strolled
into the kitchen as if to do a security check, then
noticed the suited man getting trays ready for
the meeting. Three other kitchen staff went about
their food preparations, slowly walking over to
him saying. " Who are you, sir!? " Justin waited for
an answer. " Paul Jenkins, I am the butler for
Mr. Alekvist!" Justin smiled to himself as the thoughts
came quickly. " Ge'ez! I don´t believe
I´m going to say this! The butler did it! " Being very
serious with his next thoughts, he sent the
justice machine a message from his now more active
mind. " Send a message to Maximus to get
his ass over to the outside of the kitchen, and I will
rendezvous there!! " The justice machine

replied. **" Message sent to Maximus Lindström,
and 52 minutes to potential crime scene!! "**

Showing the Inspektör the playback on the screen,
they both looked at each other. Then
Maximus opened his mouth. " The butler did it!!? " "
Thought that was just in books and
movies!? " " Get him out here, and I'll get David to
come lock him up safe. David ran all the way
from the North gate which he was surveying, arriving
at the kitchen entrance. " Maximus!!? "
" This guy in the penguin suit is probably our leak
and not a minister, he is Mr. Alekvist
butler! And don´t say it!!! " David looked at Justin
then Maximus. " As if I would do such a
thing!!?" His smile gave it away at that point.
" What is the meaning of this gentlemen!? I haven't
done anything wrong!! " " Let us be the
judge of that sir!! Now go with this agent and we will

talk in a few minutes! "
Maximus played the scene back one more time, then
both walking into the dining room, they
looked hard to see anything out of place. Nothing!
Everything looked in order. If these terrorists
were coming here, they must have some kind of
sensor telling them where the dining room was,
and that meant an electronic homing device, but
where!? " Right Justin, let´s get to that
temporary office and talk some sense into this guy!

" No! no! no! " Maximus shouted as Justin and he ran
to the table at the front of the whiteboard.
Laying on his stomach in a pool of blood was David,
he had a kitchen knife protruding from his
back. His eyes were wide open and drips of blood still
running from the wound. " David!!! Stay
with us! " The Inspektör felt for his pulse, but,
nothing, no heartbeat left in his lifeless body. A
surprised look came over Justin as he looked at his
arm. "Holy Shit!!! His justice machine is
gone!! " "Go to the dining room now and stand
guard, because for whatever reason, this is going
down very shortly, and here's what I believe,
something tells me we are going to get all 20 of the
bastards here, Stockholm was false information!! I´m
calling for back up !! They aren't here to
assassinate him, they are here to abduct him!!
SHIT!!! "

Trying to calm down a little, Justin tried to rationally
think of what to do next?
" Master instrument of justice, where is David's
justice machine? " A row of flashing amber
lights scrolled along the screen searching! " **His**

justice unit is in short grass by the fountain in the main

garden!! " " Can you control his unit from this unit!?" Justin asked with slight concern now. **" Yes, Justin, I can, and can also implement restraint and punishment sequences if necessary. I will alert you to any**

potential danger as and when it happens!! " " Thank you-you beautiful piece of metal you! " It was a relief for Justin to hear the unit was safe and might be to Maximus's and Justin's advantage when and if all hell broke loose!

Justin was now secure in the dining room, he was watching everything, but everything was still for the moment. He remembered his Glock! Getting it out from the holster was too easy, it slid from the leather holding it, then gripping it with a firm hand, he crouched down by the dining room table and waited!

Thoughts of David ran through his mind as he rested there, where was Maximus!? Justin forgot that his mind was tuned into the justice machine, and it answered him in a second. **" Maximus is on the first-floor briefing Timmy Alekvist! Also, the arriving ministers have been diverted to another location for**

safety. Back-up has been alerted, but a slight delay on the highway has slowed their progress to reach

us! Justin! Multiple possible future scenes available, evasive action needed! " Justin flinched

as he heard
that, then thought. " Fuck it!!! I can´t live forever but would have been nice to live 30 or 40
 more years! "

" David's unit is picking up multiple scenes for future events, Maximus's also multiple scenes, take evasive

action! 1 minute to first future attack!!! "
Then Justin heard the final few seconds of the countdown! **" 5 4 3 2 1 0 Crime scene happening now!!"**

A huge blinding light followed directly by an explosion that felt to Justin that his eardrums had
burst, in that frightful few seconds, debris and wood from the flying splinters of the dining table
and chairs blew across the room showering dust and rubble in all four corners of the room.
Splinters struck any objects in their path as they dug deep into anything they could find like darts
to a dartboard. Laying on the floor under debris, Justin tried to move, but the force of the
explosion had stunned all of his body; he was powerless to do anything at that point! He
managed to gain focus in his eyes as the dark and explosive dust cloud spiraled around him!
In the dining room or the remains of the dining room, the light started to pierce its way into the
room. Justin could see high powered torches with their beams moving from side to side as 4
terrorists walked and climbed over the rubble before them.
Regaining most of his senses, Justin took aim, then realized he had the instrument of justice!
" Restrain the 4 of them now!!" Four beams of light

fired quickly from the Master instrument,
each of the men with masks over their heads
shouting in a language Justin didn't understand!
Frozen within the beams, every one of them shouting
warnings and trying to break free.
Bangbangbangbangbang!!! 5 shots from an
automatic weapon rang out and started hitting the
floor and wood all around Justin. Without thinking,
Justin moved with the speed of an arrow, as
he lined up the shot to the new terrorist head. "
BANG!! " The Glock jumped into action as
Justin pulled the trigger once. The bullet indented
into the man's skull splattering blood from the
back of his mask. Then Justin saw it! As the man
started to fall lifelessly towards the ground, a
line of explosives around the man's chest in full view
of the world " Fuck No!!!" Justin was like
a hair sprinting out of a dog track as he sprinted to
the corridor outside the dining room.
" BOOOOOOMMMMmmmm!! " Yet another
horrendous explosion rocked and shook the whole
building as a flash and gust of the blast knocked
Justin along the corridor floor. **" Justin! Fugitives
have dead man switches that are wired to their
pulse, if their heart stops, the explosives will
detonate! "** Again
shaken with that second blast, Justin started to look
at the four men in the beams, it was still
working well, and the beams had protected the
terrorists shielding them, so they still lived.
" Justice machine, if you activate punishment inside
the beams, will the explosives be
exploding!? Or Imploding!?" **" Implode Justin!! "**
"Got you-you bastards! " " Activate Implosion

punishment now!!! " Four bright flashes with a sound of air traveling at 100km ph. rushed around Justin's head and ears and watched as the men looked like they were being drawn into a vacuum. Inside the beams, Justin could see the tangled mess of blood and guts clinging to the air surrounding them all.

As he leaned forward, Justin bent slightly to rest his hands on his knees, he breathed heavily as he tried to regain his strength. **" Evasive action now!! "** " Now what!!? " As he asked the question, several shots rang out from the center of the dining room in Justin's direction. He dived for cover under a corridor table against the wall, as he slid to a stop, he was pointing his gun back into the room and staring straight into the eyes of the third wave of terrorists! " Restrain terrorists now!! "

Four beams again shot from the machine, and Justin was so glad for the justice machine to exist! Eyes widened, as Justin saw the beams capture the men, but, there was five of them side by side! " Fuck!!! " Split second timing was essential as Justin gave the command for the Implosion punishment again. Repeating the scene as before, more imploded blood and guts erupted inside the beam, then immediately commanding to release the terrorists and restrain the fifth fugitive!

His command was too late, the terrorist didn't understand what just happened, but in his moment of glory, he pushed a red button on his wrist!!!.......

Darkness! Justin could hear slight feint sounds but didn't understand them. A feeling of being drunk, but had no pain. He felt at peace within his mind, and every few seconds started to see white light flashes. It wasn't his eyes that could see

them, but his mind. Color specs of light
followed the white light, then soft angelic voices in
his ears very softly spoken. " I must be
dead!" he thought to himself, as the colors started to
grow stronger and brighter. As quick as a
blink, his eyes shot open! " Don´t you die on me you
son of a bitch! " Maximus words was the
angelic voice, but he wasn't No angel!! Justin became
more aware of his surroundings and saw
he was in the main front grounds next to the small
garden plot. Looking up at Maximus, he asked
him " Is every part of my body still in one piece or in
pieces!? " " Oh, you are all there but! You
have cuts and splinters embedded in parts! You!!
Justin Webber are one lucky guy! " Justin
looked around the grounds, it looked like a world war
battlefield! " Did we win!? " Maximus
looked down at Justin with a small smile with a hint
of sadness throughout his face.
"The minister is safe! He has been taken to another
location by the backup teams. The four polis
officers guarding the front gate lost their lives in the
assault, the terrorists did multiple strikes all
at the same time. David's old justice machine took
out another four of them. " " What happened
with the penguin-suited guy!? " Maximus turned
around and pointed to a dumb looking man
sitting on a garden wall near the mansion steps. "
The machine got him with the mushy beam
then!? " " Yep!! I was quickly briefing the minister
when the asshole tried to get me from
behind, but the justice machine gave me a 30-second
heads up as to what could happen! " More
back up units arrived as he looked for a paramedic to
dress his wounds.
Justin drew on a cigarette as he looked at the black

body bags laying on the grass before him, at least Maximus and himself were still alive! Glancing at the ground he caught sight of the justice machine that belonged to David. His machine took out some of the frontal assault on the mansion, so even though David had gone, his machine took the revenge for him. Justin bent down in pain holding his back, picked up the machine. Unzipping the body bag, he placed the unit on the chest of the dead body, zipping it up afterward. With his head bowing a little, he spoke to David's lifeless body. " You did good young David! I have only known you a few days, but I know we would have been great buddies given time, but now it´s time for you to have fun somewhere in this vast space! Take care, David!! " " Time to get you to hospital Justin! " Paramedics helped Justin into an ambulance, Maximus started to shut the doors of the vehicle, saying. " Good job to-day buddy! I'll come see you later when you´re patched up! " Raising his right thumb in the air, he managed a smile as the ambulance pulled out of the bomb-damaged grounds!!!

" I managed to re-schedule my meetings, Justin, I wanted to come and thank you personally for my life! " Timmy Alekvist stood at the end of Justin's hospital bed staring at all the wires and drips connected to Justin. Sitting beside him was Bernadette and on her lap sat little Frankie! " You have a great family here Justin, and I am envious of you! " Justin looked at her and Frankie, then at Timmy. " Mr. Alekvist! You can make a difference in Sweden for the good, but remember children like my Frankie. This next generation will be looking back in 20 years and asking how things developed!? So please help them now as then they will look after Sweden in the future! I am no politician; I will leave that up to you. Just make a difference for the better! "

Timmy smiled at him. " Sounds like you could be a politician Justin!! " Smiles all round as he turned and walked through the hospital room door.

Bernadette leaned over Justin and kissed him gently on the lips. " I love you very much, Justin! After you get better, no more playing undercover spy for you!!! If you do! My master machine will turn your brain into mushy goo!!" "You got it, sweetheart! I´m too old for this shit!! ".........

Chapter 15

A GOOD MAN
DEPARTS!!

Justin sat on his grave digging machine. It was
another grave for another soul leaving this world!
Justin had asked to personally dig this one as to pay
his respects to a well-liked man. 6 Years it
had been now since the terrorists attack in Göteborg!
After leaving the hospital and trying to get
back to a normal life, (Whatever Normal was!!) he
got well enough to return to his job two
months later, that was good going for him, as some
of his injuries were serious enough to have
some concerns by the doctors. One of the bombs
splinters had penetrated his heart, and it was too
dangerous for them to remove it, so surgeons
decided it would be in his best interests to just
monitor it over time! He could do most things on a
daily basis, but an odd time he had burning
sensations in his chest when the splinter moved
slightly around the artery!
The grave had reached its depth, and Justin placed
the newly carved gravestone at the head of the
grave, then stood back to read the inscription!
**IN LOVING MEMORY OF A MAN WHO WOULD
HELP ANY-ONE!
HE WATCHED OVER PEOPLE AT A DISTANCE
BUT ALWAYS HELD HIS HAND OUT TO HELP
WHEN NEEDED
LARS SVENSSON
WILL BE SADLY MISSED BY ALL!!**
Justin and Lars didn't spend a lot of time with each

other over these last few years, that was due
to Justin always hooking up with Maximus and doing
Master instrument of justice work.
Lars did like his beers in the local bar by the
cemetery, and Justin caught up with him
occasionally. Lars never got told the true story of the
injuries Justin sustained, as he was still
sworn to the official secrets act!
Answering his cell phone, Justin listened as Maximus
started to tell him of a problem that had
come up. After agreeing to meet up at Justin's
apartment, they hung up.
After a very emotional service, Justin waited for all
the mourners to depart, then changed back
into his working clothes to cover up the coffin that
had now been lowered into the grave. " Good
bye old friend!! Have fun where ever you are! "
On the highway back to his apartment, Justin was
curious as to what the next assignment was
going to be!? Parking the SUV, he stepped into the
elevator and walked over to his apartment
door. Closing it quietly, he walked to the kitchen and
began brewing some coffee. " Buzzing!"
The doorbell came alive as he walked to open it.
" Your face is telling me something not good is about
to happen Maximus! So, what´s wrong old
man!? " Maximus went over to the cabinet where the
whiskey was kept, then poured himself a
very large one. " I have Bowl cancer, Justin!!! " Justin
put his coffee mug on the coffee table,
then poured himself a large whiskey and sat down
next to him.
Maximus as best as he could started to tell Justin
about the diagnosis he had just learned about.
" They say that it's in the last stages, and they are
not able to operate, so they have given me a

ballpark time of about 5 weeks! To go through many
years of facing knives! Guns! Bullets!
Facing murderers and rapist scum, and yet my fear is
there as I think about dark cells that are out
to kill me! " Justin held on to his arm. " SHIT!!
Maximus! I´m so sorry my friend. " The front
door opened and walking in with shopping bags was
Bernadette followed by Justin's son
Frankie! " Uncle Maximus!! Yaaaayyyyyy!! " Maximus
smiled and went to hug Frankie. " Hello, my
handsome boy! " Maximus held on to him like he was
never going to let go. Bernadette looked at
Justin, then Maximus. " Ok my secretive men, please
tell me what´s going on!? You aren't going
on another terrorist hunt, are you!? " Justin shook his
head, then put Maximus's letter from the
hospital in her hands. She stood there and started to
shake, then as tears rolled from her eyes, she
walked into the bedroom and shut the door. You
could hear the cries through the shut door,
heavy sobbing. Frankie spoke to his father. " What´s
wrong with Mom Dad!? " Frankie wasn't a
stupid boy and waited to hear is Dads answer. " Mom
has had some bad news, Frankie! But, she
 will be ok shortly! "
" Walk with me, Justin! " Maximus and Justin walked
slowly along the park river path, it was
one of the beauty spots that young lovers had visited
when they were dating! " If I only have a
few days left now Justin, I just wanted to thank you
and say goodbye before lights out! I am not
being morbid, I just want to put a few things in order
for peace of mind! You and I have come
along way since we stood in the cemetery, and
sometimes it puts the fear of God into me when I
go over in my mind the things we have come

through! I have made out my will Justin, and I´m leaving everything to you!! " " No, you are not Maximus!" Quickly replying, Maximus continued. " I have made the will so there is nothing you can do my dear friend. I have no family now, and I know you, Bernadette and Frankie will make good use of it. I want you to think carefully about maybe going back to the States and put him through University. I have come to terms today about my coming death, but somewhere in time and space, I will meet you again young man " Most people walking by them at that point would have taken them for a gay couple, but this friendship ran deeper than a river that ran along beside them.

Both smiling, they started to walk back to Justin's apartment to get a pot roast that Bernadette was making for them.

Maximus took some powerful painkillers just before he started eating the wonderful food Bernadette had prepared. " I am going to eat this even if it kills me!! " Maximus said it with a straight face, then burst out laughing with Bernadette doing the same a few seconds later. For a few seconds, Justin had this fear come over him, the fear was of being alone, and he didn't like that. The strange way that Maximus and himself met, then all the crazy stuff that went hand in glove with the Master justice machines, left an ache in his heart, he was going to lose someone to death that befriended him and loved like a brother.

It was 10.45pm a few days later when Justin got a call from the hospital. " Mr. Webber!? This is Doctor Stone. I need to tell you that Chief Inspektör

Maximus Lindström was brought into
hospital 30 minutes ago and has been asking for you!
I recommend that you get here as soon as
possible, his vital signs are decaying fast, and ...... "
Justin interrupted the doctor. " I´m on my
way now!!! " He went into the bedroom and kissed
his beautiful Bernadette, she was crying
again, she knew this was the beginning of the end for
Maximus. " Tell him I love him Justin and
tell him Thank you for his love towards Frankie! "
Justin nodded snatched his car keys from the
desk and left.
Maximus lay there in the hospital bed. His chest and
arms were wired to the ECG machine that
was monitored at the intensive care nurse station. "
You in a lot of pain Maximus? " Justin asked
with an anguished look on his face. Slow then fast
breathing was coming from him, and his
color was an ashen grey! " Not so bad now Justin,
they gave me a pain-relieving drug that should
be called I DON`T GIVE A SHIT DRUG!! It´s sending
me higher than the statue of liberty! "
Forcing a weak smile on his face, he reached for
Justin's hand and squeezed tightly. " Listen
carefully, Justin. I want you to put my justice
machine in my coffin, so when you bury me, it
goes with me. One day, you will need to dig it up,
just make sure you give it to someone good. I
drifted off to sleep earlier today and had a fantastic
dream. I dreamt I was in a mass of color in
space and drifted into some Greek looking place with
tall pillars, it was so peaceful and gave me
a sense of belonging. You had anything like that
before? " Justin smiled at him. "You are no
longer alone Maximus, you will see your dream space
again very soon, and even if you don´t

believe what I say, I am going to look for you in the
weeks or years ahead! So, listen out for my
voice you old copper, and don´t go upsetting the
beautiful ladies when you come across them!! "
Looking at Maximus's face, his eyes were smiling like
his face, and as Justin looked, the ECG
monitor peeped a long tone, followed by a doctor
entering the room, then after a few moments,
he switched the machine to the off position and
placed the sheet over Maximus's body. " I am
so sorry for your loss. We will get in touch within 36
hours for the funeral directors to collect
him!

Numb in his head, Justin walked out of the hospital
and sat on a bench. Blowing the smoke from
his mouth, Justin drew hard on a cigarette, savoring
every breath of the inhaled aroma. The
night sky was sparkling with stars as he gazed
upwards. " I will find you one day my dear
Maximus! Just you be there, or I'll kick your ass!! "

Bernadette was reacting badly to Maximus's death,
and young Frankie got upset quite often when
he thought that his uncle Maximus was no longer
there!
Yet again Justin asked to dig his friends grave, and
his boss had no problems with that request.
An honor guard from the Göteborg polis department
presented a 21-gun salute to a man that was
more popular than " Santa Claus! "
Justin once again started to fill in the grave with the
machine. Emotions ran high that day, and
the last thing Justin needed was the voice behind him
hitting his eardrums!

" So, you are the Vigilante!?" Justin heard in the tone of the voice that he just had to be a cop! He was right! Standing there with a straight face was none other than " **Inspektör Patrick Jönsson!!** "

" You and Maximus had become quite close friends Justin!!? I have been keeping my eye on you over the years, and some really strange coincidences started to appear in crimes in Göteborg and Borås!! So maybe today is a good day to come clean, and tell me how you managed to punish all the shitty assholes that were targeted by you!? " Justin like a long time ago sat down on the diggers footplate, just like he did with Maximus that first time.
It must have been all of two hours going through all the details to the Inspektör who sat next to him smoking most of the time. Just like before, they shared their smokes together. " Ok!! That explains it clearly! But just one thing Justin! Where´s Maximus's master justice instrument!!? "
Going to the box on the digger, Justin took out a screwdriver, then asked the Inspektör to move for 10 minutes.
Reaching the coffin, Justin jumped into the grave, undid the screws to the coffin, and lifted the lid. Resting on the lifeless Maximus's chest was the jeweled box! " Maximus wanted this to stay with him until someone good came along. "Inspektör! Are you good!? " " I was friends like you with him, and I knew the two of you had something going on, and I left everything alone. I knew there might come a time when he would tell me about whatever it was he hid but never did. So what do I do with this thing now!?" Justin looked at
174

him. " Keep an open mind Inspektör, and
place your thumb on the square plate at the front,
but if you do! Your world will change before
your eyes, and no turning back! " Smiles on their
faces, they shook each other's hands, then
parted company. Justin covered the coffin again and
looked at the new grave for a good man.
" See you soon Maximus!!! "......

CHAPTER 16

A NEW START
BEGINS!

Emotions were running high as Zac, Bernadette, Frankie, and Justin did enough hugging to last forever!

A new beginning for them all, and no one was more pleased than Justin's uncle Zac. Several weeks earlier, a shipment came over from Sweden, and Zac got down to getting everything prepared for their arrival, including the very large aquarium that had got there a couple days previously. A Miami aquarium installer came specially to install the tank and had received all of the seahorses and fishes to quarantine them before putting them back in the relocated tank. It took pride of place as all of them gazed at the spectacular set up.

Zac still sat in Justin's father's chair, almost like it was glued to his butt! Sitting there was also a glass of Scotch, which Zac said " Was for medicinal purposes!! " That brought some smiles. The biggest smile was young Frankie´s as he met an uncle he had never seen before, and the two of them looked like they were twins! An instant bond like a super glue!
Justin surveyed all of the house that was now their home, and feelings of warmth and welcoming shone around the place like an injection of love and closeness. Zac whispered in Bernadette's ear.
" You three are a pleasure to see in these old man's

eyes, and what a great job you have done
with raising the two of them!! " He winked at her,
and Bernadette immediately understood what
he had meant. " I´m going to take Frankie down to
the main beach, so we will get a bite to eat for
lunch when we are out. Make sure you keep the
justice machine on your arm honey!! Catch you
all later!"
Finding just the right spot to park, Justin and Frankie
headed to the sand on the beautiful well
kept beach. The sun was blazing, and a great warmth
was felt after so many years in the Swedish
mainly cold climate. Frankie ran to the edge of the
water where small waves " whooooshed "
along the sand. The blue sky was probably one of the
bluest skies Justin had seen for many many
years, and remembering the day he was told about
his parents, he smiled to himself. So many
things had happened since that day. Many new and
interesting people who had come into his life.
Thinking! He thought back to when he discovered the
justice machine and the journeys that it
had shown him. All the punishments the machine had
given out, and with a vague recollection
of the astral traveling, he had done. He watched the
sea as each wave came along and soaked
young Frankie´s feet! Justin felt alive! A new sense of
living, he so wished Maximus was here to
stand beside him. Another smile appeared on his
face.
" Dad!! Dad!! Look!!! " Justin looked to where Frankie
was pointing. About 75meters away
stood a man in the sea with water just over his
knees. He had his back to the shore, and with his
hands stretched out to the left and right of him was
three dolphins, each one of the heads looking

at the man. The noises the dolphins were making were like all three were talking to him.

" Frankie!! Come here!" His son did exactly what he was asked, and Justin lifted him up in his arms as he continued to observe the man. Justin started to walk along the beach, closer to the shape in the water. " This was fascinating! " Justin thought.

At about 30meters Justin stared at the man in the water. As his eyes looked at the man and dolphins, Justin's eyes widened as he saw the body of a native American, with a long pleated ponytail. Then it came to him!!! " JOHN!!!! " At that precise moment, a police siren blasted the beach as a 4x4 with blue and red lights skidded onto the sand and sea edge before them.

" Hey, you!! Get out of the water now!! You pervert!! " The policeman shouted at the man, as Justin noticed that he had been standing there naked!!

Getting into the police car, Justin looked directly at Johns' face. His eyes and face were smiling as he lowered his head to avoid hurting himself. He said nothing as the police car drove away and heading for the police precinct.

Frankie looked at Justin. " Who was that dad!!? Justin smiled at Frankie.

" Son!!! The world is just about to find out!!!!! "
....

END!!

" PROLOGUE "

Perfect in every way!

John Doe! The man that was. No one knew where he came from, no one knew his real name. Police at the precinct gave him that name, as unknowns are automatically labeled that way. With no memory, and a perfect body, he looked like a brightly colored rare rose in a world of thorns.

It was in the asylum that people noticed something odd going on. Insane people were acting sane! The worst of the crazies were acting normal.

Only a short time passed, and a strange power so great, revealed itself to the world. Word spread like wild fire in the jungle of life.

In the spy glass of religion, church elders kept their curious eyes fixated on events that were mystifying the world. Who was this perfectly looking man with no name? Why was he here? What was the end purpose?

Good in people surface, but at the same time, evil plays it´s part just like it always has.

Taking John Doe around the world, this wonderful power he was showing to the world, was just about to bring him down to his knees.

Should he continue to share this power? should he stop, then fade into the unknown? Maybe he would leave to go to where he came from, or maybe, the unthinkable was just about to happen!

" John Doe! The hands that could heal the world."

Ladies and Gentlemen!
Sit back and relax as you read
" JOHN DOE THE HANDS THAT COULD HEAL
THE WORLD "
A CONTINUING FROM
" THE ULTIMATE INSTRUMENT OF JUSTICE "

" JOHN DOE! " " THE HANDS THAT COULD HEAL THE
WORLD! "
© Copyright P. J. Ljung 2015 - 2019
All rights reserved. No part of this publication
may be reproduced, distributed, or transmitted
in any form or by any means, including
photocopying, recording, or other electronic or
mechanical methods, without the prior written
permission of the publisher, except in the case
of brief quotations embodied in critical reviews
and certain other noncommercial uses
permitted by copyright law. For permission
requests, write to the publisher
© Copyright P. J. Ljung   2019
Second Edition

(PLEASE NOTE!!)
This is a work of fiction. Names, characters,
businesses, places, events and incidents are
either the products of the author's imagination
or used in a fictitious manner. Any resemblance
to actual persons, living or dead, or actual
events is purely coincidental.

CHAPTER 1

JOHN DOE!!!

" Stars! " Tens of thousands of stars! Gases, colors
that don´t even match any of the magnificent 7
colors that go to make up the rainbow. Man would be
astonished if he knew what lay beyond our
immediate space! In the darkness, twinkling lights
millions of kilometers away, shining their energy and
pulsating towards any-where in their path. The paths
of light can come from any direction´s, and not just
from stars! When you look with your eyes at the
vastness of space, we stand or sit there wondering
just what lays beyond what we know. Imagine then
what it would be like to see space from space itself!!?
One such chance was for a being, a being that just
was! Alien!? Not being from our planet, I guess you
could call him an Alien! Was it a he!!? A Thing!!?
A planet long known to the beings drew much
interest over time and space. They on occasions sent
explorers to the planet, they witnessed
the growth of the species, and some-times made
themselves known. The cratered satellite shone from
the rays of the star millions of light years away! A
silvery chrome color shining to the beings eyes! Was
it his eyes!? He didn´t have a solid form, so eye´s??
It was a conscious thought process, it existed in
space, and was drifting at high speed through rays of
color after color. His alive consciousness was his
eyes. Coming up fast and bright now, the planet of
life!! A planet spinning in space, and was spinning
out of control, manipulated by the species that lived
there. Brilliant blue and glowing silver projected back

into space. From this view, the consciousness had the best view of the world! A world that was just about to know they were never alone!! A bright smile in the consciousness whisked around his misty appearance as he travelled closer to the planet surface.

Descending like a missile, the consciousness put some vibrational waves down towards the ocean, in that vicinity you would have heard the distant humming as if someone had mixed a bee and a harp together to make the sound!

There was no impact splash as the consciousness broke through the ocean surface, then slowing and slowing, until, floating 100 meters below the sea! The misty consciousness glanced around his surroundings. His misty consciousness began to change into solid form, as he looked down to see toes and feet, then legs manifesting before him. He was taking the form of the male spices on the planet. He was becoming " Man!!! " Floating under the surface for him was like the sensation of being in a mother's womb! No breath of air was needed as he wondered in this magnificent ocean. He looked in amazement as swimming around him with great curiosity, was three beautiful sea creatures. They made a talking singing noise as they felt no harm coming from this new being! Colors of silver and gold started to extend from his forehead, and gently connected with these wonderful dolphins! Six beams with two colors of each penetrating the dolphins skulls, and then changing direction, they headed straight for this radiating man!

With the new hands and fingers, he gently held the top fin of two of them, then the third put his head between the man's legs to support him as all three started to rise to the surface. His head rose to look at the blue sky above him, with very few clouds, he felt his face, touching it all over to feel the skin that had appeared from his consciousness. The dolphins sounded like they were happy and making noises like laughing as they swam fast towards the land in the distance. Taking one all-mighty breath inwards, he smiled, he could feel the skin get tight on his newly formed face. The breath was refreshing as he breathed in then out for the very first times! All of these new emotions he could feel while surfing the ocean surface as the dolphins pulled and pushed him along. His long-pleated shoulder length hair, jet black and glistening in the sunlight. He felt every second of the cool water over his body, and the star that shone heating his new face to a pleasant temperature. What a wonderful planet this was, and he was so grateful he had the chance to come here!

The dolphins started to slow down slightly as they were getting closer to the shore of golden sand. He felt a sensation on his leg, he knew it was a leg. Thoughts were entering his mind now, a mind that was sharp like a knife, and drawing on his ancient entity powers, he understood everything all at once. " Yes!! " This was an entity of such great power, and what he brought with him was packed with 101% Love!! The world was going to share some of this love, it was going to refresh parts of man that had been long forgotten, this man, was pure and awesome!

He stood in the warm sea ocean with the water just lapping over his knees and was facing into the sea where he had surfaced 10 minutes ago. The three dolphins were looking like they had smiles all over their faces, and why not, they too felt fantastic as they gazed on a being of radiant light and knowing there was something special about this man. " Man!! " He knew that was a word, a sound he had heard many days before, and understanding that man, had their own unique parts on the human male! He looked down at his knees in the water and saw the perfectly formed body with body hair that had quickly grown on to his skin. A peaceful smile rose up from his cheeks as the dolphins talked to him in their special language. One was on his right side just in front of him, and one in the center front, with the third on his front left, this was a beautiful sight. For several moments, he just stood there, taking in this new world, this beautiful planet, and some special intelligent sea creatures.

At that precise moment, a police siren blasted the beach as a 4x4 with blue and red lights skidded onto the sand and sea edge behind him.

" Hey you!! Get out of the water now!! You pervert!! " The policeman shouted at the man, as the two police officers could see he was standing naked for the whole world to see. This sort of thing was against the law at this Miami beach!!

There in front of about 25 people that had gathered to see the spectacle, looked on as this bronzed colored native American looking man, complete with a pleated pony tail, and a six pack that looked like he had been working out for several months! He turned to face the people before him, gave a warm smile to the human beings, then started to place one foot in front of the other, still smiling as he did. Both police officers were annoyed as they ran into the water ankle deep and grabbed him, using one of the officers jackets to cover the man's penis and testicles! " You sick asshole doing this in front of children on the beach. You are going to go on the sex offenders list for this you damn pervert!! "

He walked with the police officers towards the police vehicle 4x4, its lights were still flashing and drew more attention as the crowd grew in size. " Watch

your head screwball!! " One of the officers placed his
hand over the man's head to make sure he didn't
bang it as he bent down to sit in-side. Shutting the
back police door, one of the officers walked to the
front of the police car, he was still smiling as he
looked at the human beings on the beach. Then he
saw him!! The police officers had sat in the front of
the vehicle, then started to drive away past a man
holding a young child. No one saw what happened
next, as he sent an invisible blue color of light from
center of his forehead, to who he knew to be "
Justin Webber! " All that came back from Justin was
the thought of one word! " JOHN!!?? "
" What's your name pervert!? " Came the sarcastic
question from the officer not driving. John smiled at
the officer, it was a smile with love written all over it,
but the officer wasn't amused at his smile or his lack
of co-operation! Turning to the officer driving, his
partner laughed as he spoke. " OH Boy!! We are
going to have a great day with this " Jack-ass! " and
he must be a lunatic or deranged, as he hasn't
spoken a word since we picked him up! " He looked
back at John with a stern look. " You have the right
to remain silent...... " As the officer thought for a
moment, he smiled then said. " OH Yeah!! You have
remained silent Mr. pervert!! " Both officers laughed,
but looking in his rear view mirror, the police driver
saw the smile still on Johns face, and there was a
glow about him, a glow that was out of place on any
persons face, the officer just knew he was different!
As they drove closer to the police precinct, the police
driver moved his right arm and started to rotate it
clockwise as an old bullet injury was giving the officer
a lot of problems again. " Playing up again Mike!? "
Ya! I have a medical to go to in three days, and I
have the sneaky suspicion that they are going to

pension me off on medical grounds, and that will be my career finished! " Sitting right behind the driver, John stretched forward and placed his hands gently on the right shoulder of the officer. " What the fuck!!!!??? " The other officer quickly turned in his seat grabbing his night stick, then hit John several times on the head and arms forcing him back into the rear seat. His hands rested on his lap, as both officers looked at him as the vehicle had come to a stop when John had done that. " Now you are going to be charged with assault on a police officer scumbag!! " As they looked, the smile was still there, and looking at his face, there was no marks, no blood, it was like nothing had happened. " There's something weird about this dude Hank! " Replying. " You think!!? " Hank drew his gun out of the holster, then pointed it at John. " Make any sudden moves like that again pervert! And I'll put a hole in your head! "

The two police officers were standing each side of John, and just in front of them was another cop behind the booking in desk. Police sergeant Shaun O 'Clarity! With a very broad Irish accent, he looked at John, then asked. " So, what in the name of Yeezus's do we have here then!? " He saw that John was naked, except for one of the officers jackets being held by the arresting officers in front of his body. Continuing Hank started to tell him the story. " We found this guy up to his ass in the sea at the main Miami beach along the sand strip. He was playing with some fish! " The sergeant replied quite suddenly. " Playing with the fish!!? What!? " Hank tried to explain. " Both of us observed him in the sea sergeant! When we got to the water's edge, we saw 3 dolphins that looked like were talking to him in dolphin talk!! Driving here he put his hand on Mike's shoulder, so we want him charged for indecency and assault on a police officer! " On the wise sergeant´s face came a smile, one of those smiles that could tell you in an instant that he was wanting to break out laughing. " What´s your name young man? " The sergeant stared straight into John´s hazel blue eyes, but after a few seconds he realized he wasn't going to get a reply. " Ok! Take him down to the holding cell, then we will process him later, and get him a pair of overalls so he´s not giving the other prisoners idea´s about making him their prize!! "

The iron cell door clanged behind John as he walked the few paces to the bench along the cell wall. He was looking at the material that he was wearing now, and more smiles showed on his face, he was fascinated with this planet! " You would make it easier on yourself bud if you spoke and told us your name, " said Mike Hendry. Once again John just smiled, and then continued to admire his clothes. " With his locker open, Officer Mike Hendry started to change from his uniform to his evening clothes. Looking in the mirror combing his hair, suddenly he was staring at his shoulder, the one he had been shot in. He moved his shoulder in a clockwise direction, then realized he had no pain! Then his eyes zoomed in on his bullet hole wound scar! " Oh, my sweet God!! " There wasn't a bullet wound scar, nothing!! He was so confused, and how the hell did this happen!? " When I woke up this morning, I had a scar and pain, now, I don´t have either!!? " He stared long and closer to the mirror. " The native guy!!!? " He put his clothes on quickly, then fast stepped back up to the holding cell.

Gone!! " Where was he? " The officer walked to the sergeant´s desk. " Has the native guy been released sergeant? Sergeant O´Clarity looked up from his desk, then told him he had been seen by the police doctor and he decided to commit him to the local asylum, main reason being he was acting strange and didn't speak and kept smiling! " Not knowing his real name, we just put in the file. " John Doe!!! "........

CHAPTER 2
<u>Crazy in the Crazy house!!</u>

When any-one looked up at the hill to where the asylum stood, you would think it was a setting for a movie. This beautiful old castle looking building in white and cream colors stood out against the near perfect blue sky and rose bushes 2 meters high on each side of the drive way adorning the route to the main building.

Times have certainly changed since the early 1900´s, where old buildings that housed the crazy people were thrown into a locked room, then left to rot away, forgotten and neglected. On occasion, they would be brought out to an examination room, given electric shock or hot and cold bath treatment´s to help them, this was crazier than the people them-selves.

With a male nurse attendant on each side of him, John looked all around him as he walked into the examination room, and there before him sat a smiling middle aged woman in a white medical coat with the name tag on the breast pocket. " Doctor Elizabeth Channing. " This doctor had been a resident doctor for many years, and she was very clever at what she did. She could have conversation´s, even if it was just her talking to the patient´s, but she always did it with a smile on her face. " So!! Who do we have here then!? She looked straight at John, he too was still smiling, and still looked like he was at peace with him-self. Answering her own question, she read from the file and then looked back at John. " So, you don ´t talk, you smile all the time, you look like you are from a native reservation, and you look to me as if you wouldn't harm a fly!! But I guess I need to asses you, then we can get you a nice room for you to stay. " Both the nurses started to undress John, which took all of 15 seconds, as he only had the overalls the police station had given him. He stood there in front of the doctor, she smiled again as she looked up and down a golden bronze body, and a six pack that any male would have been proud to have. This body could have been entered in the " Mr. Universe contest and won!!! She started her examination from the feet upwards, apart from smiling, he did nothing. Arriving at John´s mouth, she gently moved his jaw downwards, and his top part of his mouth upwards. " Oh my God!!! " She smiled even more with a knowing look along with it. " That´s why you don´t talk, you have no tongue!! " One of the doctors skills was to sign for deaf and dumb people, so she promptly started to say " Hello and tell him her name! " John yet again smiled back at her, but, no sign language back from him. She was disappointed, because this man standing before her looked perfect in every way, and there was something more than met her eyes. He was glowing like a light bulb! He radiated a form of aura that everyone could see. Sitting back down in her chair she gazed back at him again, this time, John sat down in the chair that had been placed behind him, and without any warning, a stream of color started to shine from his forehead. Even the doctor couldn't see the colors of red, blue, silver and yellow penetrating her skin above her eyes! She so much wanted to help this man, whoever he was, if only she could find a way!

" Hello Doctor Elizabeth!! " Replying as she looked at the file. " Hello John, thank you for talking to me!! " The two nurses looked at each other with strange confused looks, as they heard her talking to him. It took 3 seconds for the shock to hit her, then she jumped back in her seat as she looked in total confusion at what she just heard. Using her very clever brain, she told the nurses to " leave her for now! " " Are you sure doctor!? " Came the reply from one of the nurses. " Yes! Just stay outside the door in case I need you! " Both nurses still with strange looks on their faces proceeded out of the office, then shut the door behind them.

" I definitely heard you talk John!! So please say something again so I don´t have to commit myself to this hospital! " She smiled again watching Johns mouth. His mouth stayed closed, but she heard more words coming from his direction. " It is so nice to meet you Doctor Elizabeth! I feel such kindness coming from you! " Her mouth was slightly opened as she heard but couldn't believe she was hearing it. She was sane, and in real terms, this wasn't possible, but it was happening, and right before her eyes. " What is your real name John!? " She asked with a calming voice. " My name is John!! The police gave me the second name " Doe! " and I like that, and it is named after one of your creatures called deer! You have such beautiful creatures here Doctor Elizabeth! " Elizabeth sat even deeper into her chair in amazement at this insane situation, but sane she knew she was! " Where do you come from John!? How did you get here!? " John with his ever-glowing smile looked at her with his deep blue eyes, they sparkled like the stars them-selves, twinkling with something that she had never seen before! " I come from far away Doctor Elizabeth! From a dimension called " Nebular 03990 ! " which would take you many of your earth years to reach with your modern technology! I traveled in a way you might call " Astro traveling through thought process! " I took this body form so people on your planet would accept me! "

The doctor now had a straight face as she realized that this man would never be accepted here or anywhere as he was so different. He was pure, he was radiating something, something so great, just for a moment she couldn't put her finger on what it was, then. " Love, pure 100% love " Never before had she seen and felt so much love coming from a person, and he certainly didn't look like any alien from outer space! Whatever they may look like! " John!! For now, I will need to keep you here for evaluation purposes, but I will need to think how I am going to be able to pass you fit enough to go into the world. Somehow, I know you don´t pose a threat to anyone, and the world here could certainly do with something as beautiful as you in it. You have a kindness pulsing from your very being, and you will start to attract people who will find it difficult for them to understand! Only a few minutes in your company, and I find it strange and new with you here! " She was looking at his perfect body, and she tried to keep looking away from him, she just wasn't used to seeing a beautiful man sat naked in her company. " Does my body form upset you Doctor Elizabeth!? " He asked. " No, no! Certainly not, if anything, you look gorgeous!! Did I just say that aloud!? She laughed as John just smiled back at her. " Nurse Collins, please get our new patient some clothes to wear, and a pair of soft slippers! " She had raised her voice slightly to get the nurses attention, which he nodded to her in reply. Newly dressed in jogging type pants, and a t-shirt, he slipped the slippers over his feet as he stared back at her still with that perfect glowing smile. The two nurses guided John from the office, then took him along the corridor to his new room. Doctor Channing started to write in her file on John, and a report that followed.

" I have examined John Doe and found the patient to be in perfect health. However, he is missing his tongue, and there-fore concluded, that was the reason for non-communication with the police officers. In addition to this report, I have concluded he has total memory loss, and I believe this to be permanent! My recommendation is for him to be assessed here for a few days, and then released into society with a new set of identity papers and new passport provided by the United States New citizen office! I personally will place my reputation on the line to guarantee this man as a potential good citizen! Signed... Dr Elizabeth Channing!

" Doctor Channing!! You had better come quick, there is something going on you should see! "

One of the patients had sat down at the old grand piano and was playing old songs that she had played before she became ill. She had been diagnosed with a severe form of schizophrenia, and she had been in that state for over 15 years, she up to that point didn't remember her name, and if you had asked her what planet she was on, she couldn't tell you! But here she was, playing beautifully with a sound of the grand piano chiming out wonderful sounds. She smiled as Doctor Channing approached her. Elizabeth was dumbfounded as she listened to her play perfect notes on the ivory keys. As she finished playing a wonderful piece of music, she stopped, then looked at the doctor. " I see by the name tag that you are Doctor Channing, I am so pleased to meet you! " She stood up, then reached out her hand to shake Elizabeth's. The patient continued. " My name is Catherine Wiseman, and John informs me that you have watched over and cared for me for 15 years. Well I can tell you I am fine and well now, and I think I want to go home to my husband! " " Nurse!

Stay with Mrs. Wiseman for a moment while I go call her husband, I'll be back in a moment! " Elizabeth fast walked towards her office, she knew that John had something to do with this, but this was incredible, and couldn't wait to tell her husband who visited once a week.

" Trinnng!! trinnng!! Click!!! " " Hello, this is David Wiseman! " - Mr. Wiseman! This is Doctor Channing. I am calling you to give you some fantastic news! Your wife has had something amazing happen to her, and you need to come and see her immediately! " " Amazing!!?? Is she ok? What´s amazing mean!?? " " Just make your way here sir! All will be revealed when you arrive! " The phone receiver was put down fast as Mr. Wiseman hurried to get to the mental hospital! Doctor Channing hurried back into the recreational area, and new music was coming again from the piano as Catherine Wiseman ran her fingers along the old ivory keys, and by golly she could play!!! The doctor looked over at John, he was sitting listening to the music, and watched Elizabeth's eyes shine as he smiled that everlasting smile.

With all the piano music, most of the patients stood or sat around the piano, as Catherine played song after song, so much, that no-one noticed a man walk up to John and place his hand on Johns, then looking at the man's face, John could see moisture swelling up in the man's eye´s. The man had not spoken for many years, and murmured sounds to John holding his hand tighter and tighter. John looked up at him, he smiled that now familiar smile, then held the top of the man's hand again. If any-one had been watching, they would have seen the golden orange glow pulsating from John, but no-one did! The murmurs became longer and longer as the man tried so hard to talk to John. " Hmmmmm eeeee! Hemmm meee! Heelll mee! Then the words formed in the man's voice! " HELP MEEE!!! " The piano stopped playing, then every person in the room turned to look at the man now talking to John. The patient fell to his knees, he held on to both Johns hands, and started to cry like a new born baby! Elizabeth had tears swelling up in her eyes too, as she looked at the man who hadn't spoken for years!

The receptionist paged Doctor Channing, informing her that Mr. David Wiseman was desperate to see what had happened to his wife. She ran to the reception area to be confronted by a worried looking man! " I am confused doctor! What has been happening?? " He looked so worried as he waited for the doctor to answer him. " Please come with me Mr. Wiseman! She wants to see you! " He looked more confused as she said that, then fast walking towards the recreational area, they both heard piano music bouncing around the walls of the corridor. David Wiseman could feel the emotion raising high in his heart and soul. He stood there speechless as he gazed on the woman playing the piano. His wife Catherine waved to him to come closer to her, then as he approached, she sat him down on the piano stool, then smiled at him as he placed his fingers beside hers on the key board, and started to play a duet, the one they had played together many times in their lives! A slight silence came over the room when she stopped playing, and they cried a thousand tears as they hugged each other so tightly.

Elizabeth Channing sat in her office chair going over the day's events, how the hell could she explain all this!? John Doe was certainly the answer, but she was intelligent enough to realize she had to make something up to cover these so-called miracles up! There was a knock at the door, and as she looked up,

she saw Mr. Wiseman standing there with a smile that could have lit up the entire Miami coastline! " I just want to say thank you so much for whatever you did Doctor, and if you have come up with a new medication, then it works!! " Elizabeth smiled gently towards David and replied to him. " Mr. Wiseman, you wouldn't believe me even if I told you, but I am releasing Catherine to your care for now, but I need you to keep in touch with me every second day, and if you need me any-time, call me, day or night! " He smiled back at her. " Thank you doctor miracle!! " She thought to her-self as he shut the office door behind him. " Me!!?? Doctor Miracle!? I want to tell them all it was John, but I would definitely end up being committed here myself!! " There had been a lot of smiles, laughter and tears to-day, and another smile just got added to the long list. Another knock on the door, and now standing there was Jimmy Rodgers! The man who now could speak. " Come in Jimmy! Sit down and let´s talk! " Strange to say, but after all these years not talking, and drifting from one day to the next just existing, she was glad to be able to have a two sided conversation with him.
During the course of the next 3 hours, there were many knocks on her door, and each time one of the patients came in and sat and talked with a doctor that was witnessing what could only be described as miracle´s! Every one of them came and opened up their hearts and not one of them had any memories to the time they had spent in the institution. Elizabeth held her hands close to her face with the emotions to go along with her tears. Putting a smile back on her face, she thought of how the board of governors were going to react with all the patients cured! " I´m going to be out of a job very soon! " She thought as she picked up her purse, then switched the office

light off.

Walking through the recreation room, she saw John sitting gazing at the " TV. " The news reporter was commenting on a Tragedy in Miami, it was a report on a lone gunman who opened fire with an automatic machine gun! He killed 14 people, including 7 children with 11 others seriously wounded! Just like before, the color beams of light extended from John to Elizabeth. " Why do the species on this planet want to destroy each other!!? What happened to the gift of love that was with man from the very beginning!? There was no smile on his face at that moment, he was confused with his thoughts. " Doctor Elizabeth! A gift of life is so precious, and yet, some-one can take that gift from you in a blink of an eye!? To-day! I have seen tears of joy on faces of man and woman, they send out hope to people who really care. This world needs the love put back into it!! As man destroys, I will heal! This is the reason I am here Doctor Elizabeth!!! " Elizabeth nodded slightly as she too thought the world to be an unsafe place now, and if she could empty an institution in one day with Johns help, then think what the possibilities could be if he was introduced to the world!!! To-day was certainly a crazy day in the crazy house!! ......

CHAPTER 3
Excited
Whispers!

Never before had there been such excitement with the TV Network. MBC. (Miami Broadcasting Company) New stories were popping up on TV screens nearly every hour about so called Miracle´s being performed in the local asylum.

Reports are flooding in to-day of mentally ill patient´s being cured of their ailments! The " Rose Castle " Miami asylum has stood on South hill for over 70 years, and never before has any patient there recovered from long term mental illness! " The TV cameras are in West Miami where our reporter Stacy Rodgers is talking to one of the long-term patients who was released earlier this week! "
" Thank you in the studio! This is Stacy Rodgers for MBC reporting live in West Miami, where with me in their home is ex patient Mrs. Catherine Wiseman, and her husband David! Please tell us in your own words Catherine what happened! "
" 15 years ago, I remembered being here in my home, when my mind started to fade into darkness. I was forgetting how to play the piano and could not even put a coffee pot on! The darkness grew longer and longer, until eventually, Nothing!! When the light came on in my mind the other day, I opened my eyes to a sight that I can only describe as an angel in front of me. I saw this native looking man

with bronze body and long pony tail smiling a smile so beautiful, I thought I was in heaven! He told me to start playing the piano again, and to enjoy whatever physical life I had left!! And the funny thing is! He can´t talk, as he has no tongue!! But I did hear him, and you can ask the other patients, as he did the same to them! He just placed his hands on theirs the same as he did to me, then a golden light shone from each hand! His name is John Doe! I believe that God sent him here for us, and my faith has been restored in love and kindness. "

" This has been Stacy Rodgers reporting for MBC in West Miami!! "

Watching and listening very carefully was police officer Mike Hendry. With a shoulder that no longer hurt from a bullet wound he sustained in the line of duty, and no trace of a scar, this started to make perfect sense to him, he just had to go and talk with him, even just to say thank you!

Yet again the phone was ringing in Doctor Elizabeth Channing's office. " Rose Castle! Can I help you!? " Doctor Channing!? My name is Officer Mike Hendry, I was the arresting officer of John Doe! Could I come over to talk to you and John please? It´s quite important! " " Officer Hendry! I have had reporters, husbands and wives calling here all day, and to put the icing on the top! I have had the board of directors yelling about the different ways they are going to fire me! So, maybe another time! " Elizabeth replaced the receiver not even saying " Good-bye! "

Mike picked up his car keys, then placed his jacket draping it over his shoulder, shutting the house door behind him.

The loud chiming sound from the door bell sounded at Rose Castle! " Now what!? " Elizabeth was becoming quite irritated now, and that wasn't like her at all! She sighed as she walked to the front door, stopping to adjust her blouse and skirt. After conversation´s with board of director´s, she wasn't sure if this was some of them coming to fire her, but she did think she would still defend John if she had to!

Standing with a beautiful smile was this good-looking man with blond shoulder length pony tail, and eyes that would melt icebergs! " Hi Doctor Channing! I am Justin Webber, and I'm quite sure if you let me come in, John will be pleased to see me! " She gazed at him with a surprised expression! " You know him!!?? Are you an alien too then!? Tilting her head to the left slightly, she looked puzzled! Justin gave a smile with some comforting words to go along with it. " Alien!!? Umm No!! But I do know John from where I met him for the first time a few years ago! " Elizabeth relaxed a little. " Then you had better come in! "

Johns eyes fell on Justins face as he walked into the recreational room! Seeing them hug tight, you would have thought they were long lost brother´s! Elizabeth looked surprised as John started to send thoughts to Justins mind, and she heard them too!!

" My dear Justin! It´s so good to see you, and in body form! "

" It´s really good to see you in the flesh too! "

" I saw you in the sea just before you got arrested, when I realized it was you, it was too late to do anything, so I waited to see how matters worked out before coming to help you! But it´s so good to see you again John!! "

" Everything that has happened Justin, has meant to happen, right down to the fine detail of being here in

202

this amazing home for mental illnesses! Did you think it was just a coincidence that I was not far from you on the beach!?? And now, I have met this beautiful Doctor Elizabeth who is very bright and clever! "

" Does she know anything about the instruments of justice John? " Justin sent out that last question in thought form, as to not spook Elizabeth.

" She heard your thoughts just then Justin! All three of us are connected by thought vibrations through the color beams! "

" Instruments of justice!!? What are they? "
John smiled at both of them as he sat comfortably in the soft arm chair.

" Many centuries ago Elizabeth, ultimate instruments of justice were placed on earth to be found by people who would carry out punishments on the criminals who committed horrendous crimes, such as murder, and rape! Several years ago, in Sweden, Justin found such an instrument, and has had quite interesting results! " At this point, Justin moved his left sleeve slightly upwards to reveal a piece of equipment that resembled a health monitoring unit.

Elizabeth looked intrigued and interested as she leaned forward to take a closer look.

" The instrument detects crime scenes and then can pursue fugitives who carried out these crimes, ending in the capture of these evil people! Their punishments are severe and swift, with similar endings to their victims! "

Elizabeth sat with a worried look on her face, as she knew what great things John was capable of, but now, he was describing a machine that took life and totally contradicted his actions.

" My dear Doctor Elizabeth! I see and feel your concern! Justice on earth has broken down, the courts and trials of suspects are getting away with these terrible crimes through smart lawyers and clever thinking! The person you should be thinking about is the victim! Where his her or his justice!? If this criminal is given justice, then many people will be spared the heartache and pain that they cause. The conscience lays with the wearer of the justice machine, and that can be tough decisions that they have to make! " The inner sense of what is right or wrong in one's conduct or motives, impelling one toward right action!! "

" Elizabeth, the world is getting a new wake up call. The evil in this world has spun out of control, now is the time to place the positive and good things back on the earth! " She was still a little concerned with the fact that someone had the ability to kill someone who had killed!

" Show Doctor Elizabeth your first crime scene you experienced Justin. "

Justin removed the machine from his arm and placed it on a table in front of them...

Night time had now come to Göteborg! The hustle of people walking around the city was like electricity, sparks of life flowing through the streets of this magnificent Swedish location. Neon lights lit up the tall shopping areas, and clubs with people eagerly waiting to have their drinking and dance time.

Walking slowly along the sidewalks, Justin stared at men and women going about their exciting night-life. Street entertainers playing many different musical instruments, each carrying their own sound, penetrating the ears, then flowing to the brain for stimulation.

As he walked, he slowly lifted his sleeve up, to reveal a little of the machine now attached to his arm.

There was a pulsating running green light, like " LED " dots running back and forward over the small screen. Justin knew that it was doing something, but what? Again, Justin felt like he was attached to it mentally, connected to the heart of the justice machine. His only goal now was to test, and see the results.

Anticipating Justins thoughts, the machine started to send messages to him, not by sound, but by a form of telepathy. " Searching for fugitives! " Justin heard so clearly the words being projected to his brain and looked at the screen to see a newly appeared diagram in thin lines, and resembled a sonar screen, just like they have in submarines. Justin walked into a red-light district of the city, where hookers were there in doorways, and bars, and were plying their trade to fill their purses with money from the perves and crazies of the city. Some-one once said. " Sex sells! " They were right! This was still one of the oldest professions in the world, and even with the fear of all the sexual diseases around, people still plied their trade for money, regardless of the consequences. Blocking his way, he saw a woman who looked like an all-in wrestler, with muscles on her muscles, and a pair of breasts that would knock you out if she turned quickly. " Want to have fun with these? " she asked smiling and looked at the large breasts in front of her. Justin smiled back at her. - Not tonight thank you, he replied, as he side stepped her and passed her now growling face. " Your loss! " she replied as she turned her back on Justin and walked back to the doorway from where she had come from.

Only a few minutes had passed, then without warning, the machine spoke to Justin again. **" Crime scene detected, analyzing data! "** Justin stopped in his tracks, as he waited for the machine to give him more information.

" Continue 150 meters, go down side ally. " He

started to walk forward with a little more speed, he was perspiring a little, still excitement in his mind, as he turned the corner into the back ally. On the screen of the justice machine, an image of the ally appeared, it was identical to the exact place he was now standing. Suddenly, an amber light started to flash Intermittently, then followed by a projected light coming from the front base of the machine. A holographic display started to project itself on to the ally wall. Justin thought this part could have come straight out of " Star Wars " movie, and pictured " Princess Leia " putting a message into " R2D2´s " memory slot. Smiling to himself, which was then wiped off his face, as a man and woman came into the ally. The projected images were that of a hooker, and a client who were obviously looking for a quiet place to have sex.

The man had a half-burned cigarette in his left hand, and the other he held the woman close to his side. The machines sound came to Justins ears, as the man's voice asked her how much she was going to charge him? -500Kr for full sex! 350 for me just to masturbate you, she replied smiling at the man.

- What if I tell you I will screw you for nothing, then cut you up into pieces? Justin was glued to the spot he stood in, he shivered to himself as he saw the man grab her with both hands tightly and threw her to the ground like a rag doll. As she hit the ground with a hard thud! she fell into unconsciousness. Underneath the back of her head, blood was running along the grooves between the cobbled stones. The man took a knife from his jacket pocket, looked straight at the razor-sharp blade, it was reflecting light from the ally lamp above him. The man smiled to himself in such a way, that it looked like he was a sadist, he gave an evil type laugh as he started to kneel down over the hookers body. Taking the knife closer to her clothes, he lifted her white blouse as far as he could, then cut the flowery bra from the straps. He tore at the blouse, he was like a rabid dog, even to the point he was drooling white saliva from his mouth.

He gazed at her breasts, pink and silky, his eyes slightly bulging with excitement. He tightly held her left breast in his hand, and with the other, he placed the blade of the knife on the top of her shinning pink flesh. She never flinched an eye lid, as he moved the blade along her breast, the trail of blood running down her side and joining the blood trail from the wound in her head. Justin at this point felt sad, as he saw the life draining out of the young woman's body. She was turning pale white as more and more blood seeped from her wounds. Blood was starting to soak in to the man's clothes, his jeans were like they had been dragged through a slaughter house, as he still smiled. raising her dress, he took hold of her underwear, then cut them away revealing her private soft flesh. More blood was gathering at her navel, then trickling down and running between her legs. Justin didn't want to watch any more, but, the machine had not finished displaying the crime yet. Just before Justin threw up, he saw the man force himself on the woman, she was lifeless, he screamed with a chilling tone in his voice, as he ejaculated inside her. Struggling to breath, Justin was choking on his vomit, as he could not believe what he just saw. Silence fell around him as his ears struggled to hear anything, not even a car on the main road at the end of the ally did he hear. He was pale white, just like the poor woman he had just seen. A horrible numbness returned to him, just like when he had been told about his parents all them years ago. As he tried to compose himself, he slowly walked out of the ally towards the main road. As he surveyed the whole street, he looked at people going about their business, and thought how unreal, but real this was. This was happening, and it had happened, as he saw a police help poster pasted to the wall at the beginning of the ally. He missed this as he walked into the ally, but he sure didn't miss it on the way out.

" MURDER HERE AUGUST 17TH. DID YOU SEE ANYTHING?
ANY INFORMATION TELEPHONE
POLISINSPEKTÖR MAXIMUS LINDSTRÖM
KRIMINALINSPEKTÖR : : : GÖTEBORG ! "

Looking at the poster, Justin thought carefully about sharing the information with the polis, but then decided that they would lock him up, as a prime suspect for the accurate information, and only the forensics and the killer would know the true nature of her death. " Not a good idea! " He thought.

Justin lit a cigarette, and inhaled the aromatic smoke, breathing deeply, and thinking about what he had just seen. This poor girl deserves for her killer to be brought to justice, but how was he going to achieve this without incriminating himself?

" I am programed to help you in any way, and I can make files available, and clues to crimes can be sent via computer without incriminating you! " Do you wish to find the fugitive of this crime? Seeing what he had seen, of course Justin wanted the guilty man to be caught, so with those thoughts, the justice instrument spoke to him again.

" Searching!!------ Fugitive located, setting directional route--------Continue walking forward towards road bridge. " Justin was now thinking what would he do? What would he say? If anything! Coming face to face with a killer was not the one thing he wanted to do this day, but, knew if he was going to be the girls champion, he had to face this fear and help her in any way he could. Walking towards the bridge, he took another cigarette from the pack, placed it in his mouth with his hand shaking a little, then struck the lighter flint with the button, and inhaled deeply again. Thinking all the time and trying to figure out what he could do when and if he came face to face with pure evil itself. **" When that moment arrives, I will activate my justice systems, and the procedure will take place to dispense the correct form of punishment. "** Everything was happening so quickly, Justin thought, and how was the night going to end? **" Justice will be served. "** The machine answered his thoughts yet again.

Reaching the bridge, the dial on the screen went into radar mode! One of the flashing running lights went from side to side, it was green in color. The light suddenly changed to orange and flashing a little faster than the green had done. A few hundred meters later, the road slightly deviated to the right, and as Justin came around the corner, he saw a bar café with all its bright lights blazing along the road. Like a very fast heart rate, the blinking light went extremely fast, and turned to red in color. Justin knew he had to go into the busy looking pub! " This was it! he thought, as he approached the door entrance, took a deep breath in, and opened the bar door....

Justin could hear the thumping of his heart through his chest, it sounded like a deep jungle drum, it pounded on his chest, and the speed increased, making him a bit breathless. Approaching the bar slowly, he asked the barman to get him a large beer, and a whisky chaser. - You sound a little out of breath sir! the barmen said, then pointed to the machine on Justins arm which was showing slightly. - Do these monitors bring you back to life if your heart stops? laughed the barman. Justin smiled through his nervousness, then picked up the beer, and took a big swallow, it cooled his throat, and ran into his stomach, which was now feeling like it had knots inside it. The cold beer hit the spot, and wiping the foam away from his mouth, he glanced around the packed bar.

A bar stool became available, as a man got up and left, Justin sat quickly before anyone else could take it. Nursing his beer with both hands, he surveyed the people in the bar area looking just over the rim of the glass. The foamy beer was leaving a scum mark around the glass, as the beer was getting less and less as Justin drank and looked slowly all around him. The voices from all the customers were deafening, as each tried to talk louder so they could be heard. At the far end of the bar from Justin, he could see a man sitting with his glass of whiskey, this man was unshaven, long shoulder length hair which did not look like it had been washed in months. As Justin looked more closely at him, the machine spoke to him in thoughts. **" Fugitive identified..... Do you wish to administer punishment now? "** Not knowing what the hell this machine was going to do, Justin panicked at the thought of this thing using some kind of ray gun on the man. **" Ray guns are for movies! I am the Ultimate dispenser of justice, and I will serve your command. When you are ready, just say Activate Justice punishment 2078!** Justins eyes bulged in his head as he heard those words, he was going to have to tell the machine himself to do whatever it was going to do. Maybe it would subdue the fugitive with a tranquilizer or sedative, maybe a stun of some kind, whatever it was, Justin was nervous about the whole situation. Bringing himself back to his reality, Justin looked as the man got up from his bar stool, then turned to head for the Toilets be-hind him. This was the time! It was now! Justin thought as he also raised his body and headed for the toilets behind the man. As Justin opened the toilet door, he gazed inside as he moved towards one of the stainless-steel urinals. With the mirror in front of him on the wall, he used it to survey the wash room. Standing at the far end, the man he was following, stood, relieving himself of his alcohol. The man looked over at Justin, and quickly looked away again. Zipping up his trousers, the man started to head back towards the exit. The man side glanced Justin as he walked passed him. Justins heart was racing fast as he knew he needed to act now, or it was going to be too late. " Activate justice punishment 2078! " Came the words from Justins mouth. The man stopped, turned towards Justin. - What the fuck did you just say? the man said angrily with his face glaring at Justin with a twisted look. In a split second, a powder blue light pulsated in a fan shape over the man. Struggling to move, he looked like he was paralyzed, he was fixed to the spot he stood in. A fear came over the man's face as he attempted to break free from whatever crazy thing had him. Moving his mouth was the only thing he could do, but when he spoke, his words were coming out quiet, as if he had a silencer on his vocal chords. Justin was shaking with not knowing what was to happen, and how this was going to play out. - What do you want? what´s happening to me? the man's voice shook with fear as the two men looked directly at each other's eyes. Justin spoke directly at the man

211

and asked the question. - Have you murdered any women lately? Looking back at Justin, the man's eyes opened wider, at that point he knew exactly what Justin meant. You could see the puzzled look on the man's face as he tried to figure out how Justin knew. The light was still pulsating, it kept him in his space, and as Justin thought back to what he had seen earlier, he got angry. _ You rape a woman, you then mutilate her body with a smile on your face and watch her die as her blood drained from her body. - You sick bastard! You had no right to take that young woman's life. The man still staring at Justins eyes looked more afraid now and muttered a few more words. - So, arrest me, and they will say I am insane! I will get 5 to 10 years, then let me out for good behavior, the man's face looked twisted with his fear. At these words, Justin was enraged! He had got the confession from the man, openly admitting his guilt. " **Ready to administer justice! Do you wish to proceed?** " Justin flinched as the machine asked the question. What was going to happen? How was the justice machine going to deal with this? With those thoughts, the machine answered again. " **Request to demonstrate! I will reveal the answer!** " Justin got a little spooked as again the machine knew what his thoughts were. - What the fuck is that thing on your arm? Who are you? Asked the man, who now looked like he was going to burst into tears with fear. - I am here to help people like the one you murdered, and this machine will help with that. Puzzled, the man smirked a little, then asked. - What's it going to do? Disintegrate me? **"Alan Iseburg, you are a rapist, and a murderer. You will pay the price for the crime. Teresa Ljung will be avenged! "** In the next split second, a red flickering beam of light landed on the man's trousers, right where his private parts were, followed by a feint buzzing sound, and then followed by a scream that would have woken the dead! "AHHHHhhhhhh! Justin looked on in disbelief as the man's groin area started to bleed profusely! Almost like someone had thrown a bucket of blood over his lower part of his body. The man was in agony, he was shedding tears as he tried to break free his restraint. With a few seconds passing, Justin looked to the floor where a pool of blood was gathering in front of him. Justin once again wanted to throw up as he saw in the middle of the blood pool the man's testicles and penis! **" Final stage! Alan Iseburg. Justice administered! "** For a split second, Justin panicked as he thought someone could walk into the toilet area at any time. Before he finished that thought, the red pulsing light moved to the man's forehead, blood filled the man's white bulging eyes, it filled every area of his eye sockets, as the man became lifeless, but still standing up straight in the restraining beam. **" Justice instrument 2078, punishment complete! "** Backing slowly away from the extending blood pool, Justin had to move quickly out of the toilet area. " What if he was caught here right now? " He thought quickly for an escape route. One thing he didn't notice when entering the rest room area, was at the far end of the urinals, was an emergency exit, and without thinking he ran to the door forcing the emergency bar on it down and forward. Finding himself in another back ally, he ran quickly to the light at the end, stumbling a little with the speed, he composed himself as much as he could, as he entered the main road along from the bridge. At a further distance from the bar, he stood at a parked dump truck, and shaking, he lit another cigarette, drawing hard on the smoke he was inhaling. He crouched down towards the ground, like a tight ball, and could not believe that he was partly responsible for the man's death.

" He asked himself, 2078? That means that it was counting up every time it dispensed justice! " White and shaking with fear, Justin moved quietly out of the area before all hell was going to break loose!....

Justin picked up the justice instrument and placed it back on his arm, then looked at Doctor Channing's face for her reaction.

" That poor girl!! And Justin!? You have had to live with that first decision all these years!? "

" When I start to feel guilty Doctor, I remember that innocent girl, and other faces that were murdered! Many murderers have been brought to justice through this instrument. Another side to the machine, was updated to predict crimes up to an hour in advance! Some fugitives had their minds wiped clean, but they were still left alive, but they will not be dangerous to any one again! Through this machine, I found my parents killer from when it happened when I was 15 years old! People need to wake up to the fact that for every murderer who is caught, 7 others get away with their crimes!! If I am helping innocent people, then that in its self is worth making those hard decisions! "

John looked at Elizabeth with a loving smile. " Doctor Elizabeth!! You have been more than kind to me since I have been here, and soon, it will be time for me to move forward in this world. I would like to give you a gift, it is a gift of fearlessness! Along with this gift will come the ability to communicate with me or any-one who has a justice instrument! "

Elizabeth now had a smile back on her face, it was a smile bringing her back to the now moment!!

John stood up and walked over to her, then gently placed one hand each side of her skull, then smiled back at her with those loving eyes! Justin looked on as Johns hands started to have a golden glow pulsing from his hand palms, and at that moment, Elizabeth gave a very feint sigh, then her body became totally relaxed. She opened her eyes, but when she did, they were shining bright, they lit up the room around her like ten table lamps! John had passed some of the universe through her mind, she had thoughts like she never had before, with a knowledge of things she never thought existed! The big thing that came to her was, a feeling so powerful, she knew it could only be the feeling of 100% love! Some people would never feel this awesome power that John had just passed on to her, but oh how beautiful it felt through every cell in her body.

" Right now, I feel like I am connected to a living psychic conscience on a higher level of thinking, I even know that in less than a minute, a police officer who called me earlier will arrive wanting to talk to you John! " John still with a smile said. " I know Doctor Elizabeth! I would like to talk to him! "

" Sorry to bother you Doctor! I know on the phone you said you were busy, but!.... Elizabeth smiled at him. " Come in officer Hendry, John would like to talk to you!! " With a surprised look on his face, he walked alongside her heading for the recreation room.

Surveying the room, he smiled at John, then looked over to Justin. John stood up, then went to where Mike Hendry was standing, placed his hands each side of his skull, with a slight jerk, he went to pull away from John, but, something told him just to relax and go with the flow! Another gentle golden glow surrounded Mikes head, information and light passed through his mind in a blink of an eye! He felt like he was plugged into the internet itself, billions of gigabyte´s running through every cell in his brain! John removed his hands: Mike stood there with a body and a mind that felt like he had consumed an entire library of knowledge! Mike had just joined the most secret exclusive private club in the world!! He leaned forward to hug John, saying. " Thank you! " to him as he looked over to Justin and Doctor Channing. " It´s good to see you with clothes on John! Sorry for arresting you! " They all started to laugh, but every one now knew that John was communicating with his mind through colored beams of light! and didn't talk. This entity, this man standing there in front of them all with a permanent smile and glowing like coals in a fire-place! had come to earth to help the world and its people, and he was doing just that in only a few days. John asked them all to sit down so he could talk of the things to come, and what plans he had for them all to help him.

" I only have a short time here on earth, and I need people like you to get me to where I am going. " " Mike! You are going to receive a master instrument of justice, Justin will help with filling you in on information about the machines, however! The new sharper mind you have can access another's thoughts and memories, so most times, you will already have that information! A chain of events will unfold very soon, I know of negative things that will try to distract us from our path, in most situations, we will succeed! There is a danger of each one of you losing your life here, but with helping each other you just might get to live through it!! " Everything boils down to what your true feelings are telling you, and if you want to be a part of this new beginning!? Life on this planet is about to change so quickly, and now it is the good guys against the bad guys!

They all looked at each other, but every one of them had a knowing smile on their faces, and each one didn't need to be asked twice! Justin looked at Mike. " Stick with me for the next 24 hours Mike!! We have to get you acquainted with the justice machines! "

Elizabeth with her new psychic senses was sensing a crowd gathering outside the asylum! They were people of enquiring minds who had heard the news on television, and reporters from all around the Miami area, even national news from New York were gathering for the exciting events.

John went over to the long oak table, he started to arrange chairs so many people could sit when he addressed the media and public. He knew exactly what was going to happen, and he was looking forward to showing the world what gifts he had to offer to the world!

Doctor Elizabeth Channing walked in front of about 25 men and women eager to know what had been going on, and each one of the media wanting to push to the front to get the best view!

" Ladies and gentlemen! I am Doctor Elizabeth Channing! Welcome to " Rose Castle Asylum! " Please take a seat and you will be able to ask as many questions as you need to discover about " John Doe!! "

Someone raised a voice anxious to get the first question in. " Doctor Channing!! I believe John Doe can´t talk!! So how can he answer our questions!!?

She smiled at the reporter, then answered. " John uses a kind of telepathy, so I will answer for him! "

Another person asked a question with a sarcastic tone in their voice.

" Is this just some kind of gigantic hoax!?

" Definitely not!! " Elizabeth answered in a stern voice

back at him.

John sat in front of them all, with a beautiful smile on his face. His pony tail hung down his back over a new denim shirt that the Doctor had given him, and also tight jeans clinging to his fantastic toned body. The one thing every one noticed was his shinning eyes, that shone right through people.

" Doctor Channing, there has been whispers of great miracles happening at this facility, what can you tell us about this!? "

She looked over at John, and then waited for him to answer the question.

Starting to answer peoples questions, she repeated what John was sending her by thought.

" I will repeat what John tells me word for word, so please bear with me while I listen to him. He tells me to say " hello " to you all, and to thank you for giving him the time to pass on positive and spiritual energy from his heart to yours! "

Most of the reporters were starting to get impatient as they wanted so much for him to get to the part of where he came from!? Anticipating that question, John kept smiling as he passed word after word to Elizabeth's mind.

" John says he has come many light years from this planet. It would take about one year with earth rockets to reach the Nebular system he comes from. He says by astro traveling, he can reach earth within a few hours! " The whole room was silent as every ear listened intently!

Every red light was on all the tv cameras as the meeting continued with message after message from John.

" John has a sixth sense and tells me there is a mother and young girl watching out-side the asylum doors. She has a terminal illness and would like to be able to see her eleventh birthday. Can someone bring her in with her mother!? " Without hesitation, Justin walked out of the room, then headed for the front entrance door.

Justin glanced around the small crowd that had gathered out-side. He fixed his eyes on a sad looking woman holding close her daughter, then stepped towards her and asked her to " come inside! " With surprise, she looked at Justin as he ushered the two of them through the corridor and into the recreational area.

Within seconds, John had caught eye contact with the young girl, then looked at her mother and smiled that trademark smile of his!

Doctor Channing started to pass on a message for the mother.

" John says that this young girl has only a few weeks left of her physical life! Is this correct? "

Her mother started to explain her illness!

" My daughter Sky has had stomach cancer for the last few months, and doctors said it was now terminal, and told us she has only about 3 weeks. I am here after seeing the reports of Johns miracles and was hoping with all my heart that he can do something to help her, she so much wants to see her eleventh birthday! "

Sky started to force a smile at John as she looked at him, bearing the pain as she stood there close to her mother.

Every single person sat or stood with anticipation as John got up and moved towards the mother and daughter.

John moved slowly still smiling at Sky, then kneeled down in front of her allowing her to be taller than he was. A glow around John shone brightly as he placed both hands on her stomach, just touching her cloth blouse and not hard, so not to frighten the ten year old.

Elizabeth came close to them, she knelt down next to John and continued to tell the mother and daughter what John was saying.

" John is going to pass healing energy into Sky´s body, then draw the poisonous cancer cells out, this will only take a few moments! " Sky and her mother watched and waited as John´s hands started to glow a bright orange, then traces of violet and blue could be seen shooting and sparking at Sky´s stomach area. If you listened closely, you could hear a rushing of air sound with a hint of humming on the under-tone! All eyes in the room tried to fix on Johns hands, they were opening their eyes wider as they witnessed the glow and colors emanating from Johns body! White bright light pulsed around him, it grew with every few seconds, almost like he was drawing power from the universe itself! Second after second came the colors, each one penetrating Sky´s body, she stood fixed to the floor, she raised one of her hands and placed it on Johns head, then spoke for the first time!

" Ohhh Thank you Mr. John!! I can feel warm feelings in my stomach, and the pain is getting less! " John looked at her eyes.

Doctor Channing spoke again through Johns thoughts.

" John is now going to draw the dark cells out of her body, and for all in the room, please don´t be afraid at what you see! " Cameras zoomed in on Johns hands as brighter colored lights dazzled the air in the room. Fading suddenly to fine pinpoints of light, the colors started to change to a dark grey black powdery look.

As the seconds went by again, the blackened smoky

looking color started to expand in front of Johns hands, a circle of spinning blackness spiraled in midair, growing a couple of centimeters every few seconds. As you looked, you could see a base line of blackness coming from Sky´s stomach area, like a flower root exposing it-self to the world!

In only a few minutes, the sphere had grown to a foot in diameter, it spun like a top filled with black gassy smoke. Apart from " Wow!! Amazing!! " and other expressions describing the event, there was just disbelief as John performed a miracle.

John stood up as he placed the sphere levitating between his hands, then moved it slightly to the right. Suddenly! He moved his arms and hands upwards very quickly, and as he did, the sphere spun faster and faster, gaining fantastic speed, then, " Whoooooshhh!!! " The sphere shot up towards the ceiling, then a black puff of smoke hung around the lighting as the sphere disappeared from view! Fading now, the black Smokey mist vanished too!

Sky stood looking at John, she had trickles of moisture running down her cheeks, the color had returned to her face, she no longer looked pale and grey! A smile came upon her face as her mouth formed that long lost smile, the smile she never thought she would get back again.

" Mr. John!! My Mom is going to always remember you, just like I will! I know you have taken my cancer away, you have given me my eleventh birthday to-day. God sent you to earth, and I am a lucky girl to be in your presence, you have shown me that miracles do exist!

Most people in the room had tears building in their eye sockets as no one could believe what had just taken place. For a ten-year-old girl, the words that came out of her mouth were that of a mature woman! A beautiful soul that was now going to have the best memory of her life. The day she met " John Doe!! "

There was a hush of silence all around, camera crews standing speechless as to what they had seen.

Sky´s mother took hold of Johns hands, she knelt down before him and placed her lips on the back of them, then looked up at him. He was radiating a glow again around him and looked at her with a sparkle coming from his eyes! He pulled her up from the ground, then embraced her still smiling that smile!

" John says that he is thanking you for bringing Sky and yourself here and giving him the chance to help where needed. Please take her to her doctor, and he will confirm her illness has gone!! " He also says to have a wonderful life and tell the world what has happened here to-day! Tell everyone that the best is yet to come and keep watching the sky's during the night!! The world is going to be healed! A new dawn is approaching where everyone will hear the new whispers!!! ".............

CHAPTER 4
To Catch
A Killer!!

Officer Mike Hendry and Justin Webber walked out
the side entrance of the asylum, they were both
looking towards the front ground garden where
crowds of people, reporters, and new TV crews who
had turned up too late to enter with the main body of
reporters.

" So! Mike! How would you like to catch that shooter
who gunned down all those people the other day!? "

" Now is just a good a time as any!! Do you really
think we can catch him!? "

" I don't think!! I know we can!! The master justice
instrument will do its job, and it does it well! "

" Your life will change a lot Mike when this begins, so
there will be no turning back, I hope you have the
stomach for it!!? "

Mike looked at Justin, he seemed so calm and
unaffected by the task they were just about to under-
take!

" I believe you dug graves over in Sweden!? How did
you manage to evade detection over there? "

" A long story Mike!! I had some backing from a
special Swedish polis officer, who at one point was
going to arrest me, but, we ended up as good close
friends! We also ended up working for the Swedish
intelligent agency, (S I A) and that was interesting
and a lot of action! I'll need to tell you about it one
day!! " Justin smiled over at Mike, then patted him on
the shoulder as to assure him it was going to be ok,
what-ever they did.

Only ten minutes passed as they drove to the filling
station in central Miami, as this is where the gunman

started his killing spree.

Justin looked down to his left arm where the justice machine was fixed firmly to his skin, then spoke to the machine!

" Diagnose crime scene! " Justin commanded, then waited for the reply.

" Master justice instrument analyzing location!! Crime scene detected as origin of first murders, awaiting data!!!! "

The voice was softly spoken, and Mike widened his eyes as he heard the machine answer Justin.

" We are just about to see a scene of the killings Mike, so brace yourself for a new Experience!! Keep an open mind like you have with meeting John, and you will settle in to it a lot better! "

Mike waited with anticipation to see the justice machine in action, as he like John had said, " You will be given a justice machine soon! " A humming could be heard from the location of Justins arm, then a beam of silvery white light shone onto the dash of Justins SUV!

Mike sat back in the car seat with a little surprise when he saw a machine gun barrel pointing out the side window panel of what could only be a delivery type van!

" The information shows that this was his first 7 victims, and then moved on 300 meters West of this location Justin!! "

" Thank you justice instrument! Play full amount of crimes for Mike´s benefit, and then inform us when you have located fugitive!! "

" Affirmative Justin! Checking for data now, stand by!!! "

Mike had at this time been checking his pistol, making sure there was sufficient bullets in the magazine, and spare magazines in his belt pouch, just in case of a long shoot out!

" Hopefully the justice instrument will do all the work on catching this guy Mike! But! Just in case, always be prepared!! "

Mike nodded to Justin as he kept his eyes on the hologram that was now showing the start of the killing spree by the murderer!

On the dash board in Justins SUV, the gunman could be seen in the holographic projection, it was plain to see he was not giving a damn on who he was going to shoot first!

Taking aim! The gunman pointed the barrel at a car at a gas pump.

Fast gun shots one after the other echoed as the machine gun burst into sound and smoke bellowing from the barrel. " Boooom!!!! A bullet had searched out one of the fuel pumps, and flames spewed up and outwards. A second explosion erupted around the gas station as the car nearest the pump erupted into a fire ball 30 feet high! Screams could be heard coming from the inside of the vehicle. The woman driver jumped out of the car with flames engulfing her whole body, she was screaming in so much pain, but then, the gunman opened fire again striking her head with one of the bullets, she stumbled and dropped to the ground, now in silence, as the bullet had extinguished her life!! 3 young teenagers ran from the service station shop, and another burst of machine gun fire could be heard, deafening the surrounding area. You could hear the screams and crying as they fled for their lives, but to no avail, as each one ran into the paths of all the projectiles. Each bullet taking their young lives.

Justin glanced over at Mike in the passenger seat, his left cheek was dripping with tears as he sat there powerless to change an event that had already taken place. " You ok buddy!? " Justin asked.

" Ya!! I´ll be ok Justin, just so hard to take in all this new stuff in my life, where before, we would get to the crime scenes after it happens, but now, you can see with this machine everything that happened! "

" I don´t say this lightly Mike!! But you will get used to all this eventually, and when you get to catch the fugitives of these crimes, it gives you some satisfaction and closure! "

As they continued to watch the horror unfold in front of their eyes, Mike and Justin saw a young married couple running towards the service station shop door, and holding tightly in the woman's hand grip, was a baby carrier, they ran as fast as their legs could carry them. The automatic doors slid open quickly, but at that precise moment, more bullets came from the gun barrel smashing some of the pains of shop glass, shards of falling glass fell around them as bullet after bullet hit several items, and then five bullets found the young couples bodies, each one falling forward to the ground with blood gushing from each wound! Her last movement in her young sweet life was to push hard the baby carrier through the shop doors, she was desperately praying that her baby was kept safe in these moments of insanity, by an evil crazy man! The tires of the crazed gunman spun fast as they made smoke plumes as he started to flee the crime scene! The smelling burning rubber added to the fire engulfed gas station! With a screeching of wheels, the gunman put his foot to the gas pedal and quickly left the carnage behind him.

Police sirens could now be heard in the distance, and slowly getting closer, and closer!

The master instrument of justice kicked into voice life again!

" Justin!! Drive 0.5kms South on ocean drive! You will then be directed to the start of the second attacks! "

Turning the ignition key, Justin drove to the main road, steering the vehicle now along ocean drive.

" This guy is certainly a son of a bitch!! " Mike´s voice was angry, he wanted so much now to catch this madman! He wanted to stare him in the eyes as he imagined putting the handcuffs on him!

Mike was checking his handcuffs as he thought these thoughts, then looking over at him, Justin knew what Mike was thinking, and then surprised him with his next words!

" Mike!! Have you forgotten about the ultimate instruments final actions!? " Mike stared hard at Justin with an angry face, his eye brows raised with a new hatred for this madman!

" Part of my training Justin is to arrest and handcuff a person, and I want to take this bastard in so much, I can taste it!! "

Justin was going to remind him what this machine was capable of, but then thought he would just let Mike see for himself the end results, after they caught this guy!

Justin reflected back to some of the first incidents he had come across! The anger he had on his own face when he saw the holograms of the first murders, the blood and pain on the victims faces, and then the punishments dealt out by the master instrument! He had come a long way from those first times several years earlier.

Less than two minutes on the drive. " Shopping mall

reached, second wave of the attack by fugitive started here! " The Hologram burst into life again on the SUV dashboard. The long streak of projected light reached the roof of the SUV, flickering, then, the machine gun barrel protruding out of the side window of the vehicle, just as before. Mike was slowly getting used to the pattern of the justice machine now, he looked patiently into the hologram waiting for the scene to unfold.

5 students sat on a mall bench, 3 girls and 2 boys, all were about 16 years old. One of the girls sitting on the bench looked up quickly as she heard what she thought was fire crackers being let off. This was no fire cracker, her friend on her left fell backwards suddenly from sitting on the back edge of the seat. As she looked to the ground where her friend had fallen backwards, she stared at her face , then screamed a high-pitched scream. Her face had been struck by one of the bullets, half of her head and face was missing with the impact of the bullet striking her. The remaining two girls were riveted to the spot in disbelief, and almost in double quick time, both girls started to fall to the ground as more bullets found their target´s. At this point, both boys ran towards the mall itself, then 3 bullets exploded in the back of one of the boys, blood could be seen splashing from the stomach and groin area. The second boys head erupted like a volcano as a bullet took most of the boys skull away as it struck him. Some people did the wrong thing, they ran from the mall to see what the commotion was all about, but that was a big mistake, as the gunman reloaded a new magazine, then clicked the trigger in to action again. He was laughing an evil laugh as he mowed down another 13-innocent people, the oldest being a 47-year-old man, to a 12-

year-old girl. The death toll was now at 14, and 11 seriously wounded. He had opened up on these people like shooting at a fair ground shooting gallery, but these were real human beings, and not metal targets!!

The beam of the hologram light, slowly faded and projected no more images.

" Locating fugitive, stand by!! " Mike looked over at Justin with disgust for the murderous fugitive, he wanted this bastard big time! " I can´t believe how he smiled and laughed as he killed and injured all those people! " Justin paused for a moment and realized that most people have this reaction to these scenes and knew that Mike would want to catch him and take him in, but, Justin knew what the instrument of justice was probably going to do when he was captured. " I have seen this type of thing so many times Mike! In time, it gets a little easier, not easy! "

As much as Mike was getting angrier, he was feeling some kind of serenity passing through every cell in his body after the new energy John had passed to him. Thinking to himself, he knew that resentment and all the anger was going to eat him alive, so getting calm and feeling good within himself was the correct thing !

Now all that had to be done was catch this murderous monster!

" Fugitive found, you must act quickly as this man is just about to go on another killing spree!! His targets is the school playground on Central avenue. You have 15 minutes to avert disaster!! " Screeching wheels spun black smoke on the ground as the rubber tires reached high revolutions, then left scorch marks on the ground behind them as the SUV moved like grease lightening!! Justin had his foot firmly on the floor of the SUV, he needed to get to the school before this fucking lunatic struck again! Slowing the vehicle to a crawl, Justin approached the outside school playground!

" That´s the delivery van there!!! " Justin held Mike´s shoulder back in his seat. " Wait Mike!! He´s got the machine gun quarter way out the window, it´s trained on the whole playground, so let me get out and walk towards it, then I will get a good contact view with the justice instrument! " Mike looked very impatient, but he agreed with Justin to go along with it his way!

Looking into the school playground, Justin could see several school children starting to exit the main school entrance.

" Justice machine!! When you have a clear line of sight with the gunman, activate restraint beam! "

" Affirmative Justin!! "

Justin thought quickly to himself, he so hoped that the instrument could activate before the killer opened fire.

More and more children poured out of the school, each one talking and laughing with their school friends.

Justins heart started to race faster, and a sharp pain could be felt in his chest as the old bomb splinter that had nearly killed him many years ago, when he served with the Swedish Intelligent Service, (S. I. A.) This splinter had moved again, and wasn't a pleasant feeling!

Justin glanced back towards his SUV, and in horror, he saw that Mike was crouching down and making head way towards the delivery vans off-side!

He started to walk a little faster, his pace was gaining ground on the gunman's vehicle, then he saw the machine gun raise slightly, he knew this was the killer taking final aim!

" Freeze!!! Move a muscle, and I'll splatter your brain cells all over your vehicle!! Very slowly, take your hands away from the machine gun!

Mike was at the far side window, and pointing his gun directly at the gunman's head.

The man started to shake slightly, but then, his hands acted calm and steady.

"I guess this is the day I meet my maker!! because copper!!! I am going to take these little darlings with me, so shoot away!! My trigger finger will act on spasm!! "

Mike´s eyes got wider when the killer had said that and started to panic.

" Make your move cop!!!

" Activate restraint beam now!!! " The words Mike heard could not have come at a better moment. The justice machine sprang into life with a powerful blue beam, it engulfed every part of the gunman's body. He was stuck fast in his seat from head to toe!

" What's happened to me!?? " The man's voice was now shaking with an unknowing, he was powerless to do anything to move or escape!

Justin peered through the driver's window to the other side, looking at Mike, and his surprised facial expression!

" You are one lucky son of a bitch Mike!! " Justin was a little pissed at Mike for acting on impulse, but they got the job done.

" Thanks' Justin, I thought he was really going to open fire on those kids! "

" He was, make no mistake, this guy is as crazy as they come, and a pure evil killer. It would have been his crowning glory to take some of the kids out, then get killed himself! So, your diversionary tactics paid off, even if I was un-prepared! "

The gunman was totally confused as to what this device was, and how was it possible for him not to be able to move!?

" Mike!! I want you to follow me with my SUV, and we need to get this guy out of the area now!

Justin pulled the man still in the restraint beam over to the passenger seat, then ran to the front of the vehicle and climbed in.

" You have to read me my rights!!! " The gunman demanded!

" I need to do nothing scumbag!! " Replied Justin looking at the man. Justin continued. " OH!!! I forgot to tell you. I'm not a cop! "

The man's eyes even though angry that he was caught, were filling with water. Yet another coward feeling emotional and sorry for himself. Well he should have thought about that before he started killing innocent people!

Mike followed Justin for what seemed like hours, but it was only 10 minutes along the highway towards the wooded road that led out of the built-up area.

Being concerned now, Mike thought hard about what might happen next, but tried to dismiss it from his mind! Having a sharper brain since john placed the new information inside his head was refreshing! In a short while, he knew that he was going to be part of an event that would involve him in a killing, but this was no ordinary killing! This was going to be an execution of great magnitude to his morals, it was going to threaten his good and sane thinking!

Values ran high with Mike, and in a few moments, he was going to have to witness a life being extinguished!

" What can I do to stop this!? Should I stop it!? Mike´s heart ran faster and missed some beats as he worked himself up into a frenzy about the whole situation!

Justin pulled off the main highway into a small forest road, which would lead to an old abandoned aircraft hangar and runway!

Inside the air-craft hanger, Justin pulled the fugitive killer out of the SUV passenger door. He was still fixed strongly into the justice instruments beam of light, then stood him up straight on the dusty dirty ground.

Mike walked slowly to where Justin and the man stood.

" I am having second thoughts Justin! " Mike said!

" I know you are Mike! So, I am going to let you have a choice of punishment´s which will be your final decision! "

" When you receive your own justice instrument Mike! You will have the choices also to give the fugitives a death, or a clean brainwash! "

The man moved his eyes as best as he could staring at Justin, then Mike.

" Ready to implement justice punishment Justin! "

Mike thought hard, then remembered back to the hologram and of the sight of the young girls getting shot, and especially the bullets taking half of one of the girls face off as it penetrated her skull!!

Mike got angry at these thoughts, then turned to Justin.

" Give him full punishment Justin!! "

" Implement full punishment justice instrument!!! "

" Affirmative!! Activating now!! "...............

CHAPTER 5
Fired!!!

In Justins SUV. Both men were quiet, as they drove back into central Miami!

Mike was going over in his mind all the events of the punishment dealt by the Ultimate instrument.

He could still see the image of the fugitive in front of him, and then the jolts of light beams coming from the machine. Several light points were shining all over his body, then in a few split seconds. Bursts of red beams penetrating the man's flesh, it was boring holes through his flesh like a hot knife through butter. Each beam went deeper until it lit up the wall of the aircraft hangar behind him! Every light that had entered his body, beamed through to the other side, and each beam sealing the wounds, so no blood escaped.

Mike and Justin saw the man give out his last exhaled breath, then his eyes fell still as his life force faded to nothing. Justice had been served again by the Ultimate instrument of justice!!!

Arriving back at the asylum, they both observed more and more people in the grounds of the old building. Very discreetly they inched their way to the back entrance door, then closed the door quietly as to not draw attention to them-selves.

Walking towards the recreational lounge they could see TV crews starting to pack up their TV and electrical equipment, then heading towards the front entrance.

Looking at Doctor Channing's office door, they could see a heated argument with three people, and these could only be board of directors personnel!

Tony Deveraux glared at Doctor Channing!
" I have never seen such a shambles as this in my life! This has turned out to be like a scene from a circus performance! There is no excuse for what has happened here, so the other board members and myself have made an emergency vote, and that is to remove you from this facility, and maybe with help from another Doctor, we can restore the good name of this asylum!! "

Elizabeth stood silent, then removing her white Doctor coat, then took her stethoscope and threw it on her desk!
" Any of various instruments used for listening to sounds produced within the body.! "
" That my dear friends, is the definition from the dictionary! So, I suggest that you place it up your ass and when it´s up far enough, you can listen to your own bull-shit!!! "

She walked gracefully to the door, opened it, spun around looking back at the board members.
" Good day gentlemen!!! "

Tony Deveraux came through the office doorway.
" And take that clown with you!! " Pointing to John!

John stood from sitting in the arm chair, turned to face the angry man, then gave that all knowing lovable smile of his!

Mike and Justin walked over to John and encouraged him to follow them trailing behind Doctor Channing!

Walking through the front main entrance door they were confronted by a lone TV crew still looking for an extra story.

An investigative journalist hurried towards Doctor Channing!

" Doctor Channing! Doctor Channing!! Can you tell us what has happened!? " The TV camera-man pointed the lens towards the Doctor and John standing next to her.

" Here beside me, you can see a beautiful man who just performed some spectacular event in healing a terminally ill child, who will get to see her next birthday!! Every single patient is now well from whatever ailment they had! Miracle after miracle has happened here, and as of this moment, I have been fired from my position as chief consultant Doctor!! "
She turned to look at the asylum pointing to it.

" The board of directors say that this has just been a farce and circus act and bringing the good name of the asylum into controversy! "
Placing the microphone closer to Doctor Channing, she continued.

" I always thought that to serve as a Doctor was to help and improve lives!? I always thought that if something revealed it´s self as some kind of cure, you would grasp at it with both hands!? So here we have a loving being who has revealed his hands to the world, and achieved things that as humans, we haven't managed!!!

" Money has once again been placed before the love and care of sick people, John here, I believe to be a being of 100% pure untainted love!!!

" Sometimes, I despair at humanity. Always placing the Buck before the heart! "

With John and Mike in the back of Justins SUV, and Doctor Channing in the front passenger seat, they all sat with sad faces, all except John!

" I am going to take John to my home! He deserves at least that courtesy. " She turned to look back at John, and as always, the ever-telling smile on his perfect face. His eyes again shinning like twinkling diamonds just seeing the world for the first time since discovered.

" My dear friends!! Whatever has happened over these last days has meant to happen. I can tell you that before we get to Doctor Channing's home, a TV crew is going to stop us and ask for me to do a TV show! This will be screened live. From that moment, your government will intervene and try to take control of my visit here! They will be frightened! Like little children not understanding, they will act in fear! "

Just as he predicted, a TV truck drove along-side of Justins SUV.

" Please stop!! We need to talk to you! " The ladies voice was raised higher as to be heard over the sounds of both vehicles.

Justin was nodding to show the TV crew they would stop.

At the roadside rest area, the woman had stepped out of the vehicle and headed for the SUV.

" You don´t need to do this John!! " Doctor Channing said, then took hold of Johns hand and held it tightly. Opening his mouth, he spoke back to comfort her fears.

" I want to do everything I can to help this world and the people in it Doctor Elizabeth!! This way has already been planned in advance! "

" Oh my God!!! You spoke from your mouth! " They had all stared at him when he was talking, but none except the Doctor had noticed he had grown a tongue!

" The chief editor at the TV station has authorized me to offer you $250,000 for appearing on a live program, and to do some of your healing! "

John smiled at the reporter.

" I will gladly appear, but I would like the money to go to these three friends! " He pointed at Doctor Channing, Mike and Justin in turn.

" That will not be a problem John!! " She answered.
She had a puzzled look on her face as he had
spoken, then realized he was talking from his mouth!
Carol Hoover was an excellent journalist, and had a
very sharp enquiring mind, and that was what
promoted her on many occasions. She started on the
mail room floor, then gradually worked her way up to
where she was to-day.
John like clockwork smiled! " It has taken a little
longer to grow my tongue, but now is fully
functioning. "
" You knew what I was thinking just then!!?? " John
nodded back to her.
Like most people, John just made people feel warm,
and feelings of calmness and peace was felt by most
around him.
As John looked into Carols eyes, she started to feel a
glow, then a tingling down her spine, it was almost
as if she was being bathed in pure light and love, the
sense of love she had never experienced before.
Music ran through her mind, then lowering through
her very soul! Every part of her mind and body felt
sudden surges and pulses of sharp and painless
energy! As she gazed back, tears of delight filled her
hazel and blue sparkling eyes.
She would have gladly spent eternity just being in
that moment. This perfect being! This beautiful man
standing before her was something so special, she
knew he was here to change this world for the
better, and somehow, she knew he was going to
achieve sending love into the world and hearts of the
beings who lived here.
Within her inner thoughts, she connected with his
visions! His plan was to let the world know it had
suffered long enough! Man was nearly at destruction
point!! She saw a possible outcome after his visit, but

the thought was diluted slightly as for now, John needed to keep that from the world! It would reveal it´s self soon enough, then man would have a second chance, it was going to be epic in its path, a world changing event. Man needed a push in the right direction and leaving all the old garbage behind, cleansing every inch of the ground that we walked on.

The soft musical notes running through her body echoed with every delicate tone. Each base note ran to her heart center, then the high pitch tones entering her unseen third eye, as they entered her body, they diverted to her central energy points spread out in a downward motion. Like waves splashing on the shore of a golden sandy beach. At that very moment, she felt like her whole body was going to explode with energized particles. She remembered back to the most wonderful orgasm she had experienced, this was a pretty close feeling to that, but in a loving way, not sexual.

Like fingers that were snapping someone out of a hypnotized state, she jolted back into reality, the now moment!!

John turned to look at his followers.

" My dear friends! So, it begins! Your life from this moment on-wards is about to go into a faster pace. You are all welcome to take this journey with me, and I will be happy to walk beside your footprints! Thank you for the trust and your good hearts!! I will return this to you 50 times! "

Without spoken words from then, they all smiled, a smile each just like John had shown from the very beginning. Each one with a slightly intense glow about them, and each one moving to their individual vehicles!! Each engine in turn firing into life as they now drove towards the Tv Station in Downtown

Miami!.......

CHAPTER 6

The light of a thousand
Stars!

Bright lights illuminated the huge TV studio. Cameras
covering every angle of the set! Technical staff!
Sound engineers testing, all getting ready for the big
event.

TV producers hovering over every aspect of the
forthcoming show. 300 seats set out like a half moon
shape so that every single person could see what was
happening in front of them.

" So this is the famous John Doe!? " Looking straight
at John was the floor director Matt Brooklyn!
Continuing. " Ok Mr. Doe! I need you to be left side
of the anchorman Brian Conlan when he introduces
and then interviews you! "

John´s smile faded a little, then came back as he
spoke to the floor director.

" Mr. Brooklyn! I came here because of an invitation
from your chief director, who had Carol Hoover ask
me this question! I would like the lady to do the
interview!! "

" That is not possible John! " He said with a hint of
sarcasm in his voice.

" I can assure you Mr. Brooklyn, that your chief is
sitting in the sound booth right now waiting to tell
you that it´s ok!! "

Matt glanced up at the booth where the chief was
sitting, then saw the nod reflecting through the
smoked glass!

" Will someone get Carol on the phone, then get her

to make up quickly please!!??

His voice sounded with a slight panic as there was only 45 minutes left until start!

With the makeup girl walking beside Carol towards the main TV set, she was applying the anti-glare cream to her face as they walked under the blazing studio lights.

John was sitting on a soft couch waiting and giving the usual smile. Looking at him as she approached, she gave a smile which contained an endless gratitude, every line in her face was saying " thank you! " The thoughts that was going through her mind, was of calmness, she knew what she was going to ask and say!

At the rear of the studio, doors swung open! Men! Women, and some children entered the studio, most of them so eager to see what was going to happen! Studio staff directed people to their seats, most wanting to sit near the front to get the best view. Coming through the doors also, was 3 wheelchairs! They each had a carer pushing the chairs towards the front of the seating area.

" 5 Minutes to broadcast ladies and gentlemen!! " Came the voice over the speaker system!

Standing at the inside wall of the studio was Doctor Channing, Justin, and Mike! Each one was waiting with anticipation.

The speakers on the walls hummed in to sound !!

" 2 Minutes to live broadcast!! Please tell all the other TV networks to standby!

Every TV that was tuned in, was just about to see an event of a lifetime!!

" 10 Seconds to broadcast! "

" 5.. 4.. 3.. 2.. On Air!! "

" Good evening ladies and gentlemen!

" Welcome to everyone in the studio audience!
" A very warm welcome to every person watching around America, and other Countries Airing this broadcast! "
" We are coming to you live from Miami, where we have a special treat and interview with " John Doe!! " To-night he will demonstrate some amazing powers of healing! Some of you would have just seen some TV recordings of just what John has done since his short time here on earth! "
" In future history of our planet, we will look back on this first time of talking and learning from an alien from another dimension!! "
" Alien!!?? When you place your eyes over John, you would not know that he was alien! Over decades now, we have imagined aliens as creatures and bringing war and destruction to our planet! "
The cameras panned over the whole of Johns body, right up to his face and head. His ponytail hanging down straight at his spine. His eyes glistened with a sparkle that emanated light.
" Since arriving here on our planet, he has done some incredible things with his healing powers, and shortly, we will get some demonstrations of this awesome power! "
" Some of you would have seen the latest film footage of curing a young girl from a terminally ill condition! This is proven fact now! John had removed the cancer cells and discharged them into the atmosphere, right in view of TV cameras and witnesses! "
" Before we continue this special live broadcast, we will take a break and hear from our sponsors! " All the red lights on the top of the cameras turned off, then!
" 3 Minutes to return! " Came the voice over the

speaker system.

Everyone in the audience had their eyes fixed firmly on John, it was almost like they were being drawn in to an inviting spa pool with knowing that the water was going to cleanse every part of their bodies! Touch their skins, then penetrate to every blemish and ailment each person had.

Doctor Channing caught eye contact with John, then turned to speak to Justin and Mike.

" John has just telepathically sent me some thoughts of the man in the wheelchair to the left of us! He mentions that the man is part of the TV crew and is there in case nothing happens!! When we return to live broadcast, he wants me to push the man to the front of the set! " Mike turned to Justin. " I will watch Elizabeth's back in case it gets ugly Justin!! " Placing his finger and thumb together to resemble a circle, he made the sign of " OK! "

Once again the speakers crackled into humming sounds.

" Standby! 15 seconds to live!! "

" In 3.. 2.. On Air!! "

" Welcome back!! I am Carol Hoover! You are watching a special live program from Miami, and here with me is our special new visitor from outside our planet. John Doe!! Ladies and gentlemen! " Extremely loud applause erupted from the audience as Carol lifted her right arm and hand and pointed to John. Carol stood up and shook Johns hand tightly. Johns face had started to get a little brighter, a silvery light shone from all around his body. He was starting to light up like a town in the sun set!

" I am quite sure every-one watching is really curious about you John!? We all have so many questions for you! "

" Thank you for letting me be here Carol, for allowing

me to give to your world what was given to me freely! "

Continuing John looked over at Doctor Channing, she knew exactly what she had to do!

Walking over to the man in the wheelchair closest to her, she smiled at the man's carer, then took the chairs handles and proceeded to push the chair closer to the front of the studio close to Carol and John. The carers face went bright red, then an anguished look came upon it as the wheelchair got further away from her.

" I see from this man in the chair that he would like to have healing energy given to him! I also know that this man is working for the TV studio!! He is here to be a backup in case nothing happens! Then!!! He gets up and pretends to be cured! " Gasps in the audience could be heard around the entire studio. Johns face smiled more and looked at the man in the chair with a knowing friendly look!

" Peter!! Your name is Peter! Yes!? "

" Yes, John it is!! " Peter looked at John with a nervous type look.

" What I do know Peter! Is you are hiding a secret from your employer!! Is that right!? "

Peter now had cold shivers inside and outside of his body, tingling shots of fear bounced to every inch of flesh:

" I am glad that the studio decided to put you here, and I will give you the healing that you need! "

" Peter here, has been living with the "HIV virous for over 13 months after having a lifesaving blood transfusion! It was 3 months after that he was diagnosed with the illness! He was not at fault, he was carrying this guilt around with him hoping he could continue working! " John walked closer to Peter, then pulled him out of the wheelchair.

Wrapping both arms around Peter, John hugged the man with such kindness, and with that, Peter broke down and fell to his knees crying his heart out! Applause erupted in the studio, the audience were standing on their feet with shouts of " Well done!! " The director behind the smoked glass was smiling, as he knew this might have gone bad for him, but! This was working in his favor!

John placed his hands around Peters chest and waist, then as he did, a glow of orange could be seen everywhere in the studio! " I am taking the contaminated cells away from you Peter! Your white cells will now take over the body to give you your life back! " A sudden glow of bright white light shot through Johns body, almost as if he had been hit by a lightning bolt!!

" I ask that the TV company get a trained blood technician in here while we are broadcasting, so by the time we finish here today, the results will be made known to everyone!! "

Peter wiped some tears from his cheeks as he looked at John and smiled. " John!! Thank you so much for this! " Peter held John close.

" You are worth every breath and day that you have been given Peter! You are living proof that life can continue if the right energy is provided! "

" Time for some more words from our sponsors, we will be back shortly!! " Carol rushed over to Peter and John and all three grouped hugged!! She had known Peter for some time, so she too like many others were surprised when John had revealed Peters illness. John held Peters hand again. " I would like you to be with my friends and myself after today Peter! You can be part of the new beginning that is going to sweep the world clean!! "

" I realize how lucky I am John to have you heal me!

But after people see this broadcast, so many, even too many will be flocking to you for healing!! "

" Everything will be revealed soon Peter! Amazing things like beyond your wildest dreams will show up in the open! Life on earth will never be the same!! This started to happen the day I came to this planet!! Love is showing a way to all who seek it! Every single person has that in a place that most never look! And that my dear friends is within themselves!! "

John with his ever-glowing smile continued!

" For longer than some can imagine, man has looked hard to discover life and love! They go to the four branches of the world! They fail to see what is right under their noses! Right before their eyes! "

" Standby! 20 seconds to ON AIR!! " Came the directors voice.

Carol smiled at the camera facing her.

"Thank you for returning to this special live broadcast from Miami! We are now going to take questions from the studio audience, John will answer as many questions as possible! "

Two thirds of the way back from the studio floor was a man standing up waiting to ask the first question to John.

" I have never been a religious man John! Through the years of my life, I have heard of many so-called miracles happening. I believe that something powerful exists in the universe that us humans can´t explain! You claim to come from another part far out in space! What is your concept of " GOD? "

John stood from his seat to answer the man.

" Thank you for your question and your honesty in that question! Your name is Sabastian yes!? "

" It is John! " The man had a slight puzzled look as to him knowing his name.

" My dear Sabastian! Do I believe in God!? " John

continued to smile like always and then addressed the audience and cameras.

" When I look at the stars from where I come from, I feel an energy so powerful, an energy with light and color surrounding every particle in space! From my very beginning in my existence, I felt the power of a feeling that I now know to be Love!! To know God! Is to know Love! Many of your fellow humans have many different beliefs of God! Through thousands of years, man has argued that his belief in God is the right and only way! What I say today, many will say I am evil, they will say I am a disciple of the Devil! People on earth are afraid of the unknown, so they believe that if something is there, and not of their beliefs, then it must be bad! I am not here to convince you of anything! I am here to give you a power that will lead you back to the Creator!! The God of your understanding, or not understanding! Each one of you can look deep into your hearts, and there, you will find that concept of God!!

Every single human has a soul, an essence, it is power in itself! Your souls are magical! They can bring a smile to the worst hurting face near them, just reach out and multiply that power!

The healing power from God that I have, I gladly give to your world! "

In the studio, you could have heard a pin drop, it was so quiet. You could look at the faces in the seats, they looked confused, they looked happy, and they looked like they understood everything he said!

John was glowing again, there was something wonderful happening around his body! Almost like a generator was starting up! The light emanated from him like a firefly in the dark. His aura was expanding and glowing brighter! Sparks of light vibrating from his skin, his hairs standing up on his arms, they became statically charged as they uncurled. Each one stood to attention like soldiers on parade. The more the seconds went by, the more colors shone from his very being! He was starting to resemble a rainbow with every color swirling around him.

Cries of. " OOooo and AHHHHhhhhhh " came from the studio. This was no trick photography or TV camera trickery, this was real as you or I. John raised his arms to chest Hight, faced the ceiling of the studio with his palms upwards!

" Great heavenly creator of all! We ask you to show us your light and your love! Reveal yourself for us now!! We are the children of the stars. We are your creation! Show us your love!

With unlimited expectations, the audience and studio crew focused on the main area where John and Carol were. With the force of 20 sky search lights, a light that was never seen before, it grew in size to the diameter of the width of the studio! Pulses of light flickering throughout the studio. Every studio light failed! The light illuminated everywhere, and everything. It´s rays shone on and through everything, from object to human flesh!

Looking at every soul in the studio was a light, a light that could see your strengths and your weaknesses. There were a few screams from some of the guests as when they had looked down to the floor!! There was no floor!!! Under them was a black space, but, the space contained stars twinkling in the distance. The whole studio and its occupants were floating in a void, a moment in space where no other material objects could be seen!!

" Do not be afraid, nothing can harm you! " John spoke the words calmly and clearly with the ever-growing smile that seemed to be a permanent fixture now!

Before each person of the studio, including the staff was a small sphere of light hovering about one meter in front of their faces! Suddenly!! the objects started to move towards the heart area of each person, slowly until they all at the same time entered the bodies and hearts of each and every one of the humans! They all went in perfect synchronization!! A smile could be seen on each face! They had just been touched by a power so great, words were not needed, just the gentle touch of a light that touched their very souls!

From the lights around John, there was humming coming from each spark of color. Looking into the light, the audience and crew could see what could only be described as " Angels!! " Each one with an angelic face and look, and just like John, a beautiful smile!

The light angels moved in a manner that could be said to be graceful! They hovered and flew in front of each person. Each wing of the angels shone with an energy of light, colors of red,orange,blue and purple! Each angel having piercing blue eyes, just like a flame had been ignited!

As the angels gracefully moved in the air, their wings gave a warmth from the wind swirling in motion to them!

Within a few minutes, every angel had formed to make a circle around the floating studio! In the next seconds, a flame of blue appeared in front of John! The flame was warm and cool, all at the same time. And suddenly!!! coming towards the blue flame from the other side of the light, started to appear a golden glowing light. This light was moving into and through the blue flame!

If you had asked each person there what they felt at that moment, everyone would have described the

light!
" The golden glowing light had joined the blue burning flame, then came through. The gold in color light, was singing a song never heard by man before. The ears of everyone heard a song so beautiful, it brought tears of happiness, it brought a feeling of belonging, and the biggest thing of all! Every single person had been touched by 100% love!!!
Gold, silver, and the colors of the rainbow lit up the space before them! A sensation of peace, of calmness, and above all else, that feeling of belonging with the glow in front of them Every person smiled and wanted to stand next to the entity! This magnificent being! They were staring into the light of God himself!!
Each human mind could hear Gods voice, and each knowing that one day, they would be in front of him again!
Looking all around him, Justin could see the serenity on all the faces, never before had he seen so many people with smiles and now, love in their hearts, no matter how much they had been a non-believer! He recalled someone saying to him once! " God denial, is only God delay! " Today he believed that to be true! He could not with all his heart believe any differently, as now he was facing the one thing he had always wondered about. Now! This creator of life was here!!
The golden light appeared to be moving back towards the blue light flame, it passed through with no burning, and sparkled as it travelled past John and all the pulsing lights of color.
The angels began to fly in a circle again, then as they did, each one was fading into a wisp of smoky air, and then swirling to a fine mist, just like spray from a water tap bouncing in a sink! Within a moment, they were gone! The floor began to appear back before

their eyes, the eyes of new energized love and light!
Carol sat there, she stared up at the smoke glass
where the director sat. He nodded to her, and she
knew exactly what to say.

" Ladies and gentleman! Each and every one of us
saw that!!?? I know I did. We will be back in a few
minutes after our sponsors!! "

" Extended commercials everyone! 5 minuets!! " The
floor manager announced!

You could hear the murmurs and talk in the studio.
Everyone was talking about their vision and feelings,
all with smiles as wide as oceans!

" 10 seconds to ON AIR!! "

The TV phone lines were red hot!! The lines to the
studio were jammed with in-coming calls, mainly
people asking if there had been special effects and
trick photography used!? Even the best phone
operator there had a problem trying to convince
people on the other end of the lines that this was real
and happening now!

" After that last demonstration by John, hundreds of
you have been calling to see if this is genuine and
making sure it´s not an April fool's joke! Ladies and
gentlemen, I can assure you that every minute you
have seen is genuine, it´s real as you or me!! " Carol
smiled into the camera as she continued.

" In my entire life! I have never experienced anything
like that before! I do know I saw what I saw, along
with the 300 others in this studio, we showed it to
you as it happened! I know if you really searched
within your hearts, you just know this to be true! This
is a wonderful time in our earth's history, we are
making history right now!! And I am grateful today
for being allowed to be part of this amazing lesson of
love!! "

A crashing door sound could be heard from the rear

of the studio! Both swinging doors swung open with a thud as the doors hit the buffers when fully opened! Two adult males and a woman in their thirties were shouting as they walked fast pushing and guiding a hospital bed towards the front of the studio towards John!

On the hospital bed, there was a white sheet covering what could only be a body! A dead body!! The woman shouted at John, and at that moment, security guards rushed at them to prevent them from reaching the front part of the studio.

" If you are the new healing miracle! Then convince me! Bring back my son! " The tears were rolling down her cheeks making her eye makeup run in black streaks! One of the guards held the arm of one of the two men, and wouldn't let go.

John walked into the audience and stopped in front of the bottom of the hospital bed.

The woman was sobbing hard, she couldn't stop, she was so distressed by the traumatic passing of her son.

She looked with begging eyes at John, all she wanted was for him to be alive and well, and being his old happy self.

Three of the cameras followed John and the woman to the studio main floor, followed by the 2 men pushing the bed in front of them. One of the men was the boy's father, he could say nothing now, he just stood along the side of the bed by the pillow end.

" Your name is Rebecka!? And your son is Richard!? " John moved to the top side of the bed, then gently removed the white sheet and stopped by the young boys chest. His face was ashen white, the lips were blue. By looking at the boy, people could tell he had slipped away. For many people there, this was the first time they had seen a dead body, and some were sad at the thought of him laying there motionless.

John turned to Rebecka. " He has passed 40 minutes ago!? " She nodded at John, then with just her eyes, you could see she was lost and pleading with John to bring him back!

John gently rested his right hand on the dead boys head above his eyes, then his left hand on the chest over the heart.

With silence again in the studio, the cameras from every angle was following Johns hands as he moved them slightly into position. Spacing his fingers about 3 centimeters apart on his head and the other on his chest, he closed his eyes. People watched as he was just about to do something that no one thought he would be able to do.

Watching his hands, you could see an orange and golden glow coming from the palm of both his hands. Johns body was starting to shake with a vibration, the body beneath his hands was beginning to show signs of color coming back into the skin.

Suddenly! There was a blinding flash of lightening streaking from 5 feet above the boy down to the hands of this healing man! Johns hands lit up like a million watts of light blasting through the space between his hands and the young boy! The next sound was of John saying these wonderful words!!!

" LET THERE BE LIFE!!!!

CHAPTER 7

Secret Service!

" One thing certain in life as we know it, is that death comes at the end!! "
Today! John just turned that statement around.
" Let there be life!!!
Gasps of air were quickly inhaled as many in the audience shot back in their seats as a coughing young man came to life and jerked his body sitting up quickly and pushing Johns hands away from him!!
" Where am I!!?? Why am I in the hospital bed in a TV studio!!??
There was raised voices as every person in the studio stood up and cheered, then clapped loudly deafening the sound crew!
Carol had tears of joy, along with several other people as John smiled and stood back as studio paramedics ran to the bed!
" Ladies and gentlemen! For those just tuned in, we have just witnessed a young man being brought back from the dead!! He was pronounced dead nearly an hour ago after his heart problem finally came to an end! As you can see here in the studio, he is very much alive, and right at this moment, paramedics are giving him an electrocardiogram test! This right now is nothing but a miracle!! I have just been informed that the hospital specialist who was treating the lad is on his way here right now! "
The raised voices, and the looks of astonishment on faces failed to see the mother of the boy quietly go up to John and throw her arms around him. She could still feel some of the energy coming from John

as the tears kept coming. She held tightly on to a being that just gave her son life! The thoughts running through her mind was of endless gratitude, and in the next breath, John answered her thoughts. " Your son is well again! His heart is now beating with the energy of a star! Each cell has renewed and grown to give him many years of life! Thank you for bringing him! " She smiled through the tears at him. " No!! With all my heart. Thank you John and thank God for you!! "

" Stand back!! Stand back!! " The voice came from the Doctor running towards the young lad. Doctor Carmichael had been the chief consultant surgeon on the boy, his face was astonished as he saw the boy sitting up in the bed, very much alive and awake! The last he saw of the boy was 20 minutes after he had died, then he had covered the boy up with the white sheet! As the Doctor examined him, he just could not believe his eyes, as this boy had severe heart complications, and it was only going to be a matter of hours, not days that he would be alive. When his heart gave up, his brain died a few minutes later, there was no way on earth this person should be sitting up and breathing!!

Carol caught the attention of the floor manager to get some cameras on John and the boy's mother, and also on the Doctor looking over the surprised lad! One camera just managed to get the tail end of the hug the mother was giving to John, and one of the cameras zoomed in on her tears and the face of gratitude.

Another sound came from the rear of the studio, and standing at each door was several men in black suits! Every one of them were dressed the same, with dark sunglasses hiding their eyes. Also, behind Carol and John were fire exit doors, and standing in front

guarding them was more smartly dressed men.
Looking up at the control box, another two suited
men stood just inside signaling to the controllers to
terminate the program!

Carols ear piece crackled into life! " The broadcast
has been terminated Carol! Tell the audience they
need to leave in an orderly fashion! " She didn't take
long to realize this was the work of government
agents, and they were now in control of the studio!
There it was again!! That beautiful smile on Johns
face. He knew this was going to happen, just like he
had known other things in the not too distant past!
Justin and Mike walked towards John, but they saw
his hand come up towards his waist with a hand
signal that just said STOP!!

John spoke calmly to the two agents approaching
him. " I have been expecting you gentlemen, I am
ready for you! "

Two more agents walked towards Justin and Mike.
" You two need to come with us as well, so please
walk out with us calmly and quietly, and officer
Hendry, give me your firearm now!! "

Doctor Elizabeth Channing glanced over in the
direction of Carol. Her personal cameraman had one
of the portable units under his arm, and no one
noticed that he had it on and recording.

" Where are you taking them!? " The Doctor asked.
The special agents just ignored her and continued
walking towards the studio exits.

In the parking lot of the studio stood 3 large 4x4
vehicles, they were polished black in color, just like
the smart suits the agents were wearing. The tinted
windows were like they were wearing sunglasses too,
impossible to see who was inside.

Between the 3 vehicles was a black stretch limousine,
and the two agents escorting John ushered the

smiling man into the back.

No matter what was happening, he kept that beautiful smile, it was looking like it was fixed to his face, and nothing could take it off!

A few hundred meters away was the main security entrance gates, and a sound of many voices that had gathered because of the TV show.

In one of the vehicles, Justin was sat next to two agents, one each side of him, as he looked to the left of him, he remembered the justice machine on his left arm. He put the thought out to the machine to ask if this was a situation of danger, then instantaneously had a reply back in his mind!

" You are in no danger at this time Justin!! John has foreseen this unfolding, and this is as it is meant to be! "

The vehicles gathered speed as they drove the short distance to the main gates, and with policemen pushing the now large crowd back from the entrance, the tires threw up the dust as all the agents vehicles rushed by!!

Sitting on a deep backed arm chair, John surveyed his surroundings! The room was the size of a tennis court, and each wall was a mirror, each one facing him. Whatever direction he looked in, he could see reflection after reflection of him-self and the arm chair.

He knew there was a door as he had been walked into the room by some of the special agents and looking in at him from all directions was the agents standing guard over him.

Like the filming of movies, and TV soap programs, the two-way mirrors were there to keep a person or persons in secret! But! John knew what was going to happen, he knew who was going to come and talk to him, so he sat back in the arm chair to get more comfortable.

Several minutes had passed, then, in the far corner of the brightly lit room, a sliding panel opened to reveal a door way with a distinguished looking man walking towards him, followed by two men carrying an office desk and chair, with another man behind them holding a tray with coffee flasks and cups. Placing his butt on the chair, the man placed a file on the desk, then opened it!

" First of all! Welcome to earth Mr. Doe! " The voice showed sarcasm, and in reply, John kept smiling! Continuing he poured some coffee into a cup, then added some sugar and followed by some cream.

" So do aliens drink coffee!!?? " Again, the sarcasm could be felt, but John just smiled back at him.

" Your name is Clinton Smith!! You are the director of the Secret Service, and I know why I have been brought here! "

" OH!! You do!? Do you now!!?? What if I told you that.... " He was interrupted by John in reply.

"You are going to tell me that I was going to be taken to a laboratory, and there they were going to perform tests of all descriptions, then if I died, you would dispose of the evidence!! "

The agent rested more in his chair and gave John a smile back.

" Ok John!! We know now that you are genuine, we have been watching you closely ever since your name has started to pop up every-where! There has been many suggestions as what to do with you, and believe it or not, I have been on your side!! " John once again opened his mouth to speak.

" Thank you Agent Smith! But! You were against me, and wanted to destroy me many days ago, unfortunately for you, everything spiraled quickly and out with your control! The man behind you saved my life here! Is that correct sir!!?? " John looked to one side of the room and mirror.

Standing with one hand in his trouser pocket, and the other resting by his side was the man in charge of everything. He looked into the two -way mirror at John. Like John, he too had a smile on his face. Nodding to the secret service agents, he walked towards the sliding door, then turned to his security chiefs.

" I will be safe with this man gentlemen!! "

Clinton Smith turned in the chair towards the now opened door.

" John Doe!! Meet my commander in chief! President Barack Obama!! "

Clinton stood quickly, then smiled as the U:S:President walked into the room and heading straight for John!!

There it was as usual! That ever-glowing smile, the smile that said ten thousand words, but mainly the unspoken words of. " I bring you true peace and the true meaning of Love!! "

" John!! Welcome to America, and earth!! " President Obama extended his hand and John replied with the same gesture.

" I have been hearing many things about you John! You have raised many eye-brows in a short period of time! And YES!! Some of the security staff wanted to hush you up and dispose of you, but! I personally wanted to wait and see what you could do for mankind. You certainly started to show the world what you can do. "

One of the security detail had placed a soft padded chair behind the President, then comfortably sat on it!

" Thank you for seeing me Mr. President! There is

many things to talk about! " The President replied. " There certainly is John!! "

In the same building, security service agents sat in front of Justin!

" Living in Sweden! Mother and Father murdered! Joined the Swedish Secret Service a few years ago! Are you still with the (S:I:A) agency!? "

Justin just like John gave that knowing smile back in return.

" It`s been a while, but I'm still on their pay-roll if they need me agent!?? "

" Smith!! I am special agent Smith! " Came the reply. Justin couldn't resist being sarcastic back to him and said.

" Smith!? Makes a change from agents called Johnson!! "

Special agent Smith got up from his chair, then slowly walked around the table.

" I could shoot your ass right now Webber!! Then say you were resisting, but, there is no fun in that, it would be over too soon! "

The other agent in the room started to raise his voice.

" Ok boys!! This isn't a pissing contest! Let´s be adult here and play the game right!! OK!? " Two nods, one from each man were acknowledged between each other.

The president sank back into the chair listening to every word John spoke!

" John! In our world here now, we have many negative things happening, and I for one see you as a ray of hope to help in healing this planet! You are standing out like a beacon of pure light, healing, and drawing everyone in to a new hope! Some people are saying that you are sent from God!! Some say you are the Christ returned!! And unfortunately, some say you are the devils disciple come to destroy us by giving the world false hope!! " The president continued.

" I see you as a newly grown rose, brilliant white and glowing, and standing between a world of thorns!! Many are frightened of you John! some have only read about the chance to live good and honest! You are real proof that pure love can exist! But is the world ready for your gifts John!? "

If illnesses could be healed with smiles, Johns would have healed the world days ago.

" My dear President Obama! First of all, I am not Jesus returned! Secondly! We are all parts of God! As we understand him, or not! God is everything, or he is nothing!! Living on earth right now, you are all in the third dimension! Everything you see is in 3D! The next realm of existence is the fourth dimension, this is where your spirit, your essence goes when the silver cord is broken from your human body!! In the fifth dimension, everything you think, will materialize!! So, if you think of a hundred white horses running through an open field, then that´s what will appear!!! At that level, you must be quite honest within your-self. If you think negative thoughts, then the negative thought you had will manifest itself!! The more love you grow in your hearts here on earth, the less you have to do in each of the following levels!! Jesus Christ is what we call the Christ consciousness, and every soul can reach that level if they become pure in heart! "

John stood up, and at that point, two special agents hurried towards John and in front of the President!

" That´s ok gentlemen! John is not a threat! " The president reassured the security detail around him, but some looked on with anticipation and anxiety! John continued.

" President Obama! You asked just now if the world was ready for my gifts!? I can say that the world has been ready for these gifts for many decades, and overdue! I am just the beginning of a wave of beings from where I came from! Each one is of pure heart, each one brings a love that most people have never felt! Very shortly, there is going to be a chance for every single person to be healed! They will still have that choice, either to grasp that love with both hands, or turn their back on it! When they arrive, an energy beam from each will fill the sky, this will enable the people who choose love over everything, will walk to another dimension! They will have only travelled a few meters but will be in an alternative time and space! The earth as they know it will be the same, but with one big change! All negativity in the form of evil and wrong doings can´t pass into this new light, so unless they accept the light, they will remain in this space and time on earth!! "

The president looked on with a little concern, then replied to John!

" So what you are saying is an old saying that comes to mind! LIKE HELL ON EARTH!!! Do we have a choice to come back John!? "

" Each soul can return at any time to this space, this earth in time! They have free will to come and go as they please! But I can assure you Mr. President, that most will not want to return to evil and darkness! Because that´s what will remain here! Can I show you what I mean President Obama?? "

" Please do John!! " The president replied to the smiling being before him!

" CODE RED!! CODE RED!!! " A secret agent held his microphone to his mouth when uttering the words.

" The alien and the President have disappeared!! Secure the whole building now!!! "

Panic could be seen on all the security agents, as man after man ran to all the rooms checking to try and locate them. Nothing, they were nowhere to be found!

In one room, officer Hendry looked shocked as coming towards him was an agent pointing his gun at his head.

" You have thirty seconds to tell me where the President is, or you´re going to have a new ventilation hole to breathe through!!! " Mike panicked as he had no idea to the location of John or the President.

" The President!!?? " Mike didn't know that was what was happening, a meeting with the President!?

" All I know is that John knew what was going to happen, and apart from telling us that, he said nothing, and that´s the truth! "

" 15 seconds left!! " The agent cocked his weapon and pushed the barrel of the gun on Mikes skull! Hearing a voice shouting from the big mirrored room, agents ran to that location like Olympic sprinters!

" They are here! They are back!! "

12 secret service agents weapons were pointing at John, then came the command from the President!!

" Stand down, stand down gentleman!! "

" Are you alright Mr. President!? " Asked the chief security agent. Continuing. " What happened sir?? " President Obama smiled at his concerned men, then started to tell of the beautiful sights that he had seen.

" We have been gone for 1 hour, and I saw an alternative earth, but without hatred and evil. You could say that it was a heavenly place! " Interrupting the President, the chief spoke.

" Sir!! You have only been gone less than a minute! You said an hour!!?? " John started to explain.

" My dear friends! Time has the ability to slow down

or speed up in other dimensions, and this is the case that just happened. The President was able to travel with me just a few meters, but in another time zone! As you can see, I have no bad intentions towards your President, it was a demonstration of what is possible! "

" I strongly advise against this again Mr. President! This constitutes an immediate threat when you are out of our site! "

" One of the most enjoyable events in my life as President, was just witnessing what I saw, and today, I trust John 100%!! "

So, what had taken place when John and the president vanished!?

The president ran the memories through his mind and savored what he had seen and felt!

At the moment of them going from the present time and space to the alternate dimension, the eyes opened wider as he and John were standing in the main grounds of the Whitehouse! The grass was soft and springy with a warmth radiating through the air. People from all walks of life on the same ground as the president and saying " Hello Mr. President! " and walking on with a smile and happiness written all over their faces! There were no body guards, no secret service agents, just the general population of people living a good honest happy life! There was no anger, no confrontations, just a warm glow of belonging with a love in their hearts! African Americans, Native Americans, Jewish folk, Muslims, Mexicans, every nationality and religious belief walking together and smiling!! That was a strange and beautiful sight to have seen! A few seconds later, they were standing under the night sky, the moon was closer and three times the size it usually was! At the sides of the moon were reflections of millions of stars, each one flickering and shining a spark of light every few seconds. President Obama stood gazing up at a sky that was always there, but he had never felt the emotion surrounding these sights before! Almost like spiritual sounds that a raindrop might make, he heard light music playing in his mind. A flowing of soft energy raced through his entire mind and body. Like standing on a movie set, and the orchestra playing epic music of feelings of love and emotions. John looked over at him. There were tears leaking from his eyes, the eyes of a powerful man, the eyes that lit up in the sparkling night sky.

A few more seconds, then being back in daylight, looking through a fine mist of vapor! The roar of thundering water falling a vast distance below them! They were suspended in midair just over the beginning of Niagara Falls!! Barack Obama floated over this fantastic feature, this was certainly a different angle to see the falls but gave him this wonderful feeling of belonging and what size he really was in comparison to these beautiful earthly landmarks. What he felt more than anything was a feeling that he thought he knew, but through his life so far, he had only scratched on the surface. And that was the power and feeling of love! Untainted, and pure running through every particle in his body.

Still suspended in midair, the scene changed to the next landmark in American history. The Statue of Liberty!! This monumental piece of history standing proud and straight up to the sky! She too looked taller, and even looked like she had developed a smile!!

He was starting to feel a difference in his very being, that life was for living, and life was for giving, and helping others that might need that little lift in life! A smile could heal a thousand hurts, and it was free to

every human being!
One of the last scenes he saw before he returned, was of a funeral. The funeral was of a woman who passed at the age of 113 but standing alongside the mourners he could see the woman smiling and knowing it was her time to move forward, so that he realized that there was life after life!! They were celebrating her existence and her life, no tears as they knew eventually they would meet up again after their life on earth!

We were eternal beings, we didn't die, we just move on! Our spiritual growth determined our next level on the plane of our travels, and life was beautiful in any dimension!

For a brief moment in time! The President stood in the moment with hope and joy in his heart, changes can be made, and humans could progress for the better!

President Obama turned to his secretary.

" I want John Doe here to have full American Citizenship as from now, by the time we leave this building, I want a passport and special letters from me to say that he poses no threat to the world, and he can go about his work of giving healing and helping Man!!

Mr. Webber and Officer Hendry will become his body guards and will answer only to me!! Mr. Webber as we know has and is a Swedish secret service agent! He can be trusted, and I want Two special agents to travel on their detail, so they will be added protection for John. The moment we allow him into the world, he will be sought after from every religious group known, and also bad asses will be after him too! From this moment! He is under my protection with the full powers vested in me as The President of The United States of America!! Two thousand years ago!

They took a life of a perfect person!! That is not going to happen on my watch!! So, gentlemen! Go to it!! Do your duty! "

Standing facing the President, John took hold of President Obamas hand and squeezed gently!

" To-day is a day that will be seen as hands across the universe Mr. President! You and I will be written in history, as history, on both sides of the dimensions! "

" Thank you for opening my eyes John! "

A special agent interrupted John and the President. " Air Force One is ready and waiting Mr. President, we need to move sir!! "

" Lead the way gentlemen! " He replied.

He looked back at this shinning being, then smiled and slid through the mirrored door.

Escorting Mike and Justin into the room where John stood, they looked with relief on their faces as he was well. Walking in behind them was two special agents, when they all reached John, one of them spoke to him in a calm and soft voice!

" I am special agent Jane Jennings John!! This is my partner Christine Murdoch!! "

Both were dressed just like all the other agents, dark suits, but because they were women, they had smart white blouses under their tight black jackets! Each one with their pistols left of their center waist.

" We are part of the new security detail the President spoke about to you, and we will be taking orders from Mr. Webber here, and special officer Mike Hendry!

Mike put a smile over his face and looked straight at Justin.

" Special officer Mike Hendry Justin!!?? And wait a minute!! Special detail from the President!!?? Can someone please fill me in on what's going on here!!?? "

John turned to Mike.

" Mike and Justin!! The next part of our journey begins! Both of you need to go put some of your items together in a suitcase, then we will be on our way to New York! Agent Jane here will pick up Carol Hoover from the TV studios, she will then be part of our team to go and spread the word and healing! I have also sent a message to Doctor Channing inviting her to come along with us, if she wishes? I need 10 minutes with agent Jane and Christine, and to give them some information on the justice instruments! " The two female agents looked at each other, in their heads you could hear the question! " Justice instruments!!?? "

They were just about to become some of the limited few people who know about the machines, not even the President and secret agents knew of such a thing existing.

Jane started to talk with Christine. Their faces were surprised and shocked when John told them that they would be receiving a Ultimate instrument of justice machine! Also, explaining what they were and how they worked!

" The secret service is certainly secret these days Christine!! " Smiling as she walked through the glass door to collect Carol Hoover.......

CHAPTER 8

Invitation from The Vatican!!

Justin held Bernadette in his arms, she pulled her head away from his, as she felt there was something he wasn't telling her.

Then she smiled, and directly stared him in the eyes! It was her usual full-frontal attack as she liked to call it!

" Everything is fine Justin! John sent me a message a few hours ago and told me of the journeys you were just about to go on! Also, he told me about the President and your new secret agent role!! " But you are only going on one condition! That you promise me you will come back alive!! Ok!? "

" You got it honey!! " Justin pinched her ass as he moved towards the kitchen to make some coffee.

" Dad! dad!! I saw you on the TV news and the TV show! That was the man we saw on the beach! Wasn't it dad??

Justins son Frankie ran to his father's arms and hugged him tight.

" Yes son it was! John did some great and good things for people, and now I have to help him with his healing work, so I will be going away for a short time Frankie! "

The boy smiled at his father and said." You are cool dad, Mom and I will miss you, and uncle Zac!! "

" That's fine son, I need to talk to your Mom, so can you go play outside for while!?

" Hey beautiful woman in my life! Now we are alone for ten minutes, we need to talk honey!! " Bernadette knew when he spoke like that, he was really serious, and that anything he spoke about had a concern with the words!

" As I said Justin, John told me what was happening, and that this was going to be dangerous! He also told me that new members for his team were being formed as we speak, and some of them might not be coming back!! "

" I had that feeling too sweetheart! I know we are going to be going into the belly of the dragon!!! So, to speak! But! I will come back Bernadette! You can bet your sweet ass on that! "

She looked him straight in the eyes, held his head between her hands, then pulled him towards her lips, just like she had done the very first time she held him all those years ago!

" Justin Webber!! I fell in love with you even before you came to Tin Tins restaurant in Göteborg! We have been through some narrow escapes with the Justice Instruments , and I know they will protect you all as best as they can, but, they aren't 100%, so there is always a chance that something can go wrong, and now John is way out in the open, he is a prime target, and anyone around him, so you really need to keep your wits about you, and closer than normal, because, I don´t want to be stood by your graveside with our son, and saying we miss and love you!!! "

Justin smiled with his eyes, he placed each hand on both cheeks. Tear drops were welling inside the eye sockets, he had never known so much with the feelings of love he held for her in his heart. This power was perfect, it was a power that John was here to give to others, if they wanted it!

Only a few hours later, the team had been assembled. When the limousine pulled up at Justins home. Special agents Jennings and Murdoch stepped out and stood each side of the vehicle rear door.

The rolls had now reversed, it was Bernadette's eyes that were filled with tears, she held him extra tightly as he kissed her tears on her cheek.

" Come back to me Justin!! Or I'm going to kill you myself!! " She forced a slight smile as he pulled gently away from her and headed to the open door of the limousine.

Stopping, he turned to her, and saw their son and Zac looking on with sadness.

Raising his voice slightly, he spoke to his uncle Zac and son.

" You had better look after that lady next to you, or I will be kicking some Butt!! " Smiling, he bent down to climb into the back seat, then both Jane and Christine followed after him and shut the door behind them. Bernadette looked as the vehicle drove from the driveway with dust swirling and following the trunk behind it. Her heart was racing faster, it was missing beats, she was wishing with all her heart that this wasn't going to be the last time she saw him alive!

The stretch limousine cruised along the freeway, it was going to be several hours before they arrived in New York!! In the vehicle sat.

John Doe! The newly appointed special agent Mike Hendry. Special agents Jane Jennings & Christine Murdoch. Carol Hoover TV Journalist. Doctor Elizabeth Channing. And of course, Justin Webber! The Limo driver was a new guy, his name was Richard Stone! Richard was one of these specialists in getting out of tight situations, he also could have been a stunt driver for the movie " Fast and Furious " and he really could handle most vehicles. On his arm was now a familiar item, a justice machine, John had picked him out personally, so everyone knew he could be trusted.

Driving along, every now and again stood bill board posters over the freeway! Nearly every one of them had a picture as tall as a building of John Doe! With the young lad in the hospital bed he brought back to life!

The posters read!!
" DOES THIS LOOK FAMILIAR FROM OUR HISTORY!!!??? "
" GOOD OR EVIL!!?? "
" YOU DECIDE!! "

They all had smiles, everyone knew John was good and genuine! A being which was perfect in looks and actions, this truly was a man of peace and love!

Carol moved over to the seat free next to John smiling like his smile was doing.

" I have arranged for the "New York" theatre to host your first tour John, we also have TV stations standing in line to broadcast live. We have seating for 4,500, and we have sold out all three appearances for the two days! We have also sold out at the Yankee Stadium on day three, and that holds over 52,000. What do you want to do with the money from the events?? "

" Share all the proceeds with our team after expenses, then book us on our government jet to Rome!! "

" Rome!!?? " She was surprised when he had said that, but, she trusted him 100%.

President Obama had placed a jet at their disposal for anywhere they had to go to, and for some reason, he was going to take them all to Rome!

Reaching the edge of New York, 8 police cars and 10

police motor cycle escorts waited at an intersection leading to the center itself.

John faced all his team, his usual smile at them all, then began to tell them about what was to happen in their next stage of this historic journey!

" In four days, we will be flying to Rome! We will be invited very soon to the Vatican! Curiosity has risen in Religious circles, and they are afraid for the world! Situations like me don't happen in real life!! But! Here I am, sitting among you all. I have as you know come a vast distance to help your world! I can feel the future, I can see where earth is heading, and I assure you my friends that things have to change now for good, or the unthinkable will happen here, but, by then it will be too late. This earth is a beautiful playground for all life! Man is forgetting his true heart! Evil! Hatred! This cancerous plague has spread and is continuing more each day! Love has begun to return to humans hearts as we speak, but there is a lot of work to do!

Our first appearance today on the theatre platform will be interrupted by an event that could stop everything! However! I need to tell you not to react to your Instruments of justice! I am aware of what is to happen, and I will make all things good. You must trust me and my judgement! What is to happen is again meant to happen, this has been foreseen! "

Every one sat motionless and silent as John finished talking, but you could see their braincells reacting as to what was in store for them all. Was there going to be an attempt on his life!? Or a worse situation!? They each had to put their trust in John, and let whatever was going to happen, happen!!

Turning on to the main central drive, there must have

been over 7 thousand people lining up waiting to get a glimpse of this amazing being!

Police in their hundreds were standing each side of the road, spaced out every 10 meters or so!

Not so long ago, people had never known of such a person, this man, this love and light healer from another world!!

The motorcade slowly moved into the sidewalk, all in the limousine were watching as they were just about to be greeted by many smiling faces!

The first two to exit the vehicle was Special agents Jane Jennings and Christine Murdoch! Very quickly then by Newly appointed agent Mike Hendry!

police were also arm to arm leading to the theatre entrance. Some of the crowd were edging forward and pushing police officers from behind. Officers linked arms as to create a tougher barrier against the surging crowd! Shouts of. " We want John!! We want John!!

As John exited the car, he had that usual smile on his face. His pony tail newly pleated hung down his denim shirt and wearing a smart pair of trousers matching. He was glowing on every part of his skin that could be seen.

At that moment, cheers and loud applause came from all around him, with chants of. " John the healer! And Mr. healing hands!! " Doctor Channing and then Carol Hoover followed behind him, and as quickly as they were out, they headed for the entrance where the Theater owner greeted John with a firm friendly handshake.

" Welcome to New York John, and my theater at your disposal! " Sam Cartwright was a jolly rounded sort of guy, large belly, short stumpy legs, his face if you placed a white beard on him would have made him look like " Santa Claus! " Apart from his overeating of

fast foods, he was genuine and a good man.
Sam continued.
" I have an extra 20 security officers John! I think you might need them with the sellout crowds, just in case of any problematic occurrences! "
There was that smile back at Sam.
" Thank you kindly Sam! They will be taking commands from my guarding agents, I am quite sure they won't have any problems with that!? "
" That won't be a problem at all John! I will get the chief officer to liaise with your staff!
Justin walked side by side with John as they proceeded through the heavy double theater doors. Walking through to the Auditorium at the rear, John started to survey this magnificent theater.
Staring at the beautiful painted ceiling stretching the width from wall to wall! With painted scenes just like painter, sculptor, architect and poet Michelangelo had done in the Sistine Chapel in the 15th and 16th centuries! Gold leaf adorned every wood panel in between the ceiling and joining the walls towards the seating and stage area.
John began to walk in the middle aisle towards the stage area. Half way down as he was walking, he glanced at a seat to his right, keeping his eyes fixated for several seconds, then looking forward to the four steps leading up to the theater stage!
4,543 people were now in this beautiful theater, with an excitement you could feel in the air!
Justin was standing about half way up the left side of the auditorium, when suddenly, his justice instrument burst into life!
" Possible future crime here in 20 minutes! Do you wish to play the scene!? "
Justin looked over at Mike, then at Jane and

Christine! Special agent Richard Stone walked quickly along the side of the wall where Justin was standing. In a split second, each one of them was getting a telepathic message from John himself! The words came quietly and calmly into their minds.

" Remember what I said my friends!! Do nothing, all will be well!! "

Justin knew this was going to be bad, he knew from experience with the justice machines that if it said " Future crime possible! " If nothing was done to alter the event, all hell was going to break loose!!

Everyone in the team was eagle eyed watching the audience, where was this going to happen?? Justin remembered John slowing down and glancing to his side when walking down the middle of the auditorium. He had been directly glancing at a seat half way down just off the middle aisle. He noticed now that a middle aged suited well-dressed man was in that seat, he had the look of nerves on his face. Justin moved slightly as to get a look at the man's eyes before the lights started to dim.

" Ladies and gentlemen!! Please take your seats, as John will be on stage in 5 minutes! " The stereo speakers all around the theater came to life with hums..

Music started to play through the speakers! With the sound of a full orchestra playing through them, the theme tune was from the movie. " Dances with Wolves!! " The whole theater vibrated from wall to wall, and floor to ceiling, the music certainly made the moment exciting and people looked onto the dark stage, with the lighting now starting to light up a point on the stage where John was to stand.

Again the speakers kicked into life!

" Ladies and gentlemen!! Will you please welcome on stage from a nebular called 03990!!

JOHN DOE!!! "

Thunderous applause came from the whole theater, people stamped their feet in appreciation on the two levels above ground seats!

John looked into the darkness of the theater, then spoke through his miniature microphone and head piece attached to his ear.

" My dear friends!! welcome!! "

Justin strained his eyes to watch the man in the middle seat row! Justins stare would have made anyone drop dead, if looks could kill!! At that point, John spoke again.

" I would like to see all the people in the audience, can the theater lights be turned back on!? " And at that moment, the whole auditorium illuminated.

" Thank you! "

Simultaneously! Every member of the teams justice instruments sent silent messages to each wearer!

" *Crime scene happening in 30 seconds, take evasive action!!!* "

They were all searching the crowd with their eyes for the approaching crime.

John lifted his right arm, then pointed to the man in the seat he had glanced at earlier!

" The gentleman in that seat has come to destroy me!! Is that right sir!!?? "

Disbelief could be seen on hundreds of faces in the audience. A fear could be seen on the man's face now, for a moment, he was unsure what he was going to do, then quickly reached inside his coat pocket. Next to his white shirt, he gripped hold of a chrome looking hand gun.

" **Evasive action now!! Crime scene activated!!** "

Shouts of " He´s got a gun!! " Screams echoing throughout the theater.

Within a few seconds, there were over thirty guns pointed at the man from every direction from special agents and security officers!

John stood there, he was smiling and standing motionless.

" I had foreseen this event David Taylor!! That is your name isn't it!!? " John continued.

" Action could and still can be taken against you David, but this is going to end the way I have seen it! You have decided that I am to die tonight, as in your eyes, I am evil and wrong for your religious beliefs!! I am giving you a chance to have your mind clear and feeling good! Healing can be given to you to put you at rest! No more will you be afraid! "

David was shaking where he was now standing by his seat. Pointing at John was a .44 Magnum!! You could see the trembles running along the barrel! A few of the security guards were edging towards the man, shuffling very slowly an inch at a time!

" You are so wrong John Doe!! " The man had raised his voice so everyone could hear him.

Suddenly!! BaaNNNGGGG!!! The shot sounded like a cannon exploding into life as the bullet ripped into the chest within half a second. " Please stay in your seats ladies and gentlemen for security reasons!! " The speakers sounded with the theater managers voice bouncing from wall to wall.

John ran from the stage towards the man now laying on the ground on his back! He was holding a wound in his chest! Gasps of air could be heard as the blood and the air mixed making a hissing and gurgling sound!

Seven security guards and Special agent Jane Jennings were still aiming their weapons at the man, but they weren't taking any chances as he still held the magnum in his other hand.

She stretched forward to him and pulled the gun from his gripped hand, he let go as the pain was getting unbearable.

Special agent Richard Stone stood from where he had fired the shot, smoke still coming from the barrel! He had made the split decision to fire, as he knew within himself that the man was going to pull his trigger on the powerful handgun!

" He was going to kill him Justin!! I had to protect John! "

" You did what you thought best Richard! And you did save Johns life today! "

John had reached the would-be assassin!!

" David!! David!! I am going to help you, don't be afraid!! " John placed his hands on the man's chest. A golden glowing humming sound could be heard from the area of Johns arms and hands, he manipulated his fingers as to open up the bullet hole, then with his thumb and first finger, pushed them into the wound! Only a couple of seconds past, and as quickly as he had put his fingers inside the man's chest cavity, he pulled them out, only this time holding the dented bullet between them!! He was still breathing badly, and now John placed just his first finger back in the wound. His breathing started to sound better, then the gurgling sound from his lungs disappeared! Guns still pointed at him, he opened his eyes wide, then looked down at his chest as he moved to sit up. John placed both his hands at the side of the man's skull, then the glowing and humming sound started again!!

" Take this healing and light into your life David!! Be free from this day of the torment you have been suffering in your mind! "

As John moved his hands away from the man's head, David put his hands to cover his ashamed face, he

sat there crying hard and loud like a small child!
John looked over at special agent Jennings, then at special agent Richard Stone! They knew from his face that he wanted them both to take David back stage to Johns dressing room and wait for later to talk to him.

Taking only a few minutes for everyone to calm and be assured that everything was now going to be ok, security were back in their original positions.

John was facing the audience once again, and just like always, wearing a smile that was contagious. Looking on that smile would have put any one at ease.

" David is going to be alright! He is resting back stage with two of my friends, he is recovering from a mental illness that anyone could have! I will not be pressing charges on this man, and later I will talk with him. " John gazed up at the two higher sets of seats, then spoke again.

" Some of you in the top back seats are maybe wishing you could be closer to the stage as to be closer to me, as to maybe get a chance for healing, because that is what you have come for!? Well!! I have some good news for you all! Every person here today will get healing energy given to them! You are all invited to see where I come from! You will not have left your seats, but you will be taken in an instant to a beautiful place in space and time! You will not feel afraid as the energy surges through and around you! You will see things that you never thought were possible! You are going to feel a peace you have never felt before, and some of you will not want to return! This will be your choice. Freewill is there for you all! "

Whispers and murmurs could be heard throughout the theater; the atmosphere was becoming statically charged!

" In a few moments my friends! Our journey can begin! Any one not wishing to experience this event may freely leave now, you always have a choice!! "
You could see excitement on all the faces there, even the security officers all looking around them to see if anyone was getting up to leave!? An older lady stood and started to walk towards the rear of the theater! She turned while still walking and said!

" I will be back in a few minutes!! If we are going on a journey, I need the ladies washroom first!!! "
At that moment, you would have thought that a comedian had been on stage and told the best joke ever!! Laughter echoed throughout the theater with deafening sounds bouncing from ear to ear! John replied.

" Certainly madam!!! " Again, laughter came back for the second time. It was amazing to think that only a few minutes before an assassination attempt had taken place!

" If we are all ready now!? I give you this gift from my world to you!! "
The speakers came to life again! The lights were turned off! A small pinpoint of light shone on the stage and on John!

John raised his arms and hands and put his palms facing towards the audience.

Music from an unseen orchestra now blaring out epic music! It started to increase in tones and volume. The resemblance to a Native American was astounding, so!! The opening music was from the movie! " **The Last of the Mohicans!!** "
Native drums could be heard from the speakers, and again the atmosphere was electrifying!

Little sparks of light began to emerge everywhere in and around the seating area! Johns body started to glow bright white and dazzled the souls sitting in their seats! The guards and special agents stood what appeared to be in space! The walls of the theater disappeared! The sparks of light settled to a constant glow! Thousands of illuminating lights shone!!

As the music sounded more, the immediate area was floating in space, as if suspended with no strings or cords attached, just suspended and now drifting in space!! Sounds of amazement and smiles came from people. They were all hoping for something good to happen this day, but this was nothing to what they expected.

While the music was playing, everything was seemingly blending in with floating and drifting in space! The music tones echoing and synchronizing with every little movement.

All the sparks of light, like little sprites moving with them, following them. As a little time went by, the speed of the surrounding space accelerated, stars in the distance were getting bigger and glowing more brightly.

A tranquility came over each and every soul travelling in this vacuum! Some even agreed at that point that to stay like this was a great idea and understood why John had said " Some of you will not want to come back! " But! This was just the beginning of the journey.

More and more smiles appeared on a lot of faces, they looked on in Awe as colors of the rainbow could be seen mixing and swirling in space! Then!! Chrome and silver mixing together in more swirls, like mixing oil and water together, making a misty smoke effect before them.

Purple! Red! Violet! All running side by side around and over them very fast. From where they sat, it was almost like they were sitting right in the center of a firework display! Beautiful!!

To every ones front left, you could see a plume of white mist with again every color flickering and shining through the mist.

John turned to face the mist, he knew where he was. This was " Nebular 03990 ! "

The seating area of the whole theater was descending through the mist. Lower and lower descending slower now, and then coming into view was what Justin himself had seen many years previously when he first met John.

Everyone could see the white and marble pillars, looking just like they did before, only this time Justin thought they had grown in size as to accommodate the theater seats and stage. And, from that stage, John looked over to Justin and smiled, remembering the first conversation they both had!

A soft cushion effect activated when the theater complex came to a stop and gentle landing in front of the Greek looking " amphitheater! "

John turned once more towards the audience, then amazing as it was, the speakers came to life once again!

" Here before you now stands a place of beauty and spiritual guidance! Many beings like myself have come to learn many words of wisdom, from teachers of every level of life!! Today! You are being privileged to be in a theater within a theater, where soon you will see things you might not understand! But! moments after, you will!! I have asked for some of my spirit friends to come here, and every one of them didn't hesitate to be able to come forward and give you some energy gifts! "

The words had not been out of Johns mouth 20

seconds when lines of lights aiming for the Greek looking stage before them descended like they had been beamed down from an episode of " Star Trek!! " Standing before them now stood male and female human looking bodies, every one of them with huge smiles, just like John himself!

There were a few laughter sounds as all the audience gazed on 12 naked bodies, each with a skin radiating golden light! It was only seconds before the crowd accepted that there wasn't anything wrong with a naked body, as that was what they had been given when each one of them were born on earth!

Only man had tainted the human flesh to make people feel ashamed! Man, over the centuries had corrupted the beautiful human form, and covered it up to hide fears and embarrassment!

Justin looked on as his eyes grew wider for what he was looking at. At the end row of the light beings, he was fixated on the 30-year-old looking man!

Justin walked a little closer to the stage. There was no ground beneath his feet, and when he walked, it was like walking on cushions of air.

As he reached the stage area, he gazed on this perfectly looking blond guy, and as all of them, smiled at him with piercing blue eyes, just like Johns did the first time!

A deep Swedish accent came from the golden glowing beings lips!

" Hello my dear friend Justin!! "

Justin shocked! Stood there speechless, as before him stood a rejuvenated Maximus Lindström!!!

" My dear old friend Maximus!! What the hell are you doing here!? How is this possible?? Are you real?? "

Maximus placed one of his hands on Justins shoulder, and the hand just passed straight through Justins arm!!

" We are all thought and light right now Justin, and only on earth can we take on a body form! You will see me again soon, and we will need to catch up on stories since I left my body!! "

" I have really missed you Maximus! Young Frankie talks about you often as well, and I'm sure Bernadette would love to see you again! "

" When you next see me Justin, there will not be time to see both of them, as you will be in a different Country, and the work we all have to do there will need to be done quickly! But! Say to Bernadette I was asking after her and Frankie. "

Maximus Continued.

" I can hear your thoughts Justin. I know you are confused as to why I am here! The truth is that I wanted to help mankind! When I was a Kriminal Inspektör back in Göteborg and then you introduced me to the Ultimate instruments of justice! I awoke from my physical death!! I always wanted there to be an afterlife, and I wasn't disappointed to find out it was true! There was " Life after Life!!! "

" There is so much to learn Justin, there are so many beautiful things and places in space to explore! What you are seeing in the third dimension is just a beginning! You are going to be truly amazed when your turn comes, and I can tell you that that is a long time away! "

" There hasn't been a day since you died that I haven't thought about you, and where you might be!? When you left, there was a void in our life! Yet! Here you are! You are just like John when I first saw him here all those years ago. I must be honest though! This is the first time I have seen you looking younger and no clothes on!!! " Maximus gave a deep quiet laugh as he smiled back at Justin:

" Being free Justin, also means having no inhibitions,

and being able to float around vast areas of star systems visiting other worlds! And yes!! There are many life systems on worlds spread out for millions of Kilometers! Some are in the young stage of evolution, and others are 15,000 years + ahead of Earth!! When a new invention happens on earth, and it helps mankind, the chances are that an un seen entity like we can be, gives the thought to someone, then the idea forms and takes shape! " Maximus looked up and towards John, who now was sending out thoughts to all the light beings on the stage area! With John and the 12 beings smiling, and sending pure love from their central body, they each lifted their arms to chest Hight, then turned their hand palms towards the audience! Some of the crowd were dripping tears, but tears of emotional happiness! Even before what was going to happen next was upon them!

The sparks of light spheres were still suspended all around the theater, each one pulsating and twinkling like distant stars.

Suddenly!! Rays of bright lines of light came from every beings hand palms! Like guitar strings straight and true! Each ray of light aiming at each light sphere! until every one of them had beams of pure light penetrating each center of all spheres! They all simultaneously started to grow another 10 centimeters. Orange, red, violet! Beautiful colors mixing like oils on a paint pallet!

John gave yet another big smile.

" Take these love and light spheres with the love that it´s intended for! Each one of you from now on, will know no fear, and your life will enhance a thousand times! All we ask of you, is to use these new healing powers where they are needed! You now will have the gift of healing! This new beginning will be the start of a new age on earth! All your negative feelings and thoughts will evaporate like rain drops in the heat of the mid-day sun! "

At the end of that last word, the spheres descended to each person in the audience! They entered the bodies of every one! You could see a sea of smiles as each person rose to their feet, they held their right hand up with their palm facing out wards! When each of the four and a half thousand hands were in place, light with enormous power shot like straight arrows to a center point above the theater! Each line of light joined to a new center above them. Looking at the spectacular event was Justin. His eyes were emotional too at this point. He felt a love so powerful, it pierced his very soul. Joy of a magnitude of 5 earth quakes vibrated in and around him! For split seconds, each person touched the divine creator with their hearts, and knowing that they were never alone, and never would be!

John lowered his arms, then followed by all the beings on stage, then all the audiences arms lowered, and each person turned to another, smiles lit up the whole theater again, and at that, every one hugged each other with a renewed love and knowing in their hearts!

" You are among the first to be given this new energy. This will be something to tell your great grandchildren, your life expectancy will allow you to live for an average 50 years longer, and when your time is right to depart earth, you will leave gladly to continue another part of your existence, then new beginnings will happen for each and every one of you!! "

As they all looked at the stage, walls started to appear again with the gold leaf from the ceiling following right behind them! Instantaneously!

Everyone was now back in the same spot they had left an hour previously. Time had speeded up! It had slowed down! It stopped! It was everything and nowhere all at the same time!

Looking at the stage, all the beings had left, there was only John standing there, and that perfect smile of enlightenment written once again all over his face!

" Ladies and gentlemen! Go in the love and light which you have been given, and pass the energy along, so all can feel what you have felt! Thank you from the bottom of my heart!! "

All the audience stood, then hands started to hit off each other, then the slaps became deafening as applause shook the very foundations the theater was built on! These were well built foundations, just like the new ones that John had laid out to all the people there!!

Opening the dressing room door, John could see a new smile on a face in front of him.

" I see by your smile David that you now know a lot more than when you entered the theater!? " David Taylor stood to hug John! Two very nervous special agents jerked into life towards him, to stop any other attack on John, but, John spoke as Jane and Richard headed in his direction.

" He is fine now my dear friends! He is now like you, all the negative energy, and trauma has been taken away! " With that moment, David wrapped his arms around John, then looked at him straight from eyeball to eyeball!

" Thank you for my life John! How can I ever repay you for your kindness!?? "

" Your mind has become well! Your heart is now filled with a love you have never felt before! That is all the repayment I need! Live well David! You are free to go!! "

Richard and Jane stared at each other with a curiousness about it!

" Before you go David, I will tell you in front of these two agents what I knew was to happen! When I looked at the seat you were going to be sitting in, I had vibrations of thoughts and pictures as to what your intentions were going to be! I also saw Richard shoot you before you could pull the trigger! You were going to pull the trigger, and I saw you fall to the ground! I knew that only with you having this event happen to you, were you going to be able to be cured! Or the alternative was your death! That would have been a waist of life, so I let it all happen, and to you Richard, thank you for my life, and you did the right thing for every one!! So, you see! More than one life was saved today! As each life is precious!! "

Without saying a word, Richard smiled and started to lead David to the back-theater door.

John faced the round large dining table in front of him. He was looking at the center where an envelope was laying, it was gold embossed lettering! At the back of the envelope was a wax seal! It was the personal seal from the Pope himself!! The ring of the Holy Father had struck the red wax firmly and indented into it with clear lettering. John had also foreseen this too! His foresight was a beautiful gift! He leaned forward towards the envelope, holding it in his hands gently, he could feel the vibration from it! There were anxious and fearful vibrations, with just a little hope that John was here for the good he said he stood for! He opened the letter, then started to read in his mind!

His Holiness
Pope Francis

**A request that " John Doe "
Come to the Vatican to have conversation
With the Holy Father.
R: S: V: P.**

Justin walked through the dressing room door to see John with the letter still in his hands!

" What I said was to happen will happen Justin! Can you reply to this for me and call the Vatican to inform them we will be there the day after we finish at the football stadium!? "

" Of course, John! " Justin took the letter from him, then proceeded to use his cell phone to contact the Vatican. " Hello!! This is special agent Justin Webber for and on behalf of John Doe from the United States! Security letter access code is #0921763. Please confirm!?::::::::::

CHAPTER 9

God! Pope Francis!
&
John Doe!

The executive jet soared through the clouds with all the team and John on board!

All the team were now relaxing for their 7-hour flight from New York to Rome!

Carol Hoover the TV journalist sat with her cameraman going over the last couple of days footage, trying to edit best they could to send back to the studio!

The best report she had done was of the Yankee stadium, where over 52,000 had attended. Of course, there would be those who would disbelieve that what the people at the stadium saw was just special effects! But then how could anyone explain what happened when the people started leaving, and people were glowing with a radiant brightness and smiles on every face!?

A few hours after that, many reports getting to the TV stations reporting healing after healing from everyday humans to love ones in nursing homes, hospitals, and private clinics!

With over 65,000 getting healing from John and his spirit beings, the amount was starting to double and treble. It was multiplying faster than a speeding racing car on a track! This was gaining pace and had no signs of slowing down. These beautiful happenings were escalating, but within complete control has to how John could envisage these events!

John sat facing all of the team now waiting to hear what was to happen next.

" Once again my dear friends, we are on our way to

another event to see the Holy Father in Rome! The Catholic church has so many questions for me to answer! They will be given them!! As we speak, there are gatherings around the world to plan an event that will threaten what I stand for! Again, I know of what is to happen, and I will let you know nearer the time as to what plans we will put into place! Right now, this is just the tip of the iceberg (As they say!). Each one of you will need to be stronger than you ever have been in your lives soon, and just know that everything is going to work out for the best! " John just like clockwork! Gave his everlasting smile. In the short time he had been on this beautiful planet, he had seen so much beauty all around, and also the dark side to the world! Sitting there contemplating on the next few days, he knew that all the plans that had been put into place, were in place, even long before he had arrived. Of course, things could change just like things could change, but, with honest and trustworthy people on his team, and the backing of the American President, he had achieved so much, in so little time!

John turned to the team again!

" I need to tell you that your justice machines will be updated and modified to take on the new vibrations that are being transmitted to earth in the next two days, so don't worry if you hear them doing strange things! You will all find out eventually what the new information is for! You have trusted me 100% so far, please keep that trust, and know that something so powerful and wonderful is going to happen, and all of you will be the first of many to experience it at close range! Your great grandchildren will know of these days and their great grandfather or grandmother being the first! Each one of you will have your names carved in stone for centuries!! "

Special agent Jane Jennings sat next to agent Mike Hendry, she smiled at him after what John had said, then winked at him.

" Do you want to have great grandchildren with me Mike!!?? " Coffee splattered over Justin as he faced Mike! Poor Mike nearly choked on the beverage, as Justin, agent Christine Murdoch laughed loudly, everyone else smiled as they saw Mike wipe the coffee drips from his face and apologized to Justin for giving him an unexpected shower!

Mike looked at his watch then said. " Is it a leap year!!?? And that is the best marriage proposal I've ever heard! "

Laughter bounced around the jet as they headed in their next direction!

Leonardo da Vinci/ Fiumicino airport is situated about 28 Km from the Vatican. The airport security was on high alert prior to Johns arrival. Four limousines were on standby to transport John and his team to the Vatican. Waiting for the jet to land, several plain clothes Vatican secret service (Swiss guards) were anticipating the crowds on the other side of the airport exit points!

"If you have ever visited the Vatican, you have seen the stoic guards that look like they missed the bus to the local Renaissance Festival. The truth is they are a high-end military force made up of top ex-Swiss soldiers. And don't let those spears fool you, they can shred you to pieces with them. If that doesn't work, they have one of the finest firearms collections on the planet to finish the job.

The Pontifical Swiss Guard is over 500 years old, making it one of the oldest standing military units in the world. Founded officially on January 22nd, 1506 by Pope Julius II, at the time the Swiss Guard was really a mercenary force. Back in the 14th century, Swiss fighters were known to be some of the best anywhere, renowned for their ability to take on far larger armies and win. In the 1400s, Swiss mercenaries proved themselves in battle time and time again, sometimes while fighting for the Holy Roman Empire. In a way, their small footprint with big results was a precursor to today's elite special forces teams."

So in other words, these boys are not to be messed with, or you will feel their rath! This was a peaceful event, but every one needed to be on guard to this new arrival of a being from another world, and days of planning had gone into organizing Johns visit to see The Holy Father!

The plane was directed to a large air craft hanger set aside for V:I:P´s. Pistols, machine guns, and sharp shooters with sniper rifles were carried by the men waiting for John and his team!

As the plane came to a halt just inside the hanger, men scrambled with the small aircraft steps pushing it into position outside the now motionless plane! The jet engines toned down and then went silent with a low humming and whistling sound! Whirring motor noises could be heard as the hydraulic door opened and slid sideways revealing the inner view.

The head of the Swiss guard officer stood with a smile at the bottom of the steps, he waited as John surveyed this new land, then slowly walked down the few steps.

" Welcome to our Country John! We have been looking forward to meeting you, and I know The Holy Father is looking forward to talking with you! "

John took the guards hand and gently shook it, John felt the good in the man, he knew he had a good heart and dedication towards the Pope! He would lay down his life for the Holy Father without hesitation if needed!

" It is an honor for me to be here in this famous and beautiful land! Thank you for letting us be here, and I speak on behalf of my team of friends with me too!! "

There it was again, always that beautiful glowing smile, it never leaves his face, even when confronted by negative happenings, just a smile upon a smile!

Driving in the motorcade towards the large airport security gates! They could see hundreds of reporters and civilians lining the outside roads, cameras clicking into action as the vehicles sped through the gates, and people cheering and smiling.

" Stop the limousine please!! " John asked in a low calm voice, the vibration of his voice reached the ears of the limo driver. The Swiss guard officer looked shocked and afraid as he asked what was wrong!?

The vehicle stopped suddenly with the rest of the guards in the other limos scrambling out of each and taking the protective stance like they were coming under attack!

Justin drew his side arm from the holster and jumped out and crouched down beside the open car door, then quickly followed by Agents Jennings and Stone! The crowd was still cheering, but, some were looking afraid also as to why all the cars had stopped!?

John started to walk towards the crowd, he was heading straight for a wheelchair, and a small boy of 7 years old!

" John sir!! We really need to be getting to the Vatican! His Holiness will be waiting! " The Officer in charge looked concerned as the crowd was moving closer to get a good look at this healing being!

" My dear friend! My main purpose is to give healing to those who truly need it! Before me now is this beautiful child, a child that we can all see needs something good to happen for him! Am I not here to give the world a healing hand or two!!?? " John knelt down to the Hight of the young boy. What greeted him would have made a glass eye cry, as a smile came back from the seven-year-old! He held out his hands to John, then in a cheeky kind voice said.

" I knew you would stop and help me John, you have come from heaven to do good, and I knew you would stop! I prayed all night for you to see me today, and my prayer was heard! "

For the first time since his arrival, John was showing a tear or two building in his eyes. He wasn't sad, just a happy emotion touching his heart! From the mouth of a child, this was good to see. The world had turned ugly in past years, and now, sitting before him was a hope! A hope of a child that a prayer might just have been answered to someone who cared!!

John winked at him! " Then I had better see what I can do for you young man!! " He said.

The nearest people around John could see him place his hands on the boys head gently. The now familiar glow of orange came from his hands. A slight breeze came from the main road lifting Johns hair to blow in the rising unseen wind. One woman near said.

" He´s glowing! He´s glowing! "

Looking on with amazement was a crowd who were witnessing a modern-day miracle! Many people for a long time had been wishing and praying for something good to happen in this now dark world of pain and suffering! And here it was!! A man stopping to help heal a young boy who had never known what it was like to walk!

" From to-day! You no longer need this wheelchair! Stand up and walk to the car with me young Anthony! " The young boy still smiling and eyes now sparkling like diamonds in the sunlight, started to raise his body out of the chair. He stood proud as his back straightened up, then balancing slowly, he moved his legs for the first time in his life!!

Cheering erupted in the road, then clapping as the boy held Johns hand, then took his first steps with a healing being!

All the Swiss guard and special agents were shedding a few tears between themselves too! John once again had shown the world what is possible with love being the reason for doing it!

The seven-year-old stood at the limousine and turned to John. With an almighty burst of speed, he threw his arms around Johns legs! " Thankyou! Thank you John the healer! " The boys smile had lit up the whole street and smiles of joy came on many around him. John replied.

" You young man!! You are worth the energy! You will grow normally now, and you might just win some running races! " John laughed a little, it was good to see Anthony with a renewed faith, and more hope in his heart, and just for meeting a beautiful man who gave him back his legs!!

" In another time Anthony, you and I will walk along a road of color, we will run and play in the fields of life! You will fly among the stars like I have done, you will reach places you never thought possible! You sent out your loving thoughts to me, and I heard you!! Thank you for that trust! We will meet again! " Hugging the boy, John stepped into the limo and turned to look at every one standing around! The boys guardian stood by the now empty wheelchair, there was tear trails marking his face cheeks! John waved to him, and then the people, then with the agents and Swiss guards returning to the vehicles, the convoy sped off again towards the highway!!

The chief Swiss guard turned to John.
" I can now see what all the excitement is about now!
You have shown to me you are genuine and real!
Thank you!! " All the team in Johns vehicle smiled
along with John, as yet again a beautiful start was
just beginning in a new country!

Outside the (" **Appartamento pontificio** ") door.
The Swiss guards in full Ceremonial attire, stood
proud and vigilant as the plane clothes Swiss guards
along with the special agents sat on the velvet and
gilded benches while John was allowed to pass
through the magnificent entrance to his Holiness!
His Holiness stood gazing at the man before him!
Johns smile was catching, as now a wonderful smile
came back from the Pope! In a calm soothing deep
voice, Pope Francis spoke to John with a sincerity
that John could feel in the room and went straight to
his heart!
" I have been waiting these last days John, and a
hope in my heart that you were as humble and full of
love as they said you were! I can see and feel that
you are! " His holiness continued.
" I am honored to be the Pope at this time in the
worlds history! To come face to face with a being
from another world! Strange words for me to say, but
good words now that I have met you! You can also
understand John why the church has been concerned
about your visit to our world!? " John looked at his
Holiness and stood closer to him and without
warning, knelt down before him, then gently took the
Popes hand and kissed the Papal ring!
" From my world to yours, thank you for this audience
with you, and for you your Holiness, I have things to
tell you that you want to know, I can hear your

questions coming from your heart, and they are wise questions! " The Pope was so overwhelmed by Johns words and gesture, from that moment, the Pope had no problem in trusting this beautiful being 100%!
" My Swiss guard chief told me of the event outside the airport gates earlier! We call these things, miracles John, because that´s what they are for us! With all the hate in this world, we pray for guidance and help from God!! And now, here is our help before me right now! 2000 years ago, a pair of hands and two feet came to earth to save man! He gave his life so we would be spared! In today´s world, people have started to drift away from churches and chapels all around the world! Their hearts grow weaker as time rushes by, and they kneel and pray for good to return soon. Hope can come in all shapes and sizes John, and I look with these eyes on you as a being from God!! Are you from God John!? "
With eyes sparkling again, John looked at this Righteous man!
" My dear Pope Francis! Like you, I talk to God every day! I ask what his will is for me, and how to help mankind! I have many gifts that the creator gave to me freely, and part of those gifts is to give healing free to those who need it! I have free will, and that is a wonderful gift in itself! In my home world among the stars and colors, magnificent thoughts and inspirations flood the space around every star! We pick up vibrations of love from every galaxy where there is so much life!! And to answer that question Holy Father, Yes!! There are many species of God's creation dotted for billions of miles! Some are in the early stages of evolution, others are hundreds of thousand times ahead of Earth! For most of time until now, man has been left alone to develop and grow! It is only now that cries of despair have been heard

as the pain of mankind gets more stronger on a daily basis! Man is just about to receive a chance and a choice to repair their hearts! That day is fast approaching, and the world will decide!

Prophecies have been here on earth for many centuries, and sadly, most of them have been misinterpreted through time, added to, and some information taken away! I know Holy Father that beneath these floors of this Holy place, there are relics and scrolls that not even you know about! God has asked me to guide you and take you to these wonderful items of Love and Light, and from God himself!! " The Holy Father smiled more as he looked on Johns honest face:

" I believe you are a child from God John! I know of many items and scrolls in the Vatican vaults!! " At that moment, John interrupted his Holiness!

" Way below your vaults, are more hidden scrolls and wonderful discoveries that the church hid hundreds of years ago after their discovery! At that time, the Pope of that time decided to keep them secret, and when he passed on to the next level of existence, the secrets were gone and forgotten as he took that knowledge with him! I can take you to that knowledge your Holiness! "

Looking a little surprised, the Pope thought deeply, then answered John.

" If this is true John, then God has meant for you to show me, then it will be decided if the world should find out about such treasures! " He continued.

" For many years people have said we have kept secrets from the world, we have kept some things from man as not to destroy the documents with pollution from the air! Many documents have deteriorated through time, and to expose them to the air would help them deteriorate faster! "

" Your Holiness! Please allow me to show you what God wants you to see and know!! "

" Then it will be so John!! "

John moved closer to the Pope, then took hold of the hands to begin their short journey!

Pope Francis held gently the hands that were healing the world, he felt a warmth from them, and felt a power that he had never felt before! He felt safe as John uttered a few words!

" Let it be so!! " John said. Pope Francis looked towards the room doors, then was waiting for John to guide him to the vaults!

But instead, strange things were beginning to happen! The walls of the Popes rooms started to fade and become transparent! The floors in all the rooms did the same! They were being suspended in midair! They could see all the Swiss guards and special agents in the next room, but they could not see back into the room as it was happening!

John projected his will for them both to go to the Vatican vaults, and to where there was a hidden section.

Floating sensations, feelings of moving towards the lower floors, but! It was like the rooms were travelling towards them and at a steady speed.

Pope Francis held a little tighter to Johns hands now, as the strange views were coming closer and closer! They could both feel the floor under their feet now, as they slowly walked along the rows of books and paper scrolls! In a few seconds, they reached the end section, where there was a solid wall! The wall was part of the Vatican's older foundations, but John knew of the secret passage that lay behind it!

" Since my time as the leader of the Catholic church John! I have been privileged to see some wonderful things, but! This is fascinating what we had just done! How is that possible!? "

John smiled yet again at the Holy Father.

" Everything is possible in Gods worlds, we just need to un-restrict ourselves from our abilities, which are hindering progression for man! "

John placed both his hands on the white painted wall in front of him. Once again the wall started to fade just like the Popes apartment ones!

In front of them now stood a 3meter cast iron vault door, on the door was a wheel of metal something like a ships wheel, but smaller. With a slight thought from his mind, John moved the wheel in a anti clockwise manner until the bolt on the same side clanged into open position!

In slow motion, the huge heavy door started to open towards them. Stone steps led downwards in a spiraling pattern. As if by magic, old lanterns jumped into life, lighting their way downwards! Shadows displayed the cobwebs left by the spiders over the centuries. Many steps they walked down, then! An open passageway stood before them! Again, the old lanterns lit up the entire area around them.

Looking back at them were two large marble statues! They were statues of the Swiss guard in full uniform! It looked like they had just been put there only a few weeks previously, but, they had stood guard there for hundreds of years! One each side of a massive double solid oak arched door with iron hinges upon the wood! As they approached the door, they saw writing carved into the right door panel. (" **Deo Ac Veritati " : For God and for truth!**)

Pope Francis placed his right hand and moved it along the fine smooth wood!

" It´s hard to believe that I am one of the first to see this secret door hidden from us for all these centuries! Maybe now the world is ready for what lies on the other side!? I am ready John Doe! " He looked at John next to him, then thought of the double doors opening in his mind, and at that! Both sides of the door started to creak and groan as they moved over the centuries of dust that had accumulated! Moving inwards, they revealed a darkness before them. More old lanterns burst into flames under each glass as they adorned the walls of this chamber. In a half moon shape in front of them, stood six pillars about two meters in Hight and one meter apart! On the surface of each pillar was different objects in all shapes and sizes, but, small enough to stand upon the top of them!

His Holiness moved towards the first pillar on the left in front of him, stood quietly gazing at an object that defied gravity! As he looked upon it with amazement, he saw before him a diamond shape crystal with a chrome looking band along the middle of it, circling the whole crystal. Above the band, the identical shape spun around reflecting the lights from the lanterns. On the walls of the chamber, you could now see sparks of lights bouncing as the object was spinning. Between the surface of the pillar and the object, there was 2 or 3 centimeters of space. " How is this possible John!? " John looked back at him and spoke softly once again.

" Anything is possible Holy Father! You just need to open your mind more as to possibilities in Gods world! Please take hold of the object! There is a secret within it and is waiting to show you! " Hesitating slightly, Pope Francis leaned forward next to the spinning shape. Slowly cupping his hands around the object, it started to spin faster, a sound of angelic music could be heard coming from it at the same time! Tones of music in perfect angelic harmony bounced around and off the walls of the chamber. Then in a beautiful deep smooth voice he heard words!

" I have been waiting a long time for this day child!! In your mind, you have always heard me and my quest for you! To-day you are hearing my voice for the first time! " At that moment! An energy burst shot in rays of light to the Popes heart area! Every spin of the object sent waves and waves of pure light to his body, mind, and began to refresh his inner spiritual awakening! He fell quickly to his knees as he knew at that precise moment, he was talking to the almighty himself!!

" My dear father God!! I am humble in your presence! Please enlighten me as to your will today!? "

You could hear the smile in Gods voice, as he spoke quietly and calmly to his chosen child. Pope Francis!!

" You are here today my child, as it is time for the world to change as we know it! John is here to help with the world change you will see very shortly! Evil has grown so much over the centuries, and now comes the time for change for the good of mankind! A brighter sunlight will be seen all over the world, a new world is dawning!! In three sunrises, you will speak to all followers of the church! You will know the right time, as I will tell you my child! This device you are holding will act as a communication passageway! The last Holy Father to hold the object you have now in your hands, thought he was going in sane!! so locked all the relics behind the doors behind you! I can assure you Pope Francis!! That you are sane and well! Your heart knows this to be true! As I speak, you are feeling the vibration of pure love and light entering your whole existence! From now on, the word GOD!!! will not be just a word for man to utter, it will mean again what it meant centuries ago!! Peace, Love, and helping hands all around this earth!

It shall be again! " With so much emotion he was feeling, water droplets were forming in his eyes, he felt so much peace and a kindness he had never felt before! He knew this was the words and sounds from GOD himself! Man was just about to get that extra helping hand in life, and it was GOD! who was stepping in to help heal a troubled world!

" The object you see on the next pillar is a small mirror! I call it the " Mirror of Truth!! " When you hold the mirror up to your face, you will see the truth develop before your eyes, it will show you truth, and falseness! Use this item wisely my child! Know that this mirror speaks the truth always!! For now, the pillar next to that has a living flame! When you hold the flame, it will grow to the Hight of the person that placed it on the ground. It is a blue eternal flame and will never go out! If someone walks through this flame, you will not be burnt, you will feel a cool breeze. This is a one-way portal and will take you to Heaven itself!! Once through the flame, it will not be possible to return to that time and place! The remaining three items you need not concern yourself with, as John knows what to do with them! " At the words of God saying that, John went to the three remaining pillars and took each object and placed them gently into his coat pocket!

His Holiness never once thought to question God about the final three objects John had picked up! After all, God was all knowing powerful, and Great!!

" To-day is the beginning of a new beginning my child! We will talk much in the near future! Take my Love and light with you! Finally!! Go over to the Holy water fountain by the left wall! There is a small chest that will hold the three objects you now know about! Sprinkle some Holy water over the blue flame, this will stop it growing before it´s needed! Place all three

310

until you need them, they will serve you well! Until we speak again My child Pope Francis! Love and peace be with you!! "

As the Pope turned to look at John, they were both wearing a renewed smile upon their faces!

" I think that secret was worth waiting for your Holiness!? "

" I am speechless John! The words that I have on my tongue is. " Love in its purest form!! "

" This is just the start your Holiness! The best is yet to come!! "

The huge doors closed behind them as they started to walk along the same dusty floor they had come along. Tracing their footprints back, they started to float towards the Popes apartments!

All the floors and walls were now re-appearing as quick as they had vanished! Hard floor now could be felt beneath their feet!

Looking at the clock on the large dining table, they could see they had only been gone 2 minutes. Again, time had slowed down and speeded up all at once!!

Pope Francis walked over to a cabinet, unlocked the panel, then opened it up to reveal a space just the right size for the small chest! He locked it afterwards, then placed the key around his neck and tucked the small cord inside his robes!

" Today has certainly been an eye opener John! Also, to have been in the presence of God himself! I certainly have been blessed! "

" Holy Father! I am going very soon, and this will be the first and last time you will see me! Your challenges are just about to start, and you will see the world changing at a good pace! The Holy flame you have, must be placed in Saint Peters Square! You will tell the people you had this gift given to you from God!! If they choose to leave this world now, their path will lead to heaven and all their loved ones who went before them! When checking the mirror of truth, you need to know who your enemies are, as some of them are close to you now! I need for you to allow one of my special agents to be part of your team your Holiness! His name is Agent Richard Stone! He also carries an instrument from God! This will only be used in special circumstances, he will know of any immediate threats to you! You can trust this man with your life your Holiness!! "

" I believe you John!! God chose well when he picked you to come to our world! "

" Pope Francis, we are all doing something that is going to change the world for the better! Each soul in this world needs to know that there is love and goodness still here, we just need to look! "

John walked slowly to the apartment door.

" God be with you always John!! "

The pope shook Johns hand, then felt more energy running through his fingers and wrist!

" It was a pleasure your Holiness!! "

Turning the golden door handles, he opened the door, the team was waiting patiently, and the Swiss guards stood straight as John walked towards the exit from the Vatican!

" Follow me ladies and gentlemen! " They did what he asked.

Carol Hoover and her cameraman followed behind while they all headed for the limo´s.

" This has been Carol Hoover live from the Vatican where a secret meeting has just taken place with The Holy Father! Pope Francis! We will be updating you as we get more information! "

Once again all the team sat in the limousine, then noticing a person missing, Justin turned to John and was just about to ask, when!!

" To answer your question Justin, Richard is on special assignment to the Pope as from now! He will not be joining us at this time! " John gave a smile more than he usually does, then continued!

" A lot of things have now been put into place for a future event that the world will soon know of! One of the final stages will mean me leaving you all for a while, but!! No matter what goes on in the next 2 days, just know that again it´s meant to be, and all will be revealed in a short time! I am placing Justin and Mike in charge as of tomorrow morning. Take notice of your newly updated Instruments of justice, they will guide you well as to the action you are going to need to take! " There were some puzzled looks as John spoke, but then that's the way John dealt with things, and he always knew what was best to know, and what wasn't at that time!

The whole top floor of the hotel was reserved for John and his team of agents, as well as Carol, and her cameraman! Security guards and police were on guard on the ground floor, and the penthouse floor. Justin knocked on Johns room door and waited for a reply:

" Come in Justin! I have been expecting you! " Walking in the room, then closing the door behind him, Justin saw by Johns face that there was a slight concern as to near future events!

" Tomorrow morning Justin, I will go to the airport in the limousine by myself. For reasons I can´t tell you of right now, you will know soon enough as to what is taking place! I can tell you that this will cut down on casualties and death! The event that will reveal itself, will make you understand why I have to do this my way! Again it´s all part of Gods plan, and I trust God 100%!! "

" And I trust you 100% John, and I always have,

right from the first time I saw you! I have known in my heart that this is all leading up to a massive event that will change the world for the good!! I also know that my heart tells me some people will be sacrificed to help the world, to save millions more! When you connected with me telepathically John, something rubbed off on me, as now I can feel some of your thoughts and concerns! I am behind you all the way, and if need be, I will die for you and God!! "

John moved to where Justin was standing.

" Your heart is a good one Justin! I knew I had chosen wisely when our paths crossed! I can only see so far into the future, but I know that some things can be changed for the good of mankind! So, I hope in my soul that you will be able to return to your wife and son eventually! There is one more thing I need to do for you before I leave tomorrow. " John placed his hands on Justins chest.

" Did you forget Justin!? The bomb splinter from your secret service activity in Sweden all those years ago!? You never did get it seen to did you!?? "

Justin smiled and laughed a little as he looked into Johns eyes. At that moment, a glowing of golden light moved through Johns hands, then started to glow with a silver light, then his hands calmed down to a pink flesh color and back to normal.

" Now you will be in perfect health to watch over your team! Thank you Justin! "

" I will see you before you go in the morning John, so rest well for whatever journey you are taking tomorrow! Good night old friend!! "

" Good night young Justin!!!...............

CHAPTER 10

John Doe!
&
Hell on Earth

It was nearly 1:30 in the morning and knocking on a hotel room door was special agent Jane Jennings!

" Hey Mike! I was getting a bit lonely. Hope you don't mind me coming to chat with you!? I couldn't sleep. "

" Sweet Jane! I´m glad you did! I was thinking of you quite a lot, and I guess to be honest, I think we have a strong connection after being around John these last few days! "

" What do you think is going to happen next with John? I mean all the hush hush stuff is one thing, but I'm sensing something bad is going to happen, along with the supposed to be good things for the world! "

" Jane!! All of us have been sensing good and bad vibes, so in most ways, we are all connected. The world as we know it is just about to change for the better, and I know it´s going to be good. I believe some shit has to happen first, then all the positive stuff can edge its way through! Want a coffee!? "

" Please Mike! "

Placing the kettle in the cradle, he switches it on to boil! " Sugar and milk? "

" Yah! Thanks! "

" In my training as a special agent Mike, I learned a lot, only now with all this new and unheard-of stuff, I feel like I'm drowning in technology! I guess it´s just change I'm afraid of at times! I am in my thirties now, and feel life is passing me by! Don´t get me wrong, I love my job, and now more so because I have such a good bunch of buddies beside me. John is one of the best things to happen to me, even leaving the Presidents detail for this special mission! And this mission is special! It´s not every day you get to protect an Alien!! "

Mike let out a low laugh, then quickly followed by Jane herself.

" What do you think he´s doing now?? "

" OH!! He could be phoning home! " That is when a knock on the wall happened! John did it to politely ask them to keep their laughter down to a minimum! " Instead of "ET phone home! " It´s JD Phone home!! "

The room extension phone rang!

" Hello agents Jennings and Hendry! This is your friendly alien here! Please keep your noise to a minimum, as I might just have to beam you into space along with ET!! "Laughing uncontrollably, they said " Goodnight to John! "

Jane smiled at Mike with a sexy look!

" Are you having the same vibes I'm having right now? " Jane asked.

Mike was standing quite close to her, his half naked body drawing closer and then brushed his skin up to her blouse!

" Does sir have madams permission to kiss her!? "

" You don't need to ask beautiful man!! We are both adults here, and I would have been disappointed if you had declined! "

Mike wrapped his long arms around her petite body, with one hand resting behind her head, then pulled her closer to get the full impact of their kiss! She ran her two front teeth along her bottom lip, then moved to his lips again to taste his warm and pink flesh.

" I have never ever wanted a man so much as I do you right now! I didn't think I would ever fall for any- one while doing this job, but, here we are! I needed you to know how I felt on the plane when I said

317

about us having Grand-children together! " Quietish laughter came from both of them as they embraced each other with a beautiful passion.

Laying side by side looking into each other's eyes, they were like teenagers falling in love!
The wall clock ticked like a hammer on every movement. It was approaching 4:45am, and they knew they would have to get up in a couple of hours to face the new day coming. They held each other gently as they tried to sleep a short time.

Room 507 was the dining room for the team and walking through the door and looking around was Special agent Christine Murdoch! She glanced at one of the tables set up for breakfast, then saw sitting at it, Agents Jennings and Hendry. They were looking at each other over their cereal bowls like love struck puppies!
" Now let me think!! My room mates bed wasn't slept in, you two have smiles like the width of the Hudson river! So, I can only guess you both couldn't sleep and !!!!!?? "
Both of them nearly choked on their cornflakes!! as some splattered over the table.
Christine continued.
" I wondered how long it would take you two to get together!? But! I´m glad for you both, just keep your eyes on the job, and not each other! Not all the time anyway! "
" Good morning all!! I hope we all slept well!? " Came the question from Carol Hoover and walking beside her was her cameraman Ray!
Justin followed a few seconds after and proceeded

over to the hot coffee jug. Pouring freshly ground coffee into his cup, he took a mouthful then breathed a gratitude breath and walked over to Mike and Janes table.

" You two look pleased with your selves!! A long night?? " He asked with a smile. Jane started to blush, and Mike looked around the room as if it was a matter of fact!

Continuing as he drank more coffee.

" As you know! Mike and I are in charge as from now, and I want you all to know that we will have every ones back covered! What is about to happen, I don't know!? But! I know John wants whatever it is to happen! It´s meant to be! " At the dining table now, every person listened as Justin spoke some more.

" At 6am this morning. John left the hotel for the airport! " What!!!? " Jane asked.

" A turn of events have meant that John is doing this stage alone! He is trying to save lives by doing this! I know he wants us to help him later, and when that time comes, we will know! A few days ago, our justice machines have had upgrades! I can tell you now that the upgrade is a one time, time and space displacer! Basically, it means that only once, you can ask the machine to move you from one space to another! I would suggest that you think very carefully before using this chance. After it´s used, it´s done! Remember that only four restraining beams can be used at the one time, and I have had past experience of having more people to deal with than the four beams being used! So, make sure your firearms are in top working order and cleaned, they might just help save your lives! "

Christine looked at Justin as he was talking. She was picking up some form of vibration from him but knew not what it was.

" Are you ok Justin?? " She asked enquiring
" I´m fine thank you Christine! Why do you ask? "
" I´m looking at you, and I see something different about you! " Justin smiled at her.
" Everything is as it should be, and thanks for your concern, but I'm good! "
The others looked closer at him too now, and each one in turn saw the same thing as Christine did! He was slightly glowing, just like John had done on occasions.
Thinking to himself, Justin knew John had passed on something to him, but he didn't know what it was, but I guess he knew he was going to find out sooner or later!
" I need every one ready at 0900 hours, some of the local police will accompany us to the airport and the jet waiting for us! "
All the team were trying to anticipate what was happening now, but no information was available at that time.

Earlier that morning!!.....
5:55am, and Justin stood in Johns room listening to a love and light being! John was radiating more now than he ever did! He was lighting up like a light bulb!
" My dear Justin. Today is going to be a day of strange happenings for you all! You will later find strengths that you didn't know you had, and, just know that once again, things will work out for the good of all! Some souls will depart today, but! Their time is over here, they chose this path a long time ago, so know that nothing that seems helpless is as it seems! For now, Justin, I'm going to miss you with me! "
John hugged Justin and held tight for more than the usual few seconds. He could feel Johns hands warm

and tingling! There was also a strange vibrational feeling running the length of his spine. At one point, Justin felt like an energy surge entered his whole body, and a new sensation that grew stronger as the seconds ticked by.

Justins body went from a pinkish color, to an orange red color! He just believed that John had given him some extra energy to deal with whatever was going to happen. Deep down, he knew things were going to change fast now, and time and the world was about to change for ever.

" It´s time for me to go now Justin! Take care of the team and remember everything you have learnt over the years with all your experiences! The rough times, and the good times! We will meet again soon! Just know that you need to trust your inner most feelings, your inner guide will take care of you and your friends! "

John gave that last smile to Justin as he left the room, then closed the door behind him.

Coming out of the elevator, John looked over to the limousine and the driver waiting for him.

Climbing into the back seat, he sat down next to someone who had already entered the vehicle.

" Are you ready for this John!? " He gazed over at the person, then answered.

" I am as ready as I can be Maximus!! It´s good to see you in the flesh here! Did the dolphins guide you well to Italy? "

Smiling back at John now, he held Johns hand, then said.

" They are wonderful creatures with much intelligence John. I am glad that I am allowed to be part of this new beginning! I am ready to help! "

" Good!! Then let's go and face this next event with no fear and God on our side! "

Driving out of the underground car parking area, two motor cycle cops rode at the rear of the limo, close enough to take any action that was needed.

Maximus had taken on the human form again after his death several years earlier! He decided he wanted the body to be younger and fitter, but. when he looked in the reflection of the limo glass, he saw the same facial features as John! He had bronze skin, native in appearance, and the same pony tail as John!

The limo driver said nothing as he drove the two entities towards the airport. He was there under orders from the President of the United States himself!!

" I need to give you a special power Maximus! You will know what to do with it when the time comes, and on your arm now, is a justice machine. When it is time to surrender it to someone, allow it to pass from you to them freely! Don´t be alarmed and know it´s meant to be! "

" I understand John!! " Maximus replied.

" I heard you had a special gift waiting for you not so long-ago Maximus!? " John asked.

Smiling back at John, he said.

" I did John!! My daughter that was murdered when I was in Sweden all those years ago was waiting for me in the Nebular!! She was well and recovered from her traumatic death, then she decided she wanted to help others still on earth, so she has taken on another human form! You will meet her one-day John! I only have to think of her, then I get pictures in my mind as to where and when she is! She is just like her old father!! " Maximus laughed!

Continuing.

" I´m aware of her thoughts and feelings at any given time! That´s good to know too!! She has

become fearless now! She has chosen to serve God more than she did when she was first alive. Looking back, I can see all the pain each one of us had in our own lives! Now!! Not having fears and troubled emotions any more, that´s fantastic! And today I'm grateful for that John! " John placed his left hand on Maximus's shoulder and smiled yet again.
" You're a good soul Maximus!! "

John and Maximus were at least 30 minutes away from the airport.
In the private jet at the enclosed hanger! Two pilots sat staring out of the cockpit glass! Standing in the doorway behind them were three men dressed in black with ski masks adorning their faces!!
 The stainless-steel floor was red in color, as blood fell from each of the pilots neck wounds where both had been cut from ear to ear!! Their life had been extinguished at the same time when the men boarded the plane with knives and automatic machine guns! Each one of the three men spoke to each other in a middle eastern language!
The leader spoke to the other two men waiting for their chiefs orders.
" The Infidels will be here soon! The false God along with them will be taken to our land and paraded as a false prophet!! Our God is great and true! Death to all non-believers of our God!! Today we will show the world that there can only be one true God! You are already dead! So, if your body dies today, you will be a true martyr! You will be with God himself!! "

The limousine came to a stop just outside the security gates to the airport.
" You need to put this cap on Maximus! Sunglasses

too! When I am out of view, walk to the terminal building. Go to the first police officer you see, then remove your disguise! When events start to unfold, use your Justice machine to come to my location! I will know just before you get to me when you are coming! Listen to my telepathic thoughts, they will guide you as to what needs to be done! God speed Maximus!!"

Maximus exited the vehicle, shutting the car door behind him. Gazed at the security gate guard hut, then walked slowly towards the path that was leading to the terminal building entrance.

" When you get to the private jet hanger driver, stop a few meters away from the open door to the right, I will not be needing you after that young man!! Drive away and don't look back! Do you understand that last part!? " John waited for the drivers response.

" Yes sir!! I have been briefed by the President! " John gave yet another smile to another human being!

All the team was ready and packed to leave the hotel. They went to the dining room on their hotel floor where they had breakfast earlier.

Justin looked at his new friends, they were waiting for his orders, and thought as what they were to be?

" In 5 minutes guys!! We will get a signal to move our asses!! I will brief you when we are on the move! We need to stick close to each other like glue today, so know that we are going to be fully active agents after the signal! Watch each other's backs and be safe as possible Let´s live through this and get home to make more babies!! "

It was good to hear the sound of laughter along the hotel floor as they picked up their bags and weapons

and were ready to move! Carol Hoover looked at Ray.
" You can get those thoughts out of your head Ray!! I
´m not going to have babies with you!! " He looked
slightly disappointed at that comment, but, he
laughed at it too!!

**" I f stars could talk! As they hover in space,
they watch with anticipation as the planet
spins in the direction of a new age! What would
they say!? Maybe it would be something along
these lines!**
**We watch the earth turning in a new forward
motion, as it spins, it rotates in a new direction
from the hate and the pain, to a free world
again! We watch, and we wait with a love for
this world that we always have had! To be born
in a new light, as the sun radiates its warmth
to the surface below! Let the whole universe
rejoice in the new beginning of love and light!!**
"(Peter James Ljung ! 2016)

By himself now! but not alone, John saw the hanger
approaching as the limo driver began to slow a little
before stopping where John had asked him to stop.
" Thank you my friend! You may go now! " John
winked at him and got out of the vehicle.
John stood proud and tall as he walked through the
aircraft hangar side door and was open just as he had
said!

Justin looked down at his justice machine. On the
screen was the numbers counting down to zero! It
showed 25 seconds to go time!
**" Zero hour!! All justice machines fully active! John
is in position! Move to stage 1 at airport now! "**
Justins machine was now primed to relay all
messages to every unit! With police escorts, they

proceeded to the underground hotel carpark.

Every team member was anxious! What was these new mystery movements that they were embarking on? All was going to be revealed in the next few minutes!

Again a limousine left the parking area, following the exact path John had taken earlier.

Two more motor cycle riders tailed the limo as it drove through the main road towards the highway, and to the airport.

Maximus walked through the main entrance of the departure lounge. To his front right, he could see three Italian police officers with automatic machine guns over their shoulders. They were drinking a take away coffee each as Maximus approached the three officers.

" Excuse me officers!! I need your help! " He started to remove his cap which allowed his ponytail to hang down his denim shirt, then removed his sun glasses from his eyes!

Standing with their mouths dropping down, they saw before them John Doe!!

They were dumb struck at the sight in front of them, as they knew he was supposed to be under a strict guard and escort with his security team and police escorts!

" What happened sir!!?? " One of the officers enquired?

" My team is on their way! I wanted to see some of Rome before I departed, and you have a wonderful country gentlemen!! "

One of the officers turned to another, then spoke to him in Italian!

" Escort John Doe to the V:I:P Lounge Giovani! Both of you stay with him until his team gets here! "

Officer Giovani replied. " Yes sir!! No problem! " The

officer pushed his button on the radio system and told control to point the American agents to the V:I:P Pick up area when they arrived! Control was dumb struck too, then replied back to the officer.

" What the hell is he doing by himself at the airport? Just make sure he´s guarded until his team gets there or asses are going to get kicked if we mess up!! "

" No problem control, it´s being done as we speak, Airport 1 Rodger and out!! "

Walking slowly towards the jet aircraft in the hanger, John smiled as he knew what was just about to happen. Again, he smiled as he thought of the greater good this was all going to achieve!
He approached the bottom of the 4 steps in front of the private jets door! Making the last step, he saw to his left, a blood trail that had run along the metal from the cockpit!
John felt a cold piece of metal pressed against the back of his head!
As he peered into the cockpit, he saw two masked men dressed in black, they still had their masks on. One was sitting in the pilot's seat, and the other in the co-pilots seat.
The man behind him started to speak in broken English, with a middle eastern accent.
" False God!! You are now a prisoner of the Arpangistan freedom fighters!! I will not hesitate in shooting you right here if you resist!! You will move now to the first forward facing seats behind me! God is great!! You are not, you are false! " He repeated in front of his men who were waiting for their orders to move.

John with the machine gun barrel pointed and pressing into his skull moved slowly backwards to the first seats, then the man forced John into the seat! Talking in his native language, the leader told the man sitting in the co-pilots seat to use his cell phone to signal they had captured the false prophet, and to prepare for the diversion in 5 minutes!!

Justin faced his team in the vehicle and smiled and started to tell them of the mission they were just going to be facing.
" As you know, this morning, John left for the airport early. This is because we had intelligence reports that John was going to be abducted, and a terrorists cell were in place to cause chaos!! There is another part to the rescue plan, but, that will be explained to you after phase 1 is complete! At this very moment, another look alike John Doe is being guarded in the V:I:P lounge! He is another love and light being who is helping John to achieve the world change!! To do that! John needs to be in the center of Arpangistan! Our mission to start with, is to overpower the diversion team that are also in the V:I:P lounge! We have a great advantage, and that´s due to the Instruments of justice! We have the upper hand right now, as they will be totally surprised when we jump into action! Another part of the mission is just about to unfold in Saint Peters square! Agent Richard Stone is as we speak guiding and guarding the Holy Father to the Square Itself. There, he will address the people, and show them a new light that came from God himself!! Richards justice instrument will tell us all when this has been done.

In the basement of the V:I:P building, the limo came to a stop! The team got out one after the other, then followed Justin up one flight of steps to the side entrance leading into the lounge.

Maximus looked over at Justin, then looked to his right, as at the other end of the lounge, sat 3 Asian men dressed in smart dark suits! They were looking puzzled, as they were waiting for a phone call to tell them their leader had John Doe captive! But this it seemed, was now not possible as he was standing next to his security team and added police guards. These men were under the diplomatic system, they were waiting with their diplomatic pouches, and unknown to them, the team knew they were carrying explosives and weapons!

The large 51inch TV screen was turned on to a news channel, then a special bulletin started to attract the people in the whole lounge.

The TV presenter opened with a statement from the Vatican!

" Ladies and gentlemen! We have some breaking news from the holy Father himself! Pope Francis is walking in Saint Peters square with his Swiss guards, and a special team of agents!

He is just about to address the world from the statue outside the Vatican! We are handing you over to our reporter there! What can you tell us Benito!? "

Benito turned away from the Pope walking towards him and the statue in the square. He faced the camera as it panned in on him and the Pope!

" As you can see behind me. The Holy Father is making his way to the statue, it is here he will make an announcement to be shown to the whole world! No one knows exactly what the speech is about, but! We believe he has some message from God himself!! This follows the visit to the Vatican by John Doe!!

Stopping a few meters away from the statue in Saint Peters square, the Holy Father stood, then bent down and placed an object on the ground. The TV camera zoomed in on the object, then managed to focus on this mysterious item!

Benito´s eyes widened. as looking at the ground, he saw what looked like a small blue flame! It was levitating just off the ground and flickered in the cool breeze blowing through the square.

" The Holy Father has placed a blue flame in front of the statue and looks like he is to address the people here! " Benito said!

" A short time ago! I had a visit from John Doe! He led me to a unknown chamber beneath the Vatican, and hidden for hundreds of years, was objects that previous Popes have kept from mankind. Until now!! God spoke to me personally and gave this gift before me to the world! It is an eternal blue flame and a passage to heaven! Anyone can enter the flame, but it´s a one-way flame! Once you enter the flame, there is no coming back to this world! If you believe in God!? And you are ready to take that leap of faith, then the gift is here for all!! "

" So, there we have something amazing in front of us, and now the Holy Father is smiling to the crowds, as more and more look towards the blue flame! "

" Look!! Look!!! " People pointed to the flame as suddenly it flared up to a Hight of 12 feet, and in a circle shape, encompassing the whole statue! It started to look like a large blue fountain of water, but this was shooting blue flames into the air above the fire jets!!

The Holy Father moved forward to the flame, he smiled as he knew what his next move had to be!

" God asked me to bring this eternal flame to you today! Today! I will be the proof you need that this is from God himself! I will be the first to walk to my father in heaven, so that you may trust what you see! " Gasps of air could be heard from people's mouths all around the square! " No Holy Father!!! You are needed here! " Came from the voice of the head of the Swiss guard.

" God has asked me my child! So, I will not refuse God, as I have spent my whole life serving him! Now it´s my time to go home to my father in heaven! " At that precise moment, The Holy Father stepped closer, then walked through the flame with a big smile on his face! Again, gasps could be heard around the square as looking through the flames, was the Holy Father! Pope Francis turned while standing in the middle of the flame!

" My time in your world has come to an end, and a part of history in the making today, will live on, just like I will now in the Kingdom of God!!

Not many seconds later, the head of the Swiss guard walked straight at the flame, then passed through to the other side. He smiled as he stood next to the Pope.

" My fears have been taken away!! I am going home with the holy Father too! I have protected him on earth! And I will walk by his side in heaven as well! Love is an eternal flame, just like you see now! " Benito looked at the camera!

" I Have never seen anything like this before! And now there are people from all over the square queuing to walk into the Holy flame!! "

At the V:I:P Lounge!
Justin looked down at his justice machine, then asked with his mind!

" Justice machine! Give me a countdown from 10 when we need to co-ordinate our movements!! "

" **Afirmative Justin!!** " The machine sent the answer

telepathically to Justin.

There was a high pitch cell phone ringing coming from one of the diplomats phones! The man reached into his suit jacket pocket to pull it out in view of every one.

" 10 seconds to activate first sequence Justin!! "

Then the countdown continued!

" 3---2---1---Activate now! "

" Mike!! Jane!! Christine!----NOW!!! " Justin shouted, as each one of the agents exposed their firearms and each pointing at the three diplomats!

" Gentlemen!! I know each one of you is carrying weapons and explosives! If you want to die today!? Make your moves! If you want to live! Place your diplomatic pouches on the floor in front of you!! "

The Italian police officers seeing the agents pointing their weapons at the three men, aimed their machine guns at the men also!

Justin continued.

" If you answer that phone! You will see a flash and a bullet entering your skull!! Your choice! "

Each one of the three men turned and looked at each other, then faced the agents and Justin!

Justin as quick as a lightning bolt! uttered some words!

" Activate Justice instruments now!!! " Came the voice, and at that moment, three beams of red light shot from each unit, except Justins! Each beam locked on to each of the three men!

An invisible forcefield surrounded and caught the three men where they sat. None of them could move, even though they tried, but each was stuck fast within the powerful beams!

Justin rushed very quickly over to one of the diplomatic pouches, grabbed a six-inch commando knife from his sock sheath, then quickly stabbed the pouch stitching, forcing the bag seem to tear and rip apart! Forcing his hands into the pouch, he carefully brought out his hands holding C4 explosives already with their detonators stuck into the explosives! Wires coming from the detonators attached to the casing of the highly dangerous material! Walking fast towards the V:I:P lounge smoked glass windows, he placed quickly 3 charges on each of the windows! The team now knew what was going to happen, and it was going to happen quickly, as this part of the plan would fail if not done straight away! Justin looked over at the three diplomats, as he forced the C4 onto the center of each glass pane. He knew that they were prepared to die for their cause and had made up their minds to attack when Justin gave them the choice! It was a great thing that the justice machines knew exactly the choice they had made!

The cell phone was ringing again. but the hand that held it was forced into a tight grip that not even his fingers could move. Justin told everyone to lay on the ground, and then shouted!!

" FIRE IN THE HOLE!!! "

BOOOOOooooommBBBBANNNNNNGGGggggg!! And then a third explosion a couple of seconds later. BBBBBOoooooooooooMMBB!! Glass could be heard falling onto the floor inside the lounge, and onto the concrete outside! The two Italian police officers looked at each other in amazement as a crazy agent had just destroyed the V:I:P lounge!! In fact! The damage had been minimal, but was it convincing enough to the Terrorist's in the Jet a few hundred meters away!? as the leader ran to the hanger door that was still open, and looked over to the terminal, where smoke and some small flames shot out the damaged windows!

Justin prized the cell phone out of the diplomats hand, then along with the broken glass, threw the phone onto the floor, and with a quick movement, brought his foot crashing down onto the phone! It lay there in many pieces, just like the splinters of glass and wood that had been blown out!

" Let´s just hope they bought that little act of vandalism!? " Justin looked through the black and grey smoke flowing fast through the open broken windows. Alarms could be heard throughout the airport as fire trucks started to arrive below the lounge.

" Get those scumbags down stairs now!! I want them kept in lockdown with the beams until I give any orders canceling them! " It looked like Justin just might have spared their lives, as usually, Justin doesn't spare murderers and terrorists!

Running back over to the floor where the lookalike John Doe was, he checked Maximus who was face down with glass splinters on and around him.

" Just like the old days ehh Maximus!!?? " Maximus, even though he was now the spitting image of John himself, looked up and blew some of his pony tail out of his eyes.

" When did you know it was me Justin!? I am identical in every way to the real John Doe! "

" OH, I knew when John sent me a message by the justice machine you old copper you!! I also know this is the type of thing the Maximus I know would do! " They both smiled at each other and shook each other's hand!

Maximus stood up, then shook his clothes to get rid of the debris from the explosions.

" Is John ok Justin!? " Max asked.

Looking back out the lounge broken windows, he could see in the distance, aircraft hangar doors now had been slid back to the open positions. A faint jet engine noise could be heard over the alarm bells ringing.

The executive jet emerged through the open doors of the hanger, and swiftly made its way to a nearby runway!

" Get this plane in the air now!! " Demanded the terrorist leader.

" Our brothers have done their job well!! To-day will see them get their reward with our great God!! " He smiled to himself, then looked down at John, still strapped to the seat.

" This is going to be your last day here, false God!! You will die in the next 24 hours! "

As always, John turned to look at the three men. The two flying the jet, and the leader who now looked so pleased with himself, but that smile, that penetrating smile that sometimes, made fearless men, afraid! The leader stood in front of John, then with a fast-downward motion, hit John straight between the eyes with a machine gun butt!!

The leader smiled as he took the gun back from Johns face, then his smile was wiped from his, as looking back at him was still a smile, and no blood or sign that he had been struck by a metal object. Justin answered Maximus.

" John is fine Maximus! I believe they have swallowed the bait, hook, line, and sinker!

" John has come a long way to have everything in place for the earth shift that's coming Justin! "

" I know dear friend! The world is in for the biggest wakeup call in its entire history! To think that in less than one more day, people will have the choice to be in with the new world or stay with the old! It´s certainly going to be different. " Justin answered Maximus, then looked at his justice machine, it was not giving any indication that things weren't right, so the plan so far was working well!

At cruising altitude, the jet levels out, and the terrorist pilot speaks to his leader again in his native language.

" Brother!! We have set auto pilot for the next 4 hours until we reach Arpangistan airspace! "

" Call our brothers at base camp, I want 50 men to greet us home with the Infidel! This will be a joyful day for us all against the evil world of false God followers!! One by one, they are all going to die!!! "

" This is Benito for channel 3 news here at the Vatican! For the last few hours now, we can tell you that the Holy Father has disappeared! If you watched the TV footage from earlier, you would have seen him give a speech and walk into the new mysterious blue flame that he says " Came from God!! " Almost 3 thousand people have followed him into the flame now, which is believed to lead to the kingdom of heaven! The flame is apparently a one-way trip, so this all boils down to having faith in God himself! We will bring you updates as and when we receive them, so back to the studio where a breaking new story of a terrorist attack at the airport has occurred!! "

The TV report continued.

" Thank you Benito! We will return to him when and if we get any up-dates from the Vatican!

News has just come in of a terrorist attack at the V:I:P terminal at the airport! "

Off the coast of Arpangistan, the calm sea had started to show signs of small ripples in the water. The saying goes!! " When you drop a pebble in the pond, watch the ripples, as they grow bigger as they reach outwards in time! "

The ripples were now getting bigger, and bigger, then dotted along the coast line, was fins, hundreds of fins making their way towards the beaches that stretched for 5 miles! These were again the special sea creatures that John Doe had encountered when he arrived on earth!

Dolphin after dolphin swam gracefully through the water surface.

Each one of the dolphins had a hand holding on to their fins! Trailing on the surface of the sea, was human shape bodies, they were holding on for the short distance to the beaches! It was only a few minutes until they reached the golden sandy shore! The sun shone brightly as body after body was standing up to their knees in the small ripples of the sea foam! Each body in the human shape, each body of golden bronzed color! Pony tails on every being standing there, hanging freely in the calm cool breeze. There were only a few people watching the spectacle before them! They gazed in awe as it mattered not to these people that they were standing naked, each skin on a body dripping with the sea droplets running from the bronze skin newly attached to them.

What a sight to see, as every face had a smile, just like the smile John Doe had when he came to earth! John Doe was just one of the first to arrive.

Before these Arpangistani´s, were 777 John Doe´s, Identical in every way!!

It was only a matter of minutes when each dolphin that had carried these entities from another world, looked like they were singing in a low and high tone sound! The sound that could be heard along the coastline, like trumpets heralding a heavenly being approaching!! 777 celestial beings had approached, and each sea creature in turn had done their job, they had introduced an army of love and light beings, and each one with the same love John had brought with him!

From the beach head, there were only 2kilometers to the central square in the town. Three town folk scrambled over the dunes at the shore! They looked on as the coastline was dotted with entities lining the beach as far as the eyes could see. They thought that this could be some kind of invasion from western countries, but, this was not possible as they had no weapons, and no clothes! What were they!?

They stood in the fading sunlight as night approached with a golden glow as the sun started to descend over the horizon! They waited, the signal was not there yet, each celestial being waited, and waited!

At the Northern end of the town, the airport which had been shut 2 years before, was lighting up a runway! The war-torn land surrounding the town was on full alert as to the new plane approaching.

30 vehicles, each with at least 3 persons riding them, heavily armed men with automatic machine guns, AK47s, rocket launchers, and hand guns! They each were smiling and chanting!

" GOD IS GREAT!!! Death to the Infidels!! "

Justin sat anxiously on a jet plane seat with the rest of the team.

After the original agents jet took off with John and the terrorists, another jet was unwrapped from camouflage in a few minutes, it was planned and prepared ready for phase 2 after the abduction of John.

" We are only 15 minutes behind the other jet now my friends! When the other plane lands in Arpangistan, we will only have 1 hour before we need to move our asses yet again! Very shortly, news will reach the town of an event happening along the coast! You don't need to know what it is yet, but the time will come when the whole world will know about it! When we land at a disused small aircraft strip 3 miles from the town, I will brief you again as what needs to be done! What I can tell you, is, cover your asses well, look after each other when possible, and rely and take notice of your justice machines! Don't get squeamish if there's a lot of blood and guts flying around, as we know, the shit needs to hit the fan first, then a hose pipe, so to speak, needs to clean after! And we are the hosepipe!! " Justin continued as he faced Carol and her cameraman.

" Carol and Ray!! I know you are press, and you have your ID passes stating that, but, you won't stand a chance if you are caught! So, I need you to carry a small pistol on you, this is a last resort situation, but, you might have to use them! " Carol looked at Ray, then looked down on her arm.

" Ray and I woke with these on our arms today Justin! John wanted us to have them, and I think soon, it will not matter who knows about the justice machines, the world we see soon, will no longer need them " She smiled back at Justin, then in turn, Justin did the same, and said.

" Don't you just love our John Doe!? " With them both giving a small laugh.

Jane was staring at Mike, she couldn't keep her eyes off him. There was a warm glowing feeling in her whole body, she so much wanted to hold him tight next to her pink skin! Mike looked over at her and answered her thought!

" Let us get through this young lady, then we will be next to each other's skin as much as we want! "
Another smile surfaced, this time on her face. The

energies were beginning to kick in well now, all the love and light that was and had been emanating from John and all the team!

Justin told them all to do a final check of their equipment, and firearms, then get ready for the couple minuet warnings to go into action. He smiled at them all, put his right-hand fingers to his lips, kissed them, then blew the kiss to all his team.

" To-day my friends, you might lose your lives!! We are going to be fighting for the right reasons, and we are the good guys!! Keep your heads up and proud, and we just might get through this day! This day is going to be like! HELL, ON EARTH!!......

Chapter 11

The world
Returned!

Word was quickly spread around the whole town, that the freedom fighter leader had returned with the false God!

He stood on the top step of the jet! Next to him stood John Doe! The man held Johns head by his pony tail and holding his machine gun pushed the barrel into his ribs.

" Here before you, the false God! The beast who claims to heal people! " The crowd cheered and shouted! " Kill him!! Kill him!! " Pushing John down the steps, John stumbled and fell onto his knees, swishing his pony tail back to his shoulders, he raised his head, instantaianiously, a foot came quickly and struck him on the face. " Die pig!! " The words were filled full of hate, just like the others standing around him now.

John pushed himself up and stood. Again, when they looked at him, he had no cuts, or blood. What was there, was the forever forgiving smile! The anger built up more in the crowd as they were wanting to see the false Gods blood!

" Bring me the land rover, I want to take him to the center of town, to the main square! There we will take his life in full view of our people! " Cheers roared again as John was pushed hard into the vehicle.

Each of Justins team were standing on the old airfield strip. He had asked them to double check their guns and ammo, then checked that each had their justice machines.

Agent Jennings, and Hendry checked each other's

equipment, Jane pulled Mikes collar straight, then uttered a few words in his ear.

" You better not die on me today lover!! I would get angry if you did that! " She continued.

" Early days Mike! But! I know I love you with every beat I have in my heart, and today, my hearts beating quickly, so that's how much I care for you! " She smiled and held his cheeks with both hands, then kissed him hard with the odd tear leaking from her eyes.

" Do you remember the immortal words from the movie " Ghost!? The unforgettable voice of Patrick Swayze!" Mike smiled back at her, then said. " Ditto!! I´ve got your ass covered Jane! Because, I love you back!! "

Synchronized words could be heard from all the justice machines!

" 10 minutes to Arpangistan town phase! Split second timing must be adhered to, as this will put the plans into a negative effect!! All instruments of justice standing by!!! "

After hearing the machines echo those words, everyone jerked their bodies to a standby stance, each one ready to move when the order was given.

On the coastline of Arpangistan, 777 entities, all resembling John Doe, started to move out of the sea where they had been standing since their arrival! They all had manifested blue denim shirts and jeans now! A sea of bodies coming over the sand dunes and towards the town a short distance away. Each pony tail swinging slightly as they moved forwards! What a beautiful sight it was for the few people who had been watching them from a distance. When the feet moved quicker to a running pace, the three citizens of the town turned quickly and ran as fast as their legs could carry them. They had no idea as to the motives of the beings and were now starting to feel more that this was some kind of invasion, but with no weapons, this was the confusing part for them!

Reaching the outside walls of the town, the three citizens stopped to look back at the advancing beings. With amazement, their eyes widened as behind them, they had vanished!! How was this possible!? Confusion again set into their thoughts.

Vehicle after vehicle drove into the town square, dust from the wheels that sped along the edge of the buildings! Some of the town folk started firing bullets into the air, still shouting! " Kill the pig dog! Also cries of, feed his flesh to the birds so they may feast today! "

The leader holding John close to him again pushed him out on to the sandy ground: John got strength into his legs again, and stood, the smile hadn't gone away, and the crowd got angrier as they thought John was insulting them by not bleeding and looking afraid!

This man, this being, was fearless! The Arpangistani 's had never seen a person who didn't fear their evil ways! The hate had burned scars into their hearts, and believed they were the righteous ones that God loved only!

The leader signaled with a hand to be quiet and listen!

" I promised you that I would bring you the false God John Doe!! His filthy skin stands next to mine now, and I also promised you I would take his life in this very town square! But first, I am going to show you his false hands, the hands that can heal! He uses

trickery to do this! So! I will show you how wrong this Infidel is, and how he has started to corrupt our world! Bring me that chair! " The leader pointed to a wooden backless chair sitting next to a water well! One of his followers ran to the leader where he stood, then placed it in front of him and John!
" So! False God!! " The leader said with sarcasm in his voice. He continued.
" Do you have anything to say before your death comes today!? " John stood with his arms at his side.

Carol Hoover had been placed in a spot overlooking the town! Ray! Her cameraman was zooming in on the square. They had a hill top section of ground, they were seeing every movement by the town folk. A small remote satellite dish was being pointed to the sky! It was sending live pictures now to the world via a " NASA " space satellite orbiting their location! The President of the US had authorized the link, and the team were given permission to carry out the mission! She started to feel frightened as she saw on the connected monitor, movement of a threatening behavior by the terrorists!
A voice came from her justice machine breaking the silence she, and Ray had both had!
" All justice instruments standing by for next phase!! 90 seconds until activation mode!! "

Every team member had got the same message! Suddenly!! Carol screamed at the justice instrument as she watched in horror as the next few seconds showed the terrorist leader pick up an old rusty sword!! On the screen in front of her while Ray was still filming.
" They are going to kill him!!! We need to move now!!

" She was shocked when Justin spoke to her on her screen with the words!

" Wait!! Wait!! 60 seconds until activation!! " She shouted back to Justin.

" He´s not going to have 60 seconds!! It will be too late! "

She looked back at the small screen, with tears in her eyes, she saw as the sword had been lifted pointing to the sky, then saw the leader say something, and then!! An evil smile came over the leaders face as quick as the blade had risen, it was falling fast with the power of the terrorists downward strength!

As the leader raised the sword, he told two of his followers to hold Johns right hand over the seat of the chair.

John just let his arm move normally and didn't resist at all! One of the men pushed Johns body down so he had to kneel, then the other tied a rope around his arm, then pulled tightly towards him, making Johns arm extend!

With sword held high, the leader shouted, then his face turned to an evil smile.

" Let us see if you can heal without this arm!? "

Even though the blade of the sword was rusty, it was still lethal and sharp as it cut through the air, then slicing Johns right hand from the rest of the arm!!!

The man holding the rope, now with the hand hanging down towards the ground, cheered with the others as he gave the hand to the terrorist leader. Only a few seconds had passed, then one by one, peoples voices started to become silent as they looked at the so called false God!

" OH My GOD!!! " Carol held her hands over her face, she was horrified at what she had just seen on the screen.

" They cut his hand off! They cut his fucking hand off!! " She shouted to Justin via the justice machine.

" **15 seconds to activation!!** " Each machine gave the announcement to their wearer.

Ray turned to Carol.

" Somethings happening Carol!! Look!! "

The town square became deadly silent!

In front of them all, stood John Doe!! He looked down at the arm where his hand had been cut off! Throughout his short journey on earth! He had always smiled through every positive and negative action. Now he stood there with a bigger smile than ever!!

The whole town looked on his severed arm. There was no blood, he had not screamed out, he just stood and smiled there! All the town had no idea as to what was happening, and they felt cheated as no blood came from the arm. The leader looked at the hand he was holding in his, then saw that there was bone inside the hand, but no blood, no fluid of any description.

" What have I done!?? " Came the concerned voice. The voice was of the leader himself! You could see the confusion on every face in the square, why did he say that??

" Allow me to tell you what has happened! " John turned to him, then glanced down at the hand in his hands.

" You maybe didn't believe in the healing powers given to me by God himself a long time ago! But as you have been holding my severed hand, you were being given healing to your mind body and spirit! You now are seeing the true light of God!! His golden energy has been flowing through you as you stood there! The insane, and evil part that fueled your hate has left you. From now, you have a choice what you want to do with the rest of your life! In a short time, you can go with the new world, or stay with the old one. Every person here will have that choice!! All your hearts need to be cleaned, and only then will you be able to move forward, except you!! Your heart has been purified along with your mind, so you have been forgiven for your crimes! God has told me your real name! Ziad Attan! Welcome to the truth Ziad!! "

To see a tough evil cruel person, start to shed tears was certainly strange, and he was beginning to see the world through true eyes for the first time in his life.

" Ziad!! The false God must die now!! "Shouted a member of the town near to the front of John. Another shouted at Ziad. " You are being brainwashed!! Kill him now, or we will kill both of you!! " Guns were being cocked and made ready to fire, then individually pointed at John and Ziad!!

" **Arpangistan square phase activate now!!!** " Came the voices on all ultimate instruments of justice machines!

Fading flashes could be seen as a second ticked by, each one of the team vanished from the airfield!! The air around them swallowed them, and it could be guessed that they were heading for the front line of the upcoming battle!!

Not two blinks of a person's eyes went by from their disappearance to suddenly!!!

Facing an angry crowd! Justin, Mike, Jane; Christine, and Doctor Elizabeth Channing! Manifested two feet away from John and Ziad!

A deadly silence arrived in the square! The men facing the team stared with hate oozing from their eyes, and the team waiting for a signal from either John or the justice machines. Each member of the team had an alternative weapon pointed into the crowd. They were heavily outnumbered, and, this might be their last day alive!! Jane whispered to Mike.

" Is this what they call a Mexican stand off!!?? " Mike gave a nervous smile back to her and said.

" I think this is what they call " Up shit creek without a paddle!!! "

" Thought you might say something like that! "

Hearing the words in the teams heads, the justice machines gave them a little hope!

" Ultimate instruments of justice are scanning all subjects in the square! 5 possible violent movements detected! Front row, third from left! Second row, 5th and 6th from left! Back row, 2nd from left, and first right! "

Each of the team members moved their eyes to all the potential attacks!

The next moment, a message came on to each screen on their arms.

" Hello my dear friends! This is your back up, John Doe the second here!! I have the rear row covered!

" There was some relief on the teams faces as they saw the words scroll over the screen. Mike whispered to Jane!

" I think we found one of the paddles in shit creek!! In all the quickened action, Justin had forgot about Maximus, but he was so pleased he was there to help.

Justin had a decision to make, as he needed to act now to deter the potential attacks.

John surveyed the crowd before him and the others, and then uttered some words to everyone.

" 5 of you are just about to lose your lives here! Your souls will continue on, but you will go to another dimension, and this is a place where dark souls end up! Call it hell! Call it what you will! But your existence will be in torment for centuries, until one day, you will see the light! That day maybe a thousand years from now, but remember, this day, you had a choice to go forward in love and light, but you chose the alternative!!

Ziad understood every word John had spoken and translated it to everyone in the square!

At the front of the crowd, the third man from the left shouted back at Ziad!

" You are a traitor to God and us!! You will now die!!! " With lightning speed, he raised his machine gun and immediately placed his finger on the trigger!!

At the very same time, Janes justice machine jumped into action with a blast of red light and fired at the man like a straight arrow! It was her decision to take the man down, she was doing her duty to protect John and the newly reformed Ziad.

The beam of light struck the man's skull! his head imploded like he was sucked in a vacuum! His body fell limp to the ground with a thud.

 This light that came from Janes machine had never been seen before now, and the crowd looked on in disbelief as the downed man fell to the ground, and a gap where his head once was.

" **Evasive action now!!!** " Came the warning from all justice machines.

The remaining four that were willing to die for their cause, like the first man, lifted their weapons to open fire!

At the rear, Maximus's machine fired two bolts of red lights hitting the two men's heads just like the first one! Again, both heads simultaneously imploding and then followed by their bodies falling to the ground. Only a split second had passed as the last of the 5 men had received the red beam directly to their skulls! The final two saw their lives extinguished as each skull just like the 3 before imploded. Mikes justice machines aim was deadly accurate as they found their target.

Only seconds had taken place for all 5 to die!!

One after the other, guns started to drop to the ground as each man realized they were up against some powerful unexplained events. And to see their friends die in the way they did, fear overtook them, and maybe, John was speaking the truth about the afterlife!

" Ziad! I would like you to tell all these people, your followers. 5 died here just now, it was their choice! But I can tell you now, that we didn't come here without back up! Your lives have been spared so that you might see the new world approaching! Each one of you would have suffered the same fate as the 5. Look behind you!! "

When they turned to see what John meant, they saw! Their eyes widened as they looked forward, then to the rear! Another John Doe standing with a justice machine on his arm!

Then John pointed to each side of the crowd!

Now! Even the team were surprised, as materializing was 77 identical John Doe´s, each standing there with a justice machine on their arms, and just like John. The unforgettable smiles.

Jane grabbed hold of Mike! She spoke to him in a calm toned voice.

" Well my lover!! I think we just found the second paddle!! " She held tight to the man, she now definitely wanted to have babies with!

John spoke again.

" And now the best is yet to come!! "

The crowd! The team! John and Ziad! All lifted their heads to see what the other 77 John Does were looking up at.

From the ground! 7 meters higher, was a ring of John Does!! Each one spaced out and above the first row, then another row! The circle of beings levitated in the air and surrounded the whole town square! John once again spoke to them.

There are 700 beings up there, waiting! They have come to help bear witness to the new world that is still to be born! They were here as the backup, and every main country in the world, has now got 777 John Does hovering over their cities! There are now 777,777 getting into place for the earth shift! "

This was certainly a wonderful sight, but slightly unusual as to say the least!

John walked closer to Justin, then put his hands on Justins shoulders!

" Do you remember I said the best is yet to come!? " With a sigh of relief, Justin answered .

" Yes! John! "

John sat on the wooden chair that was the chopping board for his hand.

" WAIT A MINUET!!! " Justin shouted at John., then continued.

" Your hand!!?? You have another hand!? I´m confused!! "

There it was again! The forever living smile on Johns face, it never left him!

The town folk started to turn and head away from the square.

On the small hill outside the town, two very happy people were hugging each other hard, then gave each other a small kiss on the lips!

" I´m still not having babies with you Ray!! But, maybe we could have some fun practicing! "

They held on to each other as they laughed, it was possible the whole country heard them laughing!

Still admiring the levitating John Does! The team had now sat on the ground looking up at the beautiful unusual sight!

John looked at Justin, then started to speak to him personally.

"Justin my dear friend! Do you remember the day I hugged you in the room!? You were feeling a different vibration from my hands? The reason for that was! When I was in the Vatican vaults with the Pope, I had been given three objects that had been there for hundreds of years! All the objects were from God himself!! Each one has a purpose, and one of them was placed on your back, then it gently dissolved into your body! You started to get more in tuned with me, and you instinctively knew of events to come, and had the ability to know deep into another mind and heart what they were doing or thinking! You were chosen by God Justin!! You are the one that will be the key to the beginning of the new world! "

Justin looked confused, but in a strange way, he knew that what he was saying was true, and something else so wonderful was going to happen, he just knew it had to be him. John continued.

" The object was a white feather! This feather is from the archangel Gabriel himself!! It was sent to Rome many centuries ago from the Knight crusaders! I can also tell you now why you have been feeling light headed and feel that you could fly! "

Now Justin thought he was in cloud coocoo land!! But as quick as he had that thought, he knew once again, that what John had said, was true again, he felt it in his heart! Was he truly chosen by God to change the world for the better!??

John answered him!

" Yes Justin!! You are! When you look up at all the beings above you. What do you think they are waiting for?? "

Justin didn't need to answer John, because deep down he knew!

" Me!! " Justin smiled at John as he answered, then as ever, the smile was returned to him.

The smiles were certainly looking to be contagious now, as John, Ziad and the team sat and watched, as Justin started to take his clothes off in front of them all!!

Standing there for the whole world to see, he had nothing to hide! His body shining in the light and hanging down the back of his neck. His full male body parts in proportion, and precisely where they should be! He had no shame as he stood there in his birthday suit! The skin that God had given him when he was born on earth!

Agents Jennings, Murdoch, and Doctor Channing's mouths dropped as they saw such a beautiful body before their eyes!

" Wow!! That I like!! " The words coming from Christine.

When John had told Justin the best was yet to come, he wasn't wrong. As they looked on, they saw something that was unbelievable and amazing!! But it was happening right then.

Justins shoulders started to part slightly from the back, just over the shoulder blades!

Coming through the skin, was the beginning of bird feathers! But! This wasn't from a bird, this was angel feathers, and wings sprouting from his body!

Bigger with every second, the wings grew to a 7-meter span!! They were brilliant white, they were glowing with a light so bright, you were dazzled when you watched them!

As Justin glanced over his left shoulder, he could see the brilliant white wings. He stood there waving the new wings, and when he flapped them faster, he started to lift off the ground slightly.

Ziad the leader, looked at this wonderful sight, he started to think on to how wrong he had been, and thought for years that God and angels just might be a myth!! How wrong he was!

John walked to Justin.

" Justin my dear friend! In a moment, you know you will have to use the wings of Gabriel to start the new world process! This has to happen! You also know within your heart, that when the new world is ready, you will be in that new world! Bernadette and young Frankie will be there shortly too! Your life here on the old world is finished now!

When the worlds split! There will be links to the new world from the old one! The main reason for us being here in Arpangistan, is that this is the center for the new light beam which will be created by the entities hovering above us! Each person from the old world, can get spiritually well, and go to the new world! The blue flame from God at the Vatican square will burn forever! It will be there for those who might just want to go to heaven early! They can bypass the new world if they wish, but only if they have truly been forgiven by God! Today!! This world will be a living hell!! It will fester like a sore wound, and it will spread like the black death that once ruled the planet! Around the world, energy points will be put in place, and when someone really has a good heart, they will be allowed to go to the new world! Both worlds will have friends and family members who will be separated, this will be due to their love or their hatred! The one thing that will not be allowed in the new world, is Hate!! If you have a true heart, even though you might struggle to find God!! You will pass through! There will be no killing, no stealing! Love is just about to find a new way to enter man's heart!! Let me also ask you a question or two Justin."

" Do you know who I am my dear friend!? "

" Yes, my dear father!! I have known since you gave me the gift from God!! "

" Then you know that you have been, and always will be loved! Your new journey will be full of joy, love, and more children, but to be able to live where there is no violence and hate. This truly will be beautiful! And you are beautiful, and you are love my dear son! There is one last thing before you go! Your new name! "

Justin knelt before his father, he looked at him and saw the shining eyes of his dear long-lost parent!

" From today Justin! God has renamed you! Your name will be known as " The Archangel Justin!! "

Two seconds past, and every entity looked as the new angel started to rise into the air, right in the middle of all the John Doe beings!

The team knew this was going to be a short time before they meet with him again, but, they were all shedding tears as this magnificent creature, this wonderful new angel rose higher through the circle of John Doe´s.

At each 10-meter interval in Hight. This new angel could be seen releasing a glowing light behind him. The light fell to the center of the circle on the ground, then every grain of sand and every stone shone with a brightness, it radiated small sparks, just big enough so you could see them. The whole square was starting to shine like a star millions of miles away! Suddenly! A circle of light 30 meters wide shot from the ground, it aimed straight at the sky, it was following the Archangel Justin! Wispy mist ran by the side of the light, it entwined with the light! The colors of violet! Red! Blue, and Gold! The angel wings stretched out as far as they could, as now the speed of the angel gathered momentum. Each of the John Doe entities were beginning to fade in to a mist too! One by one, they joined the ascending light.

" Special agent Hendry! You are now in charge! Shortly! I will be leaving you all to return to my time and place in space! When you get back to report to the President, you will notice that you are being drawn to a new light! Let the light wash over you, you will walk through to the new world that is just about to be created! Every detail of the earth as you know it, will be the same, yet there will be no evil, no hatred! People you may know and did know, might not be in the new world yet! They may just be here on the old world and are not ready to walk into the light! We will all meet again! You have been wonderful humans!! You trusted me with your lives, and I will never forget that! Thank you!! OH! Just one more thing! When you walk into the new light, you won't be needing your justice machines! They will self-destruct the moment you transfer your life to the God made new world! Again, my dear friends! Take the love and light that is here now, and bath deeply

in it! Because you will be bathing in pure love!! "
With a blink of an eye, John faded to a mist! The
wind caught him, then blew him towards the small
hill outside of the town!
Ziad looked at the remaining team.
" Sorry is an easy word! Many people including
myself, have used it, and it meant nothing! I can see
now my wrong doings, my destruction of souls and
lives! I know God has forgiven me, and I hope in my
heart that you all may be able to forgive me too!!? "
Ziad walked from them, then passed through the
glowing light circling the square.

Tears were running down both Rays and Carols
faces! They had been kept up to date by the justice
machines relaying what was being said and done!
The camera had also caught the changing body of
Justin. The new Archangel Justin!!
Behind them, John put both his hands on their
shoulders as they still faced the town.
" You two are meant to be together! I have seen
your children playing in the light!! The great thing
about you two going to the new world, is! You will
only be reporting and filming wonderful events! No
hate! What a world it´s going to be for you and your
children! I wish both of you all the love in the world!
I must say farewell for now, but like the others, we
will meet again!! "
John kissed them on the head each, then just as
quick as he came, he vanished into the air on the
wind again!

Flying!! Justin rose through the clouds, he was
gathering speed as he ascended! Each of the entities
following him to his new destination. " What
destination? " He was asking himself.

He felt the cool air run through every feather he had in his new wings! He never in a million years thought this was possible.

As the blue sky above him started to fade, he was nearing the earth's atmosphere! With every second in the air, he was feeling more connected to every atom available! " Anything is possible right now! " He thought to himself again.

Only short seconds had passed, then he had the thought to stop! As he did, he turned to look back at the earth that was now far beneath him.

He knew now why John Doe smiled so much. His heart was filling with a light so powerful, it was indescribable!

Wave upon wave of fine misty light washed over his wings and body. He knew at that point what he had to do.

To see the earth in all its splendor and glory was breathtaking, as he saw dotted around the world, 777,777 light entities hovering and aligning up in grids of 3 triangles!! Each triangle positioning it's self-ready for the new world shift!

This day was long in coming, but! It was here!! It was now!!

With a blast of powder blue light shooting from his eyes in a straight line! The beam headed for the nearest 3 beings! Each point of the triangle joined together a pulsating light! When the light had reached all three points, they projected the beam to the next set of 3! This was the start of the chain reaction that was going to encompass the entire world!!

Archangel Justin stood in space, floating with his wings stretched apart from his body. To be chosen from billions of life forms on the planet, he was so grateful that it was him that witnessed the new birth of the world!

7 minutes exactly, passed from the very first blast of blue light, until! Below him, was a grid of pure penetrating light stretching, and encircling the whole world!

It had begun!!

With a glow as bright as a thousand stars, the world started to divide!! It was duplicating as the lights shone around the world!

As the earth moved, the echo of the original earth remained in the same spot as it always did!

Joining him now, was another angel! This angel asked to be next to this wonderful man who had become an angel! The angel spoke to Justin in heavenly voice, deep, and vibrating as he uttered words to him!

" Welcome my dear brother Justin!! Your wings formed beautifully! Many centuries ago, when God asked me to give a feather from my wings, so that one day, a new angel would be born from my wings! I was smiling for years just thinking about that day!! And today! It has happened! I see before me a bright new soul willing to help save the world below! And look!!! The new one has nearly been completed! "

Justin smiled back at the Archangel Gabriel!!

" Thank you for these wings Gabriel! To see you in all your glory with your wings, is amazing!! I knew deep in my heart that you might be here to share this day, so, you are welcome beside me! "

They floated and glided gently as the new world separated it´s connection with the old world!!

At 7,000 miles apart! The new earth came to a gentle stop!

There, when they looked back at the old world, was small thin connecting beams of violet lights! Each one was a light path to the new world that had just been created!

The violet lights would only allow good souls to pass through their light! This new set of paths was still open for all souls on the old world! But! The ones that were being left there had to show spiritual progression!

Each one of their souls would have to undergo rigorous surrendering before their journey could take place!

Sighs and smiles of pure love came from the two angels in space, along with the 7,777 other entities that had now done their special job for the world! Suddenly! Each one began to fade into wisps of bright light, they shone like diamonds blinded by starlight! One by one they began to move in the direction of outer space! In turn, each one gathering speed until they vanished from sight! If hyperdrive existed, then they had gone into hyperdrive mode!!

Gabriel smiled more at Justin.

" In your heart now Justin, you feel you need to go to the new world to bath in the new worlds light!? When you get there, Bernadette and young Frankie will be waiting for you! But you already knew that! " Gabriel laughed softly as he started to wave his wings away from Justin, then built speed away from him!

" We will meet again very soon Archangel Justin! My brother!! "

Justin smiled more then waved his new wings and guided himself directly at the newly created earth, and the new Miami!!

Hovering about 3 feet over the sandy beach at Arpangistan! A glowing 2 feet sphere of pulsing white light shone!! It was nearly see-through, but it contained an object of great importance! As you gazed at the sphere, you could see radiating colors of! Violet! Red! Purple! And a chrome metal mixture! The colors swirled around inside the circle of light! Suspended in the misty colors, was something John wanted to leave for the souls still to get to the new world!

Glowing with gold and silver emanating from it! Was! His severed hand!!

If someone came close to the sphere, they could push their own hand through the bubble film protecting the hand! If they were truly ready to renounce hate, anger, and were ready for the infusion of love! The healing hand of John Doe!! They would transport automatically to the bright new world that was given back to the souls!!

Stars!! Millions of stars!!

With every known color, and other beautiful specs of light!

John looked back from his viewpoint over the world! Only now! There were two worlds!

Each one spinning as the first one always had!

At that very moment. A tear fell into the darkness of space!

He gave up that tear because he knew that it might be many earth years before

each remaining soul with a black heart, would move to a better world!

For now, they had chosen that route!

But I can assure every one!!

No One!! Will ever forget.....

JOHN DOE!!
THE HANDS THAT COULD HEAL THE WORLD!!
THE END!!

OR!
THE BEGINNING!?

CPSIA information can be obtained
at www.ICGtesting.com
Printed in the USA
LVHW031934110720
660354LV00002B/87